WHATEVER GETS YOU THROUGH THE NIGHT

WHATEVER GETS YOU THROUGH THE NIGHT

CHARLIE HIGSON

Little, Brown

LITTLE, BROWN

First published in Great Britain in 2022 by Little, Brown

1 3 5 7 9 10 8 6 4 2

A CIP catalogue record for this book
is available from the British Library.

Hardback ISBN 978-14087-1428-7
C Format ISBN 978-14087-1427-0

Typeset in Garamond by M Rules
Printed and bound in Great Britain by
Clays Ltd, Elcograf S.p.A.

Papers used by Little, Brown are from well-managed forests
and other responsible sources.

Little, Brown
An imprint of
Little, Brown Book Group
Carmelite House
50 Victoria Embankment
London EC4Y 0DZ

An Hachette UK Company
www.hachette.co.uk

www.littlebrown.co.uk

*For Richard, who waited 25
years for my new one ...*

CANNES

Pixie was dancing.

Arms above her head, hands sheathed in black latex gloves, high-heeled boots stepping – one-two, one-two – reaching for the sky, as she slowly rotated, hips snaking – one-two, one-two – stomach gently curved, honey-coloured skin as smooth as a marble statue, back arched, eyes closed, mouth open, lips wet and shining, her bright red wig swirling around her face.

The view from up here took in the Croisette, the Bay of Cannes, the distant hills, the Mediterranean – mottled silver and orange and purple in the soft, golden-hour light. But who was looking at the view? Because Pixie was dancing.

She was the most beautiful girl on Cloud 9. No contest. She knew it. Everyone else on the rooftop terrace knew it. There was an aura around her. This alien creature, dazzling and impossible and untouchable. She owned the Baoli. What did it matter if she felt like shit? Day was tipping into night and the lights were coming on in the palm trees, giving her a pinpoint of headache behind her left eye. The last hit of coke was wearing off. Her scalp was sweating under the wig. Itching. Her boots hurt her feet. She had a dose of thrush that her tight shorts weren't helping one bit.

1

The song ended and she went back to her seat as the DJ mixed in the next track. Said something. Sounding disappointed. As if he'd been playing only for Pixie. She grabbed her glass and knocked it back. The champagne had turned warm and flat. Tasted like sick. She grimaced, stuck out her tongue and ate a prawn. Bad idea. Her mouth was dry, and the prawn turned to dust. Took an age to chew and swallow.

If she stood on a table, if she could be arsed, which she couldn't, she could probably see J's yacht from up here. People got excited by that idea, didn't they? What was the kick in seeing your own place from somewhere else? On a hill, up a tower, hey look, that's our house! That was a weird one.

There were *some* things she gave a fuck about. Seeing J's yacht from up here was not one of them.

She felt a buzz. Fished the iPhone out of her bra. A message on the screen. She glanced at it.

'Please. Please. Come and get me.'

Typed – 'I'll be there as soon as I can. Tomorrow morning. Promise. Xxx.' Added a heart emoji. Sweet.

Natasha texted a heart emoji back to her. And then, there it was at last, the address.

Pixie tucked the phone back into the side of her bra, picked up her Birkin bag and danced over to the exit. Giving all the sad eyeballers one last glimpse of heaven on a stick. Look upon me and weep, you jellyfish. On the stairs she got her other phone, the shit-phone, out of her bag, and phoned Ray. Told him she was down.

Ray had been circling in the BMW, turned up a couple of minutes after she came out on to the street. She opened the back door and flopped in. It was a warm evening, the air heavy and thick. Everything felt slo-mo. She slammed the door. Grateful for the aircon in the car.

Ray looked at her in the rear-view mirror – 'Airport?'

'One moment.'

2

Ray waited. Faithful Ray. Doglike Ray. Deplorable Ray. She'd given him a hand job once. All it had taken to keep him onside. She looked up Natasha's address on her iPhone, picked out a post office a couple of blocks away from where she lived. Killed the phone. Called Adrian on the shitphone. Gave him the address of the post office. Told him to memorise it. Hung up and handed her iPhone to Ray.

'Don't turn it on until you're back here.'

'Sure.'

''kay. Let's go.'

As they drove, she transferred the contents of the Birkin into a canvas shoulder bag. Ditched the wig. Changed into a pair of trainers and wriggled into the ugly grey mac that Ray had left out on the seat. Then she shook her hair loose and wiped her make-up off with a couple of wet wipes. Finally, she stuck on her sunglasses and looked out of the window as they negotiated the crowded, early evening streets of Cannes. People wandering in the road everywhere as if they were in Disneyland or something. The view did nothing for her. You could get bored of blue skies and palm trees and endless, identical, low-rise apartment blocks lined with balconies.

They hit the Boulevard Eugène Gazagnaire on the east side of the Croisette and coasted past the sea and the boats and more fucking palm trees towards Juan Les Pins. Then cut inland to avoid the traffic.

She was humming a song to herself. Must have been the last one she danced to. Couldn't really remember. She shut down. Drifted. Mindless. Twenty minutes later they were nosing through the familiar ugly mess of development around the airport. Cranes and concrete and car parks. The crap of human progress, spreading everywhere like mould, covering everything.

As Ray coasted into the drop-off zone, she pulled on her Stella McCartney hat. A battered and faded bucket thing she used to wear to festivals before she'd met J. J didn't like festivals. She wasn't sure he even liked music.

'You good from here?'

'Sure. I'll call you when I'm on my way back.' She blew him a pornstar kiss and got out. He sort of smiled.

'You remember what to do, doll?'

'Of course.' Ray nodded.

She breezed through the airport. J's plane ready and waiting for her. That was one of the advantages of being rich – avoiding the lines, all the officials smiling at you, walking out on to the runway, having the whole plane to yourself.

She slumped into her seat and took a plastic bottle of pills out of her bag. Dropped a couple of Tylenols and a melatonin. Added a slammer of GHB for good luck. Miguel brought her a frosty glass of champagne, served with his usual professional smile and a small bowl of olives.

She smoked a blunt and dozed on the flight, slipping in and out of weird dreams that she forgot as soon as they'd done their shit. Miguel gave her a gentle shake as they started their descent and she chopped out a small line of coke with a sprinkling of Ice. Waited to come up, return to this life. Looked out at the lights of Paris below them. Travel these days was like dreaming. You woke up in another place with no sense of movement. Miguel brought her a fresh glass of champagne. And, damn, the bubbles hit her brain and she laughed. For a few seconds she was happy. And then the acid in her guts stabbed at her and she felt like throwing up. She didn't, though. She'd never been very good at throwing up. She kept everything in.

As she walked through Le Bourget airport, she checked her shitphone. Adrian had left a message. He was waiting for her in the passenger pick-up area. She found her way there, the drugs kicking in, now, her head floating like a balloon. On an upper level. Above the clouds. Below that it was all just a shitty mess.

4

Her insides felt like the area around Nice airport. Gritty, sweaty, hot. Her guts full of burning swill. Her vag on fire. She put her sunglasses back on, even though it was gone half ten.

'Luxe. Welcome to Paris.'

There was Adrian. Standing by an old Volvo with a '*Bébé à bord*' sticker in the window. He hadn't changed much in ten years. One of those guys who'd always looked the same age. Older than her, but how old exactly? Impossible to say. He wore sensible, unobtrusive glasses and his grey hair was cropped close to the skull. Suit and tie. Could have been an architect or an academic. Perhaps he'd got a little more wrinkled. Puffy round the eyes.

'You're looking well, Luxe.' Flat English accent. Unplaceable.

'I look like crap, Adrian. At least that's the look I'm going for.'

'You never look anything other than spectacular, Luxe. Even under that weird coat and hat. Good Lord, that hat! If you're trying to go incognito, you need to lose it.'

She lost it. Tossed it into a waste bin.

'And the sunglasses, Luxe.' He'd always called her that. No one else did. She'd forgotten. 'Only drug addicts, blind people and washed-up celebrities wear sunglasses after dark,' he said as he walked her to the car. Pixie took off the sunglasses. Dropped them in her bag.

'You got any clear glasses? Clear glasses would be better.'

'Nope.'

'Climb in. We'll pick some up from a drugstore.'

They got into the Volvo and Adrian pulled away. A St Vincent song spilling discreetly from the speakers.

'19th arrondissement, yeah?'

'Yeah.'

'At least we're on the right side of the city.'

'Yeah.'

'Ought I to know anything more?'

'Best not.'

5

'Sure.'

Adrian turned to look at her. She kept her gaze fixed straight ahead into the Parisian night. A blur of neon, streetlights, head-lights, brake lights. The pain was back behind her eye.

'You got everything?' she asked.

'I think so.'

'You got a smoke? A real smoke?'

'Glove box.'

Pixie popped it open and found an old cigarette tin.

'There's a little dust sprinkled on them to give them a kick.'

Pixie opened the tin. Five joints and a Bic. Neatly stacked. She took out a joint and fired it. Kept the Bic. She pulled the smoke down into her sore lungs. Felt wretched. Waited to feel nothing.

'Still living the high life?' Adrian asked. 'Letting the good times roll?'

Not really. She'd never really had any good times. She'd given other people good times. But they eluded her. Hanging just out of her reach. She said nothing. Just grunted.

The weed smoothed out some kinks, replaced them with some-thing else, something she couldn't describe.

'Here we go.'

The glowing green cross of a chemist hung above the street. Adrian pulled over, double parked. Jumped out. Pixie waited, smoking. It started to rain. Drops on the windscreen breaking up the light like mini kaleidoscopes. Fuck. She closed her eyes. Feeling her heart racing in her chest. Wanted to weep.

The car rocked as Adrian got back in. Tossed her a pair of read-ing glasses in a plastic sleeve. She took them out and tried them on. Looked at herself in the vanity mirror on the back of the sun visor. Couldn't see much.

'They're pretty weak,' said Adrian, moving off into the traffic. 'So you shouldn't bump into things. Show me.'

Pixie gave him a geeky smile. He chuckled.

'Better than the shades. You look almost like a normal person. Not that you could ever be such a thing. In my imagination you're a thousand miles high.'

'I'm just a girl, Adrian. Trying to get by in a fucked-up world.'

'Aren't we all, darling ... This shouldn't take long ...'

The 19th arrondissement. What must Natasha be thinking? All alone in the city. Stuck out of the way in a cheap apartment in the 19th. A child. Not yet sixteen. Pixie had first come to Paris at the same age, but she'd been looked after – in a way.

She'd come here to model. Everything done for her. Shared an apartment with the other girls. Private cars everywhere. Big dollars. Didn't even have to think. Encouraged not to. When it came down to it, it had always been like that, ever since she'd come into the world. And as she'd grown up it all just got easier and easier. Men had done everything for her. But there was a price. Men wanted her for one thing. She was born with it. Her meaningless beauty. Her body. The stretched donut with a hole all the way through it. They just wanted to fill that hole.

'Don't think. Let me be your guide. I am the man ...'

But not tonight. This was her thing.

She wasn't really looking now. Couldn't see clearly through the glasses, anyway. She was just letting things slide. Not listening, either, as Adrian talked quietly about the old days. Kicking over the dust. She didn't want to connect. Didn't want to go there. Didn't want to catch up. Didn't want any of this to be real. She was a ghost. It was better if she left no traces. As if all this really was a dream. She checked the time on her phone. Getting near to eleven.

'The shit's pure, yeah, Adrian?'

'Pure as the snow before someone pisses in it, Luxe. Medical grade. From the army. You be careful, yeah? You won't be used to it.'

'I'm always careful.'

'You going to give someone a special time?'

'The best. They're hurting. I want to ease their pain. Take them to a kinder place.'

'You always had a good heart.'

Adrian was one of the few men in her life she hadn't had to fuck to get something out of. He was totally asexual as far as she could tell. For him it was all only ever business. As long as she paid, he came through for her. She clearly remembered when he'd shown her how to shoot up. Clearly remembered the feeling. Terrifying and wonderful at the same time.

'Can I get it now? You got it with you?'

Adrian reached round to get a black leather holdall off the backseat. Dropped it in Pixie's lap.

'Small zip on the side? You got it? In the package? Yes?'

'I got it.' Pixie took out the very familiar looking package. Neatly wrapped in some kind of fancy Chinese paper. Adrian's signature delivery. She transferred it to her shoulder bag. Replaced it with an envelope of euros.

'There's five hundred there.'

'Five hundred? That wasn't the deal. That's way too much.'

'I'm not just buying the bonita. I'm buying you, Adrian.'

'Fair enough. I'm cheap. If you want to buy me, all you gotta have is money.'

Adrian chuckled. It was probably a joke. Pixie didn't get jokes. J often told her she didn't have a sense of humour. Well, she'd never needed one.

They were silent for the rest of the drive. After a little while, Adrian slowed down and coasted to the side of the road.

'This is you.'

'Cool.' Pixie undid her seat belt and gave him a peck on the cheek. 'I'll text you when I come out. Meet you back here.'

'You're paying.'

Pixie got out of the car and took a quick look around. A faceless street in a faceless part of town. She leaned in to get her shoulder bag. Glanced back at Adrian. He looked grey in the dim light. Older.

'Don't take this the wrong way,' she said. 'But you're the only *old* drug dealer I've ever met.'

'No offence. I guess I've just been lucky. Most die young, or get banged up, or move on.'

'Not you?'

'Back in the day, I was going to retire, but for reasons we don't need to go into here, I had to leave England in a hurry. Had to leave a lot behind. Picked up with the only job I really knew how to do. Now – I just keep going.'

'You're one of the immortals, Adrian. One of the untouchables. Like me. And Obelix. Got dipped in the shit when we were young. Nothing can touch us now.'

'They always get you in the end, Luxe. One way or another.'

'Cheerful thought. See you later.'

Pixie waited there for a moment, watching Adrian drive away, and then turned into the rain and walked. At least it was a warm rain. And it meant less people on the streets. Did she mean 'less' people, or 'fewer'? She couldn't remember what the rules were. Some people got really knotted up about such things. Correct grammar. But, in the end, being rich and beautiful, you could say what you liked. It was weird, though. She couldn't remember when she'd started thinking in English.

It didn't take her more than five minutes to get to Natasha's apartment block. A faceless sixties build on a main road above a Franprix. She found the buzzer. Pressed it, waited. Facing away towards the road. Couldn't see any security cameras but you could never be too sure.

'Hello?'

'Tash?'

'Yes ... ?' Wary.

'Tash. It's me ...'

'Who?'

'The tooth fairy! Who do you fucking think, Crystal Tits?'

'Pixie?'

'The one and only.'

'Pixie-Omigod-Pixie.'

The street door opened with a harsh buzz.

Pixie dismissed the lifts. Looked like the sort that might be filled with piss. And cameras. Took the stairs. Kept her head down as she went. Natasha's apartment was only three floors up. When Natasha opened her door, she was crying.

'Pixie, oh, Pixie, you came. I didn't think you'd be here until tomorrow.'

'Got here quicker than I thought.'

Pixie went in and closed the door behind her. Gave Natasha a big hug. The girl felt insubstantial, like she was made of nothing but twigs and rags. Pixie broke away and held her at arm's length. She was awfully thin, and her hair looked dead, her skin greasy. Sometimes when you looked at someone you saw how they were going to look when they were fifty, sixty, eighty. Pixie could see it now in Natasha. She looked like an old woman.

'Oh, little bunny girl,' she said, let go of her. 'What are you doing here, honey?'

'I made a mistake. Big time. I have so fucked up, Pixie. I'm, like, I feel like I'm totally lost.'

'Well, I've found you, bunny girl.'

Natasha started crying again and Pixie steered her to a chair, sat her down. Natasha looked up at her through blurry, pink eyes.

'I thought, I always thought you hated me,' she said, and sniffed. 'I never expected you'd be the only one who came through for me.'

'Why would I hate you, Tash?'

'I dunno. I sometimes felt that you were sometimes, you know, like, *jealous* of me?'

'Honey, I've been through what you're going through. I know

10

you're just a little girl and I know how that feels. I guess I was scared for you. Hated to see it happening. It wasn't you I was angry with. It's the system. The way things work. You know, don't you? You know that everything I did, *we* did, I had no choice. I was just like you. Just another one of The Team.'

'I know . . .'

Pixie smiled. Unbuttoned her coat. Natasha gasped and giggled when she saw what she was wearing underneath. The cut-off top, the shorts.

'You're crazy, Pixie.'

'It's layers, Tash. I've got layers. Always another layer underneath.'

She did a spin, let the coat flap wide. Rolled up her sleeves to show the full extent of her latex gloves.

'What are you like?' Natasha laughed.

'I am funky, girl! I am the funk from outer space.'

'I never knew you wore glasses.'

'It's our secret. You don't ever tell anyone else or I'll have to kill you.'

Now they laughed together. Natasha looked years younger. Her real age. Fifteen.

'That's more like it.'

'Thank you for this, Pixie. I really needed some help.'

'Raul gave you some help.'

The light left Natasha. She shivered and hugged herself.

'I fucked up there. Raul was just like – well, you know – *Raul*. I thought he was my ticket out of there. He promised so many things. And now all I've got is . . . *this*. Just this, Pixie.'

Natasha looked miserably round the bleak apartment. Lino floors the colour of baby poop. Ghastly, mismatched bits of furniture. No curtains. White walls faded to a grubby grey.

'Oh, baby girl. What are we going to do with you?'

'Can I go back? Do you think I can go back? Will he let me back?'

'Maybe. Maybe if I spoke to him. But you have to be sure, Tash. I mean. You ran away. You walked out on him. All he's thinking is how could you do that? After all he did for you.'

'Shuh ... Yeah ... All he did for me? All he did *to* me. All I did for *him*? What about that? What about all I did for him?'

'You know what he's like. It's all about the J.'

'But you'll talk to him, yeah?'

'I'll try. It's complicated, Tash. You know that. And you know that in the end – he loves you. Not like Raul.'

'I need to get away from Raul. I'm scared of him. He's going to hurt me. I know it. He's violent.'

'He's just a pimp, Tash. You should have known that.'

'He told me we'd make a lot of money. I'd sell my story to the papers. Tell them everything about Julian.'

'And have you?'

'So far just one guy, really creepy. Says he's a journalist. But he's too interested in – you know – the sex stuff. Keeps making me repeat things, add details. I don't know if he believes me. I thought we'd go to the police, but Raul says not yet. I don't know what to do, Pixie. I don't know what's going on.'

'How could you? You're just a schoolgirl, Natasha.'

'I want to go home. Back to England. But what if they don't want me back? I'm not the same person ...'

'OK, OK. Listen to me. Tomorrow I'll sort this. I'll stay with you tonight, and tomorrow I'll go straight to Julian. Fix this for you. But look at you – you're a mess.'

'I should never have started taking those pills. I know you were only trying to help, Pixie. To make the pain go away. But I should never have got into that shit.'

Pixie went over to her, lifted her arm and studied it. It was dotted with needle marks and scabs. Natasha looked broken.

'Raul gives me stuff. It's killing me. I'm so unfocused all the time. I can't believe that only three weeks ago I was playing in a tournament at the Roland Garros ... It's like I've died, Pixie. I feel dead.'

'When did he last give you anything?'

'He teases me with it, offering it, taking it away. It's only when I get too sick, he gives me more.'

'Are you sick now, honey?'

'I don't feel great. To be fair.'

Pixie put a hand to Natasha's chest.

'You need to chill, darling. You're stressed out. I can feel your heart going like a wind-up monkey drummer. You're gonna go into meltdown.'

'I've been so worried. So fucked up. Fucked around.'

'The stuff Raul's been giving you. It'll be low-grade. It'll be cut with all sorts of poisonous shit. We need to get you through tonight. Pump you clean. I've got some good stuff. Yeah? Pure. Clean. It'll smooth you out, keep the nightmares away for a while.'

'I don't know, Pixie ... I want to be straight.'

'Baby steps. Think of this as medicine ... You and me, Pixie and Tash, we'll do it together. You've got the jitters bad. You're like a little frightened bunny. This'll bring you to the good place. Straighten you out. All your problems will go away.'

'I don't know. I don't want to take anything anymore ... '

'I'll be with you all the time. Come on. Look – let's make this place nice.'

Pixie got some church candles out of her bag. Fat, stubby things. Stood them up on the table. She lit them with Adrian's Bic and cut the lights.

'Better already,' she said, getting the Chinese-paper-wrapped package out. 'It's like Christmas ... '

'Oh, Pixie ... '

'Shhh, shhhh, little bunny girl. Pixie is your fairy godmother. You got a spoon?'

Natasha went through to the kitchen while Pixie unwrapped

the package. Everything she needed was in there. A syringe. A little squeezy bottle of citric acid. Cotton wool. The heroin itself, brown and sticky, in a wrap of silver foil. That brought back a lot of memories. And, setting up the works – dissolving the smack into some of the acid and bubbling it in the spoon over a candle, sucking it up into the syringe through cotton wool to filter it – was a familiar ritual that her hands did without thinking.

She tied the belt from her mac around her upper arm and used a pair of old tights on Natasha, and, once there was a big enough vein, she leaned over, turned away from Natasha and sank the plunger. Squirting the junk on to the floor out of her sight.

She moaned, sighed, relaxed her shoulders. Faking it. Came easy to her. Then she prepared a second hit for Natasha. Cooing sweet nonsense all the while. Hoping she wasn't pushing the girl too fast. Natasha looked nervous but eager. Hungry. Her eyes glassy.

When Pixie was ready, she went over to Natasha, smiled and then quickly got the shit into her skinny, child's arm.

'There. All done.'

Natasha groaned, lay back in the chair, eyes closed. She was shaking. Slick with sweat.

'I don't feel so good, Pixie.'

'Don't fight it. Go with it. Float … Enjoy it … Let go … Just let go … Be cool …'

Natasha opened her eyes. Her pupils were tiny. She convulsed. Already her breathing was shallow. She retched, her stomach gurgling, and thin bile dribbled from her blue lips.

Pixie stroked her hair.

'Well then, there you are, no more hurting. No pain. Sleep now, bunny girl. Drift off …'

She looked around. Saw Natasha's Samsung. Took her limp hand and pressed her right thumb against the Home key.

Once she was in, she navigated to Messages. Pulled up her own contact. Ray would be outside the club now keeping an eye on her iPhone. She hoped he'd properly learned the script and wouldn't fuck up. He wasn't the brightest, but her instructions had been pretty clear.

She wrote her message.

'Oh Pixie I can't hang on any longer I've made such mistakes I've fucked everything up I lied about everything I lied about Julian I wanted him to love me and he wouldn't so I made up all those stories about him I feel so stupid so dirty now I wish there was a way out of this well maybe there is thank you for trying to helpxxx'

She pressed Send and waited. Ray was on the ball. His message pinged straight back.

'Hold on Tash. Don't do anything stupid. Please I beg you. You're special, precious. We can make things right. I'm in Cannes right now, but I can be there tomorrow morning. I'll come and get you. Hold on, babe, be strong. I love you. Px.' He even remembered to add the smiling face and the praying hands emojis.

Pixie went round the apartment. Collected some of Natasha's clothing from her grungy bedroom, some magazines, arranged them just so round the candles. Wadded up some paper. She'd tried all sorts of candles, experimented. Had cut these ones to the right length so that they'd burn for exactly five hours. Then the wax and the heat and the flame should get to the clothes and the paper. It was a crazy, half-cocked, amateur plan, but it was all she had. If it fucked up. Well, it'd be just one more fuck-up to add to all the rest. Somehow, she'd always pulled through.

She flushed the rest of the junk down the toilet. Collected her things. Took one last look around, confident that the gloves meant she hadn't left any fingerprints.

Now it was easy. Destroy the shitphone and chuck it into a river on the way to the airport. Ninety minutes back to Nice. Another half-hour into Cannes. Change her footwear in the car. Put the wig on. Make-up. Get her iPhone back off Ray and lose him when they got back to the Baoli. Hit the dance floor by 2 a.m. Boogie until dawn. Make sure everybody saw her again, knew she was there. She'd already put herself on show on the Cloud 9 terrace. Now she would own the dance floor. The goddess of sex come down from Mount Olympus. Then, boots off and walk back through town to the boat. Climb aboard, go to sleep until the police woke her . . .

It was the best she could do. She looked at Natasha. Thought she ought to feel something. Good or bad, or just something . . .

It didn't come.

FIVE YEARS LATER

1

MACINTYRE

He dropped his shoulder bag in the hallway and explored the villa. Entrance hall. Open-plan living area. Small kitchen. Downstairs bedroom opening on to the terrace by the pool on the south-east side of the house. Tiled floors throughout. Two more bedrooms upstairs. Smaller one at the front, master bedroom at the back, with its own balcony facing the sea.

He opened the doors and stepped out on to the balcony. Took in the view across to Albania. Turned to the south – there was Hepworth's compound. Up on the side of a hill, well out of town. It was partially hidden behind a curtain of mature pine trees, but he could make out a collection of modern buildings set among beautifully landscaped grounds.

He turned away from the compound. There'd be time for that. Stared down at the pool, leaning on the iron railing, emptying his mind. Closing down. It was late afternoon. The sun was on the other side of the island and the balcony was shaded now.

He let his mind drift for a while, listening to the white noise of insects, then took a deep breath of warm, scented air and went back inside. Opened the white louvred doors of the built-in wardrobe. Glanced over the different outfits hanging from the rails and neatly stacked on the shelves. All good. He checked the en-suite. Toiletries laid out for him, like a hotel. Soap. Shampoo. New toothbrush. Electric shaver.

He went back downstairs. Found the safe in an alcove between the living room and the kitchen. Punched in the code he'd memorised and swung the door open. Everything looked in order. Three passports under different names. Three credit cards to match the passports. Three phones. A wallet filled with fresh euros. A pack of USB sticks. Some miniature surveillance equipment. Including a basic listening device the size of a bottle top and a wi-fi camera not much bigger. Two magnetic trackers and some dummy car keys. A large white sealed envelope.

A Glock handgun with two boxes of rounds.

He looked at the gun with distaste. It was squat and black and functional. So far he'd never had to use one of the damned things on a job. Had managed to avoid Chekhov's rule – If in the first act you've hung a pistol on the wall, then in the following one it should be fired. Otherwise don't put it there. Only in his case it was a gun in a safe. Well, screw Chekhov, he hoped it would stay in there. He was careful. Discreet. That was why people hired him.

He took out the envelope and opened it. Inside were a new passport for the girl and various documents she might need, as well as some cash – euros and sterling.

He put the envelope back into the safe and emptied his pockets on top of it. Phone. Wallet. Passport. Keys. Loose change. Enjoying the feeling of a weight being lifted. He took off his watch. Added it to the pile. Closed the door. Locked it. Smiled.

Now he checked the technical set-up. It was all as he'd instructed. A modem with a good wi-fi connection. A high-end wireless sound system connected to speakers all around the house and pool. A virgin MacBook Pro in a small aluminium flight case on the coffee table.

He activated the sound system, fired up the Mac and clicked

on Spotify. Selected a favourite classical playlist. Neutral, unobtrusive, almost ambient. Hit play.

Packed in with the computer was a cigar box. Inside the box, a cutter, a lighter, a box of long wooden matches and two Montecristos.

One for now. One for when it was done.

He rotated his shoulders, rolled his head on his neck and stretched out his arms, turning his palms to the ceiling. Then he kicked off his deck shoes, peeled off his socks and padded into the kitchen across the cool, polished terracotta tiles. The kitchen was small but well equipped. There was a welcome basket on the counter. Bread, fruit, wine, a jar of olives, honey, some local biscuits. He selected a lemon, found a knife and a chopping board. Halved the lemon. Cut a wedge. He went to the fridge and checked the contents. All good again. Took out a bottle of Coke. Stood it on the counter and opened the freezer compartment. Two tall glasses and three bottles in a neat row – tequila, vodka, rum. Nothing fancy. El Tesoro Anejo, Grey Goose and Bacardi. He'd read somewhere about some guy who was obsessed with vodka that had been filtered nine times, through charcoal and coconut shells and pebbles from the bottom of the sea or some shit. Loved the purity. Ha. Yeah. Right. It was alcohol, mate. Pure alcohol was pure poison.

He took out one of the glasses and the rum. Poured a shot. Watched the glass turn frosty white. Cascaded some ice into it from the dispenser. Poured on some Coke. Heard the ice crack. Another smile. He barely squeezed the lemon wedge then dropped it in. Took a pull while the Coke was still hissing. Tiny bursts of spray dancing above the surface and tickling his upper lip.

He carried the glass out to the pool. Chose a lounger on the shady side under an awning. Took another drink, long and slow this time, and let out a long, slow sigh of simple pleasure. This was the part he liked. Arriving. Unloading. Emptying. Settling in. This part you could organise. Plan for. After that you had to make everything up as you went along. Get through it.

But right now, nobody could touch him.

When he'd finished his drink, he stripped off and walked over to the springboard. Stood there in the full sun and looked back at the villa. It was modern but built in the local style. White walls, blue shutters and a red-tiled roof. Purple bougainvillea climbing up the side. He looked down at the turquoise of the pool, the light breaking up and shifting like a Hockney painting.

He raised himself up on his toes and then launched himself. For the briefest moment he was suspended in air and then he hit the surface and went under. He felt the water against his skin, the cool silkiness of it, and opened his eyes as he swam a length underwater, enjoying being in this quiet, blue world. He could almost feel his body cracking like the ice, his tension dissipating. He pushed up and emerged to a cacophony of cicadas and a jet passing overhead. He stood, pushing his hair out of his face. If you couldn't enjoy your work, you shouldn't be doing it.

He quickly swam twenty lengths. A fast, steady crawl. Untangling his muscles after the flight. When he was done, he hauled himself out and stood, dripping, on the honey-coloured stone surround. He used the outside shower, grabbed his drink and then lay on a different lounger in full sun.

There was not a cloud in the sky.

When he was dry, he went back to the kitchen. Drank half a litre of water. Made another rum and Coke, took it upstairs, pulled on a white dressing gown then sat out on the balcony and lit a cigar, watching the smoke drift away on the still air.

He sat there for an hour or so, looking over the tops of dark green pine trees and the roofs of a couple of other villas to where the boats sailed past on the Straits of Corfu. Listening to the music. Settling his body. Resetting his system.

When he saw that the light was dying, he brought himself back up to operating level. His internal clock told him it was nearing six. He went inside, showered and brushed his teeth then dressed. Wanted to fit in. Chose chinos and polo shirt.

He opened the safe, selected a credit card – in the name of Robert Macintyre – slipped it into the new wallet. Picked up the house keys.

He was ready.

He left the house and headed down to the harbour.

2

HUMAN

'So, welcome to Agios Symeon and Club Corfu Villas.' The woman grinned. How old was she? Alan had never been good at guessing people's ages. And the rep had used every trick in the book to disguise hers. Her hair was dyed a tasteful blonde, professionally streaked and layered. Her face was artfully made up. He detected the touch of Botox, maybe some lip enhancement. They did that, didn't they? Injected you with fat from your arse, or something. Fake tan. Or probably a real tan, he supposed. Was there any way of telling the difference? She had immaculate, stuck-on nails. Big gold earrings to draw your attention away from the face, so you didn't look too hard for wrinkles.

She was a little on the short side and, if he was being generous, he'd describe her as curvy. If he was feeling less generous, he'd say she could lose some weight. But nobody liked skinny women. She was wearing some kind of vaguely ethnic white dress, showing a welcome bit of cleavage. Strappy sandals. Nicely presented. Forty at the most, he reckoned. There was just a shadow of tiredness about her. She'd probably come to the island for a holiday years ago and ended up staying. Got stuck here. What had once been pleasure was now work.

She raised her glass. A vivid, deep-orange Negroni. It was always Negronis these days, wasn't it? They'd all been given free ones when they'd arrived at Giorgio's bar for the meet and greet. (Or 'Meet and Greek' as it had been punningly called on the faded laminated sign that had been put up outside for the evening.)

Alan did up another button on his purple holiday shirt. He liked it, but the buttonholes were slightly annoying. You could have it either buttoned up too high or too low – there wasn't an in-between. Buttoned up higher he felt hot now and rolled up the sleeves.

He took a sip of his drink. He'd watched the cocktails being made from a Negroni mix and watered-down gin out of a fake British-branded bottle, probably called something like *Union Jack*. Probably knocked up here on the island in someone's garage. But they were free, and that made any drink slip down easier.

To be honest, though, he'd never really liked the taste of gin. He'd grown up believing that a G&T was a comedy drink that sub-urban couples drank at cocktail parties in lame seventies sitcoms. Its rise in popularity in the last few years mystified him. Now gin was a hipster thing, wasn't it? How had that happened? Actually, Alice had told him. It was to do with Instagram, apparently. Like the ubiquitous Aperol Spritz, Negronis looked sexy in photos. Provided you were turned on by lurid orange. At least they hadn't been given Aperol Spritzes tonight. He couldn't stand the swill. It somehow managed to be both sickly and bitter at the same time.

A sudden surge of anger hit him from nowhere. An explosion of acid in his stomach.

Fucking Instagram. Fucking social media.

The curse of the modern age. He wouldn't be in such a world of shit if it wasn't for social fucking media.

'Here's to you all having a lovely stay here in paradise.' The rep offered them a wide, tooth-whitened smile. '*Cheers*' from all gathered. '*Cheers*' from Alan, and he drained his glass. The quicker

25

he got rid of it, the quicker he could move on to a proper drink. He craved a nice cold beer. Wondered if that would be gratis, too. Doubted it.

There were some free snacks on the table. Taramasalata with pitta bread. Almonds. Olives. Crisps. Some rather dense little sausages.

'So, I'm Cindy,' said the rep. 'And I'll be Mum for the duration of your stay. Any problems big or small just bring them to me. You can find me here most evenings. It's happy hour from six to eight. I know that's two hours, but who's complaining, eh?'

Polite titters. Alan swirled his ice round in his glass.

'Giorgio does a very good breakfast,' Cindy went on. 'But only snacks otherwise. There are three tavernas, however, and they're all good, you can just take your pick, really. So – during the day you can usually find me in the boat hire office, which you'll probably have passed on your way here. My husband, Ioannis, runs it. I shouldn't really, it's naughty of me promoting hubby's biz, but I highly recommend you take a boat out one day. There's very high demand, so book well in advance. I can take bookings tonight if you're eager.'

Alan looked round at the other punters. You could tell who was with Club Corfu Villas as they were all drinking Negronis. There were about a dozen or so of them. He'd chatted to some of them when he'd first arrived. The usual bunch. Mostly well-heeled Brits of a certain type. Panama hats, deck shoes, chinos, crisp shorts, bum bags, espadrilles, M&S short-sleeved shirts, vaguely ethnic dresses. But there was a table of youngsters. Twenty-somethings in T-shirts, beads, sliders and shorts. Probably only here for the free booze and mezes. Not really paying attention. Plus, a serious-looking Swedish couple, a German couple and a black family – the impeccably behaved little kids struggling to stay awake.

One of the English guys had a notebook out. Was actually taking notes. What was he writing?

'All tavernas OK – take your pick.'

It hadn't been hard to find Giorgio's place. Agios Symeon wasn't huge. A single strip of bars and tavernas curving round a secluded harbour. A small general store. The boat hire place. A place to hire bikes and mopeds. An internet café, cum gift shop, cum second-hand bookshop, with a cash machine and pictures in the window of villas for sale. There were a few boats moored at the wooden jetties. Nothing ostentatious. A retired couple sitting out on the deck of one having dinner.

Alan stared into his empty glass. Assumed he'd have to wait 'til the end of Cindy's welcome spiel before he could get another drink. He'd sunk his first two perhaps just a little too fast. Notepad guy had probably already written something in his little black book – '*Man in purple shirt is a drinker. Avoid.*'

Truth was, right now he *was* a drinker. He'd polished off a good quarter of the bottle of duty-free vodka he'd bought at Gatwick before coming down to Giorgio's. And all he'd had to eat since breakfast was the table snacks.

Cindy was still talking. 'If you can't find me, just call me. My number's in your welcome pack. I've lived on the island for nearly twenty years, now, so I'm a fountain of information...'

Alan was sweating. The glass doors had been folded back and flattened against the walls so that the whole of the front of the taverna was open to the world, but it was still hot in here. He longed to be sitting outside in the fresh air.

Not everybody in Giorgio's was with Club Corfu Villas. There were a couple of locals at the bar and more drinkers on the vine-covered terrace outside. On the way in he'd noticed two scantily clad girls, one white, one black, barely older than Lauren by the look of it, getting noisily drunk. That was what his little girl should be doing. Having a fun holiday with mates. Not being up there...

With him...

His throat felt tight and he thought – *sod it*. Smiled at Cindy and went over to the bar.

'A beer please. From the tap.'

He didn't want to catch the eyes of any of the CCV types, so he looked out at the terrace while he waited. Trying not to stare at the girls.

There were two guys there, both sitting by themselves. Couldn't be more different from each other. From different worlds. One ordinary. Ordinary size. Ordinary build. Ordinary hair. Ordinary clothes. Studying a book of island walks, with a glass of white wine in front of him. Oblivious to the world. You wouldn't look twice at him.

The other was big. Hard. Watchful. An air of menace about him. Now there was a guy you *would* look twice at. Three times. Tall and solid. A little thick at the waist perhaps. Just giving off a general feeling of SIZE. Except for his head. His head looked out of proportion to his body. Maybe because his shoulders were so bulky. A little head with little eyes. Dark, like marbles. A broken nose that hadn't been properly set. Was that deliberate? To emphasise the air of menace and threat and power. Everything about him was calculated to make an impression. Like his haircut – shaved almost to the bone.

He was wearing a burgundy polo shirt that was at least a size too small for him. No doubt deliberate as well. His great muscled arms bulged out of the sleeves. A Celtic tattoo round one upper arm. Or was it Polynesian? Some tribal thing anyway. Alan was never quite sure.

It was a comical scene, really. Like two contrasting posters on the underground. One for a violent action movie – *Fist of Retribution*, or *Sudden Vengeance*, perhaps. *Mindless Violence*.

The other an ad for ... *a bank*.

Mister Average, sitting on his lawn with his Labrador, his pretty wife and bright, smiling kids. A jumper round his shoulders.

Except these days the family would probably be mixed race, or gay.

Come on. Pour that fucking beer.

28

He didn't like to think about it – *That World* – the world of bank loans and car insurance, of pensions and business meetings and commuters. The Parent Teachers' Association. Charity dinners. Waitrose on Sunday morning. Pub quiz on Monday. Listening to a podcast on the Tube to work. The latest Lee Child or Ian Rankin. Holidays in fucking Corfu . . .

The world he'd thought he was part of. Would always be part of. Boring Alan Human. Owner of an architectural salvage business that was doing really pretty well, thank you. All tickety-boo, ship-shape, pension sorted, nicely dull . . .

Until that man came into it. That poisonous, fucking man . . .

Before coming to Giorgio's, he'd taken a look around Agios Symeon. Trying to find the road to Hepworth's estate. Couldn't work out where it was. It'd looked pretty straightforward on Google Earth. He'd look again tomorrow when he wasn't knackered and half-cut.

That fucker Hepworth . . .

The beer came and he took a gulp. Paid the guy. Tried not to let on just how much he'd enjoyed the taste of it. The feel of it. The effect it had.

Fist of Retribution guy was looking at him. Very still, implacable, cradling a glass of Coke. His arms resting on the table, encircling the glass in his big forearms. Openly watching everyone in the bar. Didn't care if they clocked him. How old was *he*, then? Thirty maybe? Alan slid his eyes away from him, avoiding eye contact. Fought the urge to look back.

'Now, there *is* something I need to warn you about, I'm afraid . . .'

Christ, was Cindy still banging on? Alan returned to his seat and grabbed a handful of crisps.

'What was it Agatha Christie said . . . ?'

I don't know, Cindy, what was it Agatha fucking Christie said?

'The butler did it'?

'Even in the Garden of Eden there was a serpent.' Cindy gave a little laugh. 'I mean, really, this is the safest place on earth, but just lately there *have* been some break-ins.'

Dark mutterings from among the Negroni drinkers.

'Nothing serious. Nobody's been hurt, or anything like that. It's annoying more than anything. Passports, phones, laptops, that sort of thing. There are safes in all of your villas, so I advise you to lock your valuables away when you go out. Even during the day. And just, you know, be security-conscious – fasten all the windows and lock all the doors. Obviously. So, it's probably Albanians. They come over here, and . . . You know. It's not how it was.'

It's not how it was. You're fucking right, darling. Nothing is.

Alan sank his beer. Glanced back towards the terrace. The girls were taking selfies. Fist of Retribution was still staring. Bank loan guy had gone. As if he'd never been there. Beyond the terrace, the boats sat on the water, glowing under a bright moon. Alan thought of family holidays – him and Alice and Lauren, when nothing had been more serious than getting sand on the tiles. When the only decision had been whether to go for the calamari or the prawns. Red wine or retsina. Lamb souvlaki or chicken . . .

He wanted to upend his table, scream at the others, smash his glass against the wall, throw his shit around like a chimpanzee. He accidentally caught the eye of Fist of Retribution and gave an involuntary smile. Best to behave.

That guy could kill him with one flick of his giant hands. Could crush the life out of him. Smother him. Reduce him to nothing.

And part of him wished he would. Longed for oblivion. Instead of this constant feeling of being filled with poisonous bile. This great pressure inside him.

But not now. Not yet.

Instead, fuck it, he got himself another beer. Cindy had finally finished, was going round chatting. Alan shared a few mundane pleasantries with her. Commented on how lovely it was here. How lucky she was to live here. The usual bollocks.

Later. How much later he didn't know – didn't want to look at his phone – he stumbled back up the road to his villa feeling vile. Ashamed. His clothes rags of sweat. His underpants up his arse. Muttering to himself. Swearing. Obscenely cursing the little town and everyone in it. Heavy and bloated. His hands trembling.

But, at last, there it was, the nameplate on the wall lit by a little lamp – Villa Kassiopeia. A short driveway through pine trees. He could see his dark-blue hire car parked by the front door, looking black in the moonlight. He swore. He was sure he'd left the porch light on when he went out. When he got to the house, he dug out his keys and tried to remember which was the right one for the front door. It all seemed such an effort. He closed his eyes for a moment and swayed.

And then he felt a hand steady him. Taking his elbow in a firm, tight grip, just this side of painful. He sobered quickly, jerked his head round to see who it was.

A man in darkness. His eyes glittering. He must have just stepped out from the trees. He took Alan's keys from him with a swift, tricksy movement before he even knew what was going on.

'Let's go inside, Mister Human. I think we need to talk.'

3

LAUREN

Sigrid was crying again. It wasn't unusual for one of the girls to be crying at night. And since she'd returned from suspension it had been Sigrid's turn. This was the third night, and it was affecting the whole dorm. Nobody was sleeping well. Lauren was trying not to let it wind her up. Sigrid couldn't help it. What made it worse, though, was that Sigrid was aware how annoying it was and was trying to hide it. She held it in, making small, choked sounds, muffled whimpers. Her hand over her mouth. Head buried under her pillow. But then it would burst out, worse than if she'd just let it happen. Better half an hour of shrieking and wailing and then exhausted silence than this slow-drip torture.

Better for her. Better for Lauren. Better for everyone.

It wasn't like she'd even been suspended for that long. She'd come back real quick to be fair. She'd obviously made up with Julian. Apologised for whatever it was she was supposed to have done wrong. And now this.

Lauren wondered what was really up with the girl. During the day she was Little Miss Smiley-Face. Big eyes. Mouth wide with wonder and joy. OMG-ing all over the place. Super-friendly with

32

everyone. Soooo helpful. Sucking up to the trainers. Chatting away about nothing with Miss Lily and Pixie.

And then at night she just totally lost it. Was in pieces.

The Team were as supportive as they could be, but it was impossible to talk without being seen. The policy of 'Sharing Is Caring' was strictly enforced. Nothing was private, nothing was secret, nothing was personal. If you had a problem, the correct protocol was to bring it up at a Group Chat before dinner.

You couldn't talk in the dorm. There were cameras in here – the type that could see in the dark. Microphones as well. Julian had shown Lauren some recorded footage the first time she'd been suspended. Images of the girls at night. The picture green and blurry. They all looked like ghosts, with bright, white, reflective eyes. Cats' eyes. That was in South Africa, but the set-up was the same here. At the time she'd wondered why Julian would show her and not keep it a secret. She'd worked it out soon enough, though. It was to let her know that he could see everything, that he knew everything. He was the eye in the sky. Like, God, really, she supposed. Like on the TV show *Big Brother*.

His excuse for showing Lauren the footage was that he was asking about another girl, Roseanna. She'd been moping about, crying, getting up in the night.

'Is she OK, Lauren? Is she well? She doesn't look happy. I want her to be happy. I want all my girls to be happy. If you're unhappy, I'm unhappy. Why does she get up in the night, Lauren? Is there something wrong? Has she told you anything . . . ?'

Roseanna hadn't been well. That was all. She'd picked up a stomach bug and Julian must have known that. The Team medic would have told him. They had check-ups nearly every day. Roseanna had to keep running to the toilet during practice. Was up and down all night, going to the bathroom and back. Julian had casually shown Lauren that there were even cameras in *there*. Although he hadn't gone so far as to show that he had cameras in the actual stalls. She knew there must be, though. Why wouldn't there be?

Nothing Was Private. Nothing Was Secret. Nothing Was Personal.

There were cameras in the dorm, the bathroom, all the shared areas inside the villa, on the pathways, out on the courts, the terraces, the beach ...

For your security.

And she was pretty sure that there were microphones hidden all round the place as well. There were certainly some in the dorm. Weren't even hidden. If you were seen having too many one-on-ones, Julian, or, worse, Miss Lily, would call you in. Ask you what you'd been talking about. Though they probably already knew.

'There are no secrets here, Lauren ... ' Miss Lily would say, smiling at you over her glasses. 'This is a happy place where everyone is open, because there is nothing to hide. This is a whole new way of living that Julian has created here. We are a community.' Knotting the fingers of both hands together to show how tight knit they were. 'We share everything. If you need to say something, say it at the Group Chat. That's what they're for. And you know you can always say whatever you want. You can speak your mind ... '

No. Right. Yes. OK. I'm with the programme.

You were never told off in public, in front of anyone else. Julian never raised his voice. He floated around on a pink cloud with rainbows in his eyes. *We are all chilled here. We are all one loving family.* If anything came up at a Group Chat it was met with concerned smiles and offers of counselling.

'Thank you so much for sharing ... '

But Julian took it all in. Listening closely. Sitting cross-legged on his mat. Or, if he wasn't able to be there, Pixie, or Miss Lily would report back to him. And if it got as far as a private session with him that was a whole different story. No more smiles. No more unicorns and rainbows and heart emojis. He would yell and scream, calling you all sort of names, swearing. Really nasty words.

His language had shocked Lauren the first time. He'd used words she'd never heard before. Insults so specific, so vile, so brutal it was like he'd punched her in the belly.

So the girls had all learned never to bring up anything remotely serious at a Group Chat. You could say the coffee machine by the changing rooms wasn't working (again!), or complain that there was never enough salad, or that some of the racquets really needed restringing . . . but if you ever, *ever*, even just *implied* that this wasn't, like, being on the greatest holiday of all time and you were *so* lucky and honoured and special, then you were in deep shit, sister.

Lauren, like all the girls, tried as hard as she fucking could not to make Julian mad. You had to please him. To make him happy. Because when he was happy the whole place was happy.

'What do you say, girls, isn't this the most beautiful morning? Now, let's get out there and *play some tennis*. And if you're *good*, we'll have a party this weekend! Yes! Isn't that the best?'

But if he was unhappy about something. Who knew what? Or *why*? You couldn't ever tell. If he was unhappy, he'd go totally quiet. And then you were in trouble. And there was nowhere you could go to get away from his black mood. There was nowhere to hide in this place.

Yeah. You had to work really hard not to piss Julian off. If he got mad at you, he suspended you from The Team. Put you in 'detention'. Which meant sleeping in a small windowless bedroom next to Julian's suite. The detention room was comfortable enough, and it had a tiny bathroom – toilet, shower and sink. But the door was locked at night and it was like being in solitary confinement. A prison. A luxury prison, she supposed, but a prison all the same.

This whole place was a prison.

They'd arrived in May, after winter training in South Africa. At first, she'd been excited. She'd grown to hate The Lodge, in the bush outside Cape Town. Miles from anywhere. Penned in by high, barbed-wire fences with lookout towers and uniformed guards in red berets carrying Kalashnikovs.

'For your own security. South Africa can be dangerous . . .'

Arriving here had felt like paradise. The sea, the beach, the cliffs, the mountain. But she'd soon realised it was just another concentration camp. And in the autumn, they'd be returning to The Lodge. Julian liked to move to follow the sun. He said it was because the warmth was good for the soul. But Lauren reckoned it was actually so that he had an excuse not to wear too many clothes. Him and everyone else here. He only dressed up if he was travelling – he was always flying off around the world – or if he was going out, or when there were special guests at the house. The rest of the time it was a thin T-shirt, leather sliders, beads and loose shorts or jogging pants. She'd always called them trackie bottoms when she was growing up. Here everything was Americanised. Even though Julian had been born in Milton Keynes.

Boy, he loved his jogging pants. His *sweatpants*. Nasty, over-designed ones from designers like Gucci and Versace. Insanely expensive. Issy had told her that one Fendi pair cost more than a thousand dollars. *A thousand dollars!* For a pair of trackie bottoms! Trackie bottoms that looked like shit.

Sigrid sobbed. One of the other girls tutted. Lauren rolled over to face the other way. Then thought. *Fuck. No.* She had to do something about this. So, Miss Lily might call her in, but she could go fuck herself.

She threw back her duvet and swung her feet over the side of the bed. She shivered. The dorm was kept really cold at night. She slid into her Japanese slippers and scuffed over to Sigrid's bed.

Sigrid recoiled when Lauren got to her, shaking her head, fearful of the consequences. Julian kept dim wall lights on all night in the dorm, so Lauren could just make out the panic in Sigrid's eyes.

'It's all right,' she said, loud and clear. 'I know you've got gut ache.' And she gave a little wink. 'I'll get you some water. Go and see the medic tomorrow, yeah?'

Then, before Sigrid could protest, she quickly walked off. She filled a paper cup with chilled water from the cooler by the bathroom door. The cooler bubbled and gurgled and a girl in a nearby bed swore at her. Lauren swore right back at her in a hoarse whisper, then returned to Sigrid.

'Drink this.'

As Sigrid sat up, Lauren leaned in to pull her hair out of her face and then quickly whispered in her ear.

'Tomorrow. On the way to practice. Mob Chat.'

And once again moved away before Sigrid could say anything.

She got back into bed. Curling up into the warmth. She knew how Sigrid felt. She'd spent more than a few nights sobbing into her pillow. Not lately. She was learning to be tough, to shut her emotions off, to lock them down in a secret part of her brain.

It was her birthday in two weeks. She was going to be sixteen. But she already felt a hundred years old. She was tired. Old-lady tired. Sigrid was quiet. Then Lauren must have dozed off for a bit, because when she rolled over to look towards Sigrid, her bed was empty.

4

MACINTYRE

'You OK, Human?'

'Er . . . Yes . . . No. I don't know.'

'You're OK.'

'Fine. Yes. Right. Yes. I'm OK.'

'Good. That's settled, then. So – next question – what the fuck are you doing here?'

'I'm on holiday.'

'Do you know who I am? Do you have any idea who I am?'

'No. Yes. No . . . You're the bank loan guy from the bar.'

'Bank loan?'

'Sorry. Yeah. No, I mean – I thought you looked, kind of, when I saw you in the bar, I thought, no offence, you looked kind of normal. Like a guy in an ad for bank loans. You know – ordinary guy – nice guy . . . With a Labrador.'

'That's the point.'

'What point? What's the point? Who are you? What's going on?'

'For now, you can call me Macintyre. Robert Macintyre.'

'I can call you that. Right. But it's not your name? No?'

'It's what you call me.'

'OK.'

'Good. Now. Tell me. Why did you come here?'

'Why does anyone come to Corfu? I told you. I'm on holiday. As far as I know, that's not a crime. Ha-ha . . . You need to tell me why we're having this conversation. It's making me really anxious. Really, really anxious. I'm fighting for my breath, here. My throat's all . . . It's very dry. It's making it very hard to speak.'

'Then shut up.'

'Right. Sorry.'

Macintyre sat there in silence for a long while. Staring at Human, who was shaking. Could be fear, could be the aircon, or it could be the booze. Probably all three. He was a mess.

'Take some deep breaths, Alan. Calm yourself down.' He had to tread very carefully. Say the right thing. Not make things worse. Christ. How long had it been since he'd left the villa? Not much more than six hours and already his carefully thought-through plan had gone to shit. That had to be some kind of record.

Human rubbed his face. Made a sort of involuntary gulping, gasping sound. His skin was very red. Hadn't been here long enough to get sunburned. What was it made someone's skin go red like that? High blood pressure? His eyes were red and watery, like a little kid had badly coloured in a face and got the pink everywhere. The guy couldn't be much more than fifty, but his hair was almost white. It wasn't anything as melodramatic as shock that had turned it that colour, though. He'd seen pictures of Human from when he was in his thirties. Guy had gone prematurely grey. But, between his red face, white hair and lurid, purple 'holiday' shirt, he was certainly vivid.

The villa was cold. The air conditioning set on high. But Human was sweating.

'I'm not going to hurt you.'

'Thank you.'

'But I do need to figure out what to do with you.' He leaned back into his chair. He'd looked around the villa when he'd brought Human inside. Wanted to make sure he was alone – hadn't brought his wife along to the party. The villa was a standard build. Very similar to where Macintyre was staying. He was pleased to see there was a modem, the password handily taped to the top, and a Bluetooth speaker. He keyed the password into his phone, locked into the wi-fi and then connected to the speaker with his Bluetooth. Played a Greek rebetiko playlist through the speaker. Slightly too loudly. A distracting clatter of bouzouki, mandolins and clarinets filled the room. He very much doubted that Hepworth would have somehow got his security in here already and bugged the place, but old habits died hard.

Human's things were spilled out all over the place. Only been here a few hours and already the place was a tip. Typical detritus of a drunken man left to his own devices and falling apart, fouling his nest.

Macintyre figured telling the truth would be the best route.

'Here it is,' he said. 'Technically I work for you.' That got his attention. 'You hired me, Mister Human.'

'I did?'

'You did. We signed a deal. And it wasn't part of the deal that you turned up here.'

'You're ...' Realisation was dawning. 'You're the guy Dana Richards put me on to? You're the salvage guy.'

'Yeah – a bit like *you*, Alan. We're both in salvage. You rescue *things* and I rescue *people*. How long has Dana been your lawyer?'

'I've used her for, it must be at least twenty years, and ...'

'So, you trust her?'

'Of course, I trust her, yes. Yes, I trust her.'

He paused the music. The sudden silence was disorientating. Human looked alarmed. Now what?

'And she recommended you use my services,' Macintyre said softly.

'Well, she recommended I used your organisation,' said Human. 'There were no names. It was understood that there'd be no personal contact.'

'THEN WHAT THE FUCK ARE YOU DOING HERE?' His voice sounded startlingly loud in this quiet room full of hard, reflective surfaces. Human rocked back in his seat. Most adults aren't used to being shouted at. Sometimes it helped to shock people. It sobered them up. Made them focus. Like a slap in the face. Bracing. Macintyre could do a good simulation of psychotic rage. It was an act, but a convincing one. Of course, it sometimes went the other way and you simply shut them down. But Human was sunk so deep in his alcohol haze he took it and swam to the surface for a moment.

Macintyre started the music up again. Setting Human on edge. He was staring at him, eyes very round.

'I thought . . . I thought . . . '

'You didn't think, though, did you? Or you wouldn't be here. I do this for a living, Alan. It's my job. I sort people's problems out.'

'Yes, yes, I know, Dana told me . . . She explained . . . '

'So, she will have explained that I have my own team.'

'Yes.'

'Which means I don't need you. You can see that? Your only contribution to this undertaking would be to fuck it up. If you haven't already done so.'

'Mm . . . If you put it like that . . . '

'I put it like that because that's how it is.'

'Yes. I suppose . . . '

'Don't suppose. Just stick to the facts. You signed documents. Yes? You remember that?'

'I do, yes. I signed all sorts of stuff.'

'And you paid a lot of money. I'm not cheap.'

'Not cheap at all.'

'If you'd wanted someone cheaper there are plenty out there. Or you could have saved all your money and sorted this out yourself. As I say, you're a salvage expert yourself, aren't you?'

'Architectural salvage, that's different.'

'Aha, yes. There we have it. It's different. *You don't do what I do.*'

'No. No. I don't know how to ... I didn't know what to do, so I ... I couldn't do what you do ... I couldn't get Lauren myself ...'

'And yet you appear to be trying to do just that. Why else would you be here? Confusing human salvage with architectural salvage.'

'I couldn't sit around doing nothing. I'd had my fill of it. I couldn't wait any longer. I was crawling up the walls. And when I saw that Hepworth was here for the summer ... That he was training his tennis team here. And I pictured her. Here on the island. My Lauren. I thought – if I could just be close to her ... And I thought ...'

'No, Mister Human. We've already established that you *didn't* think. You blundered. You fumbled. You blindly, *thoughtlessly*, and, by the look of it, drunkenly, came to the conclusion that somehow you could help by being here. So, you put yourself on a plane, had some stiff drinks, and now I have to work out what to do with you.'

'It's all right. Nobody knows me here.'

'You booked a villa. Using your own name. Travelling on your own passport.'

'Yes, but ... Is that so bad?'

'It gets worse. You went all over town, trying to find the road to Hepworth's estate.'

'How do you know that?'

'It's my job to know.'

'But nobody else ...'

'Did you see that guy in the bar? Big guy? Tattoos. Dumb expression – like a bullock that's had a bolt fired into its brain?'

'I couldn't miss him.'

'You know who he is?'

'No.'

'Who he works for?'

'No. How could I? Does he work for you?'

'For me? What use would I have for a walking fridge? His name's Ray Jordan and he works for Julian Hepworth.'

'You're joking?'

'If it was a joke, surely we'd both be laughing. Do you see me laughing?'

'No ... Do you think he knew who I was?'

'He was clearly checking everyone out. Making no secret of it. But my guess is he was looking for the wrong thing. The guy's a bodyguard, muscle, not Sherlock Holmes. Sensitised to trouble. Fine-tuned to spot latent aggression. Probably not so great with faces. Not too worried about someone as *unthreatening* as you.'

'He didn't say anything to me. Didn't approach me. He left the bar before I did.'

'By the looks of you, Alan, I'm guessing everyone left the bar before you did.'

'Hm ... Can I get? I mean – is it all right if I have a drink? I have some vodka. You can have some if you like ... '

'You can do what you like, Mister Human. This is your villa.'

Human hauled himself up from his chair and stood for a moment, swaying. Breathing heavily. Then he wobbled through to the kitchen.

'Pour me a small one. Ice, if you have it.'

'Sure. No problem.'

He heard Human rattling around in the kitchen. Jumped up and hid his wifi camera on a high shelf among some Greek knick-knacks – plates and vases and little fake statuettes. Then he sat back down and thumbed his phone awake. Opened the app and checked the feed. The camera was tiny, but it had a very wide lens. The picture wasn't perfect. He could finesse it later if necessary. For now it served its purpose.

43

Human came back in carrying two glasses. One considerably fuller than the other. Bleary-eyed, mushy.

'What was this Ray Jordan guy doing at the bar?' he asked, passing a glass over.

'Hepworth likes to feel secure. As I'm sure you know, he even owns a security company. All the latest hi-tech gadgets.'

'Right.'

'Right.' Didn't tell Alan that his neat little camera was one of Hepworth's gadgets. 'That compound of his, the one you couldn't find, is vacuum-sealed. And it's not just hi-tech surveillance stuff. Hepworth has a hefty security team and Ray's in charge. I guess he probably comes down into town every Saturday to look over the new arrivals. Hepworth's the kind of guy who needs to know everything going on around him. Who's new in town? Might they be useful? A threat? Ray probably keeps on the look-out for young girls as well. Anything new to add to the mix at Patia HepKat.'

'I want to know . . .'

'That's right. You want to know. You want to know everything. What's he doing to your little girl?'

'I don't want to know.'

'Yeah. You want to know, and you *don't* want to know. Which is why you should have stayed at home. Where it's safe. Where you couldn't fuck things up. And I could have got on with my job and in time I'd have delivered Lauren back to you. You need to know, and you don't need to know.'

'Yes. No. Yes.'

'Dana transferred your money to my account. The final payment will be made when Lauren's home. That's what you *need* to know. Now I'll tell you what you *don't* need to know. You don't need to know anything about what I do. You don't need to know how I plan to get Lauren back to you.'

'I can help you . . .'

44

'No. You can't. The only thing you could do is deliver a lorryload of fuck-up. I need you to book the next flight back to England.'

'No. No, I can't do that. I was going crazy. I'll do what you say. I won't get in the way.'

'You already did. I've had to intervene. Day one.'

'Yes. I get that. And I'm sorry, but ... I can't go back. I can't. I need to be close to her.'

Macintyre thought for a long time about this. Filtering out the clattering of the music. Finally, he looked at Human and spoke. Calmly and levelly. Like he was explaining something to a child.

'OK. Then you stay here in the villa. You don't go into town. You don't show your face again. You don't use your phone.'

'But ...'

'No. Please. Just listen. What do you think, Alan? A guy like Hepworth? A hi-tech entrepreneur who owns a security firm. He'd have to be a complete fool not to use his own technology. Do you think he's a fool?'

'He's a cunt.'

'Well, he's a cunt who probably keeps files on all his girls. Photos of family and friends. Which is why you stay put. I'll arrange for someone to bring you whatever you need. You're going to have to be patient, though.'

'How long ... ?'

He put a finger to his lips – SSSHHHH. Looked at his phone. Chose a new track. A familiar plodding beat came out of the speaker. The stabbing, metallic clang of a bouzouki over the top.

'You recognise this music, Alan?'

'Yes ... Yes. It's from *Zorba the Greek*, isn't it?'

'So, you'll know how it goes? Starts slow, gradually speeds up?'

'Yes.'

'That's how this is going to work. Like a game of chess. At first nothing much appears to be happening. A few pawns take one small step at a time. Then maybe the bishops and knight might come out to play. But eventually things speed up and pieces fall all over the place, and in the end the king is defeated. You got that?'

'Yes.'

'It's going to be long and possibly tedious. With any luck, after a few days you'll get so fucking stir crazy you'll be begging me to let you fly home.'

'No. I won't. I can't stand being in that house. So close to her bedroom. Her things. Pictures of her everywhere you look. I can't even talk to my wife. I was going insane.'

'Clearly. But when I get Lauren out – which I will do. She doesn't travel back with you.'

'What? No?'

'I have my own methods of extraction. Which I'm not going to share with you. Hepworth's a powerful man. Connected. And he has more money than Mongolia. Lauren won't be safe until she's back in Henley. So, you make your own way home. And you let me deal with Lauren.'

'He has to be punished,' said Alan quietly. 'That man – Hepworth – he has to be punished.'

'Not part of the deal. Not my job. That's for the law.'

'He can't get away with it.'

'He won't. Not for ever. They always fall in the end. Weinstein, Strauss-Kahn, Roger Ailes, David Hamilton, Jean-Luc Brunel . . . But it's not my job to bring them down.'

'But you could . . . I don't know . . . '

'Have you ever seen anything about me in the press, Alan?'

'No.'

'Or seen any photographs? Had you ever heard of me before you went to Dana? Are there videos about what I do on YouTube?'

'No . . . I looked.'

'I'm not James Bond, known by every barman in the world. If I make it into the media, I'm finished. I'll never work again. I don't want publicity and I can't break the law. I fuck up and Hepworth can argue that he's not keeping Lauren there against her wishes. I fuck up and there's a danger you never see her again. I do soft extractions. I leave the toilet as clean as I found it. That's in the contract. And I will work out a way to go in there and get Lauren out safely.'

'And the other girls? What about the other girls? You just leave them there?'

The bouzouki was going crazy now, faster and faster, a whirl of noise. Zorba's dance. Out of control.

'You're paying me to get Lauren,' said Macintyre. 'That's what I'm going to do.'

'That's cold.'

'That's my life.'

5

RAY

Ray Jordan had come to the conclusion that being a psychopath was not necessarily a bad thing.

He'd made a study of it. Read many books. Well, two. Was reading a third one now. *The Psychopath Test* by some snowflake journalist called Jon Ronson. Beatty had recommended it. Said it was funny. Ray was too annoyed to find it funny. Bottom line. There just wasn't enough about psychopaths in it.

Ray was sitting outside his room under the bug zapper, listening to bugs exploding, reading Ronson's book and drinking his last Diet Coke of the night. The can sat, sweating, on the little cast-iron table next to his phone, his carabiner of keys, his holstered SIG Sauer and his SureFire Defender torch. Neatly in a row. Everything in order.

He'd looked Ronson up on the internet. Confirmed his suspicions. What, *really*, did this nerdy looking guy know about psychopaths? And he'd got it all wrong in his book. Said it was black and white. You were either a psychopath or you weren't. Like psychopaths were another breed. Well, that was bullshit for a start. As Ray understood it, from his reading and from the internet, everybody was somewhere on a psychopathic spectrum. That was what the last book he'd read had been about. *The Wisdom of Psychopaths*, by a guy called Kevin Dutton. He'd checked out Dutton on YouTube as well. Speccy, like Ronson, but spoke like a cockney burglar. His ideas made sense to Ray. Dutton said we could learn a lot from psychopaths. Plus, he talked about a spectrum.

To be fair, everything was on a spectrum, wasn't it? There was an autism spectrum. An intelligence spectrum. A beauty spectrum. A wanker spectrum –

At the bottom – total wanker – Corbyn, Blair, Greta Thunberg, Prince Harry, Kim Jong-un, Ronaldo, Scrappy-Doo, Branson, Bono, Sting.

At the top – not wankers in any way – Bruce Lee, Jason Statham, Jordan Peterson, Tommy Robinson, Steve Bannon, Pope Urban II, who sent off the First Crusade, Karl Urban – or at least the characters he played in *The Boys* and *Dredd*. Judge Dredd, although of course he wasn't a real person. Vladimir Putin, Vlad the Impaler and those off-duty American soldiers who twatted that terrorist on a French train.

BZZZZZZZZZZT.

One less insect in the world.

Made sense there was a psychopath spectrum as well, didn't it? At the top were your full-on psychos – serial killers, axe murderers, ISIS assassins and the like – but just below them were the interesting people. The people who made the world function. Business leaders, religious leaders, surgeons, generals, lawyers, salesmen, gangsters, top chefs, SAS dudes, sports stars, Formula 1 drivers, City traders, police officers, bouncers, bodyguards, spies – basically, the James Bonds of this world.

And below the James Bond level you had your ordinary soldiers, ordinary sportsmen, ordinary businesspeople, stand-up comics, firemen, the guys on *Forged in Fire* who made those cool knives – the people who did things, got on with stuff.

But then, down and down you sank into ever more wishy-washy waters, where people got softer, more gullible, more huggy-kissy, where they ummed and ahed, wrung their hands, kept cats and read the *Guardian*. These were the people who saw all sides of an argument, encouraged the homeless by giving them money, welcomed immigrants into the country and didn't laugh at men who'd had sex changes and still just looked like blokes in wigs.

This is where you found the smiling, defenceless, warm-hearted sheeple who shopped in second-hand clothes shops, tried to save the planet by dressing up as clowns on demonstrations and went on marches in support of teachers or nurses. A lot of them actually *were* teachers or nurses. They were carers, charity workers, hairdressers . . .

And it all bled out until you got to the bottom, where it was like the bottom of the ocean, full of pale, shapeless blobs with no spines, wafting about in the gloom with wide eyes and startled expressions.

Social workers.

It all had to do with something called 'empathy'. Which seemed to be about understanding other people's feelings and giving a shit about them. A proper, pure psychopath didn't have any empathy at all, while the poor sods at the bottom of the spectrum had so much fucking empathy, they could barely function. They were too anxious and weepy and feeble. *Too female.*

BZZZZZZZZZZT.

Another insect bit the dust.

A psychopath had as much empathy as a bug zapper.

A psychopath was someone who could make a decision quickly and unemotionally, rationally – 'This is what needs to be done and it doesn't matter if there's some collateral damage.'

People at the bottom of the scale *were* the collateral damage.

As far as Ray could see, empathy was a trick invented by the upper orders to get the lower orders to do the washing up.

Yes, if you wanted someone to wipe an old man's arse in a care home or push a drooling pleej in a wheelchair to the shops, or teach a Down's Syndrome kid to swim, you wouldn't hire a psychopath.

But if you wanted to sort shit out ... Well, then you called in James Bond, didn't you?

Most people were probably somewhere in the middle of the spectrum. Just ordinary. Neither up nor down. Unlikely to rob or kill you, but unlikely to make much of a dent in history neither.

BZZZZZZZZZZT.

Lot of bugs out tonight.

It was interesting – putting things into scales. He guessed there was even a scale of 'People Who Wrote Books About Psychopaths'. He'd put Dutton – a geezer – at the top, and Ronson at the bottom. Ronson was classic lower-end stuff. A nerd. Anxious. All over the place. Couldn't make his mind up about nothing. The other book Ray had read – well, half read – he'd skimmed a lot of it – was *Snakes in Suits*. He couldn't remember who'd written it, but Ray would probably put him in the middle.

Dutton, he liked best. Dutton had some cool ideas. 'Fail Fast' was one – don't fear making mistakes. Get it over with and move on. Another one was 'Decouple Emotion From Behaviour'. Which basically meant ditch your feelings, they'll just get in the way. Another rule was 'Be More Self-Interested'. That spoke for itself. It was a rule Ray was trying very hard to live by.

To be fair, he tried to live by all of Dutton's rules. He wanted to be near the top of the scale. There was a big checklist of what you needed to do to be a proper psychopath. He didn't understand some of the words – like grandiose and narcissism – but he got the gist of it. To be a psychopath you had to convince people you were intelligent, sincere, powerful, charming, witty and entertaining.

BZZZZZZZZZZT.

All attributes from the top end of the cool spectrum and the not-being-a-wanker spectrum. Which he supposed, to be fair, were both the same things, really.

BZZZZZZZZZZT.

Damn that was a big one. A great, hairy moth shot down in flames.

Yeah. Psychopaths were sure of themselves, ruthless, fearless, charismatic, manipulative, impulsive, persuasive and had a total lack of conscience and empathy.

To Ray these all seemed like *good* things. It seemed clear to him that without psychopaths the world just wouldn't work. There should be an organisation – Functioning Psychopaths For A Functioning Society.

What was the acronym? FPFFS . . . He said it out loud, making a sort of dismissive farting noise and laughed. That was funny.

But he was fired up now. It was time to speak the truth here. He was so going to tweet about this. He had to use a pseudonym on social media, obviously. A secret account with a secret avatar. He used a picture of a winged horse and the handle @security27X. Hepworth would sack Ray if he knew it was him. It would count as a massive security breach. Everything that happened around Hepworth was secret. Had to be.

So, what about Hepworth, then? Was he a psychopath? No shit! You didn't get to be one of the richest men in the world and own one of the biggest tech companies around without being a fucking psychopath. Although, if you thought about it, Bill Gates was more of a wanker than a psycho. And probably somewhere in the upper reaches of the autistic spectrum as well. Musk, too.

But Hepworth? Hepworth was something else. He was charming, could turn it on and off when he wanted. He was Number 1 in his world: dynamic, ruthless, manipulative, could sniff out a vulnerable person a mile away and home in on them, use them, chew them up, wring them out and dump them in the tampon bin by the bog. He was a good liar. Although he wouldn't call it that. He'd say he was just presenting his own version of the truth. What was it that stupid tart who worked for Trump said? *Alternative facts.* Hepworth knew all about alternative facts and how to use them.

And there was the sex. Big part of the psychopath deal, as it goes. Sexual power. Using women. And – fuck me sideways – when it came to Hepworth and sex . . .

Let's not go there, Ray.

Ray's job was to serve. To keep Hepworth safe. Not ask any questions. And in return? The best paid job he could ever dream of.

BZZZZZZZZZZT.

It was a warm night. Even this late. No problem. The aircon would keep his room nice and frosty. He never had trouble sleeping. Didn't need too much of it. Four or five hours a night was fine. He did like to sit out at the end of a day, though, like this. Look at the stars. The bats swooping over the security lights. The sprinklers dancing on the lawns. The lights dimmed in the main buildings past the terrace. Calm. Chilled. Everything locked down nice and tight for the night. Everything under control.

The only thing on his mind was the big party Hepworth had planned for the 14th. Hepworth liked to party, but it was always risky letting others inside the perimeter. Plus, Hepworth always wanted more girls. Young ones he could impress. Those two down at the taverna might be a good bet. Their first holiday without their parents by the looks of it. Easily impressed. Easily manipulated. He'd get Beatty and Herve to keep an eye on them. Vlachos was teed up to supply some more gash as well. Nice guy, Vlachos, but Ray wasn't sure he was quite near enough to the top of the spectrum to really cut it as a gangster. Someone was going to stomp on him, sooner rather than later.

He put the party out of his mind. He knew that as long as he kept a cool head, stayed on top of things, knew everyone's movements, they'd make it through OK. They'd done it enough times before.

Nothing to worry about.

No need to even break a sweat.

BZZZZZZZZZZT.

He downed a last sip of Coke. It had gone flat. Warm. And then he saw movement. Something white, flitting between the sprinklers.

He took a deep breath and blew it out slowly and noisily from his nose. Centring himself. He stood up and clipped the SIG Sauer on to his belt in the small of his back. Grabbed his torch. Woke his phone and used it to kill all the lights. Hit the thumb switch on the SureFire and aimed it at where he'd seen the movement.

A girl. She raised her hands to shield her eyes. Even from this distance the SureFire's beam was blinding. He walked slowly and purposefully towards her across the damp lawn. Didn't want to spook her, but she needed to keep still and pay attention to him.

She was one of the tennis team. Mixed race. What was her name? Something foreign. A Viking sort of name.

Sigrid.

That was it. Sigrid the mixed-race Viking. Her feet were bare. She was wearing a nightdress that was slightly wet from the sprinklers and sticking to her. She looked panicked, almost demented.

'It's Sigrid, isn't it?'

She nodded. Still covering her face. Blinking in the light that he was keeping focused on her. Maximum brightness. 1,000 lumen.

'Come towards me,' he said. 'Come out of the sprinklers. You're getting soaked, love.'

He lowered the beam slightly so that she was only illuminated by the weaker outer beam and no longer blinded.

'You know me, right?' he said. Again, she nodded. 'You know I'm not a threat.'

Nodding. Always just nodding.

'You got a tongue in your mouth? No, don't nod, love – I need you to speak. Answer me. Can you speak?'

54

'Yes.'

'Good. Now we're getting somewhere. You know the curfew rules. You shouldn't be out here at night. You know that? Say it.'

'Yes. I know.'

'It's for your own safety. We put the dogs out at night. You know that?'

'Yes.'

'So, what are you doing? Where were you going?'

'I'm not doing anything.' She spoke with a Swedish, Danish type of accent, which sounded weird coming out of a mixed-race girl. She was pretty. They were *all* pretty. Although with her wet face and hair, no make-up, she was a bit bedraggled, her eyes red and swollen.

'Where were you going?'

'Nowhere.'

'No such place. Are you all right?'

This time she didn't nod and didn't say anything either. She just stared at him with her frightened, bunny eyes.

'I asked if you were all right.'

'Please don't hurt me.'

'Why would I hurt you? It's not my job to hurt you. It's my job to keep you safe. I need to get you back to your dormitory.'

'Please don't. I don't want to go back.'

'Has something happened? Someone done something to you?'

Now she shook her head.

'So why don't you want to go back?'

'I want to go home.'

'You live *here*.'

'No. I live in Denmark.'

'Can I ask, love? Where you thought you were actually going dressed like that?'

'He takes our clothes.' Sigrid took a step towards Ray. Looked him in the eyes. Showing some strength. 'Will you help me?'

She stepped even closer. Gave him a pathetic smile. That brief show of strength disappearing. Bottom of the spectrum stuff. Victim behaviour.

'I can't help you,' he said. 'I have a job to do.'

'I could . . . do something for you.'

She got close enough to put a hand to his chest. Moved it down towards his stomach. He took hold of it and moved it away.

'Don't do that. Don't touch me, please.'

He wouldn't put it past Hepworth to have set this up. A test of Ray's loyalty. His reliability. Maybe he even wanted Ray to do something. Sort of kinky shit Hepworth might get a kick from. Ray was pretty sure there were cameras hidden in his rooms. He'd looked for them but couldn't find any. Whatever the case. He wasn't going to play Hepworth's games.

'I'm going to take you back to the dorm, love,' he said. 'And we'll forget all about this. No need for me to report it. You just need to behave yourself, not get yourself into any trouble.'

Sigrid gave a sort of gasp, almost a shriek, and dropped to her knees, wrapping her arms around his legs.

'I want to go home.'

Ray felt embarrassed. What must this look like? He hadn't felt someone hold him like this for a long while. His last physical contact had been grabbing some drunk arsehole who'd made a lunge for Hepworth in Nice.

And before that? Probably Rachel. Before the bitch had left him. Before he'd turned to Christ and taken a vow of celibacy. He spent a lot of time online, chatting, praying, researching, worshipping, watching talks and sermons. There was a lot to get your head around. Some Christian celibacy groups were really interesting, and he was quite into the whole MGTOW thing. 'Men Going Their Own Way' had a purpose about them, unlike the nerds in the Incel movement, who were classic bottom-of-the-spectrum wankers.

He was strong. He had God on his side. He couldn't be tempted.

'Come on,' he said, placing a hand on the girl's shoulder. 'You're not a prisoner here. In the morning you go and see Miss Lily. She'll sort something out. See if we can get you back to your folks. Yeah?' He prised her arms away from his legs and lifted her back on to her feet. She felt very small and fragile. Like he could snap her without meaning to. How old was she? Sixteen? Seventeen? Younger? Would be so easy to take her inside. Or round the back into the bushes where it was dark, and he was sure there were no cameras. She'd be too frightened to ever say anything to anyone.

But Ray had pride in his work. And he had pride in himself. He didn't need to take advantage of a girl that way. Girls liked him. He was a proper man. Powerful. Big, well-defined muscles. He could have his pick of any girl. He looked at Sigrid. She was a broken, sad thing. She'd made a mistake and he could fix things for her.

And he had his faith. He had to follow Yahweh's rules. Because Yahweh didn't fuck about. He'd sent down the Commandments. Wrote a set of rules. Clear and firm. Carved in stone – 'Thou shalt not kill. Thou shalt not commit adultery. Thou shalt not steal. Thou shalt not bear false witness against thy neighbour. Thou shalt not covet thy neighbour's house, thou shalt not covet thy neighbour's wife, nor his maidservant, nor his ass, nor anything that is thy neighbour's. Including the girls on his tennis team.'

'Come on,' he said, and led her across the lawn by her upper arm. 'You'll be better off in the dorm. Stick to the rules and you'll be all right. And if anyone threatens you in any way, harms you in any way, you come and see me, OK? You come and see Ray. Don't nod. Speak. OK?'

'OK.'

'There you go.'

He felt good about this. About himself. Helping the girl. But something niggled. It was the scales. The fucking spectrum.

A pure psychopath wouldn't have these thoughts. He'd act on impulse. Take what he wanted. Not consider the consequences for one moment.

Ah, sod it.

'Hold up, love. I forgot something. We'll have to go back ...'

6

AIMEE

Aimee handed over her passport and felt that familiar mild frisson. She knew that there was nothing wrong with her passport, that she hadn't done anything wrong, that there was absolutely no reason she might be refused entry to Corfu, but every time she arrived anywhere she had the same vague fear that the guy in the glass booth behind the computer would look up from his screen and say, 'There is a problem.'

There was always a moment when they seemed to take just that bit longer to study her picture than everyone else's. Did everyone feel this way? Was it just the rawness and exhaustion caused by travel-induced anxiety? Or was she not imagining it? Was it low-level racism? Was it a general mistrust of black people? Particularly in places like this where they had a very small black population.

Was he really even taking any longer?

There wasn't a problem. He passed her passport back and gave her a professional smile, was already waving the next passenger forward as she shuffled away, stowing the passport in her bag.

She went through to the baggage reclaim area and waited for her bag. Just a small suitcase. She'd have preferred to travel with only hand luggage to save time and hassle, but she had no idea how long she might be here on Corfu and what she might be required to do, so she'd packed a few options.

She looked around at the other passengers. *Holidaymakers*. Come to escape. It was funny – though not in a funny way – most people who came here didn't know anything about what was actually going on locally. Didn't *want* to know. They wanted to forget everything for two weeks downing cocktails. Sun, sea, sand, sex and squid. A holiday in the sun. How did the song go? *'Cheap holidays in other people's misery . . . '* Shit. Who was that? Mom used to play it in the car driving her to school. To wake her up.

Fuck, yeah – *The Sex Pistols*. Ha. Mom had been a bit of a headbanger in her time.

Still was.

Aimee had called her while she was waiting in departures. She'd told Aimee that she'd been to Corfu for a holiday once when the 'colonels' were still in power in the early seventies. Just before she'd joined the army.

Corfu had been cheap and easy.

'And that's what the men thought us girls were – *cheap and easy*. Wouldn't leave us alone. Three blonde English girls. As far as they were concerned, we were fair game. Free lunch. I expect it's changed a lot since then . . . '

A hundred thousand people lived here now. Aimee had looked it up. About the same number as Bath, or somewhere like Flint, Michigan. Probably grew to twice that number in the summer. There must be a shitload of crime, a lot of drugs, a lot of misery under the surface. And, let's face it, that's why she was here. To poke a shitty stick into the rotting underbelly.

The luggage was starting to come through now and she took off the top she'd worn on the plane and packed it into her hand luggage. But still felt really sweaty, even though she was only wearing a thin cotton dress. At least, so far, it wasn't showing any pit stains. It'd been cold when she'd left England. Grey and damp. Corfu couldn't be more different. A pleasant wave of heat had hit her when she came down the stairs from the plane and she'd stopped to put her sunglasses on. But it was stuffy and oppressive in the baggage reclaim area. A hard light burned through a strip of high, dusty windows, bounced off the shiny floor and hit your tired eyes like a hammer.

Her bag appeared. One of the first on to the carousel. *Luck.*

She grabbed it, hoiked up the handle and started to roll it away. She was vaguely aware of someone approaching her and the next moment a guy in a faded red baseball cap took hold of the handle.

'Hold up . . . *My* bag.'

Aimee laughed, gave him a friendly smile.

'They all look the same, don't they?' she said, not letting go.

He didn't let go either. Neither was he returning the smile. He was an older guy, skinny and pale, wearing long, baggy shorts and an old T-shirt – *I like the Pope. The Pope smokes dope.* A doctored photo of the Pope waving a fat joint. An ex-pope. At least two pontiffs back.

'This is my bag,' he said.

'Easy mistake to make.' Aimee was still smiling. 'But I'm pretty sure it's mine.'

'This is my bag,' he repeated.

'Do you wanna take a look in it?' she said. Staying calm. Keeping her voice uninflected. Not wanting to give him any ammunition.

'None of your tricks.' The guy had a tatty, blond moustache and goatee, greying and stained with nicotine. Very yellow against his colourless skin. 'I *know* this is my bag. I know what happens in airports. I know what your sort do.'

'*My sort?*'

'Yes. *Your sort.* Don't pretend you don't know what I mean, darling. You just grab someone else's gear and get out sharpish before anyone questions you.'

61

'I'll remember that next time,' said Aimee. 'Save me having to bring my own bag.'

'Very funny.'

'Listen – you've made a mistake. It'd be real easy to check. Just open it, yeah?'

'Nah. I don't trust you. I know you people work in gangs.' He was looking off to one side. Aimee checked to see what he was looking at. A young black guy scrolling down his phone screen.

'Oh, for fuck's sake,' she said and let go of the bag. 'Just open it, yeah?'

'No, *you* fuck off,' he said.

'Whaat? I didn't tell you to fuck off ... Just open the fucking bag.'

He glared at her. And then she got it.

'Ah, shit,' she said. 'You've got something in your bag you don't want anyone to see, haven't you?'

'Fuck off.'

'What is it? Dope? Coke? Pills? A dismembered body? Kiddie porn?'

'I said fuck off.' He started to walk away, wheeling the bag behind him.

'Hey!' She went after him, touched him on the shoulder.

He whirled round, raised a finger and jabbed it in her face.

'Listen, you black bitch ... '

'Whoa! I was wondering when that was gonna come out.'

'I'm warning you.'

Again the finger.

Aimee stepped in close, executed a perfect finger lock, then pulled his hand down and trapped it between their bodies. Very close now. Intimate. She could smell alcohol and cigarettes on his breath. He'd probably got into the holiday spirit at Stansted with the other early morning drinkers.

'Hey,' he said, grimacing in pain.

'Hurts, don't it?' she said, in a kindly, empathetic manner, like a mother consoling a kid with a grazed knee. And, let's face it, having your finger bent right back behind your hand *did* hurt. Nobody else could see it, though, and she kept a broad, friendly smile on her face, as if they were old friends.

She glanced over at the pair of armed policemen standing by the exit. The last thing she needed now was to get into a fight in baggage reclaim. That would not be a good start. She figured that if her hunch was right and the guy had something illicit in his bag, he wouldn't want to attract any attention either. She had to control the situation. She rotated him a little ways to make sure his back was towards the cops. He sucked in his breath. His eyes were showing shock and panic now.

'It's a good move, isn't it?' she said enthusiastically. All eyes and teeth. As if she was discussing a fun dance move. The Floss. The Futsal Shuffle . . .

'Simple but effective,' she went on. 'I'm a personal trainer and I use a lot of martial arts in my workouts. A bit of self-defence training for women on the side, if they ask. So, let me tell you this – if you stay still it won't hurt too much, but, if you try to move, your finger's either going to be pulled clean out of its socket, or snapped. Either way it'll ruin your vacation. So just stay still, yeah? And smile at me. Go on. Smile.'

The guy forced a weak smile.

'See. It's not so hard. A connection. An acknowledgement of our shared humanity. Are you familiar with the TV show *Game of Thrones*?'

'What?' Almost whispered.

'*Game of Thrones*?'

He nodded. Gulped. Sweat rolling down from under his cap.

'The big girl? Blonde goddess? Brienne of Tar?'

'Tarth,' said the guy. 'Brienne of Tarth.'

'That's her. Well, that's what my mom looked like in her prime.

Came from an army family. Long line of soldiers. What's that cool phrase she always uses? *"Tough as old boots."* But she's cool, you know? Doesn't throw her weight around. Doesn't need to. One thing she always taught me. "Aimee," she'd say. "Always stand up for yourself. Never let anyone bully you, talk down to you, or belittle you in any way." Now, I know what you're thinking. You're thinking that this girl, Aimee, doesn't look like the daughter of a blonde, British, soldier lady.'

'Uh . . .' was all he could say to that.

'Well, let me explain . . .'

He sighed. Who could blame him? This was taking a lot longer than she'd intended. But she'd started down this track and now she had to finish, or she'd look foolish. She knew she was grandstanding. Risked being seen by one of the cops, but fuck it, she was washed out and antsy, too. Up at three to take an insanely early Ryanair flight. Cramped seats. Crap food. One stress piled on top of another. She was thirsty and feeling washed out – grey – just like this bewildered jerk.

What was that quiz show her mom loved? The catchphrase? Brits used it all the time . . .

I've started so I'll finish.

And she wanted to tell this prick that she was *someone*. A person with an identity. Not just some faceless member of the great replacement.

'My daddy was a boxer from Chicago,' she said. 'Could take a man down in five seconds. Never lost a fight – until he took on pancreatic cancer. He was big. Could have killed you with his fists. Taught me how to fight. But you can't fight cancer. And I'm still angry about that. I carry around a certain low level of repressed, fucking rage. An itch inside me that I just can't scratch. So, you are one step away from being an unidentifiable puddle on the floor. You picked the wrong person to make angry today. The wrong person to insult.'

'Uh...'

'What's your name?'

'Billy.'

'Well, Billy, nobody likes being insulted. But I'm gonna be generous and give you the benefit of the doubt. Maybe it was out of character for you. It's been a long day, and it's not even lunchtime. I'm tired. You're tired. It's hot in here and travel always twists you into a knot. So, I am going to take the position that you didn't mean to say what you just did. And that you're gonna regret it later – wish you'd apologised. Well, we can change all that. Just say sorry and we'll forget all about it. Get on with our vacations.'

Someone was calling from the carousel, 'Dad ... Dad ... Dad ...'

Billy swallowed. 'I'm, yeah ... I'm sorry ...'

Aimee let go, still smiling, and held out her hand.

'My bag.'

The fucker was still reluctant to give it up.

'Dad ... Dad ... Dad ...'

Aimee looked over to where a teenage girl in crop top and shorts, straightened hair, long false nails, was standing, holding a suitcase.

'What is it, Emmaline?' Billy shouted. Angry at the world, angry at Aimee. Angry at his daughter.

'Dad. Come on. I've got your bag.' Sounding pissed off, bored and disapproving in a way that only a teenager can really pull off. Aimee looked at the bag the girl was holding.

Fuck's sake. It wasn't even that similar.

Billy looked bitter. His brain whirring. Made a decision. Walked away from Aimee. Left her bag standing there. Didn't say anything.

Aimee waved after him, smiled at his nonplussed daughter – Emmaline. An old seventies song came into her head. Something her mom used to sing, 'Emma – Emmaline ...'

'Have a nice break, Billy.'

She headed for the exit. Wheeled her bag through the automatic doors past the cops and scanned the crush of people waiting at the barrier for friends and relatives and pick-ups.

There he was. He'd said to dress conservatively. He was so conservative he was almost invisible. She'd looked past him twice before realising it was him. He gave a little nod. She went over to him and said hi. No names yet.

They talked as they walked.

'Good flight?'

'We didn't crash. Which is always a bonus.'

'You look tired.'

'Some jerk back in there accused me of trying to steal his bag.'

'You sure that's yours?'

She laughed. 'Well, it would certainly be a hilarious anecdote if it wasn't. Instead of a tedious, dreary one.'

'Yeah?'

'Tell you about it later. Haven't got the strength right now.'

When they got to the car, she slid her seat back, did up her belt and stuck her feet up on the dash.

'So,' she said. 'Who am I?'

7

LAUREN

Lauren sat next to Sigrid at breakfast, not letting her out of her sight. She wasn't going to wriggle out of this. If she didn't talk, nobody could help her. Afterwards they showered and Lauren kept close to her as they got into their tennis whites in the changing rooms. Close enough to murmur 'the Mob Chat's on' without actually looking at her or changing her bland, early morning expression. She could sense the fear and tension coming off Sigrid like a hot stink. She was panicked. Mob Chat was safe, though. Nobody had ever got into trouble after doing one. It was the only way they could talk.

Once they'd dressed, they went outside for the warm-up session on the rear terrace with their fitness instructor, Martin. It was mostly stretching, breathing, flexibility, a bit of core strength, loosening their muscles. Mats, benches and light weights. There were more intense workout sessions in the main gym every second day in the late afternoon.

The first time Lauren had done a warm-up session in South Africa, she'd made the mistake of keeping her track pants on. She was worried that her short tennis skirt would be too revealing when they did the mat work. Miss Lily had had a quiet word with her about that.

'You have a healthy young body, Lauren. There is no need to cover it up. The sunshine is good for you.'

Now they were collecting up their stuff ready to move from the terrace to the courts. That was when they'd get the chance for the Mob Chat.

The girls had all been alerted and were looking forward to it. Always up for a bit of mild subversion, getting one over on the adults. Mob Chat had been Lauren's idea. The opposite of the sincere, dreary, way serious Group Chat. It was simple, really. All fifteen of them would move as one group, walking to the courts more slowly than usual. They'd keep in a tight knot – just like Miss Lily's knotted fingers – and basically all talk loudly at the same time. Chattering away like a bunch of inane schoolgirls. Whoever needed a private chat would stay in the centre, surrounded by the other girls. With everyone talking over each other, as long as they all grinned and laughed and looked like they were chatting shit, the two in the middle could say whatever they wanted without anyone being able to overhear them.

Problem was they only had five minutes. That was how long it took to walk from the terrace to the courts, where the two trainers, Stephano and Veronika, were waiting for them.

Lauren used to love tennis. It had been her whole life. And joining Julian's juniors team had in many ways been her ultimate dream. The first few months, after she'd been headhunted from school by one of his scouts, had been amazing. Travelling the world, playing in major ITF tournaments, working with the best trainers, getting to know the other girls. And Julian had been amazing. Friendly, generous, funny, charming. She hadn't minded the weird rules. The strict regime. The Group Chats. The idea of The Team being more important than any individuals. The fact that her phone had been taken away from her and she had no access to computers, or newspapers.

'The game, girls! The game is all that's important. No distractions. We want to make you the best tennis player in the world . . .'

The only books and magazines they were allowed to read were ones they had to check out from a carefully chosen selection in the library. There were private cinemas here and at The Lodge, but the girls could only watch certain DVDs. Kids' stuff mostly, high school movies, Disney films, fantasy, some sports stuff and wildlife documentaries.

But it had been an enchanted time. She'd felt like one of those Disney princesses.

It all changed three weeks into winter training in South Africa when she'd first been suspended. It wasn't as if she'd even done anything that wrong. She'd been tired and had had a couple of bad training days. Had lost her cool and thrown a racket at the ground. Nothing she hadn't done before.

But Julian had suspended her from The Team. It was then that she discovered that the brighter the sunshine, the darker the shadows.

Suspension changed everything. You got shut away from the other girls. And when she'd come out of it that first time, everything was new. No more contact with the outside world. No more contact with her family. No phone. No internet. All there was, was The Team, the training, and Hepworth.

She hadn't spoken to her mum and dad since that first suspension. Or anyone else outside the bubble. She'd been careful lately, toeing the line, but it didn't really make any difference. She knew that in the end suspension had nothing to do with how well you played or how badly you behaved, it simply came down to whether Julian *wanted* to suspend you. It was his main method of control. The central 'Pillar' of what he called his 'Technique'. And she'd come out of her latest suspension only a day before Sigrid had gone in.

She wondered what had happened to Sigrid in there this time. What had made her so depressed. Had her suspension been worse than before? Lauren had to find out. She wasn't going to let Julian keep on winning. That was why she took centre position, grabbed Sigrid, linked arms and held on to her tight as soon as they set off for the courts. God, the girl was trembling. Lauren wasn't going to let go, though. She was going to make her talk.

Five minutes. That was all they had. She hoped it was enough.

The Team formed around her, smiling, laughing, gossiping, colourfully dissing each other, telling jokes.

'Did you hear what Roseanne said to Miss Lily? I thought I was going to die . . . '

'Oh, my God, it was so funny . . . '

'So, I think Issy fancies that new gardener . . . '

'I have got to stop eating so much porridge, I am like, totally, constipated . . . '

'Talk, Sigrid. What the fuck is going on?' Said quietly, but with a big happy grin. 'And keep smiling . . . '

'I'm getting out, Lauren.' Sigrid was doing OK. Smiling. Looking dead ahead. 'I don't want to be here anymore and I'm getting out.'

'You can't get out.'

'Someone is helping me.'

'Who?'

'I can't say. I don't want to get him in trouble.'

'A man?'

'Yes.'

'You can't trust any men here.'

'I can trust *him*. He's helping me get out. He's getting everything ready. He's going to buy me clothes. A disguise. Everything. He's even going to get me a new passport and papers. It will take long but it will be safe.'

'Sigrid – you can't trust him. It sounds crazy.'

'No. It's all right. He knows all about how to do it, but . . . '

'Why do you want to get out? What happened? Why are you crying all the time? What has Julian done to you?'

70

'No. Nothing. It's not like that.'

'What's he done?' Trying not to lose it.

'Nothing. Julian's a good man. That's why I kept trying, I try not to, to stop crying. I don't want to let him down. He'll be so upset . . .'

'Wait – you're crying because you think Julian's going to be upset?'

'I'm so scared, Lauren. Scared I'll be found out.'

'Slow down. None of what you're saying makes any sense.'

'I know. I'm so confused. He – my friend – the one who's helping me – he says I mustn't tell anyone. I shouldn't have told you . . .'

'What's he getting out of this . . . ?'

'I have to . . . *You know* . . . He's quick, though.'

'Oh, Sigrid. What are you doing? This is dangerous.'

'I'm sorry, Lauren. You know, it wasn't so bad before, when I thought I'd never be getting out. When I thought I'd never see my mum and dad again, and my kid brother, I could handle it. I just imagined they didn't exist. Now, though, when I think I *might* see them, when I know it's possible . . . that makes me cry. Everything makes me cry now. I miss them so much. I want to talk to them, to hug them. I don't want to play tennis anymore. I know I will never be good enough. I will never be good enough for Julian. I want to please him, and I know I can't. Not anymore. In suspension we talked about discipline and his Technique . . . And I knew I couldn't do it anymore. I just want to go home to Denmark and lead a normal life, be an ordinary girl. I will always love Julian and love him for the opportunities he's given me. What he made me . . . But I will always disappoint him . . . that is why I cry. Because I am leaving him.'

'Sigrid – Julian does not give a *shit* about tennis.'

'What?'

'He couldn't give two flying fucks if we're any good. That's not what this is about. Don't you see that?'

'No. Don't say that.'

'Jesus Christ, Sigrid – are you *really* telling me you're crying because you're letting Julian down? He's an arsehole.'

'No ... He said he loves me best of all the girls. I know he loves me. More than the others. I'm sorry, Lauren. He said *you* ... He said you're a problem to him. But me ... I have to go because I can never be what he wants me to be.'

'Sigrid, you are *exactly* what he wants you to be.'

'Do you really hate him, Lauren?'

'Yes.'

'Then why don't you leave?'

'If I thought there was a way out of here. Then I'd be gone like *that*. But there *is* no way.'

'There is. I will miss you, Lauren. You were always kind to me ...'

They were approaching the courts. Lauren could see Stephano and Veronika waiting for them, getting the equipment ready.

'Sigrid – you have to tell me who's helping you.'

'I can't ...'

'And then she said I was fat ...'

'I did not!'

'You so did. You are such a bitch, sometimes, Roseanna.'

'Oh, that's the pot calling the bitch black ...'

Laughter. Name calling. They trooped on to Court Number 1 and picked up their racquets.

It was already hot, and Lauren went to stand in the shade. Sigrid was in big trouble. She had to do something. She'd told Sigrid that they couldn't trust any of the men here, but there was *one* ... She might be badly wrong. He might turn out to be as bad as the rest of them, but the guy who looked after the boats, Lee Morgan, there was *something* about him. But she'd have to go carefully.

Because, somehow, she had to help the girl.

8

MRS MACINTYRE

'Been a while since I've been your wife. Must be four years.'

'Gibraltar.'

'Oh, God – Gibraltar. Don't. I'd put that out of my mind. So I'm Mrs Macintyre. First name?'

'Keep your own. It's safer. Less likely to make mistakes.'

'*Mrs Aimee Macintyre*. Had worse. So what do I call *you*, Mister Macintyre?'

'Robert.'

'That's no fun. Don't see you as a Robert. I'll work on it.'

They were driving round the outskirts of Corfu Town. Could be anywhere in the Mediterranean. A lot of concrete. Hot. She'd looked up Agios Symeon on Google Maps before she'd left. The drive would take them through town and then north along the east coast road before skirting round Mount Pantokrator and on into the more unspoilt part of the island.

'And how long have we been married, then?' she asked, looking out at a dull strip development – car hire place, furniture outlet, sportswear store, toy supermarket. 'Do we have kids?'

'It doesn't matter.'

'Oh, it does, Will. I need to build my character. I'm like

Daniel Day-Lewis, a strict adherent of the method approach. I need to know everything about Mrs Macintyre. What's her fatal flaw? What childhood trauma caused her to turn out the way she did?'

'She dicked about one too many times with a man whose patience was wearing thin.'

'You're so easy to tease, *Robert*. You know that?' The going was slow, the road busy with traffic. At least the aircon was drying her sweat and evaporating the last of her anger.

'You *know*, though,' she said, 'that you're going to have to tell me one day.'

'Tell you what?'

'What childhood trauma caused you to turn out the way you did.'

'No traumas. No dark secrets.'

'You always say that. But you have to admit – *Rob* – you *are* a bit weird.'

'Am I?'

'Doing this job. Helping people. Trying to stay anonymous. It's a funny way to get your kicks.'

'I'm not doing it to get kicks.'

'Come off it. Why does anyone do anything?'

'Do we have a choice?'

'Yes, we do, actually.'

'Debatable. You know my story, anyway, Aimee. I was picked up off the streets as a homeless, junkie teenager and trained to be an assassin by a shadowy black-ops organisation.'

'Haha!'

'Exactly. The world doesn't work like that. I helped out a friend. Found I was good at it. Got another job on the back of it. One job led to another . . .'

'Hey! Wait! Pull over a minute. I can see some paint drying over there. I wanna go and watch it.'

'I was just trying to show you that I'm not weird.'

'Being a mind-numbing bore is not the only alternative to being weird.'

'I'm so happy to see you again, Aimee.'

'I'll bet you really *are* pleased to see me. But, you know, one day I'm not going to be able to just drop whatever I'm doing and fly off to dig you out of the shit. I mean, I might have had stuff on – obligations. Responsibilities ...'

'Did you?'

'Nope.'

'Well then.'

'You could have asked, though. You never ask me about myself. My personal life. Typical man.'

'Do you want to tell me about your personal life?'

'Not really.'

'Didn't think so. That's why I didn't ask. You *know* why I use you, Aimee. You're reliable. Flexible. And I never have to worry about you. There are very few people in this world I can ask to do what you do for me.'

'Oh, now you're making a little girl blush.'

'I assume your personal trainer thing's going OK?'

'It's going. And I can do sessions from out here on Zoom, no problem. Any extra money's always useful, though. You got any idea how long this is gonna take?'

'I was hoping it was going to be quick ...'

'But things have changed, yeah? Hence me having to rush out here. I was wondering why the sudden improvisation. It's not like you.'

'I need to blend in more. A single man in a holiday town is conspicuous. A talking point. A nice, middle-class couple are part of the scenery.'

'What went wrong?'

He explained about Alan Human as they left town and

started along the busy coast road. Aimee listened, enjoying the story. She laughed every now and then. Made some choice comments about Alan. But stopped when she found out what the job was, that it involved Julian Hepworth, and felt some pity for the father.

'That bastard, Hepworth,' she said. 'Always the same old story.'

'Nothing's been proved.'

'Does it have to be?'

'We don't ask questions or make accusations. You know that, Aimee. We go in there and we get Lauren out. No trouble. No violence. We leave no traces.'

'And my role is just to be your beard?'

'You're always useful in other ways. It'll be reassuring for Lauren to deal with a woman. Someone motherly.'

'Motherly? Well, thanks.'

'It's your *job* to look motherly, Mrs Macintyre. I know full well you don't have a single particle of maternal instinct inside you.'

Aimee sniggered. 'Yeah. We make a perfect couple.'

They were passing a big marina. Rows of sailing craft of all sizes, including some super-yachts.

'You know that's why I can keep using you, Aimee,' said Macintyre. 'You're not ever going to be worried about a family back home. Kids. Anyone who relies on you.'

'I could have a new girlfriend. You don't know.'

'I *do* know. If you had a girlfriend, Aimee, someone you really cared about, you wouldn't be sitting here in this car with me right now.'

'True that. And I'm guessing you have no woman in your life? No *real* one, I mean?'

'Not at present.'

'See. Weird loner. Is that why you need my fake aura of motherliness? In case the girl . . . '

'Lauren.'

'In case Lauren's freaked out by you and doesn't want to be liberated?'

'Yeah. There's always a danger in a situation like this that the girl thinks she's being kidnapped by someone worse than whoever's holding her.'

'But you've got her father here. Can't you use him?'

'He's a liability – a loose cannon. I'm not letting him anywhere near Hepworth. Or Lauren. Not until she's safely home. That guy is highly unstable, Aimee. I've put some surveillance into his place. Camera sends a feed to my Cloud. So far he's been OK. Moping about drinking and talking to himself, but . . .'

'Is this one going to be dangerous, Mister Macintyre?'

'They all have the potential. You know that. Hepworth has heavy security. I've seen enough of them to recognise the type. Guys in love with the idea of being bodyguards, hoping and praying that something will kick off so they can show what they can do. Itching for a fight.'

They drove on in silence for a while. Leaving the built-up centre of the island behind them, moving north on to the quieter road. Aimee checked her emails and messages. And then she looked up.

'Look at all this . . .' She indicated the world outside. The sparkling sea on one side. A pebbly beach with sunbeds and umbrellas. Palm trees. Bars. People enjoying the water and the sun. A clear sky overhead. Small hotels and holiday lets lining the other side of the road. Beyond them, the green-clad slopes of hills and beyond them, Mount Pantokrator.

'Don't you sometimes think?' she went on. 'Why doesn't everybody just calm? Enjoy themselves. But, no, even on a lovely day like this there'll be men beating their wives, junkies OD-ing, cops chasing criminals, sirens wailing, murders, robberies, jackings . . .'

'Like I said, Aimee, we don't always have a choice.'

'Maybe . . .' And then Aimee started to laugh.

'What?'

'I don't even follow my own shit. Jut remembered I nearly broke some asshole's finger back there!'

She told him all about the incident with Billy. Mister Robert Macintyre was alternatively amused and appalled.

'You could have ended up in jail.'

'Don't I know it? You'd have had to find yourself a new wife. You know, one day, I need to get myself just an ordinary holiday. Sit on a beach and do nothing.'

'How long do you think you'd last?'

'About five minutes – six minutes tops.'

'I've got some things to sort out today. You can chill by the pool, get up to speed. Tomorrow we go to work.'

'Sounds good to me. I am here to *party*, Mister Macintyre. And if I get to dance with Julian Hepworth ... Well then ...'

9

IOANNIS

The Finn didn't speak Greek and Ioannis and Vlachos didn't speak Finnish. Who did? So, they talked in English. Ioannis was used to it, he'd been married to Cindy for twenty years now. Hadn't lost his accent and still made mistakes, but he could think in English if he needed to. Vlachos's English was pretty good, too. He'd spent a few years in New York and a couple in Melbourne. That's why Hepworth had hired him. He had a more global outlook than other locals. Wasn't so small-scale.

The Finn spoke with an accent that was half-Scandinavian, half-American. Ioannis didn't know much about him except that he'd been director of some kind of scientific set-up in Helsinki and had been working with Hepworth for five years.

They were in the inner square at The Big Ideas Factory, sitting at a table made of dark metal, under the shade of a fancy modern gazebo with a bamboo roof. The square was nicely landscaped. Grass that was so green and lush it looked fake. Neatly pruned olive trees. A fountain with shallow, water-filled channels radiating from it. It felt more like being in the grounds of some Californian college campus than a factory.

The Institute was newly built and mostly clad in big white

tiles that looked like vinyl. Shiny and bright and unthreatening. With random blocks of primary colours on some walls. Not to Ioannis's liking. Looked like it was designed to appeal to children.

They were all drinking smoothies. A weird green colour, but the Finn assured them it was good for you and it tasted OK. Not OK enough to ever order one in a bar, but OK enough to drink without puking.

'You're not selling as much product as we hoped,' said the Finn, taking off his aviator sunglasses and setting them down carefully on the table. He was a tall guy, a few years younger than Ioannis – everyone seemed younger than him these days – high cheekbones, high forehead, square jaw, blue eyes, blond hair and a red beard. Dressed in a loose, white cotton outfit that looked like pyjamas.

'People are suspicious,' said Vlachos. 'They dunno what Tapioca is yet. They will come round. We need time.'

'No. You need to make things happen more quick,' the Finn said, drumming out a fast rhythm with his fingertips on the metal tabletop. 'And you need to forget Tapioca. We have something new for you.'

'Oh, not again. Nobody ever has the chance to get the taste for anything we sell them. If you change it, we will be starting over again. Just like with the last shipment – "*Crumb*"? Was it?'

'Crumble.'

'Yeah, Crumble. Kids were just getting used to it and you turned off the supply.'

'As long as our customers trust the brand they will buy whatever you offer, *o philos mou*. The brand is more important than the individual product. Like Levis. Or Nike. Mercedes. Johnson & Johnson. If you can't make this happen, we will go to someone else.'

'No one is as well connected on the island as me,' said Vlachos.

'What about Genc Malecaj?'

'The Albanian? Forget him. You don't want to do no business with Albanians.'

'Maybe we do.'

'You can't trust Albanians. They're all crooks.'

The Finn laughed. 'You're a crook, Vlachos.'

'I'm a businessman.'

'So was Al Capone.'

'Listen, you have to have rules,' said Vlachos.

Here he goes, thought Ioannis. Talking too much. He looked at his phone. It was only just after eight. The day had started cloudy, but the clouds had burned off and it was going to be a hot one. He was glad to be in the shade. He pushed his damp hair back from his face. Took a sip of the iced smoothie. Was getting used to it.

'We don't want to be fighting each other,' Vlachos was saying. 'Malecaj has his places, his territory – I have mine. He has his clubs – I have mine. He has his women – I have mine. Shouldn't be no problem. You're always telling me I have to keep out of trouble, not get the police on my ass. Not get in trouble with the drugs. Keep it clean.'

'Just like McDonald's,' said the Finn. 'A business. With rules. Standards. I get it.'

'Well, Genc Malecaj, he doesn't get it. He is like the Wild West. He comes into my clubs, he sends his men, his boys. They try to sell drugs. Makes my life very difficult. A few nights ago I caught one of his boys, Elevis . . .'

'Elvis?'

'Elevis. Is different. He's trying to push pills in one of my clubs, so I had to slap him. Now Malecaj is angry. I didn't even know Elevis was one of his guys.'

'You scared of him?'

'There are stories. He killed someone – tore their throat out with his hands.'

'You believe that?'

'I would believe anything about Albanians. And Genc Malecaj – you don't want nothing to do with him.'

The Finn looked at Vlachos. 'We don't want some kind of turf war,' he said. 'Keep a lid on it, yeah? This is a small island. Everybody knows everything.'

'That's the point,' said Vlachos, waving a hand. 'It's not a good place for you to set up your business. It would be much better in a big city, in Athens or Thessaloniki . . .'

'No. This is a start-up,' said the Finn. 'Corfu is the right size for us. Easier to control. Easier to track.'

'But why do you have to keep changing the product?' Vlachos asked, sounding weary.

'Because the law keeps changing. At the moment, Tapioca is not classified as an illegal drug. The components are not illegal, but what we do with them . . . Aha! We have very clever scientists working here at BIF who know all about how to synthesise existing ingredients into something new. But as soon as any product gets known by the authorities, as soon as it gets too popular, they will ban it. So, then we have to move on. Because we must not sell anything illegal. You get it?'

'I think so.'

Ioannis didn't. Didn't have to. He was a driver. Second-in-command. He was growing bored. Needed to get out of here.

'What are these new pills called?' he asked.

'Spotted Dick,' said the Finn.

'*Ti sto diáolo?*'

The Finn slapped the table, laughed through his red beard. 'It's my joke. It's my joke. You know Hepworth likes to name the pills after desserts? What you call them – *epidorpoi*.'

'Spotted Dick is no worse than Tapioca,' said Vlachos. '*Eton Mess*. Remember that one?'

'Yeah. Hepworth told me one time that when he was at school – he went to one of those weird English boarding schools, like Harry Potter – the food was terrible. The only thing he could eat were the desserts – *puddings* he calls them. So now he makes good things for other people and names them after "*puddings*".'

'He can name them after his spotted dick for all I care,' said Vlachos.

'Well. These new ones. They are called Afters,' said the Finn.

'Aphtos? OK ... *Aphtos*. What are they? Uppers? Downers? Opiates?'

'Psychedelics, mostly, with some good vibes thrown in. They make everything *groovy*. Get peaceful, mellow and glowing – you know, sunset and sunrise, all that shit. Chill and float and see visions and forget the world.'

'I should save some for myself,' said Vlachos. 'I could do with chilling and floating down a psychedelic river with my head in the clouds. But I'll sell this shit for you. I will make Aphtos the biggest party drug in Corfu if that's what you want.'

'We don't care about Afters.'

'Why is it that every time I talk to you, I go away more confused?' said Vlachos, on the edge of anger. 'Aphtos is not important? Then what are we doing?'

'None of the synthetic drugs are important. They are just pills.'

'Oy, I don't understand.'

'It is very simple. You are Uber, Vlachos. You know what Uber is?'

'Of course I know what Uber is. It's a taxi thing. Cheap rides.'

'No.' The Finn smiled and shook his head, as if Vlachos was a naïve kid. 'No, no, no. That is where everyone is wrong. Uber is not a taxi business. Uber is a service that puts people who need a ride in touch with people who can drive them. It simply makes these transactions work.'

'That's a taxi company.' Vlachos tried to give the Finn a similarly patronising smile. Didn't really work. Vlachos had always had one of those soft faces. Friendly. A lovable rogue.

'The problem is,' said the Finn, taking a sip of his smoothie and wiping green foam from his beard, 'you have a view of things that is a long time out of date. You live in Farmville. A world where happy farmers live with happy cows and pigs and chickens in their yard and drive around on red tractors. A world of shops and banks and old-fashioned jobs. A world where men work down mines, or in shipyards, or on jolly little fishing boats hauling up nets full of happy, wriggling fish. Your head is in a world where women work in factories wearing headscarves and their bosses wear double-breasted suits and smoke cigars. A world where people actually *make things*. A world of shop assistants and taxi companies and fast-food joints. That is not the real world. The real world is online. It is all about software, IP, networks and algorithms. You can be the richest man in the world without actually making *anything*. Let me tell you about the real world . . .'

'Please don't tell me to take the red pill,' said Vlachos. 'I hate people who tell me to take the red pill. I want to punch them. And tell them – THAT! – *that's* the *fucking* red pill!'

'Yeah. The red pill is bullshit,' said the Finn dismissively. 'There is no secret alternative reality. The world is right there in front of people's noses, but they can't see it, because they believe in the old-fashioned world. They are like these Flat Earth morons. A child can see that the world is not flat. But if you have faith you can believe it is, you can see anything – or nothing. And that is how the smart people who can see clearly are able to make a lot of money. Everything and everyone here on Corfu is connected in this network, this *web* – and Hepworth wants to be the spider.'

Vlachos drained his glass and set it down loudly on the metal table.

'We gotta go,' he said. 'Listening to this just makes my ass ache. I'm a club owner. That's all. Import and export. I make booze. And I distribute these synthetic drugs for you.'

'On your little red tractor. That is why you are Uber, *o philos mou*.'

84

'Oy-oy-oy . . . Please. No more. I'll do what you want. I'll move your shit faster. But no more lessons.'

'One last lesson, then you can leave. Because you need to understand what we're doing here. Sure, Uber takes people where they want to go, but it doesn't make any money doing that. Right now, Uber loses billions of dollars every year. It was set up and financed by people with very deep pockets, who were prepared to lose a lot of money, a real lot of money, and they keep on losing money. Why do they do that?'

Vlachos sighed. 'I dunno . . . I guess they are waiting until every other taxi business goes bust so they are the only people you can go to. Then they can charge whatever they like and start to make money.'

'No. It is hard to make a lot of money as a taxi business. Because every car must have a driver in it, and every driver must be paid. Uber's plan was always to make their money by using driverless cars. They took a gamble – that soon driverless cars would be everywhere on our streets. But there was a problem. How do you train a driverless car to be a taxi? To know the best routes? The simplest routes? The quickest ways? To know how to be in the right place at the right time to find a new pick-up? These are things that only a human could know. That is why they started with human drivers. For years those drivers have been gathering the information that Uber needs to build a massive database. To create a network. All round the world. Eventually the human drivers will be obsolete and used no more.'

'And that is what I am doing for you?' said Vlachos. 'Testing your system?'

'You are building a client base. Gathering data. Creating a network. And we are using it to build a digital model for the drug business. Corfu is the perfect size. A closed system. A stable system. All the parameters are known. It is simply a test for when we go global.'

'And that is when I will become . . . *obsolete*?'

'Yes.' The Finn smiled one of his smiles and then poked Vlachos on the forehead with a finger, peck-peck-peck, like a bird. Ioannis could see that Vlachos was one step away from slapping the guy. 'You will become obsolete unless you are able to learn, Vlachos. To move out of Farmville. To adapt and grow. Tapioca and the other synthetic drugs are simply tools to help us learn about the market. There is not big money to be made out of it, because we must always be changing the drugs to keep them legal. At the moment, we are in the data-gathering phase of the business. Who wants drugs? When do they want drugs? What sort of drugs do they want? How do we get the drugs to them? How much do we sell them for? That is the data you are supplying us. But we don't want to be making physical drugs.' He gave a wave of his hand, as if he was swatting away a fly. 'They are inefficient. Using the data you gather we are building an app.'

'A drug supply app?'

'Yes.'

'Won't that be made illegal, too?'

'No. Look at all this . . . '

The Finn swept an arm round the buildings surrounding the square. 'How much of this is used for manufacturing the synthetic drugs, do you think?'

'I thought that was all you did.'

'No. Only two small rooms. It is mainly computers, electronics, coding, and testing.'

'Sounds as if you are making a digital drug!' Vlachos laughed, and then stopped when he saw that the Finn was smiling that way again. 'You are!' he cried. 'You *are* making a digital drug.'

'Yes. Hepworth is all about tech. He believes that everything in the world will be replaced by technology. Including drugs. Which are messy and dangerous and unpredictable. He lost someone close to him to drugs. An overdose. So we are building

86

clean, safe technology that will directly and harmlessly access the brain. Through all your hard work, we will then be able to plug the digital drug straight into anyone who subscribes to the app. And the app is where we make our money.'

'So how close are you to making this thing?' asked Vlachos.

The Finn stared at him for a moment, wide-eyed.

'How close are we?'

And then he leaned back in his chair and exploded with laughter, rocking backwards and forwards. Soon, tears were streaming down his cheeks and into his beard. His laughter was uncontrollable, violent. His mouth wide, showing green-stained teeth. He was fighting for breath and every time he looked at Vlachos, he just laughed harder.

Vlachos waited patiently and at last the Finn took control of himself. Sat there, panting and shaking, wiping his eyes with a napkin.

'How many driverless cars have you seen on the roads?' he asked when he was eventually able to speak.

'None,' said Vlachos with a shrug and the Finn laughed again.

'That is why we are like Uber!' he shouted. 'That is why we are fucked! The technology doesn't fucking work!'

10

PIKE

Macintyre watched the catamaran slide into the harbour, swing round in a wide arc and glide up to the main jetty where it came to a gentle stop, barely kissing the woodwork. It was a perfect manoeuvre, beautiful in its way. It reminded him of the delicate dance of the spaceship docking in *2001*. Macintyre wasn't a boat person. Preferred to have solid ground beneath his feet. But he'd been around them enough to know that he'd just witnessed a display of expert, unshowy seamanship. If that was the right word.

He checked his watch. Nine o'clock sharp. Bang on time.

A woman jumped off the catamaran and secured the mooring rope with a practised movement. She caught his eye and gave the merest hint of a smile, her face catching the sun and lighting up for a moment. And then she hopped back on to the boat and disappeared below deck. The engine burbled for a few moments more and then cut off.

Aimee joined him, carrying a bag of provisions she'd picked up from the little supermarket. Playing their roles. Husband and wife. Ready for their day's outing.

'All set, Mrs Macintyre?'

'All set, Mr Macintyre.'

They walked out along the jetty. As they reached the catamaran, a man crossed the deck and jumped down on to the planking. He was economical in his movements, with a calmness and stillness about him. He nodded a greeting. Keeping slightly aloof.

'Dennis Pike?'

'That's me.'

'I'm Robert Macintyre, and this is my wife, Aimee.'

They shook hands.

'Pleased to meet you, Dennis.'

'Pleased to meet you, Mr and Mrs Macintyre.'

That would do. In case anyone might be watching they'd put on enough of a show.

'All good?' Macintyre asked.

'All good,' said Pike and he stretched out his arms and rolled his shoulders, grimacing. 'Ugh. Not as young as I was.'

'Come on. You never age, Pike.'

In truth he had no idea how old Pike was. Could be anywhere between forty-five and sixty-five. He'd had steel-grey hair, cut short, for as long as Macintyre had known him. Covered now by a sun-bleached pink baseball cap sporting the logo of a bar in the Bahamas. He was deeply tanned and weathered from years at sea. Could have been carved out of wood. He was taller than Macintyre by a couple of centimetres. Wiry and muscular, kept fit by working on the boat all day. Dressed in grey shorts, rubber-soled boat shoes and an ancient T-shirt, washed so many times it was paper-thin. You could just make out a picture of Humphrey Bogart on it.

Pike had always been into his films. The catamaran had tightly packed shelves of DVDs. Every genre and era well represented, but perhaps leaning towards classic film noir. He'd even named the boat the *Louise B* after the silent screen star Louise Brooks.

Pleasantries over, Pike helped them aboard. Aimee looked impressed. The boat was sleek but powerful, could do thirty knots. Macintyre knew it well. Fifteen metres. Four cabins – two in each of the twin hulls, accessed by steps down from the central cabin. It was well equipped and comfortable inside. Had to be. Sarah and Pike lived on it all year round, following the sun and the summer. It was homely but uncluttered – everything in its place.

As Aimee stashed her shopping and gave the cabin a quick once over, Sarah took the tiller, fired up the engine and Pike cast off. Macintyre went forward and settled on the sun deck that spanned the hulls in front of the cabin. Once they were underway, Pike joined him, and Aimee moved to sit with Sarah at the rear. Or aft, or whatever the fuck you were supposed to call it.

Soon they were chugging out of the harbour entrance. Pike looked back at the row of buildings along the waterfront, shielding his eyes.

'We've not been to Agios Symeon for two or three years,' he said. 'Used to visit more often. Ioannis throws some work our way when we're here. Day charters mostly. We take people sailing, diving, sightseeing, whatever they want. Ioannis takes his cut. You had any dealings with him?'

'Nope.'

'You might want to check him out.'

'Yeah?'

'Yeah. Used to be a solid guy.'

'Not anymore?'

'Everything changed in Greece after the world went to shit in 2008.'

Despite leaving England a long time ago, Pike still had traces of his east London accent, but it'd been smoothed and softened by years spent bumming around the world, picking up bits and pieces of other accents from here, there and everywhere. He could still ramp it up when he needed to make a point, though. Go full *Sexy Beast*.

'There was no money around,' he went on. 'Everyone hustling to make a buck. Lot of guys turned to crime. No Choice.'

Crime. That was something Pike had a nose for. Macintyre didn't pry, but the older man often alluded to a criminal past. Violence and mayhem and broken lives.

'Rumours *are* that Ioannis is connected to Hepworth.'

'Yeah?' Macintyre looked towards the island. 'Agios Symeon's only a small town, but seems there's a lot going on there.'

'Agios Symeon's a small town, but there's a lot of money swilling around,' said Pike. 'Money's like shit – attracts flies. You want the sails up?'

'Later. Once we've taken a look at Hepworth's place. For now, we need to go slow and steady. We need full control.'

'Sure.'

Pike called out some instructions to Sarah, who nodded. She was a couple of years younger than him. A handsome woman, fit and lean like Pike, her once jet-black hair now streaked with silver. A wide mouth and wide-spaced eyes, palest blue, almost grey, set in a heart-shaped face. Cut-off jeans, brown legs, a Muppets T-shirt, pair of old trainers moulded to her feet. Aimee was sitting staring at her. Mesmerised. They were a well-matched pair. Two women who didn't take any bullshit from anyone.

Now they were clear of the harbour, Aimee took off her long-sleeved shirt, exposing her tattoos. They covered most of her arms and she had more of them all over her back. Blue-black against her dark skin. Sarah looked equally mesmerised.

Macintyre slipped on his shades and settled back in the moulded fibreglass seat, tilting his face up towards the sky. Feeling the sun on his skin. There was a smell of salt water and diesel that was oddly pleasant. And, out here on the open water, the breeze was nicely cooling.

'I get you anything?' Pike asked. 'Drink?'

'I'm good for now.' Macintyre looked at Pike, who was standing, squinting at the horizon. 'You sure you're OK about this job?' he asked. 'Might mean you become persona non grata in these parts.'

'Such is life,' said Pike with a shrug. 'There's a lot of places I can't go no more, but there's a whole lot more I can. One thing that's been made abundantly clear to me since I took to the water – it's a big old world out there. And wherever I lay my captain's cap, that's my home.'

Macintyre had first used Pike ten years ago, on one of his first jobs, when he was still pretty small-scale. He'd been recommended by a weird, seedy guy called Noel Bishop, who ran a home security firm.

Pike looked the same age now as he had then. Sarah, too. He didn't say a lot, but carried an aura of safety around with him, like some sort of sci-fi deflector shield. The effect was doubled when he was with Sarah. He'd told Macintyre once, in a rare candid moment, that if it hadn't been for her he'd probably have died in a sordid fashion years ago. She'd bestowed this sense of calm and peace on him. Before he'd got together with her, he'd had a lot of problems in his life to deal with. Now he was squared with the world.

'Once I'd sorted things,' he'd told Macintyre, 'I went to her. She took some persuading, but every day I thank God she took me in ...'

Sarah was a lot like Pike. Didn't say a lot. Always had a mysterious half-smile on her face, which hinted at deep secrets long held. And not necessarily pleasant ones. She'd had problems of her own in the past and her eyes had seen things. But, like her husband, she'd do anything for you once she trusted you.

Just so long as you didn't fuck her around.

They were motoring south, the island passing to their right. A steep rocky coastline covered with the typical, scrubby, Mediterranean maquis. Tough, dark-leaved, aromatic plants. Myrtle and thyme, rosemary and juniper. There was the occasional little pebble beach and secluded, exclusive villa perched on a cliff.

To their left, on the opposite side of the Straits of Corfu, was

Albania. It looked for the most part brown and dry and empty, slightly desolate, long ago stripped of vegetation. But then they came to a stretch of densely wooded coastline with a perfectly straight boundary. One moment semi-desert, the next, lush, green forest.

Pike handed Macintyre a pair of compact binoculars and he looked it over.

'You know why that area's different to the rest?'

'Nope.'

'Hepworth owns it.'

'Seriously?'

'He bought it when he bought the land to build his compound on Corfu. Didn't want to be overlooked.'

'That is thorough.'

'He can afford it. And he likes his privacy.'

'So, we must be nearly there, then?'

'We're there.'

Pike signalled back to Sarah over the low roof of the cabin and she eased off on the throttle until they were barely moving. Just drifting along. A couple of smart white yachts passed them heading north on the busy waterway.

Macintyre stood up and put the binoculars to his eyes. And there was Hepworth's place – *Patia HepKat* – sitting alone on a rocky promontory, the top of which had been levelled off. Terraces stepped down from the main house to the sea. There were trees and grass and rough stone walls and flowering shrubs everywhere. The main house was a long, low, white building with a pitched roof of traditional red tiles with an ultra-modern wing at the northern end. All glass and steel and concrete and odd angles. Off to the left, on a slightly lower level, were the tennis courts. Two people in track suits warming up. Below them, a smaller terrace that was walled on three sides round an infinity pool overlooking the sea. On the next level down was a collection of buildings constructed from the local yellow stone, half hidden among trees. Pines and olives mostly. Guest rooms, perhaps. Steps led down from there to a private beach with umbrellas and sun beds. At one end was a lifeguard tower, or possibly a lookout tower. Looked like something out of *The Great Escape*. Stood next to a small man-made harbour with a jetty where a smart motor launch and a rigid-hull inflatable speedboat were moored. Macintyre could see two men in matching outfits getting a jet ski ready for an outing. There were five people sitting on sunbeds on the beach. A servant in a white uniform was serving them drinks.

Macintyre focused on the guests.

'Recognise her?' said Pike.

'Who?'

'The blonde.'

'She looks vaguely familiar.'

'Ex-soap actress?' said Pike. 'Sally Spence. Made a couple of films. Recorded a couple of dance tracks. Fell out of a couple of nightclubs. Popular in the sidebars.'

'And the others?'

'The younger guy is a minor member of the Belgian royal family who owns a media company,' said Pike. 'Don't know the redhead. The older guy's a Hollywood exec.'

'And the Asian guy?'

'Finance. Banking.'

Macintyre swung the bins round to properly check out the harbour, which looked like it had been created by the liberal use of dynamite and the building of a sea wall.

'Could we use the dock, you reckon?'

'Possible,' said Pike. 'But the place is lousy with security. As well as that lookout tower, they got cameras everywhere. Plus, that RIB is fast. I've seen it in action.'

'Still,' said Macintyre, wiping sweat from his forehead. 'Got to be a better bet than the road. I'm guessing no chance of going cross-country.'

'Not a chance. He chose that spot well.'

Now Macintyre focused on the boundaries of the property. It was protected by high stone walls, with sections of wire fencing covering the more inaccessible areas.

'No two ways about it,' he said. 'We need to get inside. Take a proper look.'

Pike laughed. 'I knew you were going to say that. Would be easier to get inside the Pope's bathroom.'

'I got in there once,' said Macintyre.

'Fuck off. You're shitting me. I can never tell with you.'

'There's always a way in, Pike. We just need to find the door.'

11

LAUREN

Lauren came out of the changing rooms putting on her life vest and walked down to the jetty where Herve the Perve and Lee Morgan were waiting to take her out for her water-skiing lesson. The only part of her week she ever really looked forward to. Julian used water skiing as part of his training programme, his *Technique*. It helped strength and balance and stamina. And it gave him an excuse to have framed photographs of girls in bikinis all over the place.

Herve had all the gear stashed in the speedboat and Lauren climbed on the back of the jet ski behind Lee. She knew she wasn't supposed to call it a jet ski. Technically it was a personal watercraft and Lee got upset if you called it anything else. The Mansory Black Marlin 550 was a monster of a thing, a three-seater with a top speed of eighty miles an hour.

They burbled slowly out of the harbour, the Marlin behind the ViperMax. Lauren could have gone out in the speedboat with Herve, but Lee always insisted the girls rode with him. He knew Herve's reputation and tried not to let him get too close to them. Lee was Julian's chief mechanic. Looked after all his boats and cars. And he looked after his girls as well. The girls all said that he was 'a sweetie'. A gentle man with big, strong hands that were never really clean. Curly hair and bushy, old-fashioned sideburns. A country accent. Like a farmer. Lauren had no reason to believe that their view of him was wrong. He was always perfectly well behaved. A gentleman as well as a gentle man. But, since joining The Team, Lauren had grown to be suspicious of everyone.

Once out in the Straits, Herve and Lee rigged the Marlin, while Lauren got into the water and fitted her feet into the bindings of her slalom ski. Soon, Herve passed her the handle and climbed on to the back of the Marlin, so he could spot for Lee. The Marlin pulled away, Lauren braced herself – and she was up. First time. She couldn't stop a wide grin from spreading across her face.

This was amazing. A fantasy. Water skiing as part of your weekly routine in one of the most beautiful parts of the world. Out here on the sparkling water, under an Instagram-blue sky, cutting across the wake, bouncing, swerving, sending up a silver spray behind her . . .

Was she wrong? Wrong to question all this? To fight against it? Was she just being ungrateful? After all, she'd always been told there was no such thing as a free lunch. You paid for your pleasures.

She felt the rope pull her arms and she fought back, using every muscle to stay upright. If she helped Sigrid, there would be no going back. She might lose all this. And Julian would punish her. But what was the worst he could do? He'd already tried to break her. Just as he'd tried to break all the girls. It was built into his Technique. It was his doomsday weapon – *Suspension*.

The whole process had been carefully worked out. The six stages – *Suspension. Punishment. Retraining. Rebuilding. Therapy. Return.*

The initial suspension was bad enough. You were humiliated in front of all the other girls as they lined up and you were marched away past them in disgrace. Then you were put in the Detention Room and told to wait until Julian called.

The first time she'd waited a day before she'd heard his voice coming through a speaker and the door had been unlocked remotely.

Punishment happened in Julian's soundproofed office and involved a strap.

Retraining was the longest part. You were kept totally isolated, on restricted rations. You weren't allowed to sleep more than five hours at a time. Up at dawn, cold showers, long workout sessions in Julian's private gym. Lauren was pretty sure they put some kind of pills in the food, as well. You felt woozy and permanently exhausted, confused, not sure what time of day it was. The only real contact you had was with Julian and he became your whole world. All you wanted to do was please him and get released back to normal life.

Once you were completely zombiefied, 'Rebuilding' began. This was when Julian started the process of putting you back together. You could sleep a full night, the food was five-star hotel quality, intense physical workouts became yoga and Pilates...

Mainly, though, the 'Rebuilding' part meant long sessions in Julian's private suite as he talked and talked and talked, quietly, urgently, getting inside your head...

'Teenage girls have rampant hormones, Lauren, it can affect your play, your happiness, your life balance, and we need to deal with those hormones, we need to tame them, as you know, we don't follow any Russian methods here, we don't give you drugs to suppress hormones, or go the other way and make you stronger, faster, hairier, no, I am developing a radical new way to train female athletes, we take a holistic approach here, you *will* be stronger, but not from drugs, not from yelling and screaming, but through *love*, and you *will* be better, from my methods and treatments, my *Technique*, I want to make you a stronger person, Lauren, a better person, physically, spiritually, emotionally and mentally, most sporting contests are won and lost in the head, and in the heart, to be the best, to win, you have to follow my Technique, accept me into your life, accept my love, or nothing will work, you will only begin to grow when you accept that I know what is best for you, that I love you, and that you need to put yourself fully in my hands, everything we do here is worked out by some very clever people using super-powerful computers, you have your lessons, and you have a sports and exercise programme designed just for you and you alone, do you know how much time and money that takes? How much I have invested in The Team? All this – these amazing facilities – twenty-four-hour care – they don't come cheap, I'm a busy man, Lauren, I run several businesses, but The Team is not a hobby, it's central to what I do, you girls are the physical embodiment of my ideals, my *ideas* and my beliefs . . . *My Technique* . . . but I mainly do it because I love you. I love you, Lauren . . . So you mustn't go against me, mustn't disobey me . . . just accept me . . . '

And she'd apologised, over and over, said she'd work harder, follow the rules, take the organic health supplements. And for the next few days it was just the two of them, as he talked to her for hours about himself, about his Technique, his work, his love, his dreams – *literally* his dreams. He told her in great detail what he dreamed about. And every day the dreams he described had more sex in them than the last.

And all she'd wanted was to make him happy.

And then, once he was sure she was ready, they moved on to the next stage. Therapy. Now she was allowed to use Julian's personal spa. She had special treatments from the attendants – massage, hot stones, mud wraps, aromatherapy.

And then one night Julian gave her a special massage – to balance her hormones. Afterwards he asked her to give him a massage and when she protested that she didn't know how, he said he'd talk her through it.

Which he did.

And that was when it happened. She'd never imagined her first time would be like this. Afterwards, she was treated like a goddess. Julian couldn't stop smiling at her, touching her face, praising her, telling her how well she was doing, how beautiful and strong and radiant she was. How much he meant to her. How much he loved her . . .

Next came The Return.

She was given a new white dress to wear. A garland of flowers around her neck. The girls were all lined up again, and they clapped and cheered as she emerged. There had been a coming-out party that night. Nobody said anything. They couldn't. But Lauren could see the pity in her friends' eyes behind the forced smiles. They *knew* . . .

Suspension had felt like a weird dream. Unreal. And she'd been suspended several times since. And she never wanted to go through it again. She'd woken up. She couldn't carry on like this. She'd help Sigrid get out – and she'd go with her. First opportunity they got.

12

IOANNIS

'How many pills we got this time?' said Ioannis as they pulled away from the loading bay doors and joined the road that skirted the car park, which was as beautiful as everywhere else in BIF. With neat rows of transplanted olive trees shading all the spaces.

'Ten thousand.'

Ioannis swore. 'How we gonna move ten thousand pills?'

'That's exactly what I said to the Finn.' Vlachos sighed. Looked out of the passenger window at the perimeter wall that was built of some weird pink stone. Pretty enough, but it didn't disguise the fact that the wall was thick and high and topped with razor wire.

'And what did he have to say?' Ioannis asked.

'He said it was not his problem. Hepworth wants to flood the market with these things. He's a *malakas*. A stupid *malakas*, but he pays well.'

'But ten thousand pills? How big does he think this island is?' Ioannis waited for the main gates to open automatically.

'If it's a good product we can shift it,' said Vlachos. 'The good thing about the *prezaki* is that if you got something they want, they'll keep coming back for more.'

'Until it kills them,' said Ioannis.

'There'll always be a new generation coming up.'

They passed the metal sign – BIF – attached to a pink granite boulder, and rolled down the approach road, lined with palm trees – like being in LA. The road matched the walls, had some kind of pink surfacing.

Hepworth liked pink.

Ioannis took it all in – the high wall, the big gates, the heavy sign – a concrete fist in a pink, fluffy glove.

They went over a speed bump and the SUV rattled. The Yeti was a good ten years old and Ioannis liked to drive with the windows open as it sometimes smelt of gasoline.

'If this all pays off,' said Vlachos, 'you can get rid of this shit heap. Drive something with a bit more class.'

'It's not a shit heap. It's a good car. It's served me well.'

'It's a donkey, Ioannis.'

'*I'm* a donkey,' said Ioannis and he laughed. 'Donkeys are hard workers. Steady. They get things done. If I bought a Mercedes, or an Audi . . .'

'An Alfa Romeo. Now *there's* a car!'

'Alfa Romeos really are shit heaps, Theo. The Italians don't know how to make cars. But, no, if I bought an Alfa Romeo, or a Lamborghini, a Ferrari, the cops would be all over me – the tax guys. And I'd keep getting stuck on the mountain roads.'

'You could clean it at least. If you love it as much as you say.' Vlachos twisted round in his seat to look at the back window. Some kids had drawn pictures of cocks in the dust. They were always doing that.

'The dirt protects it,' said Ioannis. 'Makes it less likely to get stolen.'

'Who would want to steal this donkey, Ioannis?'

The road was smooth and wide. Hepworth had seen to that. It was one of the best roads in Corfu – even if it was a weird pink colour. From here, on the south side of Pantokrator, above the more

102

heavily forested lower slopes, they had a good view of the island. Ioannis never tired of the view. *His* island. The greenest of them all, they said. So many trees. From here you couldn't see any people. It was people who fucked things up. No wonder the ancients thought the gods lived on top of a mountain. All you could see from up there was the beauty. Not the grubby, squalid, day-to-day struggling of the people. Hadn't Zeus punished Prometheus for making humans? Out of *mud*. That was about right. We are all made of shit. Zeus had the right idea. Tried to stamp out mankind.

It wasn't so bad out of season. In the winter it was quiet – there were only 100,000 inhabitants – but in the summer 300,000 tourists came. Like a plague of rats.

Even so ... How many of them wanted to buy pills? They'd probably end up throwing most of this batch into the sea, like they'd done with the Tapioca. There weren't enough people here to support a major drug trade. Most people just wanted some hashish. MDMA. The kids liked to party, and the Brits down in the hellhole of Kavos ate pills like plates of beans, but still, there were only so many beans you could sell.

'The world has changed,' said Vlachos. 'Every cheap street hustler, every kid who's just learned to drive has an expensive car now. They don't *buy* them – they lease them. Some shit like that. Nobody buys anything these days.'

'I'm happy with the donkey.'

'Once a fisherman, always a fisherman,' said Vlachos. 'You think like a Farmville farmer, Ioannis.'

'I didn't understand any of that *skata*.'

'Me neither.'

'Shit. What are these clowns doing?'

Ioannis stopped the car. They were in among a dense stretch of pines. A couple of hundred metres away, just before the junction with the main road, two cars were blocking their way. A Jeep Wrangler and a silver BMW that Ioannis recognised.

He let out his breath slowly.

'Malecaj,' he said.

And there was the Albanian. Standing with four other men. Waiting by the cars. Smoking. He was wearing a dark suit and some shitty, mustard-coloured shirt. Sunglasses. He looked at the Yeti. Dropped his cigarette. Didn't bother to stamp it out.

'Are we fucked?' said Ioannis.

Vlachos grunted.

'There aren't any other roads in or out,' he said. 'So, we've got three options. We can see what Malecaj wants. We can go off-road and try to get round them, but that could just lead to a dumb car chase. Or, my preferred option, we turn round and go back to BIF.'

Vlachos's phone pinged and he glanced at a message on the screen.

'Shit,' he said. Using the English word. 'The Finn wants us to take the drugs back.'

'What?'

'It's a bad batch apparently.'

'Good timing.'

'OK,' said Vlachos. 'The decision has been made for us. We go back.'

'There's a problem, Theo.'

'What?'

Ioannis nodded over his shoulder. Two guys were coming out of the trees on to the road behind them. One of them was carrying what looked like an Uzi machine pistol.

'What the fuck is this?' Vlachos shouted angrily and he pounded the dashboard. 'Who does Malecaj think he is? Scarface? This is Corfu!'

Ioannis looked towards the blockade. Malecaj and two more of his men were walking slowly up the road towards them. It was going to take them a while.

'Do you want me to drive closer?' asked Ioannis.

'Fuck no. Let them walk.'

Ioannis got his phone out and began to swipe through the photographs he'd taken of a hummingbird moth he'd spotted at BIF.

'Put that away,' Vlachos snapped. 'And concentrate. Do you recognise any of the others?'

Ioannis put his phone in his lap and studied the men walking towards them.

'That looks like Joliffe,' he said.

'The American bum?'

'Yeah.'

Wild hair and beard. Faded denim cut-offs, tie-dye T-shirt, fanny pack with a marijuana leaf logo, flip flops, beads and a floppy straw hat. Who dressed like that anymore? Maybe it was coming back. What did Ioannis know?

Joliffe had been on the island for years. A well-known stoner. Did a bit of small-time dealing. Hustling. Stealing from kids on the beaches. House-breaking.

'What's the Albanian doing hanging out with that jerk?' Vlachos asked.

'I have no idea.'

'It was a rhetorical question, Ioannis.'

Ioannis shrugged.

Just before Malecaj reached the Yeti, Vlachos jumped out and shouted at him.

'Are you insane, Malecaj? We don't go around shooting each other. Tell your guys to stand down.'

Malecaj stayed stone-faced behind his sunglasses. Smoking. Ioannis got out and joined his boss.

'Yo!' Joliffe shouted. 'Vlachos.'

'What do you want?' They were talking in English.

'Mister Malecaj here ... '

'Does he not speak for himself?'

'His Greek's not so good. His English ain't great neither. His

Albanian, though, is magnificent! And that is a hard language to master, believe me. But I've picked up a bit on my adventures. I'm good with languages. My brain is open. Just churning with ideas.'

'What's this all about?'

'You *know* what this is all about, Zorba.'

'Don't call me Zorba.'

'Come on. I'm only having a bit of fun with you.'

'This is about Elevis? Yeah?'

'Yeah. This is about Elvis.'

'OK. Tell Mister Malecaj, that if I'd known Elevis was one of his guys, he wouldn't be in hospital now.'

'OK.'

'No – he'd be at the bottom of the Adriatic with a heavy chain wrapped around his legs. You tell him that.'

'I don't think I will. We don't want this to escalate.'

'I didn't start this. Elevis should not have been trying to sell Malecaj's drugs in one of my clubs. It's business. I hope that's clear. Malecaj would have done the same in one of his places. And I don't want this to *escalate* either. Tell Malecaj that if he starts shooting his guns like some crazy Arab wedding party, it's not going to end well for any of us. What was he thinking?'

'You know?' said Joliffe, leaning in. 'Sometimes gangsters like to behave like gangsters. Walk around with guns. Makes them feel real. *Look at this*. This is cool. Like a scene from a movie.'

Ioannis looked at Genc Malecaj. He'd never seen him up close before. The Albanian had a big, round face, thinning hair, a beard and moustache that weren't much more than glorified stubble. He was nothing special really. If it wasn't for the opaque sunglasses, the wide-legged power stance and the tattoo of the Albanian eagle on the back of his hand you wouldn't have him down as a crime boss.

Malecaj said something to Joliffe. Joliffe replied in halting Albanian then translated for Vlachos.

'He says this is about honour.'

'I have honour, too, Joliffe. I don't like Malecaj trying to sell his shit in my clubs. I'm happy for him to do whatever the fuck he wants on this island, but he stays away from my clubs. That's all I'm asking.'

'Fair point. But, you see, old Mal here, he needs to save face. Even the score.'

There was a noise from the back of the Yeti and Ioannis turned to see that the two guys who'd come out of the trees were trying to open the tailgate.

'Tell them to get away from my car,' he said.

'It's a shit car,' said one of Genc's Albanians.

'That's exactly what I've been trying to tell him,' said Vlachos with a placatory smile.

'What you got back there?' said Joliffe.

'It doesn't matter,' said Ioannis. 'I want them to get away from my car.'

'Problem is – they're the ones with the Uzi, Fishboy.'

Ioannis sighed. Joliffe smirked. The Albanians talked among themselves. Then Uzi opened the tailgate and in a moment one of the guys brought a box from the trunk round to show Joliffe. Younger guy. Red T-shirt with a picture of a Mohawk on it. He put the box on the hood. Another guy, dressed all in black, pulled out a folding knife and cut into the top.

'Hoo-hoo-hoo,' said Joliffe, and he did a little dance, miming playing the flute. Like some kind of jaunty elf. 'Seems you got a shitload of pills, dude?' he said. 'An *elephant* shitload.'

Joliffe had a word with Uzi, who was still at the back of the car. Malecaj finally showed some emotion. Smiled. He had bad teeth. Should cut out the cigarettes.

Uzi and Mohawk grabbed a couple more boxes. Lined them up on the hood.

'You can't take them, Joliffe,' said Vlachos, wearily. 'They're no good. That's a bad batch. There's something wrong with them.'

107

Joliffe laughed loud and hard.

'You gonna have to do better than that, Zorba. You expect me to believe that monie-baloney?'

'They're dangerous.'

'They're fucking drugs, man – they're *supposed* to be dangerous. That's why we love them so. If they weren't dangerous, they'd be, like . . . Just . . . ' He thought for a moment. '*Vitamins.*'

'These are poisonous, OK?'

'Jesus, man, you are the world's worst gangster. You need a new act.'

Vlachos and Ioannis watched helplessly as Malecaj's men started piling boxes on the hood. Malecaj made a call and the two cars from the roadblock manoeuvred round each other and drove up to meet them.

Joliffe grabbed one of the orange plastic pill bottles from the opened box and flipped off the cap. Peered at the pills. Took one out.

'Don't swallow that,' said Vlachos. 'Please . . . '

'It's my party and I'll swallow if I want to,' said Joliffe but he put the pill back, replaced the lid and zipped the bottle in his fanny pack.

Vlachos shook his head.

'Malecaj better watch his back,' said Vlachos, and Joliffe came closer. Whistled.

'The world is changing, brother. Things are not as they were. The axis of power has shifted. Mal is in the ascendant. You need to take the red pill.'

Vlachos slapped Joliffe hard enough with the back of his hand to knock him off his feet. The American gave a startled cry and sprawled in the road. Malecaj's men bristled. Going for their weapons. Looking to Malecaj for a steer. Malecaj stayed stone-faced.

'Hi diddly-dee,' said Joliffe, wiping blood from his face, blinking and getting his smirk back on. 'Where did that come from?'

'From the heart.'

'This ain't over, Vlachos. He's going to take you apart.'

'Tell him something from me,' said Vlachos.

'Go on.'

'Tell him to insert his rotting Albanian schlong into his hairy Albanian fundament.'

Joliffe gave a little snort of laughter. 'I don't think I better. For all our sakes.'

'Then just make sure you tell him what I told you. Those pills are bad. They'll fuck people up.'

'And I told you, Uncle Muncle, that's why you take 'em, baby, that's why you take 'em.'

13

MACINTYRE

The *Louise B* was under sail. They'd gone south, following the coastline, checking out landing sites, times and distances, and once Macintyre had seen all he'd needed, they'd turned round and headed back north, the wind behind them. Sarah had cut the engine and she and Pike had got busy turning winches, pulling chains and unfurling the sails.

Not sheets. That was one small thing Macintyre knew about sailing. Ropes were called sheets. Soldiers, criminals, coppers, games designers, organised crime, porn ... They all had their secret languages to keep outsiders at arm's length. Sailors were just the same.

Pike and Sarah were fast. Working closely without having to say anything, it had taken them less than ten minutes to get the two main sails ready. And now they were skimming over the water, the only sound the flap and crack of the sails and the creaking of the sheets, the rattling of all the little bits of metal around the boat, a steel cable clinking against the mast.

Macintyre was sitting back, feeling the spray on his face, grinning. There were worse places to be right now. He should know. He'd worked in many of them. Beirut. Syria. Some of the truly awful bits of Russia. Sudan. Malta ...

And Gibraltar hadn't been a whole lot of fun either.

Aimee was grinning, too. Standing at the front with Pike, holding on to the cable that secured the mast. It was exhilarating – the idea that they were entirely under the power of nature. Not using an engine. Not using any fuel. It was magical. Aimee turned to Macintyre.

'What are you thinking, boss?' she said.

'The people we saw on the beach below Patia HepKat. That actress woman, Sally Spence, the movie guy, the Belgian prince.'

'What about them?'

'*They* got in.'

'They're famous,' said Aimee. 'Connected.'

'And they were invited,' Pike added.

'There's our door,' said Macintyre. 'Our key.'

'If you say so.' Pike shrugged, waiting for Macintyre to explain in his own time.

'We know Hepworth's weakness.'

'Which is?'

'Classic narcissist. Loves to be talked about. Loves to surround himself with celebrities. Mixes with media types. Thinks of himself as a star already but would dearly love to be in showbiz proper.'

'It's his Achilles heel,' said Aimee. 'Get it? Greek mythology? Achilles heel . . . Suit yourselves.'

'It's certainly a Greek tragedy,' said Pike and nobody laughed at that either.

'With respect, Dennis,' said Aimee. 'I think my crap almost-joke was better than your crap almost-joke.'

'I'll give you that one.'

'You're right, though, Aimee,' said Macintyre, ignoring their banter. 'Hepworth's obsession with showbiz *is* his Achilles heel. And that's where we're gonna bite him.'

'Go on,' said Pike.

'Word is,' said Macintyre. 'Hepworth's planning to launch his own media company. Wants to have complete control of his image. Man knows the dark rumours are out there. He's hungry for good publicity. Why not just generate his own? Show the world what a nice guy he is. "Nothing to see here! Just another day in paradise!"'

'I guess if you've got as much dosh as him you can afford all that shit,' said Pike. 'Your own science institute, a media company, a tennis team – on top of all the other stuff he already runs.'

'Why d'you think that finance guy was sitting on his beach, drinking his booze? Not famous. Not glamorous.'

'And so?'

'Setting up your own media company isn't exactly cheap, Pike. And you know what they say about Hepworth . . . '

'The girls?'

'*And that.* No – I mean about his money.'

'That he's got shitloads of it?'

'No – that he's broke.'

'Fuck off. We just saw his gaff.'

'You can behave like one of the super-rich without actually *being* super-rich, just so long as people believe in your bullshit. The cash doesn't have to actually exist. That's what 2008 was all about – the illusion of wealth. A couple of journalists have done some digging into Hepworth's finances, and it doesn't add up.'

'Come on,' said Aimee. 'Hepworth made billions when he sold Ogmios.'

'Yeah. And he's lost money on just about everything else he's ever done since. Like Trump. All those useless start-ups.'

'How do you make a small fortune in the start-up world?' said Aimee. 'Start with a large fortune.'

Macintyre smiled and nodded. 'That's why he keeps doing all this other shit, he's flailing about, desperately trying to find something else, some going concern that might clear his debts. Plus, there have been some massive, secret payouts.'

'To girls?' said Aimee, with a sour look.

112

'To girls. He had *one* good idea . . . '

'Which wasn't even his idea.'

'Precisely,' said Macintyre. 'He rode piggyback on poor Angus Brodie, who was the coding genius. Then bought him out for an insulting amount when Brodie had some personal problems. Couple of years later, Hepworth sells the company for a hundred times what he'd paid Brodie. Been living off that money ever since and sinking it into ever more hopeless new ventures. He was just smart enough to keep a small stake in Ogmios, hung on to a few shares, which means he still makes money from it. Every time one computer talks to another in an online financial transaction, he takes a cut. An infinitesimally small percentage – but it adds up. And it keeps him alive.'

'So, he's vulnerable?'

'He's desperate. And desperate people make mistakes.'

They'd come alongside Patia HepKat again, and Macintyre glanced over to where a young girl was water skiing. He looked closer. Grabbed the binoculars.

'Holy shit . . . '

'What is it?' asked Aimee, intrigued.

'I think that's her – I think that's Lauren.'

Aimee took the bins off him. 'You're kidding.'

'Straight up.'

'Why don't we just sail over and grab her?' said Aimee.

'You know that's not how we work. Expose ourselves. Risk some stupid James Bond-style boat chase out here. That jet ski looks fast. We make a plan and stick to it. No improvisation.'

'But she's there,' said Aimee. 'Just there . . . '

'And so are two of Hepworth's guys. It'd be a crazy risk. She doesn't know who we are. She'd be freaked out, and . . . '

'She's good.'

'Huh?'

'A good water skier. She's got grace.'

'Come on,' said Macintyre. 'Let's get back to the harbour. I'm going to go and see Alan Human. Aimee, I need you to keep tabs on this Ioannis guy.'

'The boat hire dude?'

'Yeah. Pike says he's connected to Hepworth in some way. We need to examine all possibilities on this thing. Poke our noses into every rabbit hole. You know what they say – knowledge is power.'

'Yeah,' said Aimee. 'Knowledge is power – information is ammunition – and facts are hand grenades. What do you want me to do?'

'Stick a tracker on his car. See if you can get anything out of his wife – Cindy. She'll be at the boat-hire office. Use your charms on her.'

'Will I like her?'

'Bit old for you. But, then, I don't know your tastes. Not my place to pry. She's solidly married. Has been for over twenty years. Whether she's happily married I'll leave it to you to find out. We need to get hold of as many hand grenades as we can . . .'

As he said this, his phone vibrated in his shirt pocket. He took it out. Looked at the screen. Alan Human. He thumbed it awake.

'Yes? What?'

He listened to what Human had to say. Hardly believing what he was hearing.

'I'll be right there.'

He hung up. Sighed. Aimee looked at him.

'Trouble?'

'Human's villa's been broken into . . .'

14

LAUREN

Herve the Perve climbed off the back of the Marlin on to the ViperMax inflatable speedboat and pulled up the anchor. Lauren bobbed in the water, waiting patiently for Lee to pull in the tow rope before Herve came over to pick up the skis. Lee made sure everything was done by the book. Didn't want any stupid accidents out here.

Once Herve had taken on the rope, handle and skis, he chucked a dry towel over to Lee from the speedboat and began to motor back to the shore. As soon as he was clear, Lee manoeuvred closer to Lauren and reached over to grab her hand. He pulled her on board with one clean movement. Lauren's wet skin was slippery, and she easily slid over the side. She settled behind Lee and he passed her the towel. She sat there, pushing her hair out of her face and rubbing it with the towel. She felt nicely worn out. Once she'd got into it, she'd been so engrossed, so in the moment, that she'd been able to shut out all other thoughts.

'What's that bruise, Lauren?'

'Sorry? Where?'

Getting pulled behind this monster of a machine, it was easy to get knocked about a bit.

'On your arm.'

Lauren looked down.

'It's, oh, it's nothing.'

'Did you just get that? Did you hurt yourself just now?'

Lee was OK. Lee had a good heart. He was also nervous as fuck.

'No, it's all right, Lee.' Lauren laughed. 'It's nothing. It's old. I had it before.'

'Are you sure? If one of you girls gets hurt out here, I'm really in, I'm really in the shit, you know. You girls mean everything to Mr Hepworth.'

'Seriously. It's not your fault, Lee. We should get back.'

'Are you cold?'

'No. It's just. You know ...'

They sat on the water not saying anything for a while as Lee made a show of checking everything was all shipshape and Bristol fashion, as he liked to put it. Lauren could see that he was worried, though, turning things over in his mind. She laid a reassuring hand on his shoulder.

'Even if I had got it water skiing, Lee, I'd never say anything. Never blame you. You always look out for us.'

'I could get the blame, anyway. I get the blame for everything. Let me check it out ...'

Lee tried to get a closer look and Lauren was suddenly embarrassed – ashamed. She wrapped the towel round her shoulders. She hadn't been quite quick enough, though.

'It looks like a handprint,' said Lee. 'Like somebody grabbed you. Was it one of the girls? Has somebody hurt you? It wasn't Herve?'

'Herve?'

'I know what you girls call him – Herve the Perve.'

Lauren laughed. 'Only really because it fits. Because of his name. My dad knows this builder called Keith. Dad calls him Keith the Thief. I don't think he really *is* a thief, though.'

116

'So, Herve doesn't bother you at all?'

'Herve? He tries to flirt with us. He stares. Sometimes sort of brushes against you or touches you when he doesn't have to.'

'He *never* has to touch you.'

'You just did, Lee, when you pulled me on to the Marlin.'

'I had to . . . ' Lee stopped, smiled. 'You got me there.'

'Herve's just a man,' said Lauren.

'And you're just a girl.'

'Yeah.'

'That bruise . . . '

'It's nothing. I told you – it's nothing.'

'A big hand. Like a man's hand. Is somebody hurting you, Lauren? If somebody is, you have to say.'

Lauren gave Lee a long stare. Wondering how much she could tell him. Was this the time? She had to do something soon. *And then it hit her.* The only place she could talk with Lee was out here, on the water. Just the two of them. No cameras. No microphones. Herve was already back at the jetty. She took a long slow breath. Let it out.

'What do you think goes on here, Lee?' she said.

Lee turned round. Looked startled. Poor guy.

'What do you mean?'

'I mean – what do you think goes on? What do you think Julian does? Why he has us all locked up?'

'Come on. You're not locked up.'

'Aren't we? You ever seen any of us go out by ourselves?'

'He looks after you, is all. That's what all his security's for. A bunch of young girls. You'd be targets, pestered . . . Julian's no different. He never goes out by himself. Always has Ray with him.'

'That dick.'

Lee tried not to, but he let out a snort of laughter.

'You should show more respect, Lauren.'

'Should I? OK – quick trivia quiz. Is Ray there to keep bad things out or to keep bad things in?'

Lee started the engine. 'I think you're right. We should get back.'

They headed towards the beach. But Lee was going real slow. Lauren took that as a good sign. The conversation wasn't over.

'Seriously, Lee,' she said. 'You must think about it. What Julian's like.'

'It's fake news. Guys like Mr Hepworth, he's always going to have people jealous, saying things about him, trying to bring him down. He's a good employer, a good boss. He pays us well. Looks after us.'

'He treats you like shit, Lee. I've seen him do it. Any little thing that goes wrong, it's always your fault. Nothing's ever his fault.'

'That's just the way he is. He likes to win. Be top dog. Doesn't bother me. I let him. For me, life's not about winning or losing. It's about doing what you do well and taking satisfaction in that.'

'He said, changing the subject.'

'Listen, Lauren. We shouldn't be having this conversation. I've got my own little house here. I live a good life. No rent to pay. All the meals are free. And look at this ...' He swept an arm wide, taking in the sea, the island, the blue sky. 'I get to arse about out here on the boats. Tinker with the engines. It's a dream job, Lauren.'

'So that's it, is it?'

'That's what?'

'Pretend you don't know what's going on because you don't want to lose your job?'

'There's nothing going on.' There was an edge to Lee's voice. Lauren couldn't tell if it was anger or fear. Maybe both. She slipped the towel off her shoulders and pulled Lee round by his arm. He cut their speed as she shoved the bruising in his face.

'Take a good look, Lee. If he hurts us, he always tries to make it somewhere that doesn't show. But he didn't mean to do this. He got angry, grabbed me. And *here*. You ready for this? "This show contains scenes that some viewers may find disturbing."'

118

'Don't ...'

'"Intended for mature audiences only."'

'I don't want to know about it, Lauren ...'

'"Sensitive viewers might want to look away now. Before they get a face-full of violence and body harm ..."' Lauren raised herself off the seat, twisted her backside towards Lee and pulled her bikini bottom down a little. Lee looked alarmed, flushed bright red. Turned away quickly.

'Don't do that. What are you doing? Don't show me that.'

'He likes to beat us,' said Lauren. 'That's what those lines are.'

'I don't believe you, Lauren. I can't believe you.'

'What? I did it to myself like some kind of religious nutter? You think it's self-harm? Nobody ever believes the girl. It's her fault. She made it up.'

'All right! I know,' Lee snapped angrily. 'Of course I know. Everyone knows. Not the details, but ... Like, I didn't know he beat you ... But ... I should have known ...'

His voice had started loud and died away almost to a whisper.

'Lee.' Lauren spoke quietly, too. 'You're the only person here who could help me. Outside of the other girls I've got no friends. You're the only one who really cares about us. You're the only one who ever shows us any real kindness.'

'What can I do, Lauren? I can't jeopardise all this. It's only me. My boy's in college in America, costs a fortune. Mister Hepworth pays for it. Working here, I'm able to save – going to buy my own machine shop eventually ...' He stopped and swore, looking up at the sky. 'I guess I'm trapped here just the same as you. He's clever like that.'

'It's all right, Lee. I didn't mean to freak you out. Truly, I don't want you to do anything you don't want. I don't want to put you in any danger. I don't expect you to understand what he does. I know you just like the sunshine and the sea ... Engines ...'

'I *do* understand,' said Lee quietly.

119

'What?'

'My boy. Josh. When he was at school. He always went to boarding school because I was – because I was working for Mister Hepworth, and Josh's mum had passed away.'

'I'm sorry.'

'But at school . . . There was an incident – a scandal . . . It was the most popular teacher as well . . . That's what I can't get my head around. He wasn't, like, a monster . . . And . . . '

He pointed out a dark shape under the water.

'Look down there,' he said. 'Rocks. Hard to see, but easy to hit. They'll sink you like a stone . . . I saw something once. A glimpse. Like those rocks under the water. A few years back, there was a girl here called Natasha.'

'I've heard of her.'

'I saw something. I told myself I hadn't seen it. Told myself I didn't know it. That there was nothing I could do about it. And then she was gone.'

'If you don't do anything about it, you're part of this,' said Lauren. 'You're helping him. And one day he's going to hit those rocks and this is all going to blow up in his face. Come crashing down. He can't get away with what he's doing for ever and the people who're close to him, they're going to come crashing down with him.'

Lee turned the throttle to full power and had to shout over the noise as they raced for the shore.

'I *will* help you, Lauren. Because I can't go on like this. I'll do it. I'm not part of this. I promise you, I'm not. I just like to fix engines.'

15

HUMAN

Broken glass crunched under Macintyre's deck shoes as he surveyed the devastation in Alan Human's villa. The place had been trashed, and the words GROIN GROIN GROIN had been spray-painted on to the wall. And 'PIGGIES'.

'They've smashed the whole fucking place up, Macintyre.' Alan looked like shit. He'd been crying. And drinking. And sitting in the sun. All three activities had made his face even pinker than usual. Puffy. 'They took a dump on the kitchen floor, for fuck's sake. I scraped it up with a spatula and flushed it down the khazi. It was demeaning. I've wiped the floor and disinfected it, but I can still smell it. What do I do? Do I go to the police?'

'We'll see.'

'We'll see? We'll see? What kind of a response is that? You're supposed to be the big man. The guy who sorts things out. Like those adverts on TV.'

'What adverts?'

'I can't remember, exactly. The one where a guy comes round and sorts everything out . . .'

'Let's not get into that now, Alan. Where were you when this happened?'

'I was upstairs. In bed.'

'Really?'

'Really.' Alan turned away, hiding something. 'What else am I going to do? I can't go out. There's only so long you can sit by a pool doing nothing.'

'You could read a book.'

'I can't concentrate to read. I used to like crime books, but when you're in one . . . I've watched all the DVDs I brought with me.'

'Who brings DVDs on holiday with them these days? Can't you just stream something?'

'Lauren used to set up all that shit for me. I don't know how to do it. But that's not really the point, now, Macintyre, is it? It's not the point. I've been robbed.'

'How did they get in?'

'It's not difficult. They levered up the catch on the shutters, wrenched the window open. This place isn't exactly Fort Knox. That Cindy woman at the indoctrination told us to keep our shutters and windows locked when we went out. Fat lot of good that did. Do you think it was Albanians? Some fucking Albanians?'

'I don't know who it was yet, Alan, I've only just got here. Do you know what they took?'

'Yeah . . . they took my portable speaker . . .'

'What make?'

'JBL, I think.'

'What else?'

'My passport. My wallet. Credit cards. Some cash I had. I had my phone with me, luckily. They didn't take that. Or my laptop. I had that, too, in the . . . by the bed. But why did they have to break everything? It's utterly senseless.'

'Groin groin groin? What do you suppose that means?'

'Something sexual, I guess. Some Albanian thing . . .'

'OK. I want you to do something for me, Alan. First of all, I want you to go into the kitchen and write out a full statement on a sheet of paper. Do it now, yeah? I don't want to talk about it.'

'OK. All right. Yeah. I need to do something. I'll do that.'

'Good man.'

Macintyre wasn't sure if he needed a statement, but it might be useful one day. He mainly needed to get Human out of the way. He went over to the shelf where he'd hidden the camera. Most of the fake ancient Greek plates and knick-knacks had been broken. Not valuable items. Nobody ever puts valuable items in a rental place. But had they found the camera? He cleared some stuff off the shelf and there it was, on its side, under a pile of broken pottery. He cleared the mess away, rearranged a few unbroken items on the shelf, wiped dust off the tiny lens and put the camera back in position.

He'd quickly checked the feed before he came over. Got a glimpse of three guys in crash helmets before the camera was obscured. The best laid plans and all that...

Human came back into the room with his statement. Macintyre took it off him, read it quickly, folded it and put it in his pocket.

'I'll hang on to this,' he said. 'It's risky going to the police before we finish what we're doing. We don't want them asking questions. Trying to find the guys that did this. Sit tight, yeah? I'll sort it.'

'My passport, though, I need to report my passport.'

'I'll get it back. I'll get everything back. You've cancelled the cards, yeah?'

'Yes – I did manage to do that.'

'Good.'

'Do you think they'll come back? The burglars?'

'What for? They've had their fun. Got what they wanted and moved on. Don't be scared of them. Small stuff like this. It's usually just kids. Kids do the small stuff. It's grown-ups do the really nasty things...'

'Do you want a drink?'

'I'll take a beer if you've got one.'

He followed Human into the kitchen. Watched him get a beer out of the fridge and then fish an unopened bottle of vodka out of a carrier bag on the counter. There was a strong smell of disinfectant in here. And something more earthy.

'We'll take them out to the pool, yeah?'

'Yeah.'

The burglars had chucked the sun loungers into the water. Cushions and all. Thankfully they hadn't taken a dump in there as well. There was a wrought-iron table with two chairs by it that they hadn't touched. Macintyre and Human sat down, and Macintyre took a pull on his beer. Looked at Human.

'You weren't upstairs in bed when this happened, were you?'

'What?'

'No burglars would break in with a car outside. You'd gone out.'

'No ...'

'That was a new bottle of vodka, Alan.'

Macintyre didn't add that he'd scrolled back far enough in the spycam footage to see Alan crossing the living room in flip flops and shorts, with a towel under his arm.

'Look ... I ...'

'Go on – I'm looking forward to this.'

'To what?'

'To hearing how you can interpret the phrase "Don't Leave The House" to mean "Leave The House".'

Alan set his glass down on the table, ran his fingers through his hair and exhaled noisily.

'I went to the beach. OK? I was careful. I went up north. Well away from here. To Kassiopi. Nobody could know me there. I mean, *I went to the beach*. That is not a crazy thing, is it? That is not a weird thing. It is a normal thing to do.'

'This is not a normal situation, Alan. You're not on holiday.'

'But I'm a normal person, Macintyre. I'm not like you. This

is not my life. I only know how to do *normal* things. I suppose I wanted, in a way, I wanted to believe that things hadn't *all* gone to shit. I wanted to try to be happy . . . '

He looked over at Macintyre. He didn't look happy at all.

'If you will only let me do my job,' said Macintyre. 'I can make you happy again. I can fish you out of the shit, hose you down, pat your arse dry and dust it with talcum powder. But if you don't behave, you risk everything.'

'I've spent my whole life behaving. And where's it got me? Before this – *before all this* – my life was normal. I was a *normal* man. I watched films. I watched dramas on the TV. Box sets. Guns and drugs and explosions. Murder. Monsters. Aliens. Hitmen. I read crime stories. Jack Reacher, Jack Ryan, Dan Brown . . . But it was escapism. *Fantasy.* I never – *never for one moment* – believed that anything like that would happen to me. It was Narnia, outer space, it was Westeros – a world I didn't live in. I've never seen a gun. A real gun. In real life. Never seen a dead body. Not even when my father died. I wasn't there. And then he was in a coffin. The lid screwed shut. My life was like that – the lid screwed shut.' He took a solid slug of neat vodka. 'It's a class thing, no doubt. I'm middle class. I live in Henley-on-Thames. I rip cast-iron radiators out of old buildings, strip the paint off them and sell them for a stupid amount of money. I collect fireplaces. Tiles. Bricks. Floorboards. *Normal* things.'

'I get it, Alan. You're normal. But you shouldn't have gone to the beach. We had a deal.'

'Yes . . .' Alan stared at Macintyre with an almost comically desolate look and then started to cry.

'I just want things to be like they were.'

'You have to accept, Alan, that that's not going to happen.'

'What do you mean?'

'I'll get Lauren home. But it'll always be there. This thing that's happened to her. She won't be the same person. And look at *you*.

You're not the same person, are you? This is not the Alan Human that your family and friends, the people who work for you, your customers, would recognise.'

'Don't . . .'

'Shut up and listen, Alan. You also have to be prepared for the fact that Lauren might not want to leave here.'

'What do you mean?'

'I've done this before. I know what it's like. Hepworth will have worked on her. Groomed her like a pimp. Lauren and all his girls. Brainwashed her. Programmed her. Men have been doing that to women since before they wrote the Bible. You want to learn "The Rules", you want to be a *player*? You want to know how to manipulate and control women? Go straight to the original textbooks – the Bible, the Torah, the Koran . . . Written by men, for men. Sets of rules. What you wear, what you eat, how you do your hair, how you behave . . . All designed simply to control. And they've been refining their techniques ever since. Just about every organised religion, every cult, every guru, pimp, slave owner, sergeant-major, theatre director, film producer, CEO . . . Hepworth will have broken his girls down to nothing and remade them as his little followers. You've got to be very strong to resist that.'

'Lauren's tough,' said Alan.

'If you know what you're doing you can break down the toughest people,' said Macintyre. 'Smart people. People who think they're immune to it. If you're ruthless – if you're a psychopath – you can make them devoted to you. It's a game. Push and pull, give and take, hot and cold, the glowing tip of the cigar and the ice cube.'

'You think he's torturing her?'

'He'll be using mind-control techniques. Hard to defend against. Hard to attack. Technically, Lauren's not being held at Patia HepKat against her will. She's free to leave any time she wants. Has she left?'

'No.'

'On the surface, Hepworth's a great guy. There's a million teen-age girls on this planet who'd happily swap places with Lauren. Live in the billionaire's mansion. Swim in his pool. Play tennis, go water skiing and live the fully filtered Instagram lifestyle. Gets harder and harder now to look past the front that kids can create. They all want to buy into it. You can warn them, but they all think – "I'm OK. I know how to look after myself. It's worth it. I can put up with the other stuff . . . "'

Alan looked at him. 'What I want you to do,' he said, 'is go up there and shoot that cunt between the fucking eyes.'

'I'm not sure that would be a very good idea, do you?'

'I think it would be a *very good* fucking idea, actually, Macintyre . . . '

'It's not what I do.'

'You know – and don't take this the wrong way – I'm beginning to wonder just what the fuck you *do* do. When you came here that first night, I have to confess, I was properly disappointed.'

'Yeah?'

'Yeah, I'd pictured you as, I don't know, some hard-bitten ex-military guy with big arms and a beard. A hard man. A tough guy. Like that – what's his name – the bodyguard?'

'Ray Jordan?'

'Him. Yeah. I mean – do you even know any self-defence?'

Macintyre burst out laughing.

'Self-defence?'

'Yes. If you're going to deal with the likes of Ray Jordan . . . '

'Tell me, Alan, have you ever been in any situation, *in your entire life*, when you've thought, "You know what – if only I knew some kung fu . . . "?'

'Well, no . . . but, as I say, my life is normal, *your* life . . . '

'Alan. Listen. Even *now*. Now that you're in this world of action thrillers and Netflix box sets would karate really make things better?'

'If I knew karate, I'd take it out on someone . . .'

'And you'd wind up in jail. How would that help Lauren? Let me make this clear. I'm not Special Forces. I don't fight terrorists hand-to-hand and bite their balls off. I don't have the backing of a government. I'm not army, police, secret service . . . And, even if I was, I'd have no jurisdiction outside the UK. Hepworth is clever. He moves his circus around the world. He won't lay a finger on anyone inside the US or the UK. He knows the law. Technically he's done nothing wrong.'

'Hah!'

'It's subtle, Alan. Delicate. Complicated. And that's where I work – in the grey areas. We have to be as clever as him. We have to be careful.'

'Did I hire the right person?'

'What did you think? That I was going to drive up to Hepworth's place in a tank with a squadron of handpicked mercenaries blasting away with sub-machine guns and RPGs? Kill Hepworth and all his security guys in a bloody gun battle and swing out of there on a rope, clutching Lauren to my hairy chest like Tarzan?'

'Yeah . . .' Human smiled. A bit wonky and forlorn but a smile, nevertheless. 'I should have hired Tarzan.'

Macintyre finished off his beer and got up.

'Tarzan's retired,' he said. 'You're stuck with me, I'm afraid.'

Alan clutched his arm. Held on tight. 'No. Don't go. Will you stay? Sit with me. I get so fucking lonely here . . .'

16

PIKE

Pike and Sarah were sitting on the aft deck, playing rummy at their fold-up table. The cards were old and worn smooth, yellowed from age. It was a warm evening and various insects circled and bumped around the outside lamp that enclosed them in a friendly circle of light. Everything had a golden glow – the lamp, the cards, the moths, the bottle of Kourtaki retsina.

They weren't talking, content in each other's silence. Living in such close quarters, they couldn't exactly tell each other the events of the day they'd shared, although they would often go over something that had happened, offering their different insights. They'd already discussed today's boat trip and now they were quiet. Enjoying the simplicity of a night-time card game. The small things in life.

They were pretty evenly balanced, although, if pushed, Pike would have to concede that Sarah probably had the edge on him. She was more patient. Less impulsive. Kept her emotions out of it. Happy to wait for him to make a mistake. And you could never read her. She had the perfect poker face. Always just that hint of a smile. Nothing more. Nothing less. They both always knew what the other was thinking – until they started playing cards.

Yeah. She probably won more often than him.

And it wasn't just cards. They had a good pile of two player games stowed in the cabin – Boggle, Bananagrams, Hive, Snatch, Sequence ... They even had an old edition of Trivial Pursuit, a special movie edition. But they hadn't got that one out in a while. They'd both pretty much memorised every answer.

Sarah won the round, marked down the scores, and, as she collected up the cards for another round, Pike glanced towards the shore. Two men were walking out along the jetty. A younger guy in a red T-shirt and ripped jeans. An older guy all in black. They looked out of place. Urban types. Self-conscious but with a certain purpose about them. Business to attend to.

Pike looked at them just long enough to read the situation then gave a tiny nod to Sarah.

'Yep. Seen 'em,' she said, her attention apparently focused on the cards. 'Not yachties that's for sure. Not holidaymakers. Not locals.'

'Might be nothing to do with us.'

'You believe that?'

'Nope. We might need to play this carefully.'

'I'm way ahead of you, Pike ... as ever.'

Pike gave her a look.

The two men arrived at the *Louise B*. Stood there, looking it over, establishing their presence.

'Good evening,' said the older man, with an accent Pike couldn't immediately place. Could be Greek, Turkish, Albanian ... or anywhere from the Balkans. He was bald, but both guys looked like no matter how often they shaved they'd still have five o'clock shadow at ten in the morning.

They were attempting to smile. Polite. Pike and Sarah did likewise.

'Evening all,' said Pike.

'Is this your boat?' the older man asked.

'You interested in a charter?'

'Maybe.'

'How fast does it go?' asked the younger guy. Seemed genuinely interested.

'We clocked thirty knots once,' said Pike. 'Under sail.'

The younger guy whistled appreciatively. His T-shirt was Diesel. The image of a Mohawk and the slogan 'Only the brave'. The older guy wore black jeans and a tight-fitting, long-sleeved black shirt with one button too many undone.

'We like to take a look,' he said.

'Not now, fellas,' said Pike. Still polite.

'It's late,' said Sarah. 'We're turning in soon. Can you come back in the morning?'

'No. We would like to take a look now.' Uninvited, both men stepped aboard, glancing around, trying to own the space. Pike said nothing, just carried on smiling blandly at them.

'Welcome aboard,' he said.

'How long is it?' asked the younger guy.

'Forty-five foot. Sleeps eight in four cabins.'

'The engine is powerful?'

'As powerful as it needs to be . . .'

The older guy cut them off. Said something hard and pithy to his partner. Then addressed Pike and Sarah.

'We need to talk to you in private.'

'Yeah? You wanna come inside?'

Pike got up with an exaggerated old man's grunt, and went into the cabin; after a short pause, and an exchange of glances, the two men followed him. Sarah stayed outside.

Pike switched on the indoor lights, turned the dimmer to full. With the reflections in the windows, it was difficult to see any-thing much outside now. Pike was playing the innocent, bustling about and tidying up.

'Can I get you anything?' he asked. 'Tea? Coffee? Water. Glass of wine? We're drinking retsina. Not to everyone's taste . . .'

'Nothing,' said the older guy.

'What is it you want to talk about? Only, my old woman was right. Folks like us need our sleep. Ha-ha!' He called out to Sarah. 'Babe? Do you want to sort things, batten down the hatches and maybe join us?'

'Sure thing, babe. Give me a minute.'

They only called each other babe when there was a problem. It was a code. Be careful. Don't give anything away. Look out for the signs and signals. Stay connected. He could feel Sarah moving about the boat. He knew the *Louise B* so well he could tell exactly what every bump and vibration meant. He could feel the slight shift as Sarah got off and a few moments later another dip as she got back on, and then the little kick . . .

'You do some work for Ioannis?' asked the older guy.

'Depends how you want to look at it.'

Where was this going? Best to carry on playing dumb. Keep busy. Distract them. 'I'm gonna make a pot of tea.'

Going to the fridge. The sink. The hob. The stowage lockers. Kettle, milk, sugar, teapot, cups, water . . . Keeping the guys annoyed, moving heavily, keeping the boat gently rocking.

'Are you sure I can't tempt you? You're probably not tea drinkers. Just a small retsina . . . ?' Pushing past the younger guy. 'Babe? You want to bring that bottle in when you come?'

'Sure thing, babe.'

'You live on here all the time?' asked the young one.

'Pretty much.'

'Is cold in winter?'

Once again, his partner snapped angrily at him. Pike was still trying to get a handle on the language.

'My friend doesn't want to talk about boats,' said the younger guy, ignoring the scowl from his partner. 'I like boats. I would like one, one day.'

'And you want to hire this one?'

The younger guy shrugged.

Sarah came in, pulling the doors closed behind her. She had the retsina and the glasses.

'You having another?'

'I've moved on to tea, babe. I'm making a pot . . .' Back to the bald guy. 'So, what were you saying about Ioannis?'

'You do some work for him?'

'Right. Yes. I was saying it depends on how you look at it, really. You could say I do some work for him, or you could say he does some work for me. We help each other out. You know how it is.'

'He takes a cut? He takes a *skim* from your money?'

'Yeah. He puts work my way, takes a little something for the pot.'

'Not anymore.'

'Not anymore?'

'No. From now, you will pay *us*. You will work for us.'

'Ooh. I'd have to clear that with old Ioannis.'

'Is not necessary. You don't need to speak to him. You just pay *us*. You pay him as well if you want. Is up to you. Paying *us* is not up to you. It is up to us.'

'Well, that's all well and good, gentlemen, but I don't know you, do I? I don't know who you are.'

'Is not necessary you know names.'

'I think, if we were entering into some kind of business agreement, I'd need to know who I'm dealing with.' Pike was washing cups. 'Would you not say that was the done thing, babe?'

'I would, babe.' Sarah put the bottle and glasses down. 'It's the done thing. It's only right we know their names.'

The older guy sighed, growing exasperated. 'My name is Costel.' *Romanian.*

'This is Arven.'

Albanian.

'Well. That wasn't so hard, was it? Now we're all shored up. Everything above board. Above deck, if you like.'

'You?' Costel cocked his chin at Pike. 'What is *your* name?'

'Me. I thought you'd never ask . . .' Pike got some pistachios out and put some in a little bowl. The boat rocking with his movements.

'My name is Basil McBoatface,' he said. 'But my friends – and I hope I can count you as one, Costel – my friends call me Boaty. On account of I spend my life fannying about on yachts and suchlike. And this is my good lady wife – Barbara. She's the real skipper of this fine vessel.'

Sarah winced at his choice of name and then smiled, shook her head. She was constantly on the move, as well. Plumping cushions, straightening magazines, clearing surfaces like an anxious housewife with unexpected visitors. She and Pike working around the two men who were standing awkwardly in the small space. Pike checked. They wouldn't be able to see much out of the low windows, and to sit down would rob them of some of their power.

Not that they had any real power here, if they'd only known it.

'So,' said Pike. 'Maybe you should go through this arrangement again. I'm a bit slow on the uptake these days. Arven, you seem to understand about the life aquatic, perhaps you could explain?'

'If you want to work in this places, in Corfu, Mister Mabophus,' said Arven. 'You need to pay us. Or there will be problems.'

'What sort of problems? Not sure I follow you, me hearty.'

'You know boats,' said Arven. 'Always there are problems. They can sink. Engines can be broken. Sails can be ripped.'

'Like your jeans?'

'What?'

'Ripped – like your jeans – you salty sea dog.'

Arven frowned and looked down. Pike laughed.

'Don't mind me, I'm just having a bit of fun with you, Arven. A laugh. What's life without laughter? It's like soup without a grind of pepper.' Miming the action.

'Bad things can happen to your boat,' said Costel, who was rapidly losing his patience.

'I get it,' said Pike with a dopey, shit-eater grin. 'The penny drops with a terrible clang.' He pulled open a pistachio shell and popped the nut in his mouth.

'It's like an insurance scheme,' he said, offering the bowl of nuts to Costel, who waved it away.

'They're offering us insurance, Barbara,' he said.

'I see,' said Sarah hesitantly, biting her lip in a pantomime show of not really understanding what was going on at all.

'You mean to say ...' She put on a childish 'thinking hard' face. 'That if anything goes wrong with the boat, you'll fix her up? That's comical, Boaty. Don't you think it's comical? When we've just paid our annual premium.'

'Very comical, indeed, Barbara.'

The two of them laughed, like a harmless couple of retirees with a seaside bungalow on the Isle of Wight.

'No,' said Costel and he gave Sarah a look. 'This insurance it work in a different way. You don't pay it, you will have accident for sure. Then you fix the problem yourself.'

'That doesn't sound right,' said Sarah. 'That doesn't sound like a good deal at all.'

'It is not a good deal for *you*,' said Costel. 'Not a good deal for Ioannis. But is very good deal for us.'

'You know what I'm thinking,' said Pike. 'I'm thinking it doesn't sound like an insurance deal. It sounds more like an old-school protection racket. The likes of which I thought had gone out with the Krays. The Godfather. I used to be involved in all that shit back in Hackney in the eighties. It feels very twentieth century. I thought these days it was all internet scams and online fraud, hacking accounts, ringing old ladies and pretending to work for Microsoft.' He grinned and wagged a finger at Costel. 'Fellas, you are behind the curve. Perhaps you need to go to some kind of criminal business school and get up to date?'

'You think this is funny, Mister Mabophus? This is not funny.'

'It's amusing *me*,' said Pike. 'Like some cheap seventies crime movie.'

'You need to take it more seriously,' said Costel.

'Why?'

'Because we can make life difficult for you.'

'I bet you could,' said Pike. 'If we weren't on this boat. If we were on dry land.'

'It makes no difference,' said Costel, and he helped himself to some nuts.

'I wonder,' said Pike. 'Do you know the story of Antaeus and Hercules – or Herakles as the Greeks call him. What do you call him in Albania, Arven? Hercules?'

Arven shrugged. 'Erkili.'

'Erkili.'

Costel turned on Arven and said something to him that Pike understood enough of to know he was dressing down the younger guy for discussing Hercules. Pike was enjoying this. Wasting the guys' time. The longer he could string this out the better. The stupid sods wouldn't know what was happening until it was too late.

'Well,' he said, getting Costel's attention. 'When Erkili was on his way to the Garden of the Hesperides to steal some apples – his eleventh labour, I think. One of the last ones, anyway. He had to go through the lands of Antaeus, in modern-day Libya. Now, Antaeus was a powerful giant, the son of the sea god, Poseidon, and the earth goddess, Gaea. That's an important detail. *Poseidon*, the god of the oceans, and *Gaea*, goddess of the earth. And he liked to wrestle, old Erkili did.'

'Why are you telling me this?' said Costel, dropping some empty pistachio shells on the floor.

'Wait and see, wait and see. It is *germane*, I promise.'

'I like this story,' said Sarah.

'Yes, it's a good one,' said Pike. 'Now, any strangers passing through Antaeus's country had to wrestle him, you see? Same with Hercules. So, they went at it. Mano a mano. And to win Greek wrestling, I don't know if you know, but you have to throw your opponent to the ground. But whenever Hercules threw Antaeus down he only got stronger . . .'

'Please,' said Costel, raising his hands. 'You stop now. Stop talking. Yes? You listen to me.'

'No,' said Pike affably. 'Let me finish. I think you'll get it. Because, you see, Hercules twigged what was happening. He realised that whenever Antaeus touched the *ground*, his mother, Gaea – *Mother Earth* – renewed his strength, so the bugger was pretty much invincible. So, what Hercules did, old Erkili, he lifted Antaeus up, his feet kicking in the air, and crushed him to death in his arms. There's lots of statues. Pictures on vases. You like to see two big men wrestling naked, Costel? You like gladiator films?'

Sarah gave a snort of laughter but Costel only shouted.

'Shut the fuck up! You say one more word and I slap your mouth.'

Arven was intrigued, though. 'Why you tell us this story, Boaty?'

'I thought you'd never ask,' said Pike. 'Why don't you explain, Babs, love?'

As Sarah took over the story Pike went to pour the hot water from the kettle into the teapot, taking the opportunity to look out of the window and check that everything was going to plan.

'Gaea and Poseidon,' said Sarah. '*The land and the sea*. It's like you and us. On land you're like Antaeus, under the protection of Gaea. But on this boat, she has no power, and me and Boaty, we're under the protection of Poseidon. He's our insurance, if you like.'

Arven was nodding and smiling. 'OK. I get it,' he said and Costel shot him a foul look.

137

'Yeah,' said Pike. 'As soon as you stepped on to our boat you entered our world. You have no power here. You have options instead. You can apologise, kiss and make up, or you can fuck right off.'

'Why don't you shut up?' said Costel. 'You are giving me headache.'

'Well, I'm sorry, but you two comedians are giving me bellyache. Trying to pull a corny protection scam on us. *Boats can sink* ... What is this to do with? Some turf war with Ioannis?'

'Ioannis is what you call a cunt,' said Costel.

'That's not nice language to use in front of a lady.'

'She is no lady. She is cunt,' said Costel. 'And you are cunt, too. A boring cunt. We'll be back tomorrow at this time. Either you give us five hundred euros or you are not here. We never see you again. OK? You are gone. And you don't ever fucking come back.'

Pike took a step closer to Arven, who put up a hand and rested it on Pike's chest. Laughed.

'Whoa there, old man,' he said. 'Don't get angry. You don't want a fight in here.'

'I don't want a fight anywhere.' Pike's voice was quiet and weary. 'Can you guys swim?'

'I can swim,' said Arven. 'Costel not so good.'

Costel was looking a little concerned now, something was bugging him. Maybe he'd twigged at last.

'Wait, wait,' he said. 'There is problem with your boat.'

'No problem,' said Pike.

Costel pushed past Pike and Sarah and slid the doors open. Hurried out on to the deck. Swore. Arven followed. Pike picked up the bottle of retsina and went out with Sarah.

'Oh, *now* look,' said Pike, reverting to his South Coast retiree persona. 'How in heaven's name did that happen? Barbara, babe? Did you not tie her up properly?'

'I am such an idiot,' said Sarah.

While Pike had been distracting the racketeers in the cabin, Sarah had loosed the mooring ropes and kicked the boat away from the jetty as she got back on board. They were drifting out in the dark, open water of the harbour, a long way from the jetty and a long way from the shore.

'You guys got mobile phones on you?' said Pike. 'Cell phones?'

'What the fuck's it to you?' said Costel.

'It's only they're going to get ruined when you swim back to the beach.'

'We not swim,' said Costel angrily, and he pulled out a folding knife. Opened the blade. 'You take us back.'

Pike nodded to Sarah. 'You'd better start her up, babe.'

Sarah put on a good show of being scared, staring at the knife while she fumbled with the controls. The engine spluttered.

'Come on, babe, don't fuck about. These guys mean business,' said Pike, joining in the charade.

'I'm sorry,' said Sarah. 'They're making me nervous.'

'Yes,' said Costel, finally enjoying himself. 'You scared now, cunt? You know this is not game.'

Sarah made a show of getting confused with the controls. The boat started to swing round.

'Shit.'

'What are you doing, babe? Sort it out.'

'I'm sorry. I'm sorry. I'm sorry.'

They were heading out into even deeper waters now. Costel swore at Sarah in what Pike guessed must be Romanian.

'You know how to drive boat?'

He moved towards Sarah, putting out his free hand to steady himself.

'You're just making it worse!' Sarah shrieked.

'Babe?'

Costel took another wobbly step. Sarah jammed the throttle

full ahead and swung the boat round sharply the other way. Costel was thrown off balance. He reached for a rope with the hand that was holding the knife but couldn't grab hold without dropping his weapon.

Pike helped him out with that. Smacking the retsina bottle down on to Costel's wrist. He yelled and dropped the knife. Pike swiftly kicked it overboard.

'Never bring a knife to a bottle fight,' he said.

Now Arven came at him, but Pike was ready for him. Knew his way around a boat better. He shimmied past Costel and scurried along the starboard hull to the foredeck, hoping to draw the gangbangers away from Sarah.

They both followed him. Costel swearing and shouting. Holding his arm.

Sarah kept the throttle on full and they headed further out to sea. She was randomly shunting the tiller left and right to keep the boat unstable. Pike was used to it. Had no problem keeping his footing. The other guys were slipping and stumbling as they tried to get to him. If they'd been smart, they'd have gone straight to Sarah and taken control of the boat. But they weren't smart. They were dumb, and pissed off, and Pike had made them mad. The only thing on their minds was to hurt him badly and fix their wounded pride.

He just had to make sure that didn't happen.

He was right out on the tip of the port hull now, balancing like a circus act. Arven and Costel reckoned they had him cornered and kept on coming, one on either side of the mainstay, the steel cable that went from the front of the boat up to the top of the mast to keep it upright.

Pike took his eyes off the two mugs just long enough to nod to Sarah across the cabin roof. And as Costel came for him, he launched himself towards the opposite hull. At the same time Sarah jammed the tiller as far the other way as it would go. Pike had timed the jump just right. He grabbed the mainstay and spun round it, kicking Costel in the back with both feet. The Romanian flew into the sea with a startled shout.

Pike landed neatly on the foredeck. But, as he straightened up and faced Arven, he saw that the younger guy had taken out a gun. An old Russian TT by the look of it.

'OK . . .' said Pike. 'OK . . .'

They'd left Costel behind, floundering in the water.

'Get the boat to him,' said Arven. At least the guy had more on his mind than murder.

'Babe,' Pike shouted, not taking his eyes off Arven. 'We need to go back for Costel. Take her round. And get a lifebelt ready. We're gonna need it.'

'It shouldn't have been like this, Boaty,' said Arven. 'You have made it complicated.'

'You don't really want to start shooting that thing, son,' said Pike. 'Not out here – in the middle of the harbour. You'll end up in a world of shit.'

'Don't you start your talking again. I am trying to think.'

'Meanwhile, your pal's drowning.'

Arven glanced at Costel, struggling to keep his head above water. The boat was slowly heading towards him.

'Here!' Sarah appeared with a rigid lifebelt. Tossed it to Arven, who instinctively made a grab to catch it. It was all Pike needed. He kicked Arven into the drink.

Sarah hurried back to the helm and steered the boat towards the harbour mouth. Pike waved at Arven and Costel as they passed them and went to join his wife.

'What was that all about?' she said.

'Nobody fucks with me on my boat.'

'This won't be the end of it.'

'Yeah, I know. And Macintyre's not going to be best pleased. I'll have to call him.'

'I'll take us to one of the small bays and drop anchor there for the night,' said Sarah. 'Then we better figure out our next move.'

'I shouldn't have started a fight,' said Pike. 'But when he called you a cunt ...'

'Oh, the big man has to protect the poor defenceless little woman.'

'That's nice, I must say. What have I done to deserve this?'

'*Barbara*.'

'Barbara?'

'Yes. *Really*?'

'Thought it sounded a good fit – Barbara McBoatface.'

'Don't you ever call me that again.'

'Understood, skipper.'

Pike kissed her and she smiled.

'You haven't lost it, old man.'

'You neither, old girl ... Tell you what, though, I've wrenched something in me fucking shoulder. And ripped my hands.'

He showed Sarah his palms.

'It was like seeing Errol Flynn in action.'

'*Robin Hood*?'

'*Captain Blood*.'

'You know,' said Pike, with a touch of sadness. 'There's a lot of young people alive today have no idea who Errol Flynn was.'

A light flashed on the foredeck. There was a faint beep. Pike frowned and went to investigate.

'What is it?' Sarah called out.

'One of Abbott and Costello dropped their phone. That might come in very handy.'

17

HUMAN

'I've never locked myself out of the house. I've never lost my wallet. I've never missed a flight. I've never run out of petrol . . . and I long ago lost the ability to make my wife happy.'

They were still sitting by the pool. Macintyre had fished the loungers out and the underwater lights had turned the water a Day-Glo blue. Bats were swooping over the water, picking off insects. Macintyre had lost count of how many times Human had refilled his glass. The bottle of vodka was nearly empty.

'She's beautiful, my wife,' he said. 'Alice. I mean, you don't know her, but she has . . . She has bright red hair and faultless, pale skin. A classic English rose. And when she smiles, it lights up the whole room . . . *When she smiles.*

'Oh, she still smiles, but I can't do it. I've lost the gift. I can't make her smile anymore. Nothing I do.

'This afternoon on the beach. There was this woman there. You should have seen her. Greasy hair, sunburn, terrible clothes, and she was fat. Her body had lost all its shape, gone squashy and pale, bloated and soft-looking, like a kid's plastic blow-up toy that's been left out in the rain all year.

'And her *arse.* Her arse. I tell you. Her arse was IMMENSE. It was fucking enormous. She was waddling along with a pushchair, and I was behind her, and all I could see was this arse, this vast amorphous thing, like looking at someone through a fisheye lens. It loomed at you, that arse, while the rest of her, her tiny head and little hands and feet, receded away from it. In fact, it wasn't like a woman with a big arse, it was like an arse with a woman attached to it. I mean, I know that what with the Kardashians and all that, a big booty is a thing, but ... But, what I'm trying to say is – she was pushing this *pushchair*. You understand? You see what I'm saying? What I'm getting at here? A pushchair. *With a baby in it*. I don't know, six months old. And trotting along next to her was another child. And this woman was smiling, happy, chatting to her kids.

'Happy – *and she has kids* – which means that somebody has *fucked* her. Not just once – she has two kids, this woman with an arse that's visible from the moon.'

'Jesus, Alan, do I have to hear this? Where's this going?'

'I'm just saying ... I'm just saying ... Somebody wanted her, lusted after her, made love to her ... And I don't even have the decency to fuck my own wife. My beautiful wife. I can't bring myself to have sex with her. It's not just her, you have to understand. It's not like I'm out rutting with all and sundry. The fact of the matter *is* ... I don't want to have sex with *anyone*. My sex drive is kaput. They say, don't they, that men think about sex five times every hour, or something? Ha. Not me, mate. Not old Alan Human. No, sir. He might as well cut his useless shrivelled cock off and send it to Oxfam to help feed the starving millions.

'I mean, you're probably thinking I might be gay, right? *Gay*? That's a laugh. I'm far from gay in any sense of the fucking word. No. Sex has simply disappeared from my life. Poof! And it's *him*. It's Hepworth. I think of sex and I think of *him* – having sex. And I think of those girls and I think of Lauren. I can't stop making the connections. And I have to put sex out of my mind, because it's awful and dirty and disgusting. I'm disgusting...' He refilled his glass with the last of the vodka but set it down without drinking any.

'The idea of forcing my horrible body on to *any* woman . . .'

Alan fell silent.

'You're clinically depressed,' said Macintyre. 'Your symptoms aren't exactly unique. You're only human.'

'Oh! You think? Do you? *Really*? That's an eye-opener, Doctor Macintyre.'

They sat in silence for a while, drinking. In the end Alan got up unsteadily and looked up at the sky. The great spray of stars.

'You're right, Macintyre,' he said. 'I know it. I know it. I know it. I know it. My sorrow, my despair and desperation, my self-loathing, it's all just corny and hackneyed and old hat. I'm just a bloke who can't get a hard on.'

Before Macintyre could stop him, Alan flopped into the pool, lay face down in the water. Macintyre left him there for a while then hauled him out and rolled him on to his back.

'That was the most pitiful attempt at suicide I've ever seen,' he said, and Alan looked up at him with his pink eyes.

'I just needed to splash some water in my face.'

They both laughed and then Alan grabbed Macintyre's arms.

'Is it my fault?' he said.

'What?'

'Lauren.'

'You tell *me*.'

Alan nodded to Macintyre to help him up. Macintyre got him back on to his lounger.

'Three years back, Alice left me. Can't blame her. I wasn't bringing much joy into her life. Things were tough at work. I was stressed. Not paying her any attention. She had an affair. Moved in with the other bloke. Lauren was twelve, it hit her hard. She didn't show it. She's like that. Self-possessed. But what kid wouldn't be affected. That age. I didn't deal with it very well.'

'Well, there's a twist,' said Macintyre.

'Yeah. It's an old story and a boring one I'm sure. Started drinking ... *More.*'

Alan cleared his throat and rubbed his face. 'I was snappy with Lauren. Short with her. She threw herself into her tennis. It was what she'd always loved. Her thing. And she was good. She was amazing. Started winning everything – at school, against other schools, county level, national level. She was unstoppable. Morning noon and night – tennis-tennis-tennis. Couldn't keep up with her – no one could. To be that good – at a sport – you have to be utterly obsessed. Consumed by it. Driven.'

'And then what happened?' Macintyre asked.

'Hepworth's scouts got on to her. Started wooing her. Offering her all that free training, everything covered, state-of-the-art. She could go on his tennis camps, join his team. Top-class private academic tuition and top-class tennis tuition and the lifestyle ... Me and Alice spoke about it a lot. It was the tennis that brought us back together, you see? Going to watch her together, watch her play, up and down the country. Alice had ditched the other bloke. It was never meant to be a long-term thing. For a while it got exciting between us again. Staying in hotel rooms. Alice wanted to come back home. It was all still sticky with Lauren, though. And we thought – where was the harm? We signed Lauren up to his summer tennis camp in South Africa. It meant that for a while me and Alice could have the space to reconnect.' He looked up at Macintyre. 'Does it always start that way? Small things? Little steps? Before you know it, she's signed up for a long-term commitment. What's wrong with that? Me and Alice were happy again ... and something that appeared too good to be true, slowly soured and turned out to be rotten to the core.'

'But you didn't know anything when you signed her up?'

'No. This was before that BBC documentary. And those other things started to come out. Before anyone had started asking questions about Hepworth. Otherwise there's no way we'd have let her go. No way. We had to sign all these documents, didn't really understand the ins and outs, the small print and by the time the internet was buzzing with stories about him we'd lost all contact with Lauren. I got a new lawyer – you know her – Dana Richards. She tried. But Hepworth has bigger lawyers, better lawyers, and we'd signed everything. His team stonewalled us, blocked everything, denied us any access to Lauren. Claimed we'd given her emotional problems – *us!* I soon lost all track of what's true anymore. What to believe anymore. Some of the stuff you read online is insane ... All that conspiracy shit. Where do you start? I got together with some of the other parents.'

'And?'

'Couple of them couldn't give a shit. Dysfunctional as all fuck. Glad to have got what they saw as difficult girls off their hands. Couple of them were from really poor backgrounds, couldn't get past what a great opportunity this was for their kids, but most of them were just like me – frustrated and impotent with nowhere to turn for help. And then Dana suggested you ...'

'And I disappointed you by not showing up in a tank ...'

Macintyre finished his drink and stood up.

'Time for bed.'

'Yeah.' Alan stood up and waited, looking at Macintyre like a nervous puppy that wants petting.

'What?' said Macintyre. 'You want me to put you to bed?'

Alan made a sad face and nodded.

18

RAY

People were often surprised that Ray wasn't a racist. They always assumed that a guy with his build, background, accent, general manner and job must be one. But once they got talking to him, they pretty soon realised he wasn't. Wasn't now, and never had been. At school he'd hung out with the black guys, because they were generally cooler and funnier and smarter and tougher than the white boys. Not all of them, some of them were wankers, obviously. But they accepted him, and he accepted them. He had no reason to hate them. When it came down to it, if you thought about it – which most racists didn't, to be fair – racism didn't make any sense at all. There was no *logic* behind it. Why would you automatically hate someone simply because their skin was a different colour? How did that work? How could they be, in any fundamental way, different from you, lesser than you? It was the knee-jerk, instant nature of the judgement that was ridiculous – *oh, he's black, therefore I don't like him.*

He *was* a xenophobe. Admittedly. But xenophobia was at least logical – the French were wankers, the Italians were childish and overexcitable, the Greeks were peasants and the Albanians were all bandits. That was fact.

Herve the Perve, on the other hand. He was a pure racist. Only had to look at a black guy and he went into a steaming meltdown. Herve was ex-French police. And, as far as Ray could tell, you had to take a racism exam before they let you join the French police force. If you didn't hate the blacks enough, they wouldn't let you in, but Herve had still somehow managed to get kicked out for being substantially more racist than his fellow cops, which was quite an achievement. Some kid had died in his custody. It had all been hushed up, but Herve was out of a job. With his record, Ray sometimes wondered if he should have hired him. But, the racism aside, and the way he was around the girls, he did a good job.

He could really get on Ray's tits, though. Like now, here they were in church, in God's house, St Spyridon, a place for quiet reflection and peaceful worship, and all Herve could do was bang on about the harmless young black guy sitting with a pretty white girl on the opposite side of the aisle. A black man with a white woman was an affront to Herve's pride. To his innate, racial superiority.

'They come here from Africa, because their country is a shithole, but it's them who have made it a shithole, and so they come here and they want what we have got, what we have made by being more civilised, they want our cars, and our houses and our computers and most of all they want our women . . .'

'She's not your woman, Herve.'

'She is white, so she's more mine than his.'

'In your dreams, Herve. In your dreams.' Ray always pronounced Herve's name the English way, as it was written, to rhyme with perve. Herve had long since given up correcting him. Accepted it was a status thing. As his boss, Ray could pronounce his name however he fucking liked. Back in the day, though, he'd get really shirty – '*It is pronounced Air-Vay, not Hurv. Air-Vay.*'

It was the girls who'd started calling him Herve the Perve, and when they were being particularly lively, they called him Air-Vay the Pair-Vay. They were always complaining about him in Group Chats. How he stared at them, how he made inappropriate comments, how he'd try to touch them. Ray used to wonder why Hepworth tolerated him and didn't tell Ray to get rid. But then he twigged. The girls could focus all their resentment on Herve. He was a useful scapegoat who could draw their flak. And so far, at least, he hadn't gone any further than walking unannounced into the changing rooms *'to check on security'* or letting his hands wander when he was helping the girls in and out of the boat during water-skiing lessons, or on to the minibus.

'That girl is a slut – dreaming of a big black cock!'

'Yeah. All right. Don't get salty. Remember where we are, Herve. Forget about him. Simmer down, yeah?'

But Herve was on one now and there was no stopping him. 'You know our governments? They are part of it. They want to replace us, Ray – the EU, George Soros, the World Bank, the Jews. It is a plot – they want to replace us proper white people with blacks and browns and yellows, with the Muslims, it is a plan to destroy white civilisation. And also, to fuck our women.'

Ray had made the mistake before of trying to engage with Herve on this subject but had quickly learned it was a total waste of time. It was like a religious belief. Unshakeable. Best thing was to just keep schtum and wait for Herve to fizzle out. Ray let him carry on, muttering and mumbling, and tuned him out.

He just wanted to connect with the spirituality of St Spyridon, which was tricky, because the place was slightly nuts, all cluttered up with paintings and gold and mad chandeliers and silver candelabra. The nuttiest bit was the far end, where, behind the altar, like something out of a fantasy movie, was what looked like the front of a second, smaller church. Like a church within a church. It even had a little dome on the top. Who thought of these things? What went through their minds?

Whenever he was with Hepworth on a job, visiting some new

city, he'd try to find time to check out the local cathedrals and such like. That was something else that surprised people about him – his love of visiting churches. His faith. He wasn't so big on organised religion, all the dressing up and rigmarole. He'd always thought he could come to God his own way. But he liked the atmosphere of spirituality in these places, of being one step closer to God. They were cool and dark, and you could properly unwind, de-stress. And fucking Herve, acting like a moron, was in danger of upsetting Ray's equilibrium. Maybe it was time to let him go. He'd have a talk with Hepworth when they got back.

It was Ray's job to look after the two girls from The Team – now four – who were Christians and wanted to worship. The original two were for real. The American girl, Avery, was a true stars and stripes fundamentalist, and Chioma, the Nigerian, was proper, straight down the line, evangelical. The other two. They were different. Sigrid had started coming a few weeks ago. Had thrown herself into it like she was here to wet herself in the front row of a Korean boy band concert. Praying her arse off. And now Lauren had joined them. Ray hoped this wasn't going to turn into one of those teenage hysteria things, like the fainting epidemics. He didn't want the whole team to find God.

He didn't trust Lauren one bit. She was up to something. And Hepworth knew it too, had told Ray to keep a special eye on her. The last thing anyone wanted was another Natasha.

Herve and Miss Lily made up their God-bothering gang. Miss Lily had been brought up Christian in the Philippines and Herve claimed to be a devout Catholic. So why he didn't go to the Catholic church here Ray had no idea. And wasn't interested enough to ask him. It was probably because he'd seen one too many non-whites in the congregation.

What a bunch they were. Ray had his faith. And it was strong. But Herve didn't really have a Christian bone in his body. And Miss Lily . . . Ray had found out a fair bit about her past. Born in a knocking shop. Her mother a whore. The girl following in her mother's footsteps before it was exactly decent. Marrying some born-again Yank flyboy from Clark Air Base who'd wanted to save her soul for Jesus, and her ass for himself. Hepworth had shown him some photos once. Miss Lily as a young girl. Pretty under all the make-up. So different from the mean-faced old witch she'd matured into. And once she'd got to America, she'd clawed her way up the totem pole. Ditched the husband and ended up running a security firm that Hepworth had bought out a few years back. He had a knack for surrounding himself with useful fuck-ups. Ray wondered what Miss Lily really thought about God, giving her that childhood. If you could call it a childhood.

He closed his eyes and bowed his head. Tried to clear his head and get in touch with his god. Things had been getting on top of him lately. It was bloody Sigrid. She was more needy than an actual girlfriend. Had all that teenage shit going on. Worrying about the small stuff, obsessing over feelings, as if the two of them were on *Love Island* or *Big Brother*, with nothing to do but talk about relationships. He wished he'd never got involved with the silly cow.

Perhaps he wasn't taking a very Christian attitude towards Sigrid. But when it came to faith, he'd figured out that Christianity was on a spectrum like everything else. And the Christianity spectrum was actually very similar to the psychopath spectrum. The upper half of the scale – *the alpha half* – that was the Old Testament. The blood and guts half of the Bible. The action movie part. Full of thunderings and lightnings and the noise of the trumpet and the mountains smoking.

Jehovah, Jahweh, Yahweh, God – call him what you will – and he *was* a 'him', not a 'her', or some sort of mystical cloud. Or, *God forbid*, gender fluid, a 'they'. The Holy Bible was clear about that. GOD WAS A MAN. And he was a *hard* man. The *hero* of the Old Testament. It was his book.

And Jesus was the hero of the New Testament. A whole different story. The New Testament was the lower half of the scale, the beta half, the wishy-washy half, the date-movie half. A weepie for MILFs, starring Ryan Gosling, or that new guy, the wet blanket, Timothée Chalamet. You only had to look at how he spelled his name. You couldn't get more bottom of the scale than Timothée. That was a wimp's name if ever there was one. Timothy was bad enough, but Timothée.

Yeah. The New Testament was bottom-end stuff. Yahweh was top end. And, let's face it, Yahweh would be right at the top of the psychopath scale, as well, wouldn't he?

Because Yahweh didn't fuck about.

'You will sacrifice animals to me, you will sacrifice your children to me – hell, I will even sacrifice my own son to you show you how hard I am. I am Keyser fucking Soze!'

What was it he'd said in the Ten Commandments?

'The Lord thy God is a mean motherfucker – visiting the iniquity of the fathers upon the children, upon the third and the fourth generation of those who hate me . . .'

Jahweh was Samuel Jackson in *Pulp Fiction*. He was Liam Neeson in *Taken*, calling you up and telling you he was going to fuck you in the ear. He was Russell Crowe. The Terminator. Gerard Butler. Old-school. Hard. Unforgiving. Kick-ass.

And Jesus, the hero of the Woke Testament, with his snowflake, 'turn the other cheek', victim vibe – he was Woody and every other fucking character Tom Hanks had ever played, he was Harry Potter, WALL-E, mister nice-guy, sticking flowers in a soldier's gun barrel.

Yeah, Christianity was on a spectrum, all right. At the top you had Yahweh, the Crusades, the Spanish Inquisition, all those crazy saints, Cortés, early popes, back when they had armies, Hitler, probably. Then down from them, you had creationists and fundamentalists, the orthodox brigade, flagellants, faith healers, missionaries, the Jesuits, Welsh Baptists, Puritans, modern popes, then down you went through monks, nuns, evangelists . . .

In the middle were probably the Catholics. A huge great wodge of them. Then, below them, you sank down through more liberal waters – first your regular Protestants, then on down through Anglicans, C-of-E wankers, gay vicars, the people who thought all religions were all kind of the same, so, let's be nice to the Muslims, the people who thought *there must be something out there but I'm not sure what it is* . . .

And right at the bottom you had Jesus.

Ray wished there was a name for Christians who didn't roll with Jesus but were really into the Old Testament.

Perhaps he was a fundamentalist?

He wished some divine understanding would be passed down to him. What to do about Sigrid? Before it all got too messy. Perhaps he should pray. Ask God for guidance. She'd been getting really needy in the last few days. Panicky. Anxious. He hated anxious women. He wanted to slap them. Couldn't she see he totally had his hands full at the moment, organising everything for the party?

Perhaps he should ask the Big Fella if he could see his way to zapping Sigrid with a bolt of lightning. She had, after all, broken many of his most sacred rules. Girls had been stoned to death in the Bible for less.

Once they were all done praying, they all trooped outside. The entrance to the church was on a narrow side street, lined with tourist shops selling fake icons and gaudy religious knick-knacks. It was a few minutes' walk down through the old town to where they'd left the minibus in the car park. Ray was checking his phone for messages and wondering if they should stop off at a café somewhere en route when Herve shouted, 'Hey!'

Ray turned, too late, to see a black guy in tatty old T-shirt and shorts approaching Avery with a begging cup. Ray cursed. A lapse in concentration. The beggar wasn't a threat, but Herve was. He was on the beggar like a Jack Russell on a rat. He grabbed the poor sod and shoved him back against the church wall, smacking his head into the stonework. The guy groaned. There was blood in his hair. More on the wall.

'Mister Jordan, Mister Jordan ...' Miss Lily had a very irritating high-pitched voice. Ray tried to cut her out.

'Leave him, Herve!' he shouted. 'I got this.'

'I will kill him.'

'That's what I'm worried about. He's harmless. Let him go.'

'The blacks, they are all muggers.'

'Come on, Herve. He's just a beggar.'

'Mister Jordan, Mister Jordan ...'

Shopowners, a couple of tourists, were looking at the scene with growing interest.

'It's all right,' Ray announced with some authority. 'I've got this. It was an accident. *Ena atychima*. He's all right.'

'Mister Jordan ...'

Ray got between Herve and the beggar, who looked woozy and confused. He took some tissues from his pocket. Wadded them up and guided the guy's hand to clamp them against his wound. Then snapped at Herve.

'Give the guy some money. A few euros. We don't want any fucking trouble here, Herve.'

'Mister Jordan!'

'I've got it, Miss Lily.'

'Mister Jordan. The girls. They run away ...'

19

PIKE

'*Peppa Pig.* It's *Peppa Pig.* Remember, Pike?'

'Remember what?'

'It was all over the family WhatsApp last year.'

'I don't always keep up with that.'

Sarah smiled and shook her head. Turned to Aimee and Macintyre.

'Do you know *Peppa Pig*?'

'I know *of Peppa Pig*,' said Aimee. 'Can't say I know him personally.'

'Her.'

'What?'

'Peppa Pig's a her.'

'If you say so.'

They were sitting drinking coffee at a metal table on a little terrace under the shade of a linden tree. Place called Old Perithia on the north-eastern side of Pantokrator. Pike had suggested it. It was quiet and out of the way, no chance of bumping into anyone they shouldn't. And it was cooler up here. A fresh breeze blowing. Good place for a team talk. Hardly anyone else around. Some older tourists wandering around taking photos. Little old guy selling honey from his hives, and beeswax candles. Not such a bad life. No responsibilities. In the end, all you really needed was enough to eat and drink and a roof to keep the rain off.

'I know *Peppa Pig*'s not a big thing if you don't have little kids,' Sarah went on.

'Rules out me and Mac,' said Aimee.

'Exactly, but my lad Darren,' she looked to Aimee. 'From before Pike came into my life. He lives in Dubai, works for an English-language TV station out there. Anyway, his little girl . . . '

'Wait,' said Aimee. 'You're a grandmother?'

'That's sweet of you,' said Sarah. 'But, really, you don't need.'

'Come on,' said Pike. 'We wanna know where *Peppa Pig* comes into this.'

'I'm getting to it. So, Darren's little girl, Pearl, she's really into *Peppa Pig*. And her mum bought her this *Peppa Pig* backpack online. She found a real deal. So cheap. But when she got it, *there* was Peppa and *there* was the word "groin" plastered all over it.'

'Groin?'

'It's French for oink apparently.'

'Ha-ha-ha!' Aimee laughed. 'Groin.'

'She'd bought a cheap French knock-off.'

Macintyre was smiling. 'So the graffiti in Alan's villa was written in French.'

'Yeah,' said Sarah. 'Nothing to do with any Albanians.'

'It's a start,' said Macintyre. 'But we still don't have a lot to go on.'

'Nothing in the footage you got?' asked Pike.

'They looked young. They had crash helmets. Probably got there on motorbikes. Mopeds. Whatever.'

'Doesn't narrow it down much on an island like this.'

'Nope.'

Macintyre ran through the arrangements for the next few days. Pike sipped his coffee. Looked around at the old stone buildings, the gnarled trees, the tops of the hills brown in the summer sun. He knew Old Perithia well. Just after the crash of 2008, he and Sarah had rented a little house in Avlaki on the north coast for the winter. They'd had a tough year and had had to put the *Louise B* in for repairs and refitting in Kontokalis. It had felt good to be grounded, in both senses of the word, and they'd enjoyed the peace and calm of being on Corfu out of season. They'd enjoyed long walks in the countryside and one day had rented bicycles and struggled up the mountain to visit what was then a ruined town. For hundreds of years, it had been a prosperous place, built high up in the hills to keep its inhabitants safe from marauding pirates. Most of the larger buildings were Venetian, old stone walls and tiled roofs, and back in the day it made sense to build towns inland close to the most productive, arable land. Once tourism became the main industry, however, the previously worthless land on the coast had become the most valuable, and life in Perithia had got tough. The town was eventually abandoned in the sixties and left to quietly fall into ruin. It was a piece of untouched old Corfu. And there wasn't much of that left. In the last twenty years people had started to return and renovate some of the buildings. Mostly foreigners, who hankered after something unspoilt – *authentic*. There was the honey man, a little taverna, a chic B&B. Pike and Sarah had drunk wine at the taverna and fallen in love with the place. Shared the fantasy of buying a semi-derelict building and doing it up themselves. Working side by side, rebuilding, wiring, plumbing, plastering... They'd talked of developing it as another B&B. A place to sit out their days quietly in the hills and toast the sunset.

They'd got *that* close to selling the boat and signing the contract on a place.

But, in the end, it had felt a bit like a defeat. Giving up on their sea-gypsy life. Settling down. Getting tied to a place. Plus, it could get bloody cold up here in the winter.

Pike liked the sun.

The reality of actually living in Perithia, 365, was something else. And on their last visit to the place, in late January, it had been freezing and grey and bleak and windswept and Pike had had a vision of smoking a fat spliff on the beach in Jamaica.

Come the spring, they were back at sea. It had been the right decision. Although they both knew that one day they'd have to give up the seafaring life. They were neither of them getting any younger.

Coming up here today he'd felt an unexpected lurch in his guts. A nostalgic kick from the past – the sweet memory of a life he'd never actually lived, only imagined.

He looked at Sarah, in the dappled sunlight, the grey in her hair shining silver, more beautiful than she had ever looked, and he thanked God, like he did every day, that she had come into his life.

'You listening, Pike?'

'I don't need to know all the technical stuff,' said Pike. 'Sarah deals with that. But what about that mobile? The one that Abbott and Costello left on the boat?'

'My guys in Korea have managed to remotely hack into it,' said Macintyre. 'Translated it all for me.'

'Anything interesting?'

'Phone contacts. WhatsApp conversations. Crudely coded texts. They're a bunch of bums, basically. Small-time. The usual – girls, drugs, clubs ... '

'Extortion,' said Sarah with a wry smile.

'Extortion. Guy called Genc Malecaj in charge. We may be able to use them somehow. Working on it. We've got the tracker on Ioannis's car.'

'I got lunch with Cindy tomorrow,' said Aimee.

'Good. So we just have to hope that the next stage goes smoothly, and we get Lauren out of there with minimum fuss.'

20

LAUREN

They were running. Down the narrow street, almost an alleyway really, a dark canyon, the buildings on either side so close they seemed to be leaning towards each other. The paving slabs shiny, worn smooth and slippery by so many people over so many years. This was the old part of Corfu Town, the streets mostly too narrow for cars, or blocked off to them. It was all tourist shops, pottery and cheap jewellery, brightly coloured ukuleles, T-shirts, takeaway places, clothes shops, with summer dresses and sunglasses, leather shops, racks of postcards, embroidered tablecloths, sponges, crap everywhere. Hardly any locals, just tourists, wandering around, blocking the way. Lauren couldn't remember how they'd got to the church or which way anything was. But right now she was following Sigrid. Did *she* know where she was going? Or was she just running blindly, like a rabbit from a dog. *This was crazy. It wasn't going to work, girl.* Lauren shouted at her to stop, but Sigrid was too far ahead.

It had started to go wrong in the church. The four of them, kneeling there, praying in a row, like good little girls. They'd had a chance to talk quietly, not much more than a whisper. Miss Lily dozing, Ray and Herve the Perve on the opposite side of the aisle. No CCTV in here. Nobody watching you – unless you counted

God's great all-seeing eye. All-seeing, all-knowing, all-powerful. Lauren had long since stopped believing in any kind of god, though. If there was a God, then he was one almighty wanker.

Avery and Chioma had already figured out that something was up with Sigrid. The whole team knew it. And Sigrid had been crying again, pooling tears and snot on to the tiled floor of the church.

What is it, Sigrid? – You can tell us. – Tell us, babe . . .

And she'd told them. It had all come gushing out, emotional snot.

She couldn't stand it anymore, she was going clear, getting away, she loved Julian and she hated him, she was going insane, she didn't know what she wanted, it was too confusing, too complicated, she just wanted to be home, with her family, that's all she wanted, she couldn't stay on The Team, she wasn't up to it, she didn't deserve to be on The Team . . .

And then Chioma had got into it.

'Me, too – God, I'd go with you – do you have a plan?'

And Lauren trying to cool the situation down. This wasn't the way. They weren't ready yet. Had to have a proper, thought-through plan. She was working on it. Give her time.

And then Avery had said something that chilled her. Avery was the oldest on The Team, had been with Julian the longest. Rarely got suspended these days. She'd joined up when she was thirteen, was now nearly eighteen. And she told them that when she'd first arrived, all anyone was talking about was this girl, Natasha. Natasha who'd tried to get away. Told everyone she was going to blow the whole thing up. She was going to go to the media. Expose Julian.

And what happened? – I've heard rumours – Omigod, I don't want to hear . . .

'She ended up a junkie. Nobody would talk to her. Apparently, this, like, pimp got hold of her in Paris, a dealer. She took an overdose and burned to death in a fire.'

'Shit.'

'You can't get out. He'll get you in the end. You can't get away.'

'I have to. I have to go. I'll go home. Nowhere else. Just home. I won't say anything.'

Sigrid had got really weird, jittery, hyped up, and when they'd gone outside and Herve had started in on the beggar, Ray distracted, Miss Lily, too, she'd bolted. Just upped and raced off. Fast in her tennis shoes. A moment's hesitation and Lauren had followed. Not sure if she was just trying to save Sigrid or get away herself. She'd glanced back briefly to see whether Avery and Chioma had stayed. They had. It was just the two of them.

Sigrid came to a junction, looked quickly left and right and then disappeared out of sight to the right. Lauren was catching up, hard behind her. Swung round the corner, had to jump over a pile of boxes some guy was delivering to a shop. Cleared them easily. Her legs were strong from training. The delivery guy shouted after her – bloody teenagers – bloody British tourists – probably drunk.

Lauren laughed, out of control. But it felt good. Rushing through the streets. At least for one wild moment – free. The two of them were well away from Ray and Herve. Pushing past tourists. Grumpy and cow-like. GET OUT OF THE WAY!

She could see bright light ahead, wide-open space, greenery, blue sky. And there was Sigrid, a flash of white, nipping in and out of the crowds.

Lauren emerged from the end of the alleyway on to a wide terrace. A park of some sort ahead. Trees and grass and parked cars. A café to the left, people sitting out on the wide pavement drinking coffee, eating pastries. A covered arcade to the right with more tables and chairs in the shade. Past the café a road. Cars and buses and lorries fuming in the heat. It was confusing. Loud and busy. She wasn't used to it. All this time Lauren had been here on the island, she didn't really know the place at all, hardly left the compound. Apart from three days in Rome for a competition.

Sigrid looked equally confused. Wasn't sure which way to go. Hesitated just long enough for Lauren to catch up.

'Sigrid. Not like this. This is crazy. This won't work.'

'No. We did it, Lauren. We're away.'

Sigrid was off again, walking fast, to the left, towards a big arch further down the road.

'How?' said Lauren, keeping pace with her. 'How are we away? What do we do?'

Sigrid saw a taxi, ran into the road and flagged it down waving her arms and getting in its way. Holding up the traffic. The driver looked pissed off, but he stopped. Sigrid jumped in the back. Lauren climbed in after her. It was hot in there. Close and sweaty.

'Where?' The driver was glaring at them.

Where? They had no money.

'To the airport.'

'Sigrid? Don't be stupid. What'll we do at the airport? We've got no money. Passports. Tickets. We can't even pay for the taxi.'

'You got no money?' The driver was twisted round in his seat.

'We're fine. We're good,' said Lauren. 'We have money.'

'Where you go?'

Sigrid was peering through the windscreen, keeping a lookout for Ray and Herve.

'Just go,' she said, almost shouting.

'They'll arrest us, Sigrid.'

'Then we can tell the police.'

'Tell them what? We're girls from Hepworth's tennis team. They'd just take us back there.'

'Get out my taxi.'

'Wait, wait, please ...' Sigrid was crying again.

'Julian has contacts in the police,' said Lauren. 'That creepy Captain Karagiannis who's always hanging around. How can you prove any crime's been committed?'

'They can call my parents.'

'And who's going to get to you first? You parents, or Julian? Ray and Herve? Miss Lily? Tokyo?'

'I THOUGHT YOU WANTED TO HELP ME!'

'Get out my taxi. You crazy bitches.'

Cars behind them were hooting.

'We have nothing, Sigrid. No phones. No money. No ID.'

'You don't want me to go.'

'Remember Natasha.'

Lauren couldn't believe that she was the one being a wimp. Scared. Wavering. Backing down.

'You got money? No money, I kick you out.'

'We have money,' said Sigrid.

'You show me.'

And then Sigrid spotted Herve, skirting the tables of the café. She grabbed the driver's shoulder, pointing to the road that went round the park.

'There,' she said. 'Go that way. Just go.'

The taxi driver pulled across the road, yelled at another driver out of his window and started to skirt the park.

'Stop!' Sigrid shouted. 'Stop here!'

The driver swore, braked sharply. Sigrid jumped out and started to run along the pavement. Lauren sighed, followed, the driver cursing them.

To their left was another strip of park, a children's playground, some statues and monuments. Beyond them a big old castle of some sort. And the sea. Blue and cheerful. Sigrid ran through some open iron gates and crossed the grass towards the castle and the sea.

'Sigrid!'

'Leave me alone.'

And then Sigrid was climbing some railings.

'Sigrid, stop! What are you doing?'

'You're right, Lauren. We can't escape. There's only one way.'

164

Lauren reached the railings. Looked down. There was a drop on to a lower concrete walkway next to the sea.

'Oh, don't be such a bloody drama queen, Sigrid. You're not going to kill yourself.'

'I am.'

'No. What I mean is, from this height, you'll probably just break your legs. Just stop it, yeah? Climb down. Be smart. We'll work something out.'

Sigrid was halfway over the top of the railings.

'I'm doing it.'

'No, you're fucking not!' Lauren grabbed her and pulled her back. They tumbled in a heap on to the ground. Sigrid groaned, rubbed her elbow. Lauren felt bruised all over. Sigrid was crying again, shaking, hyperventilating. Lauren took hold of her. Held her tight.

'Calm down. If they didn't spot us running over here, then we might be OK for a few minutes. Let's just sit here for a bit and talk, yeah?'

'What's the point?'

'There *is* a way to do this.'

'But you just said . . . '

'Not here, not now, not like this. Without a plan.'

'You're as bad as Ray!'

'Ray?'

'Shit.' Sigrid looked embarrassed. Caught out. It was Ray, then. Ray who was supposedly helping her. No wonder she was in such a state.

'Oh, Sig . . . Not Ray. You must have known . . . '

Sigrid said nothing, just gave a small nod.

'OK. Forget Ray. You listen to *me*, now.'

'OK.'

'So. There was this old movie Dad used to make me watch. Every Christmas, right? He had the DVD. God, he loved it.

Sometimes he'd march around the house banging out the theme tune at the top of his voice.' She remembered it vividly. And the thought of her dad sent a stab of pain to her gut. He could be a bit of a dick, but he was her dad and she loved him. Loved him even more when he was being daft. As long as there was no one else around to witness it, to film him on their phone and break the internet.

God. That world seemed so far away. She hadn't looked at any social media for nearly a year now. But that old movie of Dad's was still fresh in her head.

'It was called *The Great Escape*, and it was about these soldiers in the war, or were they air force? They had blue uniforms – did that make them different? Doesn't matter, anyway, they were all in this prisoner-of-war camp in the Second World War. The one against the Nazis, yeah? Hitler and that. And, actually, it looked quite cool in there, it was in the woods and they could walk around outside, get lots of fresh air, sunshine, and they all slept together in huts with bunk beds, not that different from the set-up at HepKat, to be fair ...'

Sigrid had calmed down. Lauren managed to manoeuvre her to a nearby bench and they sat there looking out to sea.

'These soldiers, they were, like, the best escapers in the British army, yeah? They'd escaped from everywhere else, all the other camps, so the Germans put them all together in this one place, Stalag something or other. It was meant to be escape-proof, but the prisoners made a plan to all escape at the same time, you get me? It would make it ten times harder for the Germans to catch them, they'd spread out all over Germany and the German army would be tied up searching for them.'

'Why are you telling me this?' Sigrid sounded flat, tired.

'Don't you get it, Sig? Maybe *we* could do it? All or nothing. *It could work* – we all escape at once, a mass breakout, our own Great Escape ...'

'Maybe ...'

'One of us – two of us – we're just two stupid little kids running away from school. Nobody would listen. But all of us. *All at once.* Together. What could Julian do? He couldn't do another Natasha on all of us. And even if some of us got caught, if the others got away, like in *The Great Escape*, they'd be able to tell the world what's actually going on here. Come back and rescue the rest of us.'

Sigrid sniffed. She was smiling at last.

'Yes,' she said. 'I like that plan. We show them, yes? We show Julian. We show Miss Lily. We show Ray. He was never going to really help me. I can see that now.'

'Good girl.'

What she didn't tell Sigrid was that, at the end of the movie – spoiler alert – the British soldiers all got caught except for about two of them. Even Steve McQueen, the cool one with the motorbike, was captured. And the Germans killed them all in the woods, with a big machine gun on the back of a lorry. Not Steve McQueen. She didn't know why they didn't execute him. But the others ...

But – what the fuck – it wasn't like if Julian caught them he'd shoot them all to shit with a machine gun.

Would he ...

She stood up.

'Let's sort this crap out, then, shall we?'

'Yeah.'

She pulled Sigrid up and they walked back through the park and over the road. Nipping between the cars. And there was Miss Lily, waiting by the café with Avery and Chioma. And there was Herve, darting about and looking in all directions like a dog who'd lost its ball. And there was Ray, stalking along the pavement with his back towards them. Lauren waved, took hold of Sigrid's hand. Called out.

'Hey!'

Ray spun round, ran up to them. Furious.

'What the fuck do you . . . ?'

'Sorry, Ray, we just wanted to see the sea. And the castle. You know us, we're like highly strung racehorses. Sometimes we need to just run!'

'You need to behave.'

'What's the big deal. We're here, aren't we?'

'You ever do anything like that again you are so going to regret it.'

'Do anything like what?'

'Run off like that. I am *this close* to murdering you two.' Holding out a hand with narrowed fingers.

'Oh, don't murder us, Ray. Girls just want to have fun.'

'Lauren . . .'

'We were just mucking about. I mean, God, it's lucky for you we didn't *really* run off, isn't it, Ray? That would have looked pretty bad for you and Herve.'

'Lauren . . .'

'But, listen, we promise not to say anything about it to Julian, OK?'

'Don't try it on, Lauren . . .'

'We say nothing, if you say nothing. Is that a deal?'

'You don't tell me what to do.'

Lauren moved closer to Ray and put a hand on his chest. Smiled up at him.

'You say nothing to Julian, and I say nothing about you and Sigrid.'

Ray's lips went white. There was a moment of panic in his eyes, which was replaced by anger. But he said nothing.

Lauren started walking back to the others. Avery and Chioma were staring at them, amazed. Wide eyes, open mouths, cracked smiles. Lauren felt Ray's eyes on the back of her head. She swung her hips and sang – 'Girls just want to have fun!'

168

21

EMMALINE

Emmaline was walking down the middle of the road with her gang, arms stretched out towards the sky, half shouting, half singing the chorus to 'We Are The World'.

She wrapped her arms around Debs and laughed. Laughed and laughed. Laughed so much she thought she was going to be sick.

And then Debs *was* sick. Just a little bit. She managed to swallow most of it before it came out, but there was a little dribble. That made her laugh more.

'Ahhh, you dirty cow!' said Livesey. 'Debs, you are a dirty cow.'

'What a specimen!' said Thommo.

'I know . . .' Debs was swallowing and spitting. 'Oh, that's disgusting. Ohhhh – it tastes like . . . *coconuts*.'

Debs and Emmaline screeched. Livesey shook his head. Thommo roared.

'We should never have done them Malibu slushies,' said Emmaline.

'They tasted like frozen cum,' said Debs and that set Emmaline off again.

'You'd know.'

Emmaline loved Kavos. There was always something

happening, always something on the go. It was after midnight, but the Strip was bright as day, music and lights everywhere. Red light, pink light, purple light, black light, neon, glowing from every bar and club they passed – Snobs, Scorers, Pulse, The Necro, Wembley, Genesis, HQ, Future, Rolling Stone, the Barn, SOS. Music thudding, wailing, banging. As if the Strip was actually alive, its massive heart beating loud enough to knock you down. Oh, the Strip was *amazing*. Every bar and restaurant open-fronted, so that dancers spilled out into road, bouncing up and down, as motorbikes and scooters weaved in and out. It was like one huge, open-air club. Anything you wanted to eat, as well, anything you could imagine, it was there – pizza, kebab, Real Greek, Chinese, Thai, Tex-Mex, burgers, Subway. And everything was in English, the signs, the talk on the street, the DJs shouting out to the dancers.

'Come on! Come on! Do it!'

They pushed on down the street. People buying water in a supermarket. Kids looking at sunnies in a gift shop. Bulldog, the tattoo parlour where Emmaline had got the word 'Oops' tattooed on her ankle, first day.

'Here! Here!' said Thommo. 'We've got to have a go!'

Between two bars was a strip of floodlit AstroTurf with a goal at the back end. A big sign above it – Penalty Shootout – under a row of Union Jacks.

Thommo read the sign. It was funny. His Liverpool accent made it funnier. Specially the way he said 'euros'.

'4 euros, take 1 shot, score and win a bottle of champagne. Pay 2 euros, take 3 shots, score them all and win the champagne. No ricocheteds!! No rebounds!!'

They all laughed at the misspelling of 'ricochets'. Stupid Greeks.

'Go for the four euros,' said Emmaline. She was pretty good at maths and reckoned it was a better deal with a better chance of winning. The others were too drunk to argue. They all chipped in.

Thommo was elected to take the shot. Claimed he was the best, and Livesey didn't argue.

Whack! Thommo hit it hard and to the right. Easily beat the goalie, hardly even tried, just stuck a foot out, and they all cheered. The guy in charge got them a bottle of Greek prosecco from an outdoor fridge. It tasted foul. But who cared?

They stood in the road to drink it, passing it round, watching the other kids go past. So many of them. The Strip was packed. Gangs of boys and gangs of girls. The boys all dressed the same – T-shirts, shorts and trainers with no socks. Some with their shirts off, shouting. Lots of the girls were dressed the same as the boys, but some wore short dresses or skirts, tight leggings. Flat shoes. Lots of sunburn.

It was buzzing. *Literally buzzing.* There was even a club called Buzz. When you went to bed you could hear the hum all around you like you were inside a hive of bees. She found it comforting. Last year, Dad had taken her on holiday to another Greek island. She hated it so much she'd actually forgotten the name. They'd flown to Athens and then got a ferry boat to this, like, shitty, old-fashioned dump in the middle of the ocean. A taxi took them to their villa. Took ages. And when they got there, there was nothing. Just this house on rocks and some steps down to a little, stony beach. Dad said he loved it. Sat down there on the beach all day and night in his Pope with the dope T-shirt, smoking himself stupid.

'It's so peaceful,' he'd say. 'So good to get away from everything.'

But she could see in his eyes that he hated it, too. She couldn't sleep there. She imagined killers roaming around outside in the dark, ready to attack them in their beds. Stab them, like, a thousand times, and do terrible things to their dead bodies. Like some Netflix true-crime series. There were weird animals that made weird noises at night. And mosquitoes. So many bloody mosquitoes. And the sea. You could hear it in the bedroom. So close. She

171

imagined it rising in the dark and drowning her in her sleep. Not that she ever slept. Least that's how it felt.

Dad had been running away from something. There was always something to run away from. He'd stitched somebody up, done somebody over, ripped somebody off. Take your pick. And he'd gone about as far away as he could from anyone he knew. Once, a helicopter went over and he ran inside to hide. Silly twat. Every couple of days they'd walk to the nearest supermarket. Twenty minutes along a winding road. In and out in five minutes and back to the house. Light up some shit and disappear in a cloud of smoke.

This year was different. This year Dad was on one. She reckoned he'd made a good score. They were staying in a posh apartment, with their own bedrooms. A shared pool. Right next to the Strip. It was heaven.

Dad hung out drinking pints all day with an older crowd in a British pub called Churchill's, with two giant screens showing sport all day. Union Jacks on the walls. St George flags. Pictures of the Queen and Churchill, who'd won the war, or something. Framed England football shirts. A big photo of Nigel Farage raising a pint of beer and laughing. Even the bottles of spirits had Union Jacks on them. Dad held court in there. Telling stories. Telling jokes. Buying rounds. Shouting things at the women who howled with laughter. They all knew his name and would shout it out when he came in.

'Billy! King Billy! Legend!'

Early evenings, as the Strip was starting to come awake, he'd put on his signature red baseball cap and go to sit outside the Atlantis beach bar on a plastic chair where a steady stream of kids would approach him. They'd chat and then go off together, back to the apartment. The Atlantis was cool. Day and night, it was wild. Free drinks with your ticket. Foam parties, paint parties, pool discos, fancy dress, guest DJ sets. Everyone up for it. Everyone out of it. And that's where Dad came in. Helping keep everyone high.

Back home he was Billy Onions, Emmaline had no idea why, but the kids in Kavos all called him Uncle Charlie, because it was charlie they came to score off him. That or some pills. She remembered leaving the airport. He'd been pale and sweating, totally rattled. Convinced that an American DEA woman had been on to him. Had tried to get him to open his bag. He was strung out, totally paranoid. The dick. What would a DEA agent be doing in Corfu airport disguised as a passenger? But once they'd got to the apartment he'd settled down. Made himself at home. He polished off their duty-free and now he was Mister Middle-Aged Party Dad Guy. At least he never tried to dance.

He bragged to Emmaline about the drugs. How they'd pay for this holiday and any other holidays they wanted this year – and next. It was a good life. She already had her routine. She thought about tomorrow. Up at twelve. Full English breakfast. Sit by the pool, or down the beach. Sunbathing. Looking at her phone. Maybe a swim. Or a bash round the inflatable obstacle course at the little aqua park. A munch of some sort late afternoon. But it was the nights she really lived for. Once the evening kicked off, she kept out of Billy's way. Left him to his deals. She'd met Debs, Livesey and Thommo on the first night. Had met so many other great people. Expected she'd bump into them all tonight in some bar or other. Thommo had copped some pills earlier. Given her a couple. Debs and Livesey weren't interested. Stuck to cheap shots. The wimps.

Emmaline never took any gear off Billy, except maybe some weed now and then. It was just too uncool to score off your old man. Too embarrassing. She'd asked Thommo where he'd got the pills.

'Some foreign guys were selling them.'

'Everybody here's foreign, you dope.'

'Yeah. I mean they weren't Greek. Reckon they were Spanish or Italian or some shit. Stupid accents. Thinking they were so cool in their designer shades. Bunch of wankers. But the pills were cheap.'

'What are they?'

Thommo had shrugged.

'They're meant to be good, though.'

'They got a name?'

'Something Greek – *Aftos*.'

So now it was party central, and Emmaline was coming up. A nice warm glow. The colours pinging. Her heart racing. They'd come to The Necro. More exclusive than most of the other joints on the Strip. Not open to the street. Just one central door. Two bouncers, hustling the kids as they went past.

'Hey, come on! Come in! You want to party?'

Most places had at least one person outside telling you how theirs was the best place on the Strip, cheapest prices, best food, best cocktails. Emmaline and her gang had come here last night. The bouncers had made a big show of checking IDs, which they didn't do anywhere else, and they'd tried to touch her up as they'd searched her. Debs, too.

'Hey! Girls. Is free drinks for one hour! Come in quick. Only for one hour!'

Emmaline showed her fake ID. Dad had got it for her. Dad could get anything. It was a shame he was such a loser. If he hadn't been a loser, he could have been a winner. Once they'd got past the bouncers' hands, they hit the bar. The bouncers hadn't been exactly telling the whole truth. Only the cocktail of the day was free – something called a Fuckface. Vodka, lemonade, pomegranate juice and kombucha.

'It's practically a health drink, ladies,' said the Aussie barman as he handed them out. 'And as you're my favourite customers you can have a free round of shots!'

They all cheered, even though they'd heard him give the same line to the girls who'd been served before them. They downed the shots. Some unidentifiable shit from a weird, generic bottle. Then they did a big 'cheers' all round as they got stuck into the cocktails.

Tasted exactly the same as every other cocktail Emmaline had had since she'd arrived. Sweet and fruity and watery. But what the fuck did that matter? *They were free!*

The music was way loud in here and they had to shout at each other to be heard. Emmaline still couldn't really hear and had no idea what they were talking about – probably just how drunk they all were. She laughed and said 'Yeah' and 'Crazy' and whatever else came into her head and just went with it. Riding on a wave of euphoria.

The lights were bouncing around inside her head, sparking off mad colours. The bass on the track the DJ was laying down – some crappy Euro summer hit from last year – was hitting her gut like she had a baby kicking inside. The hi-hat hissing right up close and personal – Tss-tss-tss. The whack of the snare sounded like gunshots. She closed her eyes for a moment and followed the sound, down and down and down, through twisting tunnels and into a weird kind of fleshy room with pulsing red walls.

Whoa!

Where had that come from?

She snapped her eyes open. *That was like – I dunno – suddenly being in a dream.* She sunk some more of her cocktail. Bad idea. She felt hot in the face. Burning up.

'I'm going to the loo!' she yelled and walked off. Stumbled. Bumped into someone. Laughed. Real trouble keeping her balance. Shit. This was half fun and half scary. She didn't usually get wankered like this. It was the cheap, fake booze, the sun, a bad kebab . . .

She had to push right across the dance floor to get to the bathroom. Squeezing past all the kids bouncing up and down. Bouncing. Bouncing. Bouncing. With one arm reaching up to the ceiling, as harsh white lights strafed them. The DJ must be using some funky new tech. One moment the music sounded like it was crashing right inside her skull, the next it was a million miles away.

She looked at the bathroom sign, spelled out in green neon. It was dimming. She looked back at her friends, chatting, not looking at her. Everything was going away from her, like she wasn't there. And then everything was too close, too loud, too big.

Come on. Come on. You're not such a lightweight.

She made it to the bathroom and couldn't remember why she'd come. While she was here, she thought she might as well have a pee, though. She had to wait a while for a cubicle to be free and then got in and got her shorts down. The pee seemed to go on for ever. She imagined a shimmering golden column of pee between her and the water in the loo. Like a pole-dancing pole. Some of the bars had poles. She saw herself swinging round this golden piss-pole. No. Nobody wants to dance round a piss-pole. She giggled.

Shit. She had a terrible headache. She stared at the crap on the floor, mushed up loo roll, a hippy crack canister, a Biro, puddles of dirty liquid . . . She went for a swim.

No. *Fuck*. Keep a hold of things, Emmaline. She pulled up her shorts, banged out of the cubicle, ran the cold tap at one of the sinks, splashed her face, felt a little better.

There were two girls there, talking about salad. They sounded Scouse.

'Woo-hoo!' she said to them when she caught their eyes in the mirror.

'Woo-hoo!' they replied. 'Go, girl! You are flying.'

'Are you guys from Liverpool?'

'Bootle.'

'You're the Bootles!'

'Yeah!'

'Thommo's from Liverpool. He's totally jokes. Debs and Livesey are from Southend, which is near me. We met some squaddies last night. They were mad. Fun, but they got into a fight. And some Welsh lads . . . Big up the Welsh crew . . . big them up . . . '

Emmaline looked around. The girls had gone. Hadn't even seen them leave. She looked at her hands, there were lumps on the back of them, under the skin.

'Big up the Welsh crew!' she shouted, trying to sound like a DJ.

She left the bathroom and struggled back across the dance floor. The DJ seemed to be playing the same song still. Hard to tell. They all sounded the same. Dancepartygirlovebabydanceparty-give-it-to-me-do-it-do-it-do-it... Halfway to the bar, a fast snare beat kicked in like a machine gun, synched with a strobe light that flashed violently like explosions going off... And then came the drop...

Boom!

All the sound cut out and Emmaline was in a world of silence. Like being at a silent disco, or underwater. She looked around. Everyone was still dancing. The lights were going dim. Everyone was way far away. It was getting dark and cold. And then with a painful, piercing ping the sound came back on. Deafening. Smashing into her eardrums. She yelled in pain and shock. Clamped her hands over her ears.

'I need some fresh air,' she said when she got back to her friends. Thommo said he'd look after her.

'You look well done in.'

He walked with her down a side street to the beach. There were a few people around, sitting on the sand smoking and drinking, more out on the pier. Emmaline leaned against a wall.

'Did somebody spike my drink?'

Thommo laughed. 'Why would anyone need to spike your drink? You took those pills. You spiked yourself, girl.' The way he said it, it sounded like *Gail*.

'Do you feel weird?' Emmaline asked him. 'They're making me feel weird.'

'I didn't take mine yet.'

'What?'

'Saving them for later.'

'You didn't take them?'

'Well ... I kind of ... You know. I wanted to see what they did, first.'

'Did? You mean – *to me?*'

'Kinda.'

'So, I'm a guinea pig.'

'A cute guinea pig. Yeah. Ha-ha-ha.'

'Honestly, Thommo, I don't feel right. I feel ...'

'Yeah, I know – *weird* ... But to be fair, Emma, that's what they're for. Yeah?'

'I wish I knew what they were.'

'Don't worry about it, babe. Everyone was taking them. Go with it, yeah ... Coast the vibe.'

'What?'

And he made a move on her, started kissing her, pushing his hand down her shorts. She shoved him away.

'Fuck off. I'm fifteen.'

'Fucking hell? You're joking me?'

'Seriously. I'm fucking fifteen. How old are you?'

'I'm twenty-two.'

'Well, go and find someone your own age, you perve.'

'I didn't know, did I? You don't look fifteen. You never said.'

'Just leave me alone.'

'I'm looking after you, aren't I?'

'No, you're not. You're trying to fuck me.'

'I'm not trying to fuck you.'

'This is shit ...'

'Emma ...'

Emmaline screamed. And then she was shouting and cursing, so hard her throat hurt. But Thommo wasn't there anymore. When had he gone? Emmaline's head ached like a bastard. She was crying. The stars in the sky were all streaks and smears. A jagged flickering halo of white light had appeared in front of her eyes, broken up around the edges like a rainbow.

Shit. Shit. Shit.

She wandered up and down the beach breathing in the night air, but it felt heavy and damp and warm. Thick and solid, like soup. Made her head spin even worse than before. And the halo of light pulsed and the thud from the bars made her teeth hurt.

Someone spoke to her, but when she turned round there was no one there. She closed her eyes. The jagged halo wouldn't go away. When she opened her eyes, she was surrounded by people. All chatting away in a language she didn't understand, smiling at her. As she tried to talk to them, they, one by one, slowly disappeared right in front of her eyes. This was fucking annoying.

'Fuck,' she shouted. 'Don't do that. Stay with me … Stay with me.'

She moaned. Someone had taken an ice-cold metal bar and rammed it into the top of her skull, forced it down through the middle of her spine. It hurt like hell. She sat down on a low wall and put her head between her knees. There were tissues and puddles, a pen … Was she still in the bathroom?

It must be. It must be that.

She blacked out. When she came round, there was a pool of puke between her feet, some had splashed on to her shoes. She looked at her hands. Weird, soft rubbery spines were coming out of them, like thorns on a rose. Must have been what those lumps were. She tried to brush them off. They just bent. Annoying. She stopped bothering. What did it matter? She just hoped they weren't all over her face.

Shit.

She had to get back. She couldn't stay here. She looked around for her bag. Her things. Her phone …

Had she left them in the club?

Shit. Shit. Shit.

She stumbled up the road back to the Strip. The club wasn't there. Wasn't where it should be. Had she come up a different street from the beach? The Strip ran parallel. Fuck, The Necro could be anywhere.

And then she was dancing with Debs and Thommo and Livesey. Screaming and whooping. Shaking her head. And Debs was looking at her.

'You all right now, babe? You sure you're OK?'

'I'm good . . .'

'You were having a predicament.'

'I'm good. I'm so good . . .'

What track was this? Sounded like Lizzo.

What? What did you say?

She was back at the apartments. The pool looked so inviting. Bright blue and glowing. She was so hot still. It'd be good to cool off.

She took a deep breath. Dived in. Hit the road with a horrible smack.

Someone was leaning over her.

'Oh, fuck. You OK?'

'Do I look OK?'

'You fell in the road. We saw you fall in the road . . . Are you OK?'

'No, no . . . I went for a swim.'

'Sorry, we can't understand you. D'you speak English? Inglese?'

'I'm speaking fucking English . . .'

'Are you OK . . . ?'

'Stop asking me if I'm OK.' She propped herself up and looked at her messed-up clothes. Wiped her face. Her hand came away red. She was covered in blood.

'I need help.'

'Do you speak any English at all?'

'Where you staying, love?'

'I'm speaking English. Please. I don't feel right. I need my dad . . . Can you get my dad . . . ? I'm scared . . .'

Everyone had gone. She was sure she was back on the beach.

And then she was in a car. Or a van. Maybe a bus. There were flashing lights. They made the halo worse. She couldn't see straight at all.

And then there was her dad. And she cried out with relief. Tried to get up. Couldn't move. The lights were very bright in here. She was in a bed. But not at the apartment. Had they moved? Had Dad booked her into a five-star hotel? She laughed. If only she could just wake up properly, she could make sense of things.

'Oh, my baby, my baby girl, what have they done to you, love? What have they done?'

'Dad, I feel sick. I think I'm gonna throw.'

'Baby ... You'll be all right. You're my baby. I'll look after you. You're gonna be OK. What did you take? What are you on?'

'Dad. It hurts. Real bad. I think something broke. Inside ...'

'What's that, baby? Are you trying to speak? You're OK. If you can speak, you're OK. Don't worry. I'll be here. I'll look after you. I'll look out for you.'

'It hurts, Dad. I'm hurt.'

'That's good. Try and speak. Stay with me. You're OK. Stay with me. Speak louder. I can't understand. Who were you with? What did you take?'

'We were drinking a cocktail called a Fuckface. Guaranteed to blow our mind. Get you wrecked. Was it the cocktail ...? Practically a health drink ...'

Her brain felt like it was splitting down the middle. The jagged halo was back, shimmering, twisting, sparking and flashing with rainbow colours. Like a unicorn had rammed its horn into her back. A spike into her skull.

'Fucking unicorns ...'

'What? Say it again, love. Fight it ... You have to be a fighter for me ...'

A high-pitched whine in her ears. Hard to hear what Dad was saying.

'Dad, it really hurts. Help me, Dad . . . '

He can't help you.

What? Who was that? She turned her head, turned it right round on her neck, like that freaky girl in *The Exorcist*. She'd seen it on a Halloween sleepover when she was twelve. Felt like her neck was going to snap. There was a dark shape here. She didn't know who it was.

When she turned back, her dad had gone, and she was all alone. And she was scared. The noise stopped. The halo flicked off. Everything stopped.

Shit.

22

HEPWORTH

The Finn was looking at the huge full-length portrait of Hepworth on his office wall. Arms outstretched and the word PANTOCRATOR written across the bottom of the frame in gold lettering. Julian was smiling in the picture, a world-eating smile. He wasn't using that smile right now. He was giving the Finn a textbook blank look. Had been staring at him for a good long moment. Letting him sweat. Letting him shit his little Finnish pants.

The Finn was standing by the door. Ray by the windows, also giving him the blank look. Julian's South African lawyer, Tokyo Masombuka, sitting at the desk. Poised, pen in hand, loose sheets of paper on the desktop. Don't commit anything to digital. Paper can be burned. Julian on his pure white sofa. One leg stretched out along it. Waiting. The Finn looked shifty. Embarrassed.

'It's not my fault,' he said eventually. Quietly. Julian said nothing. Dragging it out.

'I told Vlachos to bring the contaminated batch straight back.'

'Why did he ever have it in the first place?'

'There was an error in despatch. In the warehouse. You know nothing's named, only numbered. Well, there was an error.'

'I get it – an error.'

'There was one pile of boxes ready for the incinerator, one pile for Vlachos. The numbers on the two batches were very similar. One box got mixed up – *only one* – went on to the wrong stack. As soon as we realised the mistake, we called Vlachos back. It was minutes. But when he came ... He didn't have *any* of the boxes.'

'You didn't check the batch as it went out?'

'The despatch guys do all that. It was only after Vlachos had gone that the despatch clerk called me to say there was a discrepancy. And we checked the boxes, and ... '

'So, the mistake was made by the despatch clerk?'

'Yes ... The *main* mistake. I accept we all could have done better. But, you know, Julian, it's not my job to test batches. I am the director of BIF ... '

'And you killed someone.'

'It is regrettable.'

'It is very regrettable. What have you done with the clerk?'

'He's still there. I know the protocols. I follow policy. We keep people close. He is more harm to us on the outside.'

'Sure. What's his name?'

'Thanasis Alexopolos.'

Hepworth looked over at Tokyo. He was writing. When he glanced up, Julian nodded at him.

'You'll go up and have a talk with him, Toke?'

'Un-hnh.'

'Scare the living shit out of the fucker, yeah? Anyone else involved in this clusterfuck. Make sure it's clear to Mister Alexopolos – that if the truth gets out, he's liable for manslaughter. Who knows, maybe even murder.'

'Un-hnh.'

Julian turned his attention back to the Finn. 'This was two days ago?'

'Yes.'

'And you're only now telling us?'

'We hoped it would not be serious.'

'A kid died, buddy. Three more in hospital. God knows how many out there still puking up on a beach.'

'We didn't know how dangerous the contaminated batch might be. We hoped it might do nothing worse than give someone a bellyache, a bad trip, massive downer, you know ...'

'Yeah. And as I say – a kid died.'

'It's possible the death was not related to the bad batch. Kids die from drugs all the time. It may be nothing to do with us. And if it is ... Let's hope she's the only one.'

'You should have come to me before.'

'We wanted to see if we could fix it at our end first. It was just one box among twenty. It was possible there would be no problem. At first we hoped Vlachos could fix it with the Albanians ...'

'This Genc Malecaj guy?'

'Yes. Him.'

'Do we need to get to him?'

'From what we have found out, he is an ... ah, shall we say, an unknown quantity. Not a businessman like Vlachos. But it is not in his interest to let this get out.'

'The police are going to have to be seen to be doing something about this. They're going to have to find out where the drugs came from. And if it was our drugs, then would you not say that it's only a matter of time before it all comes out.'

'It is a confused network,' said the Finn. 'And nobody wants to talk. Vlachos. Malecaj. The guys who actually sold the drugs. The kids who bought them ...'

'At least the girl who died can't talk.' A withering, sarcastic smile.

'No. But her friends. They will be scared to talk. The junior guys who sold the drugs. They won't know the chain of command above them. If the investigation does get to Malecaj, and then from him to Vlachos, and from Vlachos to us ... that could be months ... if ever.'

'It's not a risk we can take. This is a small island. Which is why I've already put some measures into place.'

'Already?' The Finn looked confused now.

'You know how I work. It's my job to know what's going on.' Julian offered him a condescending smile this time. 'I have security up your ass. I have security to keep an eye on my security. This meeting – it's like a meeting of SPECTRE in a Bond movie. I can pull a lever and drop you into a fucking shark tank. I knew your mistakes before you made them. It's always been a strong possibility that something would go wrong with what you're doing up there. So, we have – yes – we have *protocols* in place. We've been following this whole thing, waiting for you to come to us. But we couldn't wait for ever, so we've already put our own story out there which, if our involvement ever does come to light, everybody will buy into. We've created a fake digital trail.'

'What's the story?'

'We'd packed up a batch of experimental antidepressants. We were shipping them to the testing labs in Finland. Our truck took them to the airport on the 6th – a shipment did go out then, so the truck's real at least – the packages were checked on to the plane. But when they were checked off at the other end, there was a discrepancy.'

'A discrepancy?'

'Some items on the manifest weren't present. We've been investigating it. As yet we don't know. Was the problem at this end? Were they stolen at the airport? Somewhere in transit? At the Finnish end?'

'Antidepressants?'

'Yeah. This whole micro-dosing thing's getting to be a big deal these days. Not far off what the Albanians stole, really. Except those were macro-doses. Yeah?'

'I guess. So – in this story there's still a robbery?'

'Yes. The Albanians are our loose end – the only guys outside our group who know the truth. What do we do? D'you think we should be working with *them* rather than Vlachos? They play harder. Should we bring them in? Keep them close?'

The Finn looked over to Ray. 'Don't ask me. That's not my area.'

'No. It's not. We may need to have a quiet word with them, all the same. Get our stories straight. Find someone between us to take the fall if needs be. But for now, we've created a trail of red herrings, some emails, some enhanced packaging and shipment documents, some enhanced digital records. Our arses are covered. Vlachos isn't part of the story. *You're* clear – for now.'

The Finn nodded.

'But always bear in mind that you can be replaced at any moment.'

'You're not worried I know too much?' The hint of a smile – a nervous little laugh.

'You come out with anything, you implicate yourself in a whole fucked-up world of pain and madness and sheer wrongdoing. We all need to stay as one big happy family. Isn't that right. Tokyo? Ray?'

Nods and smiles all round. Julian leaned back on the sofa.

'This story has all the ingredients of a classic conspiracy theory, don't you think?' More nods and smiles. 'The death, the illness, the hallucinogenic experiences of the survivors, the mystery surrounding where the drugs came from. It's perfect. Alongside the antidepressants story, we're already clogging the internet with bullshit. Twenty different theories – who supplied the drugs – what they looked like – what they were. Only a matter of time before we get the antivaxxers piling in with some typically inane theories about a vaccine gone wrong. We'll have the "One World Government" mob endlessly posting about thought control, the CIA and their mind experiments, George Soros, David Icke, Big Pharma and the fucking Matrix.'

'The Matrix?'

'The red pill, my friend. We've put the story out there that the drugs were red. Those who survived have seen the truth! Before this is over with, there'll be a massive demand for them. Ha-ha-ha! Maybe we should make some more?'

'No. Please. I feel terrible enough already.'

'Good for you. What I'm saying is, the Greek police will disappear down a rabbit hole. Karagiannis is helping to see to that. By the end of this we'll have them believing that the sun's the size of a beach ball, the world's as flat as a pancake and those drugs came from Atlantis.'

Hepworth got up, gave a dismissive wave and left them to it. He walked outside, on to the upper terrace, looked out over the Straits towards Albania. It was going to be a lovely day.

As if by magic, Miguel appeared at his elbow. Damn, the guy was good. He had a silver tray with a can of Diet Coke on it – already opened – and a frosted glass of crushed ice. Slice of lemon. Julian smiled at him. Miguel filled the glass and handed it over. Julian took a sip. Turned back to enjoy the view.

God, he loved conspiracy theorists. Those eager jerks looking for meaning in a meaningless world. He secretly gave a fair amount of money to fund all sorts of cranks. I mean, come on, nobody in their right mind seriously believed the childish theories of QAnon – Satan-worshipping, baby-fucking, baby-eating, baby-trading from pizza basements, satanic rituals, harvesting organs and adrenochrome. Liberal Hollywood A-listers, elite businessmen and Democrat politicians locked in an *Avengers: Endgame*-style war against Trump. Where We Go One We Go All. Jesus. Come on. No sensible person believed any of that shit, just as nobody in their right mind believed in a flat earth, or that the American government had actually blown up the Twin Towers, or that the royal family were lizards, or that man hadn't walked on the moon – indeed, that the moon was actually just a fucking projection, *man* . . .

The whole of existence is a simulation!

What a crock of silly bollocks.

Useful silly bollocks, though. That was the thing. You get a load of people marching and shouting and tweeting and spending every waking hour watching ludicrous YouTube videos about shit like QAnon and you completely distract them from what's really going on in the world – right there in front of them. In full view – GOOD, OLD-FASHIONED, FERAL CAPITALISM. Give me all your money and fuck off!

It was a classic sleight of hand. You've got a magician up on stage with his dick up a kitten's arse, right there in plain sight, but he's doing fancy card tricks and pulling coins out of thin air and communicating with dead spirits and sawing women in half, so nobody's looking at the poor fucking kitten.

When it came down to it, the conspiracy theorists were the kitten and capitalism was the magician – rogering them rigid up their soft, willing, pink arses.

No, no, no! Can't you see it? What's really *going on? The world is run by the Freemasons and the Illuminati and the Knights Templar.*

'Shut up and pass me the lube . . . '

It was un-be-fucking-lievable.

He, Julian Hepworth, had been in business for a good while and made a whole lot of money and met a lot of rich people, a lot of extremely powerful and influential people, politicians and bankers and oligarchs, CEOs, dictators, warlords and every other type of hard motherfucker out there, but, you know what, he'd never met a Knights Templar, or one of the sodding Illuminati, never been offered a secret handshake.

Why didn't Trump ever try to discredit QAnon? Because they were doing his work for him. Distracting the idiots from the shit-show of his presidency and his shitty business deals and his shitty property developments.

But for pity's sake, think of the children! Those poor little babies. Raped and then eviscerated. Sold for spare parts . . .

It was everywhere. Right in front of you. The *real* bad things in the world – burning rain forests, melting ice caps, air pollution, species extinction, rich executives earning more than the entire population of small African countries, the incarceration of just about the entire black population of America, the Chinese digging up coal to burn in the power stations that kept Bitcoin going, good old capitalism shitting on everybody – but you don't want people to get angry about that, *no sir*, you want them to believe that they REALLY KNOW WHAT'S GOING ON IN THE WORLD. That they're privy to SECRET INFORMATION.

Don't you see it, sheeple? The fault with America isn't Trump, and Amazon and gun manufacturers and opioids and the lack of free health care. No, the problem is crazy fucking lizards and a secret international one world cabal who are SECRETLY RUNNING EVERYTHING. And they're all involved, you know? NATO and the EU, the UN, the IMF and NASA and the World Bank and the RSPC-fucking-A.

And, of course, you only had to scratch the surface of every conspiracy theory on the table and what did you find?

The Jews. Always the poor fucking Jews. They were to blame. For *everything*. Communism? – that heinous plot to enslave America – it was the Jews! And rich bankers? *Jews?* They were all Jews. The Jews were simultaneously the communists *and* the rich bankers. Clever bastards.

It was brilliant. It was perfect. It was comical. You want to know what the *real* conspiracy was? That the capitalists – *people like Julian* – had fooled everyone into believing in conspiracy theories. Tricked them into believing that none of this was their fault. And that suited Mister Julian Hepworth just fine, thank you. Shut up and pass the lube.

Yes. Let the people believe a ridiculous, totally unworkable, theory that the Democrats were harvesting babies and you could quietly get on with whatever shit you wanted to without the glare of publicity, without the tiresome burden of scrutiny and the fear of retribution.

Let the people waste their lives – hours and days and months and years – online, reinforcing their meaningless, pseudo-science twaddle and shite instead of actually looking into the real problems in the world. He'd even set up his own smokescreen, spread a few conspiracy theories about himself. Got some Ukrainian kids to start posting shit on social media and write stupid blogs. He'd had fun coming up with some of the ideas with Pixie and Tokyo. He'd tried to get Miss Lily on board, but she had no sense of humour.

Take your pick.

Hepworth was a Freemason.

Hepworth was Jewish.

Hepworth was assassinated in 2015 and replaced by someone who'd had plastic surgery.

Hepworth was a digital simulacrum. He didn't really exist, and his company was actually run by Kim Jong What's His Face from North Korea.

Hepworth used to be an international criminal. A hit man for the Russian mafia. A mercenary who'd massacred a whole village in Africa . . . Or was it the Far East?

Hepworth was Bill Gates's son.

Hepworth helped fund ISIS.

Hepworth worked for the CIA.

The main purpose of HepKat was to run the massive digital operation that perpetrated the lie that the earth is a globe. BIF was where all the number crunching was done. And the moon projections as well, probably.

Hepworth was gay, and the beautiful girls he was always seen with were 'beards' to make him appear hetero.

Hepworth was a transsexual.

Hepworth was a hermaphrodite who was born with both male and female genitalia.

Didn't matter how crazy the idea was, in a very short time people were making earnest YouTube videos proving that IT WAS ALL TRUE.

The stories were growing, circulating, being elaborated on, linked up, collecting mass, like so many shitballs rolling down a hill. Which meant that less people were thinking about underage girls.

Because, all right, he had to admit, some *were* younger than was strictly legal. Those that wanted it. The mature ones. The ones who liked to have fun. The Lolitas.

He was getting excited just thinking about it.

It was fashionable to say about powerful men who had lots of young women, that it wasn't about sex, it was about *power*.

What shit. Only an ugly, old, dried-up middle-aged witch could be self-deluded enough to believe that.

It was so totally the other way around.

There was only one reason to gain power.

For the sex.

23

CINDY

Cindy was having lunch with Aimee at the fish taverna. Cindy had no idea why it was known as the fish taverna as it served pretty much the same food as both the other tavernas in Agios Symeon. It was just the way it was. Always had been. The Keration was known by the locals – and therefore also the tourists – as the fish taverna and was classified on TripAdvisor as a 'Seafood Restaurant'. Gianni's Taverna was the 'traditional Greek' place, classified on TripAdvisor as a 'Local Family Restaurant'. The Apollo was known as the kebab place and classified on TripAdvisor as a 'Grill Restaurant'. Even though Gianni's and the Keration also did grilled meats, all three served fish, they were all family run and you could get traditional Greek dishes like moussaka, keftedes, spanakopita, stifado or fried courgette balls, kolokithokeftedes, in any of them.

And chips. Chicken. Greek salads, of course. Cindy didn't know a restaurant in Corfu that *didn't* serve horiatiki. She simultaneously loved a horiatiki with all her heart and would be happy never to see another one as long as she lived. Sure, they did other salads, but the ingredients were just variations on lettuce, olives, tomatoes, peppers, feta, onion and grated carrot.

Sometimes a hard-boiled egg.

The only thing that was different in each taverna was the view. It was how the world was going. Everything becoming – what was the word? – *homogenised*. Once upon a time, way back when, she supposed they'd done things differently. Maybe even when she'd first arrived, twenty-five years ago, the menus had been different. She'd forgotten so much. The slow creep of change meant that you lost track of how things were. You'd be driving down a road one day and see a new building you hadn't noticed before and you couldn't remember what had been there before.

But the food, round and round, year in year out, never seemed to change. These days, unless it was something to do with work, she tried to cook and eat at home whenever possible, using ingredients that friends brought over from the UK – if she couldn't get them in the posh supermarket in Corfu Town. Just so she had some *variety*. Once in a blue moon she and Ioannis would go for a night out in the Town. There was even an Indian restaurant there – Tandoori Bites – that catered mainly to Brits. But it wasn't like an Indian restaurant back home.

Back home . . .

Even after twenty-five years she thought of England as home.

She envied Aimee. This was fun for her. *Different*. She was living the Greek dream. Two weeks in the sun eating horiatiki and drinking ouzo and then back home to Blighty. She envied her casual ease. Her nice long-sleeved top and chic sunglasses. Her cool. Her normal life.

They were sitting outside, under a rush-covered pergola, on the northern side of the harbour, the water coming right up to the wall at the edge of the terrace. Everything painted white and 'Greek blue', as she called it. The Keration was busy. A tourist boat had put in and disgorged its passengers to eat here. Two of the couples from her villas were here as well. The Samuels and the Karlssons. The girls who were staying at the Vines Guest House were at another table – Juno and Taz. Cindy had got to know them a little. She was jealous of them, she had to admit. They reminded her so much of herself when she'd first come out here. Young and happy and naïve and looking ahead to a future full of infinite possibilities. They could still get excited about a Greek salad.

Big difference was she'd never have been able to afford to eat in a proper restaurant like this. She'd survived on bread and cheese and olives, cheap rubbery ham from the supermarkets and sometimes – *sometimes* – if she was feeling flush, chips or gyros. She still loved gyros. The girls had probably made a withdrawal from the bank of mum and dad. What was it Jane called them? *Gap yahs* ...

No. She didn't want to be mean. She liked Juno and Taz. They made a change from the dull, middle-class, middle-aged couples in their Panama hats, pressed shorts and clip-on sunglasses. The girls' youthful energy and sense of fun were nice to have around.

She wondered if she'd ever get back there herself. Regain *her* sense of fun? *Real* fun, not the fake, 'good-time-girl' exterior she put on for the holidaymakers, all those brittle laughs like glass cracking, which irritated even her.

'What are you going to have?' Aimee asked.

'Maybe just a salad?' *God, not another fucking salad.*

'What about the fish of the day?' said Aimee. 'Do you think it'll be good?'

'I think it'll be expensive,' said Cindy. 'For what it is. The Greeks export all their good fish, they can get a much better price elsewhere. There are so few fish left in the Med. The phrase "plenty more fish in the sea" is becoming fake news. Ha-ha-ha-ha-ha ...'

'I do *like* fish, though,' said Aimee.

'It'll be *OK*,' said Cindy. 'Just prepare yourself for a shock when the bill comes. Oh, listen to me. I really shouldn't be saying this. I get a tiny commission from the tavernas if I point customers in their direction. The more they spend the more I get. I always say to them – "Tell them Cindy sent you".' She tapped her nose and

winked at Aimee. 'They think it's so that they'll get special treatment, but it's actually so I get my commission.'

'Then I'm gonna get all the most expensive items on the menu!'

They both laughed. That felt good. Cindy liked Aimee. She was
so straightforward and open, but there was something naughty
about her as well. She was one of those people you could talk
to. Tell secrets. It had been fun getting to know her these last
couple of days.

'How about a bottle of wine?' Aimee asked.

'I shouldn't really.'

'You can have just one glass. I'll make the rest disappear. I'm
on holiday! Nothing counts. I don't need to go anywhere. Do
anything. I can just lie by the pool and snooze . . .'

'Well . . . maybe a nice cold white?'

'Now you're talking, Cindy. That's my girl.'

It was so different living here from being on holiday here. That
was why so many expats fell apart when they came out here to
retire. They approached every day as if they were still on holiday
and usually drank themselves to death in a couple of years.

'Or, I guess I could go for swordfish, maybe?' said Aimee,
frowning at the menu. 'What about the prawns? Squid?'

'They'll all be from frozen,' said Cindy. 'The squid will probably
have been shipped over from the Falklands, and the prawns from
some habitat-destroying farm in the Far East . . .'

'You are doing a terrible job of selling this place, Cindy. This
was your recommendation! You are going to ruin my holiday with
all this reality.'

'Sorry. Tell you what. If you're OK with the price, let's share
the fish of the day.'

Aimee put down her menu with a slap. 'Done.'

It was easy for people like her. They could fly in and fly out again
without ever having to engage with what was actually going on
here on the island. She could be happily oblivious. Cindy couldn't

hold it against her. She'd said it herself, Aimee was on holiday, and she deserved her break. It sounded like she worked hard with her fitness business. She could enjoy the sunset cocktails, the olive trees and the pines, the blue water, the boats and the beaches. The worst she could fear was being annoyed by a mosquito. Or she might fall off a rented moped. Tourists were always doing that, scraping all the skin off their bare arms and legs.

Aimee wouldn't see any further than the picture postcard views (did anyone send postcards anymore?), the cheerful locals, the picturesque old ladies in black. She wouldn't see the pollution, the corruption, the crime, the domestic abuse, the drugs . . .

Oh, stop it, Cindy. It wasn't that bad. This was Corfu, not Istanbul.

But then – there was that horrible news about that poor girl . . .

No. Don't think about that. That was nothing to do with her. Kids were always getting into trouble with drugs. Wherever they were. *Talk to Aimee. Distract yourself.*

'Any problems at the villa?'

'God, no. It's a dream.'

The Macintyres had taken Villa Chelona. One of the nicest in Agios Symeon. Cindy would dearly have loved to bring it into the Club Corfu Villas portfolio. It would be a real money earner. Bump up her commission no end. The owners were a German couple. They rarely visited and had no interest in joining the club. Why would they? They rented it out themselves via their own website. It was hardly ever empty, even in the bad years.

'I've been dying to ask,' she said. 'And I hope you don't mind, but what's your accent, Aimee?'

'I guess you'd call it mid-Atlantic. My mom's English, my dad was American. They split up when I was a kid. I went to live with my dad in the States. He died when I was sixteen . . .'

'Oh, I am sorry.'

'Thank you. Anyway, I moved back to England. So, I'm a bit of both and a lot of neither. You haven't lost *your* accent at all.'

'They don't say that if I ever go back to Manchester,' said Cindy. 'They reckon I've gone all posh.'

'Not Greek, though.'

'Not Greek, no. I speak it fluently but with an awful English accent.'

'How's business doing here?'

'So, it's still not back to how it was before the crash and all that nonsense with the EU. I mean – it's *hard*. Both our jobs are reliant on tourists. If they don't come, we don't eat. Ha-ha-ha.'

'The crash hit things pretty bad here in Greece, didn't it?' said Aimee.

'It was awful. The whole place went batshit. The worst part was, when the Greek economy nosedived, because we were tied to the EU and the euro, there was nothing the government could do. In the past they'd have simply just devalued the drachma and the tourists would have come flocking with their cash worth ten times what it used to be. But the opposite happened. You can't imagine. There were horror stories of hotels no longer accepting credit cards and marching guests to ATMs to get cash. And then the ATMs started running dry . . . '

'Jesus.'

'Yeah. We've been buggered left right and sideways. And – put it this way – we don't have any savings anymore. Nothing set aside for a rainy day. Luckily it doesn't rain here that much! Ha-ha-ha. Not like Manchester. At least we haven't lost our home. It's all a bit of a nightmare, though . . . '

The waiter came over with some bread and water and they put in their order. Cindy was glad of the distraction. She hadn't been telling Aimee the whole truth about the state of their finances. Ioannis seemed to have more money than he used to lately, even though boat rentals were slow. They'd always had separate bank accounts and never discussed money – that would hurt his male pride. If she ever tried to bring up the subject he'd become even more – what was the word? – *taciturn*. But *something* was going on. He'd started doing odd jobs with Theo Vlachos after the crash, anything to get some cash coming in, and he was spending more and more time with the old rogue. That man had his fingers in so many pies he should be on *MasterChef*. She liked Vlachos, he was always friendly, always smiling, but she knew he was dodgy. Forever ducking and diving. A real Del Boy.

She looked over at Aimee, tearing a strip off a piece of bread. Cindy bet she'd never heard of Del Boy Trotter. Before her time. Funny how quickly things disappeared when they weren't on the telly anymore.

Vlachos's main job was selling cheap booze to the bars and nightclubs. He knocked out bathtub gin, vodka and rum in an industrial unit in Kontokali. Cindy had boxes of the stuff in the garage. Cheap and cheerful was the best way to describe it, if you could ignore the mind-blowing hangovers. Vlachos sold it for half the price of the well-known brands. Disguised in some sugary cocktail you couldn't really tell the difference. Best not to drink it neat, however, unless you were already pissed. It was variable quality, weak and lacked any real character, but bartenders could make a big show of sloshing the stuff around, ignoring any official measures, so the tourists loved it. Especially the booze-obsessed Brits in their compounds down south, who'd grown up with the parsimonious shots so pedantically and joylessly measured out in British pubs.

Yes. In the Union Jack party bars, with their round the clock happy hours, Vlachos's rotgut was drunk like water. The young-sters could drink all night and spend their days lying in bed until they had the strength to go out and start all over again.

Thank God it was all so different up here in the north-east. The exclusive part of the island. Another world.

The wine came and Aimee poured out two generous glasses, they clinked and giggled like two schoolgirls bunking off, and

Cindy had to admit that the first sip was bliss. Vlachos had tried his hand at winemaking once, using pulp he bought in bulk from the mainland.

The least said about that the better.

There were a lot of other rumours about Vlachos. They said that it wasn't just cheap booze he sold. There was talk of drugs, and girls. Cindy laughed it off as island gossip. Didn't want to think about Ioannis being involved in anything – what was the word? – *sordid*. And then there was this talk about killer drugs, and that girl . . .

'I suppose in a way,' said Aimee. 'It must at least be a bit easier to cope on less money here than if you were back in the UK.'

'You're right,' said Cindy. 'But you get used to a certain way of life. In the good times we were DINKY rich.'

'No kids?'

'Afraid not. We got tested . . . turns out neither of us is fit for purpose! Ha-ha-ha. Can you imagine that? Maybe that's what attracted us to each other? A couple of duds. What about you and Robert?'

Aimee looked blank for a second, then lit up. 'You mean Mac?'

'Yes. Of course. Do you have any kids?'

'Not yet.'

'Sometimes I'm glad we don't have kids,' said Cindy.

'Yeah?'

'I'd be so scared all the time. Worried. Being responsible for someone else. There are so many things that can go wrong.'

'I know what you mean,' said Aimee. 'Shit, I guess you heard about that teenager?'

Cindy blurted something, stammered, not wanting to talk about it.

'The one who took those bad drugs?' said Aimee, not letting it go.

'Oh, yes,' said Cindy. 'That was awful. They say it was

contaminated drugs of some sort. Several clubbers ended up in hospital.'

'I feel so sorry for that little girl . . .' said Aimee.

'It's the dealers,' said Cindy, reaching for her glass. 'The Albanians. There are rumours they stole some stuff from . . . Well, from somewhere . . .'

Cindy knew she should have shut down this conversation. Her job was to sell Corfu as an island paradise. Which in many ways it was. But she wanted to impress Aimee. Make her world sound more exciting and interesting.

'Even here, I guess,' said Aimee. 'There are bad things going down.'

'That's life,' said Cindy, inanely. Not her life, though. Please God, not her life. Nothing to do with her and Ioannis. The rumours and gossip were just that. There was no truth to it all. She'd always trusted Ioannis.

He wasn't the same man she'd married, though. He'd turned in on himself. I mean, let's face it, he'd never been the most demonstrative type. She'd liked that at first. Found it mysterious and attractive. There had been a Clint Eastwood, Man With No Name, vibe about him. Nothing seemed to faze him, she'd never seen him scared or angry or sad. A rock. Tight-lipped. Didn't bang on about himself like so many men. Happy to let her talk. Now she just wondered if he wasn't actually just a bit dim. No, that was unfair, there was a lot going on under the bonnet, he just never shared it with her.

He was thirty when they met, five years older than her. *A man.* And, *God*, he'd been hot. Jet-black hair, deep liquid-brown eyes, a great physique from working on fishing boats all his life, a smile that could turn your knees to jelly and refresh the parts that other smiles couldn't reach.

So, he'd been a little on the short side. She could live with that. To be fair, Cindy was no Cindy Crawford. More of a Cindy

Lauper. A pocket rocket. She was only just over five foot tall and way back when she'd been Juno and Taz's age everything had been in the right place. In old photographs she looked stunning, like Scarlett Johansson, just so long as there was nothing to show scale. But then, Scarlett Johansson was no beanpole. Weren't all movie stars tiny? Small people tended to be better proportioned. Until they started to put on weight. As Cindy had been doing steadily in the last few years.

She had to admit it. She was going off, like an over-ripe peach in the sun, turning all wrinkled and mushy. Ioannis hadn't aged well, either, but at least she made an effort. Ten thousand steps a day. Furious, angry steps. Yoga, tennis, jogging, Pilates, hair, make-up, Spanx. She'd even had a little Botox and a teeny lip injection.

Ioannis had long since stopped doing any physical work and grown steadily more chunky. Stolid and lumpen. His face puffy. His eyes no longer clear. They'd lost their sparkle. He looked at least *ten* years older than her now, not five.

So everyone said.

Of course, it didn't help that he'd been massively depressed since the crash of 2008 and was on all sorts of drugs. The Prozac seemed to numb him and make him withdraw even further from the world. She wished she could persuade him to have some therapy. To be honest, though, it was hard to find a decent therapist on a small island like this. With a population the size of Rochdale or Leamington Spa back home. She bet it was pretty hard to find a good therapist in Rochdale as well. And they couldn't afford for him to go off to Athens every other week.

She was on beta-blockers herself. Still hadn't recovered from the bad years. It had been so *scary*, as if Greece was collapsing into chaos. Golden Dawn, the anarchists in their black masks, the far right, the far left, the boatloads of immigrants and asylum seekers crossing the Med, the awful things going on in Lesbos and other islands, terrified that it could happen here . . .

And money. Always money at the back of her mind.

She probably wouldn't have come to lunch if Aimee hadn't offered to pay. 'Her treat', she'd said. Cindy was in danger of clinging on to Aimee. She was so lovely. So straightforward. So strong.

Cindy took another, larger, sip of wine. And then another.

'I'm really feeling like I might take the afternoon off,' she said.

'We could hit the beach,' said Aimee.

'That'd be bliss. Sometimes you just have to say – fuck it!'

'Fuck it!' Aimee raised her glass and they clinked. And then Cindy spotted Ioannis, storming out of the boat hire office and bustling towards the Keration.

'Now what?' she muttered.

He pushed between the tables, his face dark. She hadn't seen him this animated in years. Just when she'd been thinking he never showed any emotion. He blasted Cindy with a tirade in highly colloquial Greek, laced with curses and colourful threats of violence. She exchanged a look with Aimee, who seemed concerned.

'His car's been stolen,' she explained.

'Oh my God, that's terrible.'

'He loved that car more than he loved me,' said Cindy and she laughed nervously. That just set Ioannis off again, thinking she was laughing at him. She tried to placate him, but he was livid. It was quite exciting in a way.

'It's probably Albanians,' Cindy told Aimee. 'It's always Albanians. They're ruining this place. They break into the holiday villas. They steal hire cars and ship them back to Albania ... '

Ioannis was still ranting. Threatening bloody revenge.

'Would you excuse me,' said Aimee, getting up from the table. 'I need the bathroom.'

Bless her for being discreet. Leaving Cindy and Ioannis to talk this through in private. But Cindy didn't want Aimee to go. She didn't want to have this conversation. She wanted to run and hide and bury her head in the sand. As she got older, she was finding it harder and harder to deal with stress.

And then she did the thing she really hadn't wanted to do.

She burst into tears.

24

HEPWORTH

Be charming. Always charming. Charming and funny and generous. Grease the bastards. Grease them and flatter them and dazzle them. Julian Hepworth. The emperor in his palace by the sea. Midas and Croesus and Apollo all rolled into one knockout package. He caught sight of himself in the huge floor to ceiling glass doors on the way out. Looking like something out of *Vogue*. An advert for men's perfume, or one of those stupidly expensive watches. Patek Philippe. He'd stopped wearing a watch years ago. Old tech. Antediluvian shit.

Dominic Beard was walking across the lawn towards him. Grinning.

Grin back. Disarm the fucker. Get in the first shot.

He waited on the terrace. Three steps above Beard. He knew the effect. The modern extension at the end of the house rising above him and framing him in glass and steel. He timed the moment then stepped out of the shade of the jutting roof extension into full sun, spread his arms – The Golden Boy – Pantocrator. The hairs on his brown arms *were* actually golden. Glowing in the sunlight.

He held the pose a moment and then stuck out his hand as Dominic trotted up to him. He gripped his hand – firm but not too firm. He wasn't some macho wanker trying to crush Dominic's knuckles to dust. Didn't have to. This was his world, after all. The house and the estate did all the hand crushing for him.

'I love what you do,' he said. A wide smile, showing his teeth. He'd practised that smile in front of the mirror. Making sure he didn't show any gums. 'Me and my girlfriend sit and watch it together,' he went on. 'We binge the box set on Netflix. You know what it's like?' Going into a breathy, Marilyn Monroe, girly voice. "Oh, baby, can't we watch just one more . . . ?" I'm a little worried she has a thing for you, Dominic.'

'Ha – I'm only ever a disappointment in real life,' said Dominic. Was he blushing? 'I'm even more geeky than on the TV. People realise it isn't an act. I really *am* like this.'

'Some girls go for the geeky types,' said Julian, not denying it. The guy *was* a geek. Tall. Glasses. Floppy schoolboy hair. Dressed to blend in. Button-down grey Oxford shirt with some texture in it. Dark jeans that met his shoes just so. Kissing them. Old, but well-kept brown shoes. The two of them must be about the same age. Thirty-two, maybe thirty-three.

'So, your girlfriend?' said Dominic. 'That's Philippa von Crantz?'

'Philippa Pennington-Bausch-Hohenlohe von Crantz, to be precise. Everyone calls her Pixie, though. *Her* choice.'

'You've been together a long time.'

'Have you started the interview already, Dominic?'

'Sorry. Ha. I'm always doing that. Never get the best bits on camera. I reckon I'm always going to be a hopeless amateur.'

'Some people find that endearing.' Not denying that one either. He was having fun. This was going to be a fun day. 'So where do you want to do this, Dominic?'

He spread his arms wide again to indicate the almost untold possibilities of the estate.

'Be great to have the ocean behind you,' said Dominic. 'That view . . .' Taking it in. 'Be cool to show some of the house in the wide, though. I mean, we'll see it all, obviously. We'll grab some GVs of the whole place and cut them in.'

'General views.'

'You've done this before.'

'A few times. I'm interested in television. How it all works.'

'You know your stuff. Me – I'm still learning,' said Dominic with a boyish smile. 'GVs is just one of those bullshit terms you have to learn when you do this. You know what it's like? Every organisation has its set of clubby acronyms.'

'Don't I know it.'

'A few years back I did a doc on the porn industry for the Beeb, and when I told one of the performers that I worked for the BBC she gave me the funniest look.'

'Ha-ha-ha. Tell me about it. When I first had to have dealings with money people – bankers, financiers, investment managers – they started straight in with the jargon, hoping to bamboozle the fuck out of me. I'd done my homework, though. Shoved that jargon straight up their arses. They found that impressive.'

'Are we talking about porn again?'

'Ha-ha.'

'You know, when I started out,' said Dominic, 'I didn't even know what a two shot was. I hadn't been to film school, hadn't done media studies like every other bugger. I thought a two shot was part of some kind of complicated numbered system I'd have to learn – assumed there was some kind of manual with all that shit in it. A one shot, a two shot, a three shot, a twenty-seven shot, a ninety-nine . . . Turned out it just meant a shot with two people in it! Jesus. I was such a virgin!'

'It's what people like about you, Dominic. There's no bullshit.'

Dominic was perfect for Julian. Who knew everything there was to know about him. Started out as a reporter for Vice, then became an unlikely star at the BBC before being poached by Netflix. Had his own show – poking around the homes of the rich and famous. He didn't have a mega news corporation on his back wanting big, exclusive, news stories, scandal, controversy, forensic journalism. His viewers wanted bling and fluff. It was strictly entertainment. Lots of young people watched it. Lots of clips on YouTube. Lots of memes. Mucho chatter on Twitter. Exactly the sort of exposure Hepworth wanted. Stay away from the MSM, the big, toxic corporations like the BBC and CNN, Sky and MSNBC with their fake news.

The chief cameraman joined them. He'd been wandering around, checking light levels, looking at the sky, all that shit they did.

'Where's good?' Dominic asked him after they'd done the introductions.

'Here on the terrace, I think, Dom. In the shade. The sun's good at the moment. I'll chuck a couple of lights on you both to balance things, so the background doesn't burn out ... That all right with you, Mister Hepworth?'

'I'm in your hands. If you need anything just wave something. My staff are all on standby.'

'Good-good-good. I'll give you a shout when we're ready to go.'

Julian watched the cameraman rejoin his team and turned his attention back on Dominic again. 'Do you prefer Dom, or Dominic?'

'Happy with either ... So. You obviously know the sort of interviews I do, Julian? And I know you must get a lot of requests for this kind of thing ...'

'And you must know I turn most of them down, Dom,' said Julian. 'But we've already established I like your stuff. You always say what you want to say – face to face – there's none of that snidey voiceover some people put on afterwards.'

'I'm not here to take the piss,' said Dominic. 'You've been good enough to invite us into your amazing home. And people want to see it. They want to see *you*. As you *are*. It's very English to sneer at the rich, to think it's vulgar to talk about money, but, deep down, it's what we all want. We all want *this*, Julian.' Looking around at the spectacular surroundings. 'I give ordinary people a glimpse into another world. And they love it.'

Who wouldn't love this?

From here on the upper terrace, whichever direction you faced, past the house and grounds, all you could see was trees and sky, rocks and ocean. Even when you looked over towards fucking Albania all you saw were densely wooded slopes. It wasn't natural. None of it was natural. It had all been designed for maximum effect. Painstakingly landscaped. He thought of it as terraforming. Most of the rocks had been imported, the mature trees planted with cranes, the streams dug out and plumbed in. The system of ponds with their lush vegetation had been created with dynamite and careful planting. Stocked with those fish that ate mosquitoes. What were they called? Oh, yeah, mosquito fish. Some Californian pillow biter had designed it all. Done an amazing job.

And the real beauty of it was that Julian still hadn't paid the sad-ass prick.

The trick was to have good lawyers. That was one of the first things he'd learned. You want to get anywhere in this world, get yourself some good lawyers. They'd drawn up all the contracts for the work, all the specifications, guarantees, deliveries, and had made sure that they'd be able to run rings round the uphill gardener and delay payment almost indefinitely.

Same with the house. The architect and the builders were still flailing about, drowning in a quicksand of paperwork, under the charmingly quaint illusion that one day they were going to get paid.

That was one of the first things he'd learned about how to amass great wealth. Don't fucking pay anyone – except your lawyers. He even had a second team of lawyers secretly keeping an eye on the first team. Any slip-ups and their payment would freeze out, too.

Miguel brought them over a tray of soft drinks. Smoothies and juices and iced water. Stood there patiently while Julian and Dominic made their choices. Then went over to the rest of the crew.

As Julian and Dominic chatted about the island and the house, Julian studied Dominic's clothes. They were chosen to look casual, normal, man of the people. But they weren't cheap.

Julian had dressed to look normal as well. Nothing flashy. Stylish but cool. Rich but tasteful. All fresh out of the box. Pale grey Prada slacks. Dark blue D&G T-shirt. Pink Yves Saint Laurent sweater artfully draped across his shoulders. Chalmers calfskin suede, burgundy, penny loafers – Purple Label from Ralph Lauren. He still felt slightly restricted, though, preferred shorts and sliders in the heat. He'd toyed with the idea of going full casual. Surfer T-shirt and beads. The barefoot tech genius. The rich man who dressed like a slob. Just like those Hollywood directors in their tatty baseball caps, the worst dressed people on set.

In the end, though, he'd wanted to project the image of the suave, effortlessly stylish, metropolitan, cosmopolitan, metrosexual plutocrat. The Great Gatsby. The Last Tycoon. Master of all he surveyed. Clean lines. WYSIWYG. Cool and straight with no odd angles or dark corners.

The important thing was not to look *weird*.

That was where Whacko Jacko had gone wrong. He'd started to look more and more like a weirdo. And people believed that weirdoes were capable of anything.

No. Julian was not weird. He was clean-cut. Sexy – in a conventional way. He had good hair. Lush. So many guys his age were starting to lose it. Blond, but not in a fag way. Carefully streaked and waved and kept in shape with a haircut every week. A dye job every month.

His T-shirt showed off his tanned arms, good muscle definition. That came from playing a lot of tennis and working out twice a day in his private gym. He made a big effort to keep in shape. He appreciated the admiring glances he got when he went out anywhere. The men jealous, the women turned on, wet. He'd had to learn how to deal with the fact that people were always a little bit overawed by him. He was *attractive*, in every sense of the word. A man who would never have to *pay* for sex. He could bed any girl he wanted, even if he wasn't fucking rich. All right, so he was never going to punch above the musicians and the movie stars, but, among the men who actually had to work for a living, he was firmly settled in at the top. And he was only thirty-two. He had years ahead of him. He could mature into a suave middle-aged guy like Brad Pitt, and then mellow into a silver fox like Clooney. He had the right features for it. Handsome rather than cute. Chiselled. Classically masculine. His face wouldn't go to seed, run to fat. He didn't have that boyish, Leonardo DiCaprio thing going on, where you started to look kind of freakish as you got older. He had the portrait over the fireplace in the living room here to prove it. The big one in his office – The Pantocrator. Other portraits in all his homes. And this interview was only going to polish his lustre. Show him as one of the gods on Mount Olympus.

'So – I want to talk a little about how you got started,' said Dominic. 'Your first company. We'll talk about Ogmios, of course. Then how you expanded from there. Your inside tips on how to get rich. A little about your home background, growing up in England . . .'

'Bore-ring.'

'We'll skate over it. But the fact is – there aren't that many English tech moguls out there.'

'There's Tim Berners-Lee. We'd none of us be here without him.'

'But he gave it all away for free.'

Julian leaned in close to Dominic. Conspiratorial. 'What a fucking idiot.'

They laughed.

'But I mainly want to talk about *now*,' said Dominic. 'What you *do*, what you *are*, how you *live*. As you know, my show's about lifestyles not life histories.'

'Always look ahead, Dom. Never look back.'

'Right. That's the sort of stuff we want. You could talk about how you move around all the time. Your different homes – thanks for the clips you shared of your American house and The Lodge in South Africa, by the way. And, ideally, we'd love to do a second day of filming – I know you've said no – but just to pick you up doing all the cool things you do. Jet skiing, out on the yacht, playing tennis, of course.'

'You can't film the girls playing. It'll disrupt their training programme. And their privacy is sacrosanct. Rather you didn't film them at all, actually.'

'Of course. This is about you. But we're gonna talk a bit about The Team, yeah? I mean, it's such a big deal for you.'

'Sure.'

'Swimming.'

'Come again?'

'Do you do lengths? You obviously work out. I'm very envious, Julian.'

'I'm not obsessive about it. You know. What about you?'

'Not really. I jog now and then, is all. Listen. We've brought a drone. Be great to get some aerial footage. Really sell this place. You know, the classic helicopter shots.'

Julian looked over to where a junior member of the crew was unpacking a drone from a flight case.

'Maybe. But you'd have to stick to very tight guidelines. As I say – privacy is sacrosanct.'

'Yeah. Of course. You can see everything we shoot, vet it all.'

'I'm sure we can work something out.'

Show willing. Be affable. Accommodating. He'd get Ray to sit with them while they filmed with their drone. Didn't want them shooting anything they shouldn't. Wouldn't let them stray from the public areas. Security here was tighter than an elephant's cock-ring. Keep it all wide – light and sunny and lovely – no dark places. This interview was going to be good for him. Show him for what he was. A *good* guy. But his lawyers were still going to crawl all over this little puff-piece like flies.

Dominic's producer/director, Ali Jensen, an efficient Australian dyke with big legs and short hair, was in with Tokyo Masombuka right now. And Tokyo could be absolutely terrifying when he needed. He'd be hitting Ali with all sorts of apocalyptic warnings and arcane documents to sign that she hadn't been expecting. Take it or leave it, darling. You want to film today, you sign here ... here ... here ...

And here.

In fact, there was Ali now, coming out of the house with Miss Lily. She'd have just learned, among other things, that Miss Lily would be sitting by her side watching proceedings like a shark.

Ali looked a little shell-shocked. She sat down carefully in a folding chair under a big umbrella and stared at a small monitor, while Miss Lily settled in beside her and got out her own video camera.

The Nice Young Girl With The Clipboard – every film shoot had one – invited Julian and Dominic over to where the cameras had been set up facing a couple of chairs on the shaded part of the terrace. Dominic had the standard crew. Honestly, if you'd asked Julian in advance to describe them, he'd have been pretty much spot on. He knew about these things. As well as Eager Clipboard Girl, there was Nondescript Soundman, sat by the trolley that held his gear, wearing headphones. Older than the others. Steel-framed glasses. Not the most stylish dresser on the planet. Comfortable would best describe his look. He even had on a pair of green Crocs. The type of guy you forget as soon as they've gone. Apart from those fucking Crocs. The main lighting cameraman – Top

Gun – was fussing about with his lights, looking important. Macho black cargo pants. Boots. Black T-shirt.

Sidekick – the second cameraman – looked like a local. Functional. T-shirt and jeans. Very much second fiddle. Did what he was told. Modern digital cameras were so cheap and portable now they could afford as many as they wanted, but it was expensive to fly too many crewmembers around the world. Made sense to pick up locals for the dogsbody stuff. His camera was set up to do an oblique two shot. It'd be pretty much locked off, the guy just had to keep Julian in focus if he moved around in his chair.

The third camera guy had a cheap, handheld thing. Was filming all that jerky handheld stuff, fidgety, flitting around, getting texture. Crash zooms. Close-ups on hands and feet, an ear, a dog wandering into shot in the background, all that sort of 'edgy' shit. He was the Required Hipster of the crew. Loud, short-sleeved shirt with a pattern of lizards on it, baggy shorts, trainers with no socks. They were going to stink later. It was illegal for a TV crew to work without a hipster these days. He had the standard beard, heavy black plastic-framed glasses. Michael Caine glasses. They were coming back in a big way. Why advertise the fact that you couldn't see? Might as well wear a T-shirt saying, 'I'M A LOSER'. Mind you, some of them *did*. Fucking irony. Hepworth used not to have the greatest eyesight, but laser surgery had fixed that. Like he'd fixed his teeth and his slightly beaky nose.

Hipster had started filming almost as soon as they'd come through the gates. Ray had shut him down sharpish until he'd laid down the rules – where they could and couldn't go, what they could and couldn't film. They were to stick together, and nobody was to wander off out of sight of the rest of The Team unless accompanied by a member of staff.

Hipster was also their drone guy and Ray was talking to him about it, asserting his authority. Drones were everywhere now. Helicopter shots used to be insanely expensive to pull off; the appearance of one in your production told the world that you had money, that this was a prestigious film. Now you just sent up a drone and that was that.

Ray finished with Hipster, who came over and filmed Julian as Nondescript Soundman fitted a radio mike and battery pack on to him. Typical of Dominic's style. The behind-the-scenes/making-of stuff incorporated into the main documentary. Short-attention-span TV.

'Is it all right to lose the jumper?' Sound Guy asked. 'It'll interfere with the radio mike.'

'No problem.' Julian took off the jumper and held it out until Miguel came and took it away. He sat down.

'All set?' asked Dominic, settling into the other chair.

Julian switched on his thousand-kilowatt smile. 'Let's do this.'

25

PIKE

The Piaggio Beverly 300 was making the noise you heard everywhere in Greece – the farty, rasping, lawnmower-whine of low-powered motorbikes, mopeds and scooters. Next to the cicadas it was the most evocative sound of the islands. Whenever you heard it on the streets of London or Paris you were instantly transported back to a summer holiday in the Aegean. Pike hadn't ridden a scooter like this in a long while. Had to admit it was fun. Especially with Sarah riding pillion and holding tight around his waist. They were young again. A couple of teenagers.

A group of actual young people on scooters appeared, coming the other way, and Pike felt his age. The illusion of youth shattered. There were maybe six of them, taking up the whole road, weaving all over the place. They passed Pike and Sarah on both sides, laughing. Careless and carefree. Some not even bothering with helmets, as if they were untouchable. One wore a plum-coloured bucket hat. Stuck his tongue out, heavy metal-style, as he passed, leered at Sarah.

Pike couldn't be angry. They reminded him of the days when he really *had* been young. The first bike he'd ever rented was on Ibiza towards the end of the seventies. A Honda C70. He could vividly recall roaring – well, *buzzing* – in a very similar pack along the coast road with the lads. Fuelled by amphetamines and dope. The full cliché – open road, sun on his face, wind in his hair. Nobody wore helmets back then. Or any kind of protective clothing. Just tiny shorts and flip flops. Tank tops. It was a few years before Ibiza became the world centre of clubbing. Back then the place had been a cheap, funky mix of weirdos, hippies, drifters, up-for-it lads and arty types. The clubs, like Ku, Amnesia, Es Paradis and Pacha played mostly disco. Pike and his mates had spent a week there, getting wasted, sleeping on the beach, trying to shag every girl they met.

Dennis 'the Menace' Pike, Chrissie Boyd, Colin Shakespeare, Mick Beadle, Chemical Al ... Most of them were dead now. Chemical Al had gone first. Didn't exactly go out in a blaze of glory. Went nuts in the early eighties. Wound up in a mental hospital. Managed to top himself. Inevitable, really. He'd lived his life with more drugs in him than Boots.

Mick was killed in a small-time gangbang thing in Miami in the nineties, trying to live the Hollywood dream, become the next Scarface. Chrissie became a landlord, lost his pub through drink and then lost his life the same way. Colin got the bike bug – and a job in the City. Bigger and bigger bikes and then – a lorry drives over him.

Then later, Patterson and Chas Bishop and the others ...

But that was all a long time ago.

It was funny the different lives he'd led. Thinking about it was like watching different films. *A season of British cinema*. Like you used to get on the BBC back in the day. Maybe kick off with a coming-of-age film from the seventies. Cheaply shot, grey and gritty, with odd splashes of colour here and there. Ken Loach, maybe. *Scum. Bronco Bullfrog. Quadrophenia*, maybe. Then, when Patterson came down from Scotland and tried to mould them into a proper gang, it was more like one of those British gangster

217

films. Grim and nasty with flashes of glamour. That film would have a *Long Good Friday* vibe, *Brighton Rock*, *No Orchids for Miss Blandish*, *Get Carter*, or Guy Ritchie before his time. Patterson had big plans, had set up 'The Business'. They even had their own printed cards – 'The Business. For all office cleaning'. It'd been a doomed venture and the only one who'd profited from it had been Patterson.

Then, to cover Pike's loner years, after it all went tits up, you'd have to watch something more dismal and arty. With a title like *It Always Rains on Sunday*. Something black and white from the sixties with a melancholy jazz soundtrack. Hiding from the world. And then it was *Sexy Beast* time ... Noel and Chas Bishop turning up out of the past and dragging him back into the life. But at least one good thing came out of that time. Meeting Sarah. Late-flowering love like *Shirley Valentine*. Yeah. That was more classic British romcom territory. Although, not so much of the com, when it came down to it. More bittersweet. Could have ended up as *Brief Encounter*. But he'd persevered. She'd been a single mum, with a ten-year-old boy. Darren. Darren who worked for a TV station in Dubai now and had kids of his own. Shit, it was all so long ago.

And for a while it became a family film – first bringing up Darren, and soon there was Jessica. Even Jessica was grown up now. In her twenties. Maybe that one was a Mike Leigh, or another Ken Loach. Not much money, setting off from a difficult start. But they *had* had a laugh – they'd got through it. Were there any happy films about families? It had all felt quite small-scale, domestic, quiet after what had gone before. More like a TV show than a film. And all the better for it.

And now look at them.

Two old people on a scooter.

What was this? *Best Exotic Marigold Hotel*? *Quartet*? That Michael Caine film about a pensioner going full Rambo and cleaning up crime on his local estate? *Harry Brown*. That was it.

He turned to shout over his shoulder to Sarah.

'Check the signal again. Make sure the car hasn't moved.'

She slipped his phone out of his jacket pocket and looked at it.

'Still just sitting there.'

When Aimee had called Macintyre to tell him the news that Ioannis's Yeti had been stolen, he'd been busy, so he'd called Pike.

'Check it out, Dennis. Let's be thorough.'

Always thorough. The magnetic, nano GPS tracking device that Aimee had attached under the Yeti was communicating with an app Pike had downloaded on to his phone, so that they knew exactly where the Yeti was. Right now, it was parked just outside a little town called Karousades in the north-west of the island, near Sidari.

'This could all be just a massive waste of time,' Sarah shouted, slipping the phone back into his jacket.

'Who cares?' said Pike. 'I'm enjoying this.'

They passed a strip development, then a café next to an open-fronted shop with a colourful display of fruit and vegetables and gaudy plastic things for the beach. Now the road straightened out, widened. Pike put on some speed. Sarah yelled.

'Yeah!'

'Don't pretend you're not enjoying this,' Pike called to her.

They'd rented the scooter in Kassiopi. Had had a bit of an argument about who was going to ride pillion. In the end Pike had won. He'd ride it there, and Sarah would ride it back. He'd been a bit shaky at first, much to Sarah's scornful amusement. But he'd grown more confident as they'd got away from the town, and now, spurred on by Sarah, he was picking up speed. She whooped semi-ironically whenever they overtook someone or hit a bump or sped up into a bend.

The scooter handled well and while it was no hog it was a fun ride and had a bit of poke. The road along the north of the island wasn't too busy and mostly wound through open countryside, following the contour of the coast. The sea was off to their right, tree-covered hills to their left – scrubby kermes oaks, cypress, juniper and myrtle. Clumps of Spanish cane by the roadside.

They passed the hand-painted sign for the taverna in Old Perithia, up on the side of Pantokrator, and headed on towards Sidari. In less than half an hour they were turning off the main road towards Karousades. There wasn't much to the town. The usual little supermarket and café, an Orthodox church. No spire. Like a large chapel. Its walls that familiar, pale-yellow stucco. Many of the houses in the town were painted the same colour. Others were the deep red so typical of Greece.

The streets narrowed, the noise of the Piaggio echoing off the walls on either side. There were a few old women out and about. Old men sitting at a table drinking. A dog barked at the scooter half-heartedly. As they came to the end of the town, they turned right on to what looked like a country lane.

The Skoda was parked a little further along, next to a high, grassy bank where agaves and yucca grew. It was just up the road from a single-storey building with a blue and white Greek flag hanging limply outside.

On closer inspection the building turned out to be a police station. There were no squad cars around and the place looked empty. Sleeping in the afternoon sun. Pike cruised slowly past, then pulled into a small dirt car park just beyond. He stopped the bike, kicked down the stand and they took off their helmets.

The car park overlooked a valley filled with olive trees, a dusty haze hanging in the air.

'What do you reckon?' said Sarah, getting off the bike and stretching. 'Did the police pick it up? Has it been impounded?'

'Doesn't feel right,' said Pike. 'This is a one-horse operation in a one-dog town. Just a local substation. If the car had been impounded for some reason, they'd surely have taken it to the main station in Corfu Town.'

'In that case,' said Sarah, 'if I had to take a guess, I'd say whoever left it here wants it found by the cops.'

Pike looked up and down the road. 'I'd have to agree.'

'Do you think it was the Albanians? Is this part of their turf war?"

'They do tend to get the blame for everything,' said Pike. 'But in this case, they're the most obvious suspects. This is their way of getting back at Ioannis. Maybe I shouldn't have hit them so hard.'

'It seemed reasonable at the time,' said Sarah. 'I think we'd got about as far as we could with polite conversation. Come on. We should take a closer look.'

They got back on the bike and buzzed back up the road to the car. First thing they spotted was a pile of small cardboard boxes in the boot. One of them was open, and they could see orange plastic pill bottles. A few more bottles and some loose pills had been scattered around. It all looked very deliberate.

What it meant, exactly, Pike and Sarah couldn't decide, but Pike felt responsible. Wanted to get the car back for Ioannis.

'So, I guess *we* steal it now.'

They'd picked all the tools they needed in a hardware store on the outskirts of Kassiopi. But to get into the car, all Pike needed was his phone.

Always thorough. Macintyre had told Aimee that when she fixed the tracker to the car, she should go the extra mile and clone Ioannis's key. She'd used an RFID amplifier to copy the signal from Ioannis's key through his front door. Relayed the data to a laptop and then uploaded it to Pike's phone. Pike opened another app and – pop.

Pike looked up and down the road – quiet as death in the heat – opened the driver's door and got in with his backpack. The Yeti had an old-fashioned key ignition rather than a push-button starter, so the phone wouldn't actually get the engine going. He'd have to do the next part the old-fashioned way. Old school. Low tech. He took out a screwdriver, jammed it into the ignition and then knocked it home with a hammer. He smiled with satisfaction. This was getting to be a very nostalgic day. He was right back in east London, 'Taking Without Owner's Consent'. Twocking. The simple screwdriver in the ignition trick had worked most of the time in those days, otherwise it meant removing the steering wheel cover and then cutting and reconnecting a couple of wires. It'd been a whole lot of fun. He'd felt in control. Could run rings round the Old Bill. Invincible. Joyriding through Hackney, Whitechapel, Dalston, Stokey, Clapton, down to Hackney Marshes, the Lea Valley, up round Victoria Park, then leaving the car on a rival estate and torching it.

He didn't feel half so invincible now. He was stiff and rickety after the ride, and the heat was getting to him. Plus, he was so much more aware of just what a massive pain in the arse it must have been for all the poor car owners whose days he'd ruined. Ah. He was getting old.

Next problem was the steering lock. There were two ways to go. One was to jam the screwdriver in behind the steering wheel and snap the lock. The other was simpler and quicker and would cause less damage to the car – if it worked. He opened the door. Stepped out. Yanked down as hard as he could on the steering wheel, anti-clockwise and felt the lock give way. He smiled at Sarah.

'Still got it.'

'You're a hooligan, Pike. Always have been.'

'That's why you love me so.'

'You gonna drive it, then?'

'I know you've been itching to ride that scooter.'

'Yeah. But go easy, Pike. You always were a shit driver.'

'Another reason I won your undying love and devotion.'

'Screw you. I'll take the bike back to the hire place in Kassiopi. Meet me there, yeah?'

'OK. Maybe we should swap phones just in case. Mine's got

the tracker signal for the Yeti on it. In case anything goes wrong, you'll know where I am.'

'In a ditch probably, or endlessly trying to do a three-point turn up some dead-end street.'

'Ha-ha. Just wait 'til I get the engine started.' He put his phone close to the ignition, activated the app and twisted the screwdriver. The Yeti started first time and he left it idling.

Sarah swapped phones with him, kissed him and got back on the scooter. Pulled away whooping and beeping the tinny horn. He watched her go, grinning. She looked like a teenager. And he felt like one again. They were like two kids misbehaving.

He drove down to the car park, did a quick circle and then stopped. Waiting to let a car go by before he pulled out. A big black Mercedes coming from the direction of Karousades that looked out of place on these country roads. As it drew level, the driver glanced at him. He looked startled, eyes and mouth wide. An expression that quickly changed to anger.

It was Arven – Abbott – who Pike had last seen floundering in the harbour at Agios Symeon. And he was pretty sure that the guy in the passenger seat next to him was Costello. There was a third guy in the back, who also eyeballed him. Not anyone Pike knew.

Not anyone Pike wanted to get to know. It looked like the bloody Albanians had returned to check whether the police had picked the car up yet. Whatever the case, it wasn't something Pike wanted to get into a conversation about.

The Merc carried on down the road and pulled into a driveway. Probably planning to turn round. Pike didn't wait to find out. He gunned the engine and skidded out on to the road sending up a shower of loose stones and grit.

Things had taken a definite turn for the worse.

26

MACINTYRE

Macintyre adjusted the focus on his minicam and scratched his hipster beard. Hoping the sun wasn't melting the glue. Seemed to be holding up OK. Hot, though, and itchy. Did he really need it? Ray Jordan hadn't given him a second glance as he'd explained the security situation when they'd arrived. Had been more interested in checking out the equipment and showing how important he was. Rattling off a string of rules and regs. Macintyre had started filming almost as soon as his feet hit the ground. Knew that would rile Ray. Distract the big idiot from actually looking at him. A classic piece of misdirection.

He looked at the tiny screen on the back of his camera. It was a pleasure watching Dominic in action. Funny how his victims never felt it when he quietly slipped his knife into them. He chose his interviewees well. Went for narcissists and sociopaths with zero self-awareness. People, and they were usually men, who had no idea how they came across to other people. Who were so far up themselves they could see nothing but their own sweet-smelling shit. Dominic had once told Macintyre how he'd learned the trick early on that he didn't really need to say anything; in fact, the less he said the better. The work was all done before he got there – you simply had to choose the right person. Pick the right questions. Scatter his shiny marbles on the floor and let the cockwombles slip and fall. He never needed to add anything after the interview. He just let them rabbit on. Stayed quiet so that they filled in all the silences. Nobody liked an awkward silence. Held up a mirror for the interviewees to admire themselves in, dazzled by their own marvellousness. And afterwards, when the interview dropped, because it was all their own words, the arseholes were happy to see themselves on-screen, happy to hear their pearls of wisdom, happy to think that everyone watching believed that they were as fantastic, clever, witty and gorgeous as they believed themselves to be.

Dominic – never 'Dom' – simply edited out the boring stuff and peppered the interviews with telling details he'd shoot during the day, added without comment. It didn't take long for most of his interviewees to start coming out with the sort of jaw-dropping bollocks that his viewers loved. If they clammed up, said nothing stupid, then the interview was never aired.

The TV show was not universally loved. Some people didn't get it. You can entertain some of the people all the time, you can entertain all of the people some of the time, but you can't waste your time trying to keep *all* of the idiots out there happy.

The type of morons on social media who thought they knew best how the world worked.

'Why do you give those obnoxious dickwads so much airtime and free publicity?'

'I hate to see you sucking up to these rich bastards.'

'Your as big a jerk as the people you so-called interview.'

There were even a few humourless TV critics and social pundits who couldn't see what he was doing. Dominic didn't respond to any of them. *Never apologise, never explain.* Which, of course, just made the idiots madder.

Hepworth was one of the smarter ones. He was doing OK so far. Hadn't said anything too outrageous. Was trying really hard to be bland and uncontroversial. Normal. Which just made him seem weird. And he was oozing vanity. It was hard to concentrate on what he was saying because he was so unnatural looking. Like a 3D simulation of a person in a computer game. His perfect, pristine clothes still creased from where they'd been folded in the box they were delivered in. There he sat, with his too-tight T-shirt tucked into his high-waisted trousers. His glossy, golden hair. His flawless, evenly tanned skin. His teeth so blindingly white Macintyre had had to check his camera was set up correctly. It was like looking at someone on a knackered TV, skin tone too orange, teeth too white, hair too yellow. It was a shame Hepworth had had to lose his preposterous pink sweater. But Dominic had made sure he'd taken lots of footage of him with it draped over his shoulders before they'd started the interview.

Right now, Hepworth was off on one about Theodore Roosevelt and security and his bland veneer was starting to crack.

'Roosevelt – the macho one, the bruiser, not the moonbat wimp in the wheelchair – famously said "Tread softly and carry a big stick".'

Nope. Wasn't what he'd said. He'd said *speak* softly and carry a big stick, and it was to do with diplomacy, not guarding your property. But Dominic wasn't going to correct him. Despite the fact that several of his previous interviewees had quoted – or misquoted – Teddy Roosevelt's zinger. It was the doctrine of the hard man. Il Duce. The functioning psychopath.

'Well, I've updated his philosophy.' Hepworth was smiling – look at me, sharing my awesome words of wisdom. 'I say, "creep around a lot and carry an RPG".'

Hepworth laughed. Dominic nodded and smiled, sharing the joke. Said nothing, though. Left it hanging. Macintyre knew what he was thinking – *give me more, baby* . . .

He swung his camera away from Hepworth, zoomed in on the building, looking for security cameras, listening to the interview in his headphones. He was getting good footage. Useful stuff. Once he put it all together with what they'd get from the drone he could build a good picture of the layout here. The drone was a marvel. Latest generation. Had a load of extra spyware on it as well as two different cameras.

He caught a movement and swung his view back to the terrace. Kept filming. That was the beauty of digital. You could film for ever. A girl had come out of the house to check out what was going on. She was carrying a small white chihuahua.

'You're in my shot, babe,' said Hepworth, half joking, but with an edge.

'Whoops!' Doing a sort of Marilyn Monroe 'silly little me' thing. She was late twenties, wearing a T-shirt that said 'Die Another Day' and a cowboy hat in rainbow colours. No doubt about it. This could only be Philippa Pennington-Bausch-Hohenlohe von Crantz. The famous Pixie. Born in Luxembourg. Father a minor aristocrat, mother from an English upper-class family distantly related to the queen. A model in Paris before she was sixteen. Married a superstar American DJ at eighteen. Rehab at twenty. Widowed at twenty-one. Met Hepworth soon after. Rarely out of the magazines and sidebars.

Unreal.

Mac didn't want to objectify her, but it was hard work – she'd objectified herself. Turned herself into a living doll. Unreal. If this was how she looked before she added all those layers of filters and effects to her Instagram posts he understood why she had so many followers. He wondered if there was some kind of secret, locked, Dorian Gray-style Instagram account out there where in all the photos she looked rough and haggard, because in real life she was breathtaking. An all-over, even, creamy-coffee tan. Her skin unblemished. Long limbs, short shorts, flip flops . . .

She even managed to make flip flops look sexy and elegant. She threw out a girlish smile and sauntered off.

'I'm going for a swim, baby.' She had an Anglo-European-American accent that marked her as a princess of the world.

'Cool.' Hepworth gave a half-wave. 'I'll catch you when I'm done here.'

Hepworth was basking in the effect she had. That was *his girl*. Not yours. Mac knew that every man here – apart from Hepworth, who'd turned away – was surreptitiously sneaking a look at her behind. Mac deliberately swung his digicam away, back to picking out security cameras. What must it be like to be born that way, he wondered? And it was pure, blind luck. We have very little say in what we look like, when it comes down to it. To know all your life that everyone – male and female – was looking at you in dumbstruck awe.

You'd have to be a very special kind of person to not get fucked up by that.

27

PIKE

Pike was forced to slow down as he negotiated the narrow streets of Karousades, anxiously checking his rear-view mirror every few seconds. So far, no sign of the Merc. And now, as the road opened up, he risked putting on a bit more speed. He couldn't overdo it, though. Couldn't risk being stopped. He was in a stolen car with a screwdriver for a key and a boot full of what looked like designer drugs.

As he drove, he weighed his options. He could stick to the plan and head back to Kassiopi. He could bypass Kassiopi and head straight to Agios Symeon, staying on the busier roads where he'd be less vulnerable to attack. Or he could try to get off the road somewhere and hide . . .

First thing. He needed to warn Sarah. He fumbled her phone out of his pocket and into his lap. Woke it up. Realised he was going to have to enter her passcode. It had seemed like a good idea exchanging phones. Now he wasn't so sure, but at least she could track him. Find his bullet-riddled body by the side of the road . . .

Shit. What was her passcode? Sarah was very security conscious and was always changing it. Nothing as simple as date of birth for her. Under stress the brain can go either way. It can panic and lock down, or it can suddenly and miraculously open up as if a light was being shone into your head . . .

Hallelujah!

Literally. He remembered her telling him about it the other night. Psalm 104, verse 35 was the first appearance of the phrase Hallelu Jah in the Old Testament. She'd told him it would make a cool passcode. She'd just stuck an extra 1 on the end so there were enough digits. It was 104351.

Sarah loved cryptic games like that. She'd once had 737263, which was what you got if you typed the word 'sesame' on a numeric keypad. But she'd changed that one – worried it was too easy to guess.

Yeah, right.

Keeping half an eye on the road he slowed down and keyed in 104351. The phone came awake.

Hallelujah, indeed.

'Hey Siri . . .'

'How can I help you . . . ?'

And then he saw a black shape coming up fast in the rear-view mirror.

Shit . . . The Mercedes was close enough for Pike to make out the faces of Abbott and Costello. They did not look best pleased.

'Hey Siri,' he yelled. 'Send a text.'

'Who do you want me to send it to?'

'Send it to Sarah . . . no – fuck it! – scrap that . . . Jesus. Hey Siri . . .'

'What do you want me to do?'

'Send a text to Dennis Pike.'

'What would you like it to say?'

'Big problem. Change of plan. Abbott and Costello following me. Track the car but be careful . . . *Send.*'

As soon as he sent it, he regretted it. Now he'd drawn Sarah into this mess. They were going to end up like Bonnie and

Clyde if they weren't careful. Both of them riddled with bullets. Roll credits.

As he headed back along the north shore, he managed to keep just ahead of the Mercedes but was having to edge steadily faster. The four-wheel drive would have the advantage over bad roads, but on more major roads like this he was fucked.

He overtook a lorry carrying terracotta roof tiles. Saw the Mercedes swing round it, narrowly missing a car going the other way. This was ridiculous. It was turning into a fucking car chase. His hope that he'd be safer on a road where there was more traffic and people seemed an empty one. The Albanians were reckless. And he was still at the disadvantage of being totally illegal in a car that was full of weird shit.

Then he saw the sign for Old Perithia and made a snap decision. The Yeti would easily outperform the Merc on the twisting, switchback, hill roads, which were pretty basic, in some places almost a dirt track. If he could get away from the Albanians and pull far enough ahead it might buy him enough time to figure out a plan.

He pulled a hard right and skidded off the road, nearly losing control. A few hairy twists and turns later and he was on the steep road winding up the side of Pantokrator. It was only when he was some way up the road that it struck him. One way up – one way down.

Yeah. Good work, Pike. Another stupid decision. It was essentially a dead end.

28

MACINTYRE

'You were talking before about how important security was, Julian, but you all seem very relaxed here.'

'That's because my team are second to none. They work very hard behind the scenes to make this all look effortless. It takes hard graft and a shitload of cash to create this fantasy, Dom. This playground. Which *everyone* wants. This – call it what you like – Shangri-La, Nirvana, Seventh Heaven ... the Dog's Bollocks! Ha-ha-ha.'

'It just seems all so perfect. *And* you. You seem almost *too* perfect.'

'We all have our flaws, Dom.'

'Not *you*. You're regularly featured in top ten lists of the world's most desirable men.'

'Oh, you're making me blush, now. Are you coming on to me?'

'Ha-ha-ha.'

'Ha-ha-ha. I mean, let's not get carried away, Dom – all I've got is looks and money. Ha-ha-ha.'

'Ha-ha-ha. Yes. And when it comes to the world's hottest *tech* billionaires ... You hit the number one spot every time.'

'Yeah, well, come on, it isn't hard, when you look at the competition. Musk, Gates, Zuckerberg, Bezos, the Larries ...'

'The Larries?'

'Larry Ellison and Larry "Bugs Bunny" Page. Jesus, that guy is all teeth. Sergei Brin. Ma Huateng . . . He might be a Crazy Rich Asian but he's never going to be asked to join a K-Pop band, is he? And – holy cow – Jack Ma! Tech guys tend not to be hot. I mean, Jesus, if you're young and have the looks, why waste your time learning coding?'

'Have you ever made it to the number one slot in the *general* billionaires' chart?'

'Always just missed out, Dom.'

'So, you're not the world's hottest billionaire?'

'No. There's that Norwegian stud, Gustav Magnar Witzoe. He regularly beats me. But his wealth is inherited. From fish farming. Who wants to be a *fish* billionaire? Same with the young Braun guy, Ludwig. Family money.'

'And not a techie.'

'Not an anything. Now, Steve Jobs. He was presentable. Had a certain style. At least when he was older. Tell you the truth, I've stolen quite a lot from him – the black turtleneck, jeans and trainers look always works. You wanna know the trick?'

'Go on.'

'The trick with jeans is that they should look like every other pair of jeans on the planet but cost ten times as much.'

'I'll remember that.'

'You'll have to if you ever want to get into the billionaires' club.'

'But even Steve Jobs. He was more the thinking woman's crush,' said Dominic. 'The intense, intellectual type. He was no beefcake.'

'True that. Jobs was more of a geek god, than a Greek god – like me! Ha-ha-ha.'

'Ha-ha-ha.'

Hepworth liked that line. Macintyre, who'd researched the fucker extensively, had seen it quoted in several interviews.

Macintyre looked over at Ali, Dom's producer, staring intently at her monitor, making notes in a pad. A small sixty-something Asian woman was breathing down her neck. Weird 1950s school-girl hairstyle. Severe glasses. Expressionless. Hadn't even so much as cracked a smile since she came out. She looked like one of those people who had zero sense of humour.

She was scarier than Ray. That was for sure.

'You're not the usual tech head on any level, are you, Julian?'

'No. I am not.'

'I love the name you use for your parent company – HepKat.'

'Cool, isn't it?'

'Did you ever consider going with something a bit more *sciencey* sounding? More digital? Like, I dunno, Microsoft, or IBM – INTEL – something like that? Or even one of those meaningless "*international*" names, like Consignia, or Aviva? Something more corporate?'

'Apple.'

'Sorry?'

'Apple doesn't fit either of your categories.'

'Yeah. Maybe.'

'You don't need to give a tech company a tech name. Everyone knows it's tech. Think about it, Dom, *everything* these days is tech. It's taken as read. Our *world* is *tech*. But people don't think of it as that, they just think – that's how things are. It's the way things work. When someone uses a tablet, they don't think, "Wow, look at me! I'm using tech!" Well, some wankers do. Ha-ha.'

'Ha-ha.'

'Most people just think, "I'm playing Minecraft", or "I'm checking my mail, or the weather, I'm doing my accounts, I'm watching a movie, I'm drawing, I'm writing..." Tech has become part of who we are, the boundaries between bio and digital, between flesh and circuitry, are blurring, disappearing. Tech is now an extension of our bodies. You look at a little kid with a tablet, they can tap and touch and swipe and pinch and click before they can read and write, before they can talk. You give them a book – they don't know what to do with it. You see them angrily swiping the pages.'

He mimed a pissed-off toddler with a paperback. Laughed – 'Ha-ha.'

'Ha-ha.'

'When that kid is interacting with their tablet, though, they're interacting with the world. And they don't think about it. Just like you and I – we don't think about talking. We just do it. Talking is the earliest technology humans used . . . '

Macintyre had first worked with Dominic five years ago. Back in the days when he was just another security consultant and Dominic was an eager, but inexperienced, and, to be honest, totally reckless, young reporter for Vice. Crashing around major danger zones and reporting back from the heart of darkness.

He'd approached Macintyre to ask if he could get him access to a renegade Ukrainian general.

He could and he did. That had been the interview that really put Dominic on the map. Particularly the scene where the two of them had got pant-shittingly drunk and shot the general's Lexus to pieces with a Kord 12mm heavy machine gun.

Dominic had used Macintyre a few times since. And had always returned the favours. Like getting him access and inside info on an American evangelist/cult leader, and a Thai casino owner/human trafficker. Now they were both in a position to mutually help each other. Hepworth wasn't to know it, but it was Macintyre who'd brokered the deal for this interview.

This was very much an information-gathering exercise for Macintyre, who hated to go blind into anywhere. He needed to know about security. Such as the double entry-gate system with the no man's land airlocked between them. Like the dead zone between the US and East German borders in Berlin during the Cold War. The cameras. The staff. The access. The pathways.

When the time came to get Lauren out, he wanted to know his way around the place.

And he'd wanted to get a close-up look at Hepworth. That was important.

Know your enemy . . .

'When they're using computers, or cell phones, tablets, laptops, I don't know, calculators, people don't think of it as some sort of weird, fancy, future, sci-fi interface with technology. They think of it the same way our ancestors interacted with a spade, or a knife, a hammer. An extension of their own bodies. A tool that was just – *in the tool shed*. The very idea of "tech" feels old-fashioned. We're over it.

'You know what I'm saying, Dom. When you drive your car, d'you think about what you're doing with the front part of your brain? No. You can talk, and listen to the radio, think about sex, make a hands-free call, and you're not even aware that you're driving. The car becomes an extension of your brain, a part of your body. So, when you name a company you don't have to bang on about the tech side of things. It's taken as read. *All* modern companies are tech companies, you can call them what you like. Tech is at the heart of everything anyone does these days. It's at the heart of everything I do. It's what I do.'

'That and tennis.'

'Even the tennis, Dom. We've gone beyond just physical training. I'm developing a system, The Hepworth Technique. That's as much why I do it as winning trophies.'

'The girls are your guinea pigs.'

'*You* can put it that way. *I* don't.'

'How do you respond to criticism that you bring the girls into your team more for how they look than how they play?'

Macintyre glanced over at Miss Lily. Her eyes had narrowed, but Hepworth didn't miss a beat.

'They're all world-class athletes, Dom. Top tennis players.'

236

'You haven't *actually won* any trophies, though.'

'We *have*, actually. And when my method is fully developed – nothing will be able to stop us.'

Macintyre liked that. Hepworth had just flat-out lied. He *hadn't* won any trophies. All he had to do was lie and move on. No more questions. No discussion. Shut it down. Dominic hadn't picked him up on it, but he'd have spotted it. He'd come back.

'Tim Cook wants Apple to run our lives, Musk wants to go to the moon, Gates wants to cure every disease on the planet ... And you want to teach young girls to play tennis.'

'I'm interested in sport, Dom, because I'm interested in the human body. I'm interested in how technology can take the human body to the next level.'

'Sounds like you're working on a new vibrator.'

'Ha-ha.'

'Ha-ha. Seriously, though, Julian. Are you talking about bionics, implants?'

'We're exploiting every possibility. Drugs are banned in sport. Rightly so. But we're working on ways to use technology to enhance the sport brain. The winning brain. If you have two sportsmen of equal ability, it'll be the one with the superior psychology that wins the match. The winner will be the one who wants to win most. We work on the girls so that they want to win above all else.'

'This is what you're developing at your secretive Institute? At BIF?'

'My "*Secretive Institute*"? You say that as if there's something clandestine going on up there, something dark and dangerous. All research centres are secretive. Because of the immense value of what might come out of them.'

'So, are we looking at a kind of William Gibson, cyber punk future? Inputting data directly into our heads? Like *The Matrix*?'

'Of course we are. We can't have all future technology based around ... *typing*!'

'And how close *are* you? To brain implants?'

'It's a secret. Ha-ha-ha...'

'Ha-ha-ha...'

'A secret kept in our *Secretive Research Institute*. But when it happens, you'll be the first to hear about it, Dom. You can be our first client. I will input my data directly into your squirming, pink brain...'

29

PIKE

He'd have to get far enough ahead of the Albanians to get off the road, hide the car, wait for them to pass him and then sneak back down without them spotting him. Too many variables in that plan, too much risk involved, but it was the only one he had. The worst outcome would be not finding anywhere to get safely hidden and ending up driving all the way to the top. He'd be trapped in Perithia where there would very likely be nobody around at this time of day. He should have stayed out in the open and confronted the Albanians in Kassiopi. He couldn't believe they'd risk open violence in a busy town centre. But he didn't know enough about these guys to be certain.

And *there* was the fucking Merc, moving up close behind him again. Not struggling at all on the road. Sarah was right. He wasn't a great driver. Didn't do it often enough. And he was certainly no rally driver. He was 'Old Pike', slow and careful, too aware of all the risks involved. The guy driving the other car was 'Teenage Pike', convinced of his own immortality, no sense of risk, laughing at danger, ha-ha-ha, getting high on the sheer joy of driving way too fast.

Shit, shite and derision. You're a fool, old man. You've made a

239

series of dumb choices. Not least of which was telling Sarah to keep track of him. She was perfectly capable of looking after herself, but he didn't want to drag her any deeper into this stupid mess.

The road had quickly deteriorated into a single, winding lane, some of which was tarmacked, other parts appearing to be just bare concrete. The going was mostly open but there were pockets of greenery around the few stone farmhouses they passed along the way. High walls round their property. Dusty trees overhanging the road.

The bends were getting sharper. He pulled round one too fast and nearly lost control, fighting to keep the car in line, cursing and skidding. He was now climbing up an even steeper stretch, the land falling away to his left. A clear view down to the sea and over to Albania. The Yeti gripped the road well and Pike risked putting on some more speed. He had to get away from his pursuers. He was sweating. His hands painful where he was gripping the wheel too tight. It was a good year since he'd last driven at all and the Mercedes wasn't struggling nearly as much as he'd hoped. He had to concede that Arven was a better driver than him. Probably loved boy-racing around the island, scaring the girls and pissing off the locals.

The other guys probably hadn't thought through how this was going to end, either. They were all committed now, though. Like a cat automatically going after anything that moved, they'd started this ridiculous chase and there was no way of it stopping without something drastically violent happening. And like a kid with a piece of string teasing a cat, Pike had encouraged them to keep after him. He kept expecting to see Costello leaning out of his window and taking potshots at him, like some dumbass Hollywood movie. Pike had always thought that the best way to get out of a car chase was simply to stop. The car behind was always at a disadvantage.

Crunch.

What!?

Jesus H. fucking Christ on a moped. Arven had rammed him. *Actually fucking rammed him!* The idiot definitely hadn't thought this through. Had definitely seen too many films. Ramming someone from behind made no sense at all. There was nothing much to damage at the back of a car, especially an old 4x4 like the Yeti. There was a lot at the front, however. Delicate stuff, easily broken. It was like a headbutt. Except they were butting his Eastern European, steel, Yeti arse with their easily crumpled, safety-conscious, Western European head.

A new plan was forming. Probably as dumb as all his other plans.

He had nothing better, though.

He just had to find the right bend.

It had to be particularly sharp with limited visibility. And he needed to go into it as fast as he could, which risked him spinning off the road. The drop was getting scarily steep now, falling away to rocky scree. The view was spectacular – going over the edge would be even more spectacular. The Yeti was an unlovely thing. A workhorse. Nothing sweet or fancy about it. But it felt solid enough for his plan to have at least a slim chance of success.

But if he fucked it, then he was *completely* fucked. No plan B. He really didn't want to try to get back down from here on foot with a bunch of irate gangsters on his arse.

A couple of gentler bends came up, visibility too good. He swerved round them as fast as he dared, the car just holding the road, his hands starting to slip on the wheel. A short, straight run. And then he saw a farmhouse ahead. Right on a corner. The road curving up and round it. Trees all around the buildings. Nothing to the left except the drop. Not exactly awe-inspiring – this wasn't the Swiss Alps – but it would do. And he didn't want to actually kill anyone, after all.

He accelerated. Going into the bend much faster than he'd risked so far. The Merc accelerated, too, keeping pace with him.

241

The Yeti heaved around the bend, slipping and sliding, throwing him against his door, his seat belt digging into his neck.

Now to do it.

Pike braced himself and stamped hard on the footbrake. The Yeti skidded to a halt and a moment later there was an almighty thump as the Mercedes slammed into the back of it. The tinkle of broken glass. The racing whine of a thwarted engine. He saw the shocked faces of Abbott and Costello in his rear-view mirror, their mouths goldfishing. He imagined the interior of the Merc hot and thick with filthy curses. It wasn't over yet, though. He'd already wrenched the gear stick into reverse and was now powering the Yeti backwards. This was where its tough, four-wheel-drive and solid road grip came into their own.

If the Albanians were thinking clearly, they'd go into reverse as well and try to get round the bend and away from him. If they were dumb, they'd try to fight it. Pushing back at him.

They proved to be dumb. Smoke rose from under their bonnet. Their engine shrieked as it over-revved. But he steadily drove them back. Didn't let up. In a few seconds the back of the Mercedes was off the edge of the road and into the loose dirt. Costello opened his door and jumped out. Smart move. He was fumbling for something in his pocket. A gun, no doubt. Pike couldn't worry about that now. One final push and the Mercedes left the road completely, teetered for a moment and then dropped sharply out of sight.

Costello was distracted, watching it go. Disbelieving. Then he turned, shouted something, and fired randomly at the Yeti. The rear, right-hand window shattered. Pike couldn't tell where the bullet ended up. Not in him, luckily. He stopped the car and yanked up the handbrake before the Yeti followed the Merc over the edge. Costello fired again. Missed anything vital. Pike was already getting out of the car – putting its bulk between him and the shooter.

He got a glimpse of the Mercedes rolling backwards down the slope. No huge explosion, no ball of fire, just a cloud of dirt, bouncing stones and a great thumping, clanking, crumpling noise. It hit a rock, twisted, flipped and started to slide down on its side.

'Motherfucker!' Costello shouted. Fired clumsily. He was having to use his left hand. His right arm was in plaster where Pike had hit him with the wine bottle.

Out of the car, Pike was aware of all the sounds – the rumbling from the Merc, bees, cicadas, wind in the trees, distant sheep, and that most evocative sound of the islands – *the buzz of a wasp* . . .

Costello gave a sort of weary shrug. As if he had to go through the motions of what was expected of him. He stepped closer to Pike, raised his gun and then Sarah came up round the bend on the Piaggio, behind Costello. She stuck out a foot and kicked him over where the Merc had taken a chunk out of the roadside. Costello yelled, sliding down the loose ground that had been churned up by his car.

The kick had unbalanced Sarah: she nearly hit the Yeti and threw herself clear as the bike left the road. Pike grabbed her. Watched as the bike flew out into space. It hit the ground with a thump and careered down the slope.

'Hooligan,' he said. 'She-devil on wheels.'

Someone was coming down the road towards them. An old guy. Maybe the farmer.

'Let's get the fuck out of here,' said Sarah.

'Good idea.'

They bundled into the Yeti. The engine still ticking over, Pike got it into gear and awkwardly manoeuvred the car around until the nose was facing down the hill. Rolled forward. They waved to the farmer and soon they were speeding back down towards the coast.

They drove in silence for a while, a pleasant breeze blowing in through the shattered window. Pike turned on the radio.

Ioannis had it tuned to a trad Greek station. Raw rebetiko music filled the car. The mix of the twangy, stringed instruments and the harsh throaty vocals suited his mood. Jangled. Gritty. His heart pumping.

'Lorry driver music,' said Sarah and she looked around at the damage. 'Poor old Ioannis is not going to be happy with the state of his car. It's a wreck, Pike.'

'Nice you've got some sympathy for Ioannis,' said Pike. 'And a soft spot for his car. No need to ask how I am.'

'No need at all. You're like an old boot, Pike. You're going to go on for ever.'

'That makes us a pair of old boots then.'

'Ha ... So, what do we say to the rental guys about the bike?'

'Tell 'em it was stolen. They'll blame it on the Albanians ...'

30

HEPWORTH

The 'stinking rich' had arrived. The French kids from the de Surmont perfume family estate up the hill and their entourage. Led by the brothers, Gabriel and Sacha. They were churning up the lawn on their scooters and motorbikes, mopeds, a couple of those trendy electric bicycles. Like a party on wheels. They must have been held at the gates until filming had finished and then they'd come racing in, French rap pumping from a portable speaker precariously balanced on the handlebars of Sacha's bike. Whooping and screaming. A carnival riot of colour, orange and pink, purple, lime-green, hats and sunglasses, shorts, bare flesh. Boys and girls, young and alive. Hepworth was laughing and waving at them. He'd forgotten he'd invited them to the barbecue. Was actually quite pissed off by what they were doing to his grass but didn't want to show it in front of the film crew. They'd been packing their gear away when the kids arrived.

Dominic had lit up. 'Can we film this?'

Julian had shrugged – waved a hand – it's all yours . . .

And, boy, had they got up and running again fast. This was good. It'd make Hepworth look young and plugged in. A clubber. Generation Z, or whatever the latest generation was.

The de Surmonts had money coming out of their arses. They'd created the Sur la Mer perfume company in the eighteenth century, built it into a global luxury brand and had diversified into chemicals in the 1950s. This lot looked like they were heavily into chemicals right now. They may have been high on life, but they were also high on coke and MDMA, and whatever else they'd managed to get their eager little paws on.

They were a fun crowd, the boys always had some new, young, coffee-tanned bikini girls with them. And they didn't disappoint today. There were a couple of older girls, one with the haunted look of a junkie about her, and a couple of younger ones, teenagers by the look of them. One white, one black. They fitted the description of the young English tourists Ray had spotted in town. And now the stinking rich had obligingly picked them up for him and delivered them to his doorstep. This was going to be a fun evening.

The oldest brother, Gabriel, heir to the de Surmont millions, rode on to the driveway, stood on his saddle for a moment without letting go of the handlebars. He was wearing a deep red bucket hat and circular mirror shades.

'Ep Cat! Ep Cat!' he shouted. 'Are you filming a movie? Are you a movie star now?'

'It's an interview. TV. They're doing a feature on me.'

'Are we going to be in it?'

'If you like?'

'Hey! I know that guy!' Little brother, Sacha, was wearing a baseball cap on backwards. Was that still a thing? Maybe in France. He was pointing at Dominic. 'He is the English con!'

The cry went up as they circled. 'Film us! Film us!'

And, of course, Dominic's crew carried on filming and now Julian ran over and climbed on to the back of Gabriel's bike. The boy roared across the lawn, cutting it up even worse. Fucking wanker. Hepworth would have to get it fixed. He kept on smiling, though. He was a party guy. Gabriel did another circuit and then delivered Hepworth back to Dominic, who was grinning appreciatively.

'Just some friends of mine,' said Julian. 'They're crazy.'

'As only the French can be,' said Dominic dryly.

The kids posed for the cameras and arsed about, making those hip-hop hand gestures and sticking their tongues out in cokey leers.

Julian put an arm round Dominic.

'Can I ask you something off the record, Dom?'

'Go ahead.'

Wouldn't get him that easily. Julian took off his mic and battery pack, handed them to Boring Sound Guy, led Dominic away across the terrace, away from the cameras and towards the view. His arm round his shoulders.

'You're gonna stay for the barbecue, yeah?'

'If you're sure. Love to.'

'Good man. 'Cause I've got a small proposal I want to put to you.'

'Really?'

'Not now. Save it for later, yeah?'

'I'm intrigued . . .'

That was the point. Tee them up. Flatter them. Break them down. Use them. Flush them down the toilet.

'You ever been on a jet ski, Dom?'

'What . . . ? Yeah. One time.'

'It is a blast. You want to come out with me now?'

'Could we film it?'

'Don't you ever stop, Dom?'

'Don't you?'

'Ha-ha. You wanna do it?'

'Why not? Let me get the guys set up.'

Dominic walked over to his crew. Julian had him now. He'd seduced him. Won him over to his side. Dominic had thought

247

he was so clever, slipping his little comments in, trying to find a chink in Julian's armour. There were no chinks. His mind was a steel trap. Solid-state. Nothing out of place. In charge and on top of things. He wasn't ever going to be tricked into saying anything stupid. No danger of over-sharing. And he knew what Dominic had been after. Kept looping back to the tennis team. How *young* the girls were. How fit. How good-looking. *Of course* they were good-looking. Just about every fifteen-year-old girl on the planet was good-looking. And his girls were *athletes*. Perfect physical specimens. What did people expect? That he was going to hire hefty girls? One-legged asthmatics with Coke-bottle glasses, to tick the diversity box?

Come on . . .

There was no point arguing about it. Younger girls were prettier. Fact of life. Nothing improved with age. It was all downhill. Every artist since the invention of oil paint knew it. They painted young girls. Girls with no pubic hair. No blemishes. Small, high breasts. Skin you wanted to bite, it was so creamy. Worst of all, when girls got older, their personalities started to show through. All that piss and vinegar women brewed inside themselves. They wanted to take over. Young girls did what you told them. And every time Dominic had thought he was getting close to something . . .

Change the subject. We are not going to be talking about that today, thank you, Dom. Fuck off, Dom. Look at the nice view. Look at my money. Look at my perfect teeth.

In the end, Dominic had given up. Defeated. If he'd come here to collect dirt, he'd failed. Hepworth never lost. He aimed to stay at the top. He wasn't going to cock it up like all those other fools who'd let go of the tiller. It was all about public perception. He'd done nothing wrong, after all. Hadn't broken any laws that he was aware of. He wasn't a paedophile. He had no sexual interest in children. That was sick. He was an ephebophile. That was the technical term. He'd looked it up. An adult who's sexually attracted to adolescents. And – *come on* – every man wanted to sleep with teenage girls. But the world had tilted off kilter. You could still get cancelled. Normal behaviour was now seen in some quarters as suspect. He was waiting for the United Nations to propose a ban on human nature. It was like all this fuss about Prince Andrew. Why was everyone getting so worked up about that? He may or may not have had sex with a sixteen-year-old girl? Since when was that fucking illegal? Jesus, fucking, Christ, the prudish, prurient, uptight, repressed general public had a lot to answer for. They were so easily whipped up into a hypocritical moral panic . . .

'Look at that evil bastard, *behaving in exactly the same way as me* . . .'

Dom came back and Julian slapped him on the shoulder.

'Come on, hombre. I've got swimming things down in the beach hut. Brand new. Still in the cellophane. Won't be catching crabs off anyone. But I'm warning you. My jet skis are MONSTERS!'

31

CINDY

Somehow, they'd drifted on into the evening, worked their way through two and a half bottles of wine between them and were still sitting at the table. Cindy couldn't remember the last time she'd drunk this much, or the last time she'd laughed so much. Oh, she'd needed this. Letting go. Speaking to someone. Properly. And, just as she'd suspected she would, she'd poured her heart out to Aimee just as Aimee had poured the wine out into Cindy's glass.

Ioannis had hung around for a while, beefing and moaning and making phone calls. What was his problem? The car was insured, wasn't it? They could get another one. A decent car. Maybe one of those nice hybrids. Finally, he'd got bored and mooched over to Giorgio's taverna where he was now – knowing him – getting twice as drunk as Cindy. Showing everyone photos on his phone of some insect he'd photographed, or a moth. Or, no, he'd be tearily showing them photographs of the bloody Yeti.

Cindy and Aimee were the only two guests left from lunch. The day trippers had piled back on to their boat, packing themselves together like sardines, and chugged away. The rental couples had drunk a civilised amount and strolled off in a purposeful manner.

A group of youngsters on bikes had turned up. The French boys from the de Surmont estate. Had a bit of a reputation for being out of control. But they were so young and smiley and good-looking you could forgive them almost anything. They'd flirted with the young girls, Juno and Taz. The girls laughing and exchanging looks and flicking their hair. The boys jostling each other, physical, bursting with sexual energy. In the end, the boys had paid the girls' lunch bill and the girls had climbed on to the backs of their bikes and they'd all zoomed off.

And now, the sun was going down. The harbour was in shadow and Michalis, the taverna owner, was lighting candles, getting ready for cocktail hour.

Was this fun? Was this a release? A wild and crazy thing to do? Or was she just falling apart, dissolving further into a sort of middle-aged mush. Letting go. That meant two things, didn't it, *'Letting go'*? In the end, she just wanted Aimee to like her, to think she was special and interesting. But she wasn't special and interesting, was she? *Except . . .*

'Can I tell you something?' she said.

'Something else? Is there anything left to tell?'

'Oh, you have no idea! Ha-ha-ha-ha-ha . . . '

'You have hidden depths, Cindy.'

'Yes. Black lakes in deep, dark caves . . . lakes filled with wine. Ha-ha-ha-ha-ha. I don't know. I've never told anyone this. Maybe I'd better not tell you. I know what'll happen. You'll only laugh.'

'I promise I won't. At least I promise I'll try not to. Actually, Cindy, I can't promise anything. But if you don't tell me, I'll kill you. I love secrets. The sillier the better.'

'I'm . . . well, I'm part of an online group. People from all round the world.'

'That's not so unusual. I used to belong to a biscuits forum. Not anymore. I try to avoid biscuits. And you'd be amazed how toxic it got. People have strong feelings about biscuits.'

'It's not about biscuits. My group – my *groups* plural ...'

'Plurial?'

'Yes, plurial. I'm going with it. Works for me. We're all very supportive of each other.'

'That's nice.'

'Us against the world!'

'Woo-hoo! You're going to have to tell me where this is going, girl.'

'So. Well ... It's just. I've got into this thing. It's all just a bit dangerous, in a way, once you find out more about it.'

'I'm hooked. Look at my face. Not laughing.'

'So, I was sceptical at first – people are always sceptical about any alternative views, but why aren't we sceptical about the science we're told at school?'

'Mm – I dunno – maybe because it's true ... ?'

'Is it?'

'I *think* so ...'

'The thing is, Aimee, I used to be, when I was at school, I was ... Well, I was brought up a Catholic. Went to a convent school with nuns and everything. St Mary's. I'm not sure how much I believed in it back then. All the God stuff. The sisters told us all the stories, and that's just what they felt like – *stories*. The Garden of Eden and the serpent, the Ark, the parting of the Red Sea, you know, burning bushes, water into wine and Jesus walking on water. *Stories.* And I had no choice. It was just *accepted*. We'd drone along to the Psalms, and sing hymns and recite things about how we were worthless and corrupt and full of sin and we would give ourselves to God and he was all powerful and only he could cleanse us. We did that. We gave ourselves to him. And it was sort of ... It was sort of sexual.'

'I always found the Garden of Eden sexy when I was younger,' said Aimee. 'That bad old devil-snake, all that nudity ...'

'Yeah. I know what you mean. But this was different. It was

deeper. The whole time I was, like, I had this feeling that God was – I don't know how to explain it – God was always there, always with you. Even when I was having a bath.' They both gave a snort of laughter at that.

'And not in a nice way,' Cindy went on. 'He was always *judging* you. It was forced into us. Guilt and shame ... I'm sorry, I don't want to sound like a religious nut, because I'm not. I'm really not. It was just the way things were for me. We went to mass as a family. And not just at Christmas and Easter.'

'That's going some. You were practically the Pope.'

'You know, sometimes I think Catholics are stronger when they're not in a Catholic country, yeah? Because you feel there aren't that many of you left and you need to preserve your heritage. Your *culture*. It's like, I know a Jewish guy here, Leo Adler, quite dishy. *Very dishy*. We play tennis together ...'

'Oh, yes? Sounds like a euphemism, Cindy.'

'No. Ha-ha-ha-ha. It's true. We *do* play tennis. Just tennis. And he ... Well. He looks after our business affairs. But that's not important. I'm sorry. I'm rambling. Anyway. What Leo says is, he never felt very Jewish before he came here, it wasn't important to him. Even though he'd grown up in Israel. Can you imagine that? But as soon as he came here – there aren't a lot of Jews in Corfu.'

'I wouldn't know.'

'The Germans deported them all to Auschwitz. Only a handful escaped. There aren't much more than a hundred of them left on the island.'

'Right.'

'So, Leo started going to the synagogue in Corfu. He'd never really gone before, but his faith got stronger when he left Israel.'

'Where's this going, Cindy? Are you saying you've become more devoutly Catholic? That you've become Jewish? Or that you want to do the dirty with Leo?'

'No.' And Cindy couldn't stop herself from giggling. 'It's not that. I've become ... No. You'll laugh.'

'*You're* laughing already.'

'I know, because it still feels odd to me. I don't talk to anyone about this.'

'You're going to have to tell me. Talk, Cindy.'

'I was online one night. Ioannis was out. He works late a lot now. With Vlachos.'

'The dodgy guy you were telling me about?'

'Yeah. Yeah ... Anyway. I was just losing myself on YouTube, one video leading to another, clicking random things, seeing where it took me, down the rabbit hole ...'

'Porn. It's porn, isn't it?'

'*No. Listen.* I went on – remember, you promised not to laugh?'

'No, I didn't.'

'No, you didn't. It's just – I think they've been lying to us.'

'Who?'

'NASA. The government. Everyone.'

'About what?'

'Aimee – the world is actually flat.'

Aimee didn't laugh. She just sat there. A perplexed look on her face. Her mouth slightly open. And then she said, slowly and calmly and carefully, like someone trying to pretend they weren't drunk.

'Wow. Stalking, Farmville, Quidditch, soap carving, self-harm, cross dressing ... I mean, like, wow. Of all the things I thought you might say you were into, like, I don't know, swinging, dogging, freebasing, base-jumping, black mass, S&M, trolling, nudism, that thing where you dress up as a baby and wear nappies and get someone to suckle you ...'

'Is that a thing?'

'Everything's a thing. But of *all* the things ... I never for one second thought you were going to say the earth is flat.'

'There's so much proof online.'

'Cindy! You live by the sea. Look out of your window! You can see the horizon. You can watch a boat disappearing over it ...'

Aimee was almost shouting.

'That can all be explained,' said Cindy. 'It's to do with density.'

'Density?'

'Yes. It bends the light. Or something ... I'm still learning. But you can do experiments ...'

'Why would you need to do experiments? It's just ... I mean, *it's there*. What about day and night? Summer and winter. Australia ...'

'The sun is nowhere near as big as we're told, or the moon. They circle around above the earth, which is a flat disc, and the circles sort of spiral outwards through the year ... It explains everything.'

'And the edge?'

'A twenty-foot ice wall protected by NASA. If you go too close, they have armed guards at the top – they'll shoot you.'

'OK ... Right ...' Going slowly again 'But why? What's in it for them?'

'It's part of a massive conspiracy going back thousands of years. It's all NASA fakery. NASA is a fake god. A golden idol. There is no *space*. The earth is all there is. We're in an enclosed system, like a ... what are they called? A terrarium.'

'God, they're so trendy, aren't they? All over Instagram.'

'Yeah.'

'I bought one,' said Aimee. 'It got all mouldy and this one plant took over, filled the thing up with giant leaves. I gave it away.'

'Did you know that Pythagoras, the first man to claim the earth was round, was a Freemason?'

'I have to confess I didn't know that, Cindy. My knowledge of the ancient world's a bit rusty.'

'And Galileo, and Copernicus ... all of them.'

'They were all in on it?'

'Yes.'

'And, sorry ... *Why?*'

'It's all pseudo-science. None of it makes sense. And the lies were started by the Freemasons, and NASA is a front for them ...'

'Cindy. Cindy. Stop! WHY ARE THEY DOING THIS? Why the big lie?'

'Because it's ... because the Bible was *right*. They weren't just stories. There *really was* a serpent in the Garden of Eden. A snake demon. A devil. The Great Satan.'

'Satan's behind it?'

'Ultimately, yes. It's part of an eons-long plan. Unfolding through history. We have to stand up to him. Stand up to the lies. Expose the truth. But it's difficult, because they're so powerful. I sometimes think – Leo ...'

'Your Jewish pal.'

'Yeah. Has he been sent here? To spy on me? Are his stories about the Germans even true? We have to be so watchful.'

'Cindy? Why would Satan and his disciples and NASA, and ... well, just about everyone else in the whole world, why would they go to so much trouble to convince us that the world is round?'

'So that we won't believe in God. It says in the Bible that the world's a flat disc, you see? And the devil's tricked everybody into thinking that it's actually round ... Which makes no sense, when you think about it – a round world. People would fall off. Ha-ha.'

'Right ...'

'It's a conspiracy to make us believe that God doesn't exist. That the Bible's a lie. That our lives have no meaning. That we're just stuck on a pointless blob of old rock flying through space at a million miles an hour ... I mean – can you feel the movement? Can you feel it spinning?'

'Right now, something's spinning, Cindy. I don't know if it's the wine or my brain trying to process all this.'

'It *is* mind-blowing when you look into it.'

'It's quite a plot ... But, I mean, Cindy, tell me – last time you went back to England. Did you fly?'

'Yeah, of course.'

'Did you get up from your seat on the plane? To, like, go to the loo?'

'I guess so. Why?'

'Did you feel that you were flying along at five hundred miles an hour?'

'No, well, yes, well ...'

'You and the plane were travelling at the same speed. You were in a bubble. So, you didn't feel any movement.'

'It's different.'

'How?'

'Please ... Aimee. Don't try to bring me down. I've discovered something amazing. And, you know what the most amazing thing is? My faith has come back. And it makes me so much happier. Isn't that all that's important? Science can't make us happy. Only miserable. All that global warming and pollution, and black holes ... I mean, as I said, I was like you at first, it all sounded so daft, and I was a silly old woman looking for friends online ... But now, the only thing that's keeping me going is my flat earth groups. When I talk to them, *I know I belong*. I feel a part of something. I don't want to be a speck of dust, Aimee, in a soup of nothing ...'

Shit. Shit. Shit. She was crying again. She really hadn't meant to cry. How could she be so weak? Letting Aimee see her like this. Aimee passed her a tissue from her bag. Less grubby than using a napkin.

'I'm so sorry,' said Cindy.

'Don't be sorry,' Aimee said kindly. It's good to have a good old blub sometimes. Let all that snot out.'

'It's just ... I don't want to feel that all this is just ... *nothing*. That we spin through cold, empty space and then ... we're *gone*.

And what for? We might as well be germs. Bits of dirt waiting to be wiped away by a cosmic anti-bacterial wipe ...'

Aimee gave her a warm smile – eyes, teeth, the works – and put her hand over Cindy's where it lay limp on the table.

'Well, you know what they say, babe – "Whatever gets you through the night".'

32

HEPWORTH

'You asked me earlier, Dom, why I don't live in England, and this is the answer.'

Julian took in his world with a wide sweep of his arm. The pool, glowing aquamarine, the sea, the sky, the three chefs in white manning the barbecues, the bottles of beer and wine and champagne stuck into a mountain of crushed ice.

The party guests.

'What's England compared to this? he said. 'Tea and baked beans and porridge.'

He laughed. Dom laughed. Julian could feel the drugs beginning to kick in. He was ready to take flight. 'England is the *Daily Mail*, the *Express*, the fucking *Guardian*. Piers Morgan and Nigel Farage and *Good Morning Britain*. *The Antiques Road Show*. *Countryfile*. *Songs of Praise*. *Come Dine With Me*. *The One Show*. *Strictly Come Dancing*. *Ant & Dec* and *Britain's Got* fucking *Talent*. *Has it? Really?* Radio 4 and *Just A Minute*, *The Archers* and *Woman's Hour*. The Royal Mail. Gatwick Airport. Green wellies. Croydon. Guildford. Harrogate. Durham. Swansea. *Football Focus*. The weather forecast – 'Another grey, dull, damp day . . .' Pub grub, the Grand National, *cricket*, dog walkers and bags of dog shit hanging from the trees. Battersea Dogs Home. The RSPCA ... '

What he didn't mention was the age of consent. One year older than here in Greece. In Germany, where he'd set up his first training camp, it was fourteen. You didn't hear much about that, did you? And Germany were in the fucking EU. They *were* the EU.

Thing was. He'd loved being a teenager. Getting off with teenage girls. That was bliss. Why was he now supposed to fancy old women? It was perverse. And as to consent ... He knew several teenagers who were more sorted, more aware of the world, more in control of their own sexuality, than most thirty-year-olds. In fact – women got more and more nuts as they got older. He'd met too many thirty-year-olds who weren't in any fit state to decide whether they should have sex with someone or not. Give any kind of valid consent. Too out of it on drugs, or just fucking *mental*. Throwing themselves at him at parties, slobbering all over him, puking and cross-eyed. And when he went to bed with them, they were like these *THINGS*. Big, heavy trolls, like sacks of coal. Swamping him. Suffocating him. So unlike a lithe, light teenager.

Not that he could ever say any of this to anyone. Least of all, Dominic Beard. He was about to ask Dom if he needed another drink when he saw Dom look away.

Yeah. You want to think about sex? Well, here comes Pixie ...

All heads turned. Boys and girls alike, as she sauntered down the steps from the upper terrace. Like an angel descending from heaven. Her silver outfit glowing, sparkling, lighting up the world.

Julian nudged Dom. 'Get ready for a close encounter of the fifth kind ... '

She was in many ways a picture of perfection. But nothing lasts. Least of all youth.

It was going to be a shame when he had to say goodbye to her. *Man*, that girl worked hard. Would do anything for him. She was so good with the tennis team as well. In every way. He wondered if he'd ever find another one like her. Someone who could just make things happen the way she did. Her days were numbered, though. And the thing was, she *knew* it. She was thirty now, practically a pensioner in girl years.

And she knew too much.

It was going to be tough, but he'd have to work out how to fix it sooner rather than later. Pixie was minor Eurotrash aristocracy. Her family thinned out by heroin, fast cars and inbreeding. The only one she'd been close to – her little brother, Georgy – had been found drifting in his yacht in the middle of the Atlantic two years ago, his body so decayed and rotten it had melted into the floor. Nobody would miss her.

Yeah. Girls like Pixie, who burned as bright as a roman candle, didn't last long in this world . . .

'Enjoying the view?' Julian asked and Dom turned back to him, guilty at being caught out.

'I don't suppose we could interview her?' asked Dom.

'You're done here.'

'OK.' A face like a disappointed schoolboy.

'Unless . . .'

' *"Unless"*? I like the sound of unless – is this to do with the thing you wanted to talk to me about?'

Julian smiled. Put an arm round Dom. Led him away from the other guests.

'So. I couldn't talk about it earlier, on film. It's all still a bit hush-hush. But I'm setting up a new streaming service . . .'

'I've heard rumours.'

'You've heard nothing. The truth is so much better than the rumours, compadre. It's gonna be the bomb – quicker, better, stronger, cooler.'

'And?'

'And how would you like to come and work for me?'

'Oh … Well … I'm surprised. What do you say to an offer like that?'

'You say "yes".'

'Ha-ha, well …'

'As much money as you want. Make whatever show you want. You'd call the shots.'

'Well, wow, amazing. I'm flattered. That's a very interesting idea, Julian. The only thing *is* – and don't take this the wrong way – I'd feel nervous jumping ship from a successful streamer like Netflix, that's taken years to get into the position it's in now and end up tied to something unproven that might not work. It can take for ever for these things to get established. Takes an insane amount of money. I mean, I know you're not exactly poor, Julian, ha-ha, but you don't have the clout of Disney or Amazon.'

'Forget them. This'll be something new – young – exciting. You'd get in on the start. I can offer shares – the full package.'

'Don't get me wrong. It's an incredible offer – and totally out of the blue. I just don't want to burn any bridges, though. I'm contracted to Netflix for another three years, so …'

'I have good lawyers. They can fix all that shit.'

'Yeah, but …'

'Not just the money – you'd be one of the faces of the service when we launch – right there on the Home page every time anyone logs in.'

'Mm. It's tempting. I can't deny it, but …'

'I'd pay you enough so you'd never have to work again.'

'I like working, though, Julian. Don't you?'

'Yeah. I love it.'

'I'm not saying no. I will definitely think about this. If you can get me some more details …'

'You have to understand I can't do that, Dom. Not at this stage. It's all very top secret at the moment. You know how it is – you say anything, I have to kill you.'

'Is this why you agreed to the interview?'

'Did you like it? Go well for you? Get good stuff today?'

'It was perfect. Brilliant. The best.'

'Well, if you want to use it, you need to be nice to me, Dominic.'

'You're quite an operator, Julian . . .'

'I am. So. OK. Listen. Enjoy yourself here tonight. *Mi casa es su casa.* Things can get pretty wild at Patia HepKat. And keep telling yourself – you could be part of all this. I'm gonna introduce you to Pixie later. And, let me assure you – she likes to party . . . Know what I mean?'

'OK. Well . . .'

'Think about it, Dom. Think about having a golden ticket to paradise . . . party on, dude.'

'Party on.'

And maybe I can get some compromising photos of you, Mister Dominic dome-head Beard. Then we'll see about whether you want to work for me or not, you belly-crawling, low-status, parasitic, condescending, cocksucking motherfucker.

33

PIXIE

Pixie was dancing on the springboard, clutching Little Pixie, her tiny, white chihuahua. He was trembling. He didn't like the water. She had to be careful not to drop him in. He'd fallen in the pool one time and shat in it. A real bad runny gut-emptying underwater jet. A lot of poop for a little dog. They had to drain the whole thing. Problem was he suffered from chronic diarrhoea. The vet told her she shouldn't give him so many treats and needed to stick to a proper eating plan. She had to buy these insanely expensive bags of dried crud which he hated. Called 'Science Plan', or 'Bio Wonder', or something. But – get with the plan, Stan – what was the point of having a fucking dog if you couldn't give him candy and little juicy scraps?

A feeding bowl of grey-brown dried grit and a bored dog looked like nothing on Instagram. You had to have fun with your dog. Even if he did end up crapping everywhere.

She'd actually managed to get a couple of good pics of him looking ashamed after squirting in his bed. Once she'd cropped out the actual, unphotogenic shit and made up another reason for his embarrassed expression, she'd had a great reaction online.

'Who ate mommy's shoes?'

'Aw, it wasn't me . . . '

He wanted everything from the barbecue. She'd given him a sausage (specially flown over from Italy) and some steak – which he'd taken from between her teeth – *adorable* – a couple of prawns and a bit of sea bass. He was still licking her fingers, which she found frankly revolting, but it looked cute.

She held him above her head and whooped to make sure everybody was looking. They clapped and cheered, and someone shouted, 'Yay, Pixie!'

It was quite hard dancing in her silver, high-heeled wedge sandals on a slippery diving board. It was a case of just bending her knees in turn and lifting one foot carefully at a time. The main thing was to keep wriggling her body. That's all they really wanted.

The sandals were part of her magic pixie outfit. Julian had told her to wear it. Super-big lashes, tiny, silver bikini top, skin-tight, silver Kylie hot pants with nothing under them – didn't leave anything to the imagination – her pink wig, pixie ears and wings. The diamond stud in her belly button caught the light and twinkled alluringly, and she had glitter all over her body, silver make-up, thick around her eyes and on her lips. She glowed and shone and sparkled. Underlit by the colour-changing LED pool lights, she was a human glitter ball.

She'd hoped she could dress down tonight and just enjoy the BBQ and have a dance, but once the French boys turned up with those girls in tow, Julian had told her to get on it – 'the full fireworks'. She had to be prettier than the other girls, sexier, more outrageous. He'd even sprayed her with musk.

'You'll be my bitch on heat,' he'd said. 'And tonight, only I can fuck you.'

That's what he'd said, but, knowing him, he'd probably drop some more pills and try to get at least one of his guests into bed with them. He lost control easily. Maybe he'd try to get the

English TV guy involved. He was kind of cute, in a preppy way, she supposed. But it was all such an *effort*.

An old song was playing through the big hidden speakers that Julian had installed everywhere. It was part of his chillout mix. Always listened to it by the pool. The mix needed updating. This song must be twenty years old at least. From when she was a little kid. It sampled some ancient nightclub singer singing about sand dunes and salty air.

Round and round, over and over, slightly creepy. Julian loved it. He was singing along loudly with the Belgian sort-of-prince-guy whose name she could never remember. Arms round each other, swaying, like a couple of frat boys, in danger of falling into the fire pit. David Hamlish, the American TV exec, was hovering on the edge of the circle around Julian. Trying to get in. The Brit actress, Sally Spence, was chatting with Dominic Beard. Typical Brits, sticking together. Sally had been here for three weeks now, didn't seem like she was ever going to go home. She'd definitely be staying for the big party on the 14th. Julian's annual summer bash, as he called it. All the people he wanted to impress would be there. Including his pet cops.

Ray was standing behind Sally Spence and Dominic, big arms folded across his pumped-up chest. She grimaced. Ray had no idea how grotesque he looked, and he'd got worse lately, pumping himself up. All those muscles, that throbbing maleness, was nauseating.

The French boys were clustered round Julian, moths wanting to be near the hot candle. Jesus, how Julian loved that. They were drinking beers and negronis. Pixie had had a couple of cocktails. Pietro, the Italian barman, knew to mix them weak and sweet for her. She didn't really like the taste of alcohol. Didn't like what it did to her head. Julian gave her pills – what he called his 'happy' pills. And they didn't mix well with booze – made everything spin and twisted her melons. Made her confused. The pills were

Julian's own invention. Or at least someone working in his labs up at the Institute. She didn't really know what they did or how they worked. She didn't understand chemistry or biology, or whatever science it was you used to make pills. Physics? Medicine? Was medicine science? And then there was homeopathy. What was that exactly?

WHO FUCKING CARED?

'Whoo-hoo!' she shouted, pressing Little Pixie between her tits.

'That dog has it too good,' Sacha de Surmont shouted, and Pixie leered at him, stuck out her tongue.

Julian lifted his bottle of beer to his mouth, took a glug. Eyes fixed on her.

Little Pixie started to bark. Too scared of the pool. Julian's look turned disapproving. She climbed down from the board. She'd done her bit. Put on a show for the guests.

'Whoo-hoo!' she shouted again as she came over to join Julian and his gang. Little Pixie was still yapping. Which earned her another dirty look from his highness, Julian Hepworth, Fucklord No. 1. Junior highness, Prince Belgian boy, just grinned and his eyes flicked down to her boobs.

Julian had changed out of his smart interview outfit. Was wearing loose pyjama trousers – lounge pants – and a thin cotton shirt made of what looked like some kind of Indian fabric. She hadn't seen it before. Way too many buttons undone. A lot of beads and leather bracelets.

Little Pixie snapped at him and Pixie laughed.

'Can't you keep him quiet, honey?' Julian asked and she shrugged, gave him a helpless little-girl-lost look.

Julian hated the dog. Truth was, *she* hated the little bastard, too. She hated him shitting everywhere, hated his yapping, hated the way she had to put him in his stupid fucking coat in the winter, hated the fact that he was just a fucking dog and not an actual baby.

The only thing she liked was dressing him up and photographing him. Humiliating the shitty fucker. She had several matching outfits – her and him – Big Pixie and Little Pixie. He even had his own pixie wings and silver hot pants.

He had his own Instagram account, too, with 130,000 followers, and she was working real hard at getting more. Her target was a million. A Pomeranian mutt called Jiff Pom had the most – seven fucking million.

She was fed up with carrying him around. She held him out to Hamlish.

'Would you hold on to my little boy? Just for a minute?'

Gave him the big-eyed, open-mouth face that always worked. His whole face lit up. The pussy-stoned fucker would do anything for her. He took Little P and cuddled him. Little P looked miserable.

'He's so cute,' said Hamlish.

'Isn't he?'

He was holding the dog slightly awkwardly. Wasn't used to holding pets. Looked like he was scared of dropping him. She wished he would. That would be so fucking hilarious.

'He's shivering.'

'He gets cold.'

Yeah – in the winter. Little rat was just a nervous wreck.

She spun away and joined the girls, who were dancing on the pool terrace. One of the French guys had managed to persuade Julian to put on something more upbeat. Was choosing the tracks now on Julian's phone.

Right now, that Calvin Harris thing he did with Dua Lipa was playing. 'One Kiss'. She sang along . . .

'One kiss is all it takes . . .'

She gave it her best. Trying to outdo the other girls, who were all younger than her. She knew she had to be sexier than them. Hotter. Wetter. More desirable. More fuckable.

268

She had to hold the men between her thighs. Hold Julian mesmerised.

Come on. You want me. Don't you . . . ? Don't you . . . ?

Want me.

I am sex.

She knew what Julian liked and she worked very hard at it. She called him Daddy and pretended to be a schoolgirl, or an elf, or a princess in a fairy tale, lost in the woods. And he was the hunter. Kept her captive. Her wrists shackled. And he would spank her and make her kneel before him, hands pressed together in prayer. Don't hurt me, Daddy – I'll do anything for you – I'll be your slave . . .

And she would open her eyes as wide as they would go and stare into his eyes with a look of such utter innocence he would start to tremble like Little Pixie.

And when he fucked her, she would gasp and moan and writhe and tell him how good he was, how good he made her feel, and she would fake an orgasm, not too big, no shouts and screams – Julian hated that – just . . . a loss of control. Tiny whimpering sounds. Jerking her body. Rolling her eyes back. Acting almost ashamed.

And he would come on her.

It was hard work. It would be so much easier if she actually enjoyed sex. She'd never come. Not once in her life. She'd read so many magazine articles and books and online forums, she'd tried meditation and massage and drugs, she'd tried to pleasure herself, as they called it in the magazines. Usually with Julian watching, she had to admit. And that wasn't ideal. She'd tried enough times by herself but always got bored and lost concentration and gave up. She'd made every effort to understand her body and try to work out what felt good – but it was never *good enough*. She could never tip herself over the edge. The most she'd ever got was a pleasant tingling sensation. No. She didn't know how to please herself. Instead, ever since she was fourteen and a friend of her father had taken her virginity on holiday in Capri, she'd learned how to please men.

And, in return, men had given her things. Everything she wanted, everything she asked for, was hers.

But that was the thing. She'd never really known what she wanted. Her mama and her papa used to say to her, back in Esch, 'what do you want for your birthday, schnecke?'

And she said what she thought they wanted her to say.

A doll...A pony...A dress...Jewellery...A car for my sixteenth... A life...

What *did* she want? Happiness? But that was so fucking trite. What did it even mean? Was there really such a thing? Happiness was like an orgasm – just over the hill or around the bend, never close enough to feel.

People said that to be happy you had to live in the moment, didn't they? But that was all she'd ever known. No past and no future. Just endless, empty – NOW – NOW – NOW...

And it didn't make her happy. She was living in a little fairy bubble. She was Tinkerbell, she was Dorothy in Oz, she was Alice in Wonderland. She'd gone down the rabbit hole. She didn't know what anything was anymore.

She just had to dance. Harder and harder, 'til her feet bled.

She looked over – Little Pixie was shitting all down the executive's shirt. A thin, yellowish-brown stream of sticky liquid. He hadn't noticed yet and was still grinning like a dope, jigging in a feeble sort of half-dance and staring at her. She turned round and wriggled her ass at him, mainly so that he couldn't see her laughing.

Work, work, work. This was her job. Being The Girl.

She worked hard for Julian. Had to keep him happy. She'd learned how to choose other girls for him. When they went out to a club or a party or some glitzy reception. She could smell them out – the damaged ones, the unhappy ones who smiled too wide and too hard, the out-of-control ones, the young ones who could be manipulated.

If it meant that Julian would love her and need her, she'd do anything for him. She knew he would never truly love her. The best he could manage was desire. Obsession. And that wouldn't last. She was already too old for him. Next year she'd be thirty.

Thirty fucking years old! How had that happened?

He couldn't let her go, though. She knew too much. He'd have to keep her close or pay her off with so much money and set her up somewhere so fucking amazing that she'd lose too much if she ever opened her sweet little lip-glossed mouth.

Another one of the girls would become a favourite, step up and take her place. She did everything she could to keep them down, to undermine them, to report to Julian about them, what they'd said, how he couldn't trust them.

Lauren was the most threatening. She was smart. Strong. You could see her scheming. Too much going on behind her eyes. Julian had failed to break her. He'd tried. He'd broken all the others. But not Lauren. She was like Pixie – she knew how to work Julian. He thought he was in control of her, but Lauren was in control of him.

It was like Natasha all over again. That had been the closest Julian had ever got to being in love. Such total fucking obsession. Tangled up in her. Natasha could have brought the whole thing down, but Pixie had dealt with her. Now, it was like she'd never existed. Pixie would deal with Lauren when she found her moment. Not in the same way. Back in the day she'd been young and reckless and had only just got away with what happened in Paris. She'd learned a lot since then. She'd be so much more subtle this time. More careful. It had to be soon, though. Lauren was tough. She would rise up quickly. She could be princess here. Queen. Empress. And Pixie would end up as the withered old wicked stepmother.

Before then, she had to get pregnant. She needed a baby. Of course, that would be the end of it with her and Julian. He had no interest in a girl once she'd become a woman. So she'd lose Julian, but she'd have the kid.

She'd tried so hard to get knocked up. But Julian was clever. He knew that Pixie regularly skipped taking the pill. When it came to finishing, though, he had amazing self-control. He'd never once come inside her. When she skipped out to the bathroom she'd once or twice tried to scoop some of his junk off her and jam it up inside. It never worked, though.

Maybe she should just turn her back on all this? Get away from the madness. Yeah. Right. Who was she kidding? There was no escaping Julian and his big fat ego. Even if he no longer wanted you himself, he'd make damned sure nobody else could ever have you.

There was a shriek. Hamlish had discovered what Little Pixie had done. One of the staff was wiping the shit off him. Hamlish was appalled. One of those Americans who was insane about dirt. Julian was smirking. Pixie came over and kissed him. Exchanged a look – *see* that dog can be fun.

Julian put an arm around her, pulled her close.

'Isn't she spectacular?' he said, showing her off to everyone. 'But, in the words of . . . whoever said it! You ain't seen nuttin' yet! My bash on Saturday is going to be the Best. Party. Ever. A night of revelations! You just wait. It'll be a night you will *never* forget. Bring one. Bring all. Bring it on!'

34

PIKE

Ioannis was crying. Running his hand along the side of the Yeti as if it was a sick horse or something. A favourite cow in a TV vet programme.

'What have they done to her?'

'She still runs . . . ' Even as Pike said it he knew it sounded feeble.

'But she is shot to pieces.'

'She sure is, mate.'

Pike and Sarah had parked the car up here yesterday. Up a dead-end, single-track country road in the hills behind the village, in a wooded area where it was well hidden among the trees. Ioannis had let out a cry of shock and pain when he saw the state of it this morning.

Pike watched as he walked around the car another time, tutting and muttering and inspecting the damage.

'They have killed her . . . ' he said. Then he looked inside and saw the screwdriver jammed in the ignition. 'They have raped her.'

Pike had cooked up a half-arsed story about hiking in the woods with Sarah and coming across it.

'Why would they do this?' Ioannis shook his head.

'You know who it was, then?'

'The same Albanians who tried to scam you.' Ioannis opened

the boot and looked inside. 'They want to hurt me ...' He stopped. He'd seen the solitary box of pills that Pike had left in there. The rest of them were securely stashed in the garage at Macintyre's. 'What is this?'

'Drugs by the look of it, old chum. The boot was full of them.'

'There were more?' Ioannis looked really confused now. Not sure where this was going.

'Loads.'

'Where are they now?'

'I thought I'd better put them somewhere safe.'

Ioannis moved in on Pike, bristling. His dark eyes angry. Pike stood his ground. Sarah glanced up from where she was sat on a rock reading a book. Keeping her place by resting her finger on the page. Ioannis prodded Pike in the chest.

'What is this? What are you doing?'

'How long have we known each other, Ioannis?'

'I don't know, ten years?'

'It was before the crash. More like twelve, fifteen. I know you're a decent bloke. Fundamentally. And what about me?'

'What about you?' Ioannis was still up in Pike's face.

'Would you say I was a decent bloke. Fundamentally.'

'I don't know all these words.'

'*Vasika*,' said Sarah, and she went back to her book. '*Vasika, Pike einai kalos malaka*.'

'Hnh ... OK.' Ioannis shrugged. '*S' Oreos.*'

'I don't want to screw you, Ioannis. But you've got yourself in a shitty situation with some shitty people, haven't you?'

'This is not your business.'

'Isn't it? They already tried to menace me and Sarah on the *Louise B*, as you well know. Would you rather I'd left the drugs in there for anyone to find?'

'I don't know anything about drugs. They are nothing to do with me.'

'No?'

'*Ochi*.'

'You don't recognise those pills?'

'*Ochi*.'

'You don't need to lie to me, Ioannis.'

'I'm not a fucking liar!' Ioannis came back at Pike. 'Stop playing this game with me. Tell me what you are doing here?'

'We can get the rest of the pills back to you, yeah? Put all your problems to bed. You won't have to worry about the cops finding them. You can put things straight with Hepworth – hold up – row back – don't get your knickers in a twist.' Pike gently pushed Ioannis away. He'd boiled over again. Had tried to grab Pike.

'Just hear me out, or we'll be here all fucking day. I'm offering you the chance to make the pills go away. Nobody will be any the wiser. *Katalavaineis*? Nobody will be able to connect them to you.'

'But I don't know anything about the fucking pills. They are not my pills. The Albanians put them there.'

'I think, Ioannis, that, like everybody else, you're not a fundamentally bad man, you're just doing what it takes to get by. But your Albanian friends clearly wanted to stitch you up – frame you.'

Ioannis had walked away, was fuming and running his hands through his hair. Still had a good head of hair on him.

'It's clear there's a war going on here. You tell me to mind my own business, but we're caught up in it. They threatened to sink our boat. So, when we found your car . . . '

'I don't want her. She is *fucked*. I don't want even to look at her.'

'And the drugs?'

'I know nothing about any drugs, they are not my drugs.'

'They were in your car.'

'I didn't put them there.'

'Fair enough. I don't want them, though. The rest of them. We'll just take them to the police, yeah? Let them work out what to do with them.'

'No. Don't do that. If there are any more drugs – you might get in trouble. It's not good for you. You don't want to get mixed up with the police and the Albanians. You just said it – is not your fight. You give the rest of the drugs to me and I will deal with them.'

'If they're not your drugs . . .'

'JUST GIVE ME THE FUCKING DRUGS!'

'We can make a deal.'

'What? What kind of a deal? Jesus Christ. My head is going to break. I am beginning to think you are a fucking shit, Pike.'

'I need some information.'

'Information. I don't have any information. Information about what?'

'About Theo Vlachos and Julian Hepworth.'

'Now what are you talking about?'

'Come on. It's no big secret. Everyone knows Vlachos is connected to Hepworth.'

'I don't know anything about Julian 'epworth.'

'Then we don't know anything about any drugs. And you won't see them again. We're just going round in circles here.'

'Are you in this? Are you against me? Are you the enemy?'

'Oh, fuck off.'

With a great roar, Ioannis launched himself at Pike, who just sidestepped. Ioannis slammed into his own car. Recovered and charged again, like some enraged bull. He was a powerful man. Stocky and solid. But he had a sedentary lifestyle and Pike was light on his feet. He danced away from him, always moving. He had no desire to fight Ioannis.

'Are you police? Are you gangster? What are you?'

'I'm like *you*, Ioannis. Just a bloke trying to get by in a fucked-up world. You know – bobbing and weaving – like a boxer. Rolling with the punches.' And he had to roll, leaning out of the way of a hefty swing from Ioannis.

'What? You're gonna hit me, now?'

Ioannis slumped. The air went out of him.

'No. I don't want to hit anyone. Except maybe Genc Malecaj. And Arven. Costel. Adrian the pimp . . . '

'Ioannis,' said Sarah, not even bothering to look up from her book this time. 'We're not the enemy.'

'What do you want from me . . . ?'

'Just a little inside information on Vlachos's dealings with Hepworth.'

'He is my boss. He is my friend. I cannot do this to him. How do you say it in English . . . ?'

'Grass him up. There's no need for him to come to any harm. Nor you. Specially not you. It's only Hepworth we're interested in. OK?'

'Why?'

'That's our business. But this can work both ways. We can tell *you* stuff, too.'

'Yeah? What can you tell me, you motherfucker?'

'That the Albanians are moving in on Vlachos's territory.'

'This is not news.'

'That Malecaj wants to do a deal with the Englishman. That they'd all like to cut your Vlachos out. He messed up big time, Ioannis. That's why I've now got a shitload of weird drugs knocking about. And they're yours to do with what you want if you just answer a few questions about Hepworth . . . '

'OK. OK. OK. Everything is fucked up now anyway . . . '

And then Ioannis changed as his attention was taken by something. He was looking up at the sky with an expression of wonder on his walnut face. A big yellow and black butterfly was floating down from the trees. Ioannis held out his hand and it landed on his fingertips, stretching its wings open and closed. Ioannis was smiling like a little kid.

'A swallowtail.'

'Do you ever long for the simple life, Ioannis?' Pike asked. 'Do you ever wish you were just a fisherman again? Out at sunrise, back before lunch? Nothing to worry about except your nets and keeping your boat painted.'

'Fuck no. It was hard work and very boring. I had no money. I had no life. You should see my TV now, is big as a truck. Fuck fishing. And fuck the fish.'

He lifted his hand, and the butterfly flew away.

35

LAUREN

Lauren and Roseanna were packing up their kit. Stephano and Veronika, the instructors, were chatting at the other end of the court. Things were strangely normal, strangely quiet. All of Julian's thoughts, all his energy, were directed towards the party. Getting everything just right. He'd been drilling the girls on their routine. What to do on the night. That was all he cared about, showing them off. No more suspensions. No more one-on-one time. He wanted them fit and healthy and unblemished.

Nothing had been said by anyone about Sigrid's escape attempt. Ray was keeping away from them. Keeping away from Sigrid. She'd scared him. But Lauren was worried he'd be plotting against her. She had to push things forward quickly now. She'd set the date – Saturday – the 14th – the night of the party.

'This is one of yours, I think ...' Roseanna rolled a ball to her. Lauren glanced at it before picking it up. It was split along the seam.

'Thanks.' Lauren stuffed it in her bag. 'Here ...'

She chucked another ball to Roseanna. Similarly split along the seam. She'd hidden a note inside it. Just as she knew that there was a note inside the ball Roseanna had passed to her. The tennis

279

ball exchange had been Lauren's idea. A way of exchanging information that was more detailed than they were able to manage in a Mob Chat.

They scooped up the last of their stuff and joined the other girls who were waiting at the gates. The loud chatter had already started, and it continued as they moved off in a tight group.

'I'm sure Veronika let one off when she served in that last game.'

'No way! It was just her shoes. They squeak. She needs new shoes. Those ones are so *old*.'

'You have such a lezzer thing going for Veronika. You are *in love*.'

'I am not!'

'She farted. It was a definite fart. I smelled it.'

'That was just your own pits . . .'

Carmen got into step with Lauren. Linked arms. These days, almost every time they walked to the tennis courts or back, they had an MC. There was always another girl wanting to talk to Lauren. She'd thought it was going to be hard to sell the *Great Escape* plan to the others. They all kept up a front of being in awe of Julian, of loving The Team, the system, the technique, the life. Little brainwashed zombies. It was impossible to know what any of them really thought. But they'd gone down like dominoes. Each one secretly dreaming of going free. First on board were Avery and Chioma. Then Roseanna. Then Issy, Ho-Sook, Abigail . . . Today, it was Lauren's chance to convince Carmen. She liked this. The girls were changing, becoming closer. Usually they were like cats in a sack. Prepared to scratch each other to death if it meant survival. Julian kept them that way. Him and Miss Lily and Ray. Even Pixie. All of them. It suited them to have the girls at each other's throats, ratting on each other, climbing over each other to get to the fresh air and light.

But now Lauren had managed to unite them into a proper gang.

'You got second thoughts, Carm'n?'

'I'm just scared that if it goes wrong, Julian will punish us.'

'He punishes us anyway. Not for doing anything wrong, but just because he likes punishing us. He gets off on it.'

'He might do something worse. Like with Natasha.'

'What do you know about her?'

'She got away but he had her killed. Some kind of fake drugs overdose. Like Marilyn Monroe, when President Kennedy killed her.'

'It's a risk, Carmen. I know it is. But it's worth it. Isn't it? It's *us* – kicking back . . . '

Lauren didn't say it, but the biggest risk of all was the other girls. The more of them who were in on it, the more likely one of them would be tempted to go to Julian, or Ray, or Miss Lily. Score some points. Another reason why the mass breakout had to happen soon, before anyone wimped out.

'I'm not backing down, Lauren. I'm still in.'

'Good. OK. So we need a signal, at the party, so we all know when to make our move.'

'"Shots",' said Carmen.

'What do you mean, "Shots"?'

'You know – "Shots". LMFAO. Julian always plays that track. It's on all his party mix tapes. He plays the same playlist at every party. When "Shots" comes on, we'll know it's time for everything to kick off. "Shots". You remember it?'

'Yeah,' said Lauren.

'Their panties hit the ground every time I give 'em shots.'

Some of the other girls joined in, shouting 'shots' and laughing.

'It's really old,' said Carmen. 'I was like five years on this earth when that dropped. But we can use it.'

'Yeah,' said Lauren. 'He'll be up on stage with a microphone when it comes on, because he always loves to sing along and get everyone going. Same every party – everyone drinks shots and shouts, and he loves himself and they all love him.'

'Yeah,' Carmen nodded. 'See what I'm saying? Everyone'll be there – on the dance floor – by the stage. Busy having fun. That's the time to go.'

'All right. Cool. Good plan.'

'But fifteen of us, Lauren ... You sure it's gonna work?'

'I'm sure. I'm pretty sure. I think I'm sure. But I can't tell you everything, Carm. I have to keep the final part of the plan secret. I can't risk it getting out there.'

'You don't trust us ... '

'Nope.'

Carmen laughed. 'You are *wise*, Lauren. You are one wise bitch.'

Was she? Was any of this wise? Lauren just hoped she could trust Lee Morgan. He was the key. As long as he was still on board, they had a chance. She'd talked it all through with him out on the jet ski once she'd been sure she could trust him. She was going to do it properly. A proper plan. Lee had a friend in Corfu Town with a big boat. As far as Lee knew, Lauren and Sigrid were going to sneak down to the beach during the party, move away from the harbour along the rocks and swim out to a buoy, out of sight of the cameras. Lee would then make some excuse, go out on the ViperMax, pick the girls up at the buoy and take them out to his friend's boat. His friend would then take them back and keep them hidden at his place while they got in touch with their parents.

The hardest part was sneaking down and getting along the rocks. They'd have to do it mixed up with all the guests coming and going. And then Lee was going to have to distract Herve the Perve somehow. She had to admit it was pretty thin. So many things could go wrong. Particularly as she hadn't updated Lee yet and told him that there were going to be more than just her and Sigrid. She wouldn't let him know until the last minute, so he didn't have time to panic and back out.

And, oh yeah, Lee – there's going to be fifteen of us ... '

He was going to FREAK. She already *was* freaking.

Because – shit – it was a *terrible* plan, wasn't it? But she didn't have anything better. And the least they'd do would be to show Julian he hadn't broken them. They could still fight.

She just wished she didn't keep picturing that big machine gun at the end of *The Great Escape*.

All those men dead.

36

RAY

Duh-duh, daa-daa, da-da daa-daa, duh-duh, daa-daa, da-da-daa-daa, diddly-oh, diddly-oh, diddly-oh, dah-dah! Ray turned his volume control up and sang along to the *Mission: Impossible* theme. Hepworth's favourite piece of music. They were out on the Straits on the jet skis. Or personal watercrafts, if you wanted to be accurate. But, let's face it, a hoover was a fucking hoover, and a jet ski was a fucking jet ski, even if it wasn't made by Kawasaki.

Lee Morgan would get all pedantic about it and Ray deliberately called them jet skis just to wind him up.

Hepworth was on his new toy, the Mansory. Ray was on the green and black Kawasaki Ultra 310R. It had a real kick to it – the 310 was for the amount of horsepower – and could do almost seventy, but the Mansory Black Marlin 550 was a monster: 550 horsepower and a top speed of eighty. Like being pulled along by five hundred horses. That was something else.

It was supposed to be a race. Hepworth had grabbed Ray while he was giving a party-focus talk to the two pool guards at the house.

'The main point to remember, boys, is that we don't want any of the guests to drown. Right? It would really spoil the party. They're going to be off their tits. Some are going to be young and stupid. It's gonna be noisy, chaotic, hard to keep track of things. We don't want to wake up in the morning to find some motherless arsehole floating face down in the pool.'

In the background the familiar twat – punk – twat – punk from the tennis courts.

Next thing Ray knew, a hand on his shoulder.

'Come on, big man, jet ski and then some lunch, yeah? I'll race you to that place I like.'

Twat – punk – twat – punk . . .

Hepworth never paid any attention to that sound. Never watched the girls practise. Ray sometimes wondered if he actually had any genuine interest in the sport, or if he just used it as a way to keep the girls occupied, distracted, exhausted, mouldable. And as an excuse to keep them all here in his compound.

Twat – punk – twat – punk . . .

Hepworth had already been in his swimming shorts. A baggy, retro pair with pictures of 1950s pin-ups all over them. Slip-on rubber shoes. A fluorescent yellow vest. Red baseball cap.

This wasn't spontaneous.

Just as the race wasn't really a race. Not once had Hepworth chosen the Black Marlin. He didn't like to lose. The last thing he'd said before they'd got out on to the water was, 'I warn you, Ray, you don't stand a chance, mate.'

'We'll see, boss.'

They *would* see. Hepworth had no interest in a fair competition. Cheating was all part of the game. He'd once told Ray that everybody was free to cheat in the same way, so it was a level playing field. Cheating was good – encouraged, even – in his world. *'Yeah – I've got better running shoes than you. What's the matter? You only got Adidas Boost? I've got a new pair of Alphaflys.'*

Shit. When Nike launched the Vaporfly – the shoe that broke running – their shares tripled overnight. Hepworth loved that.

Loved business. Loved making money. Loved the shoes. Had bought one of the first pairs.

'Yeah – I've got better shoes than you. I've got a better training facility than you. I've got a better tennis racket than you. Where does it say in the rules that's not allowed?'

Only thing was – The Team never won anything.

Ray nearly caught up with Hepworth, who clocked him, yelled and jerked the throttle, struggling to hang on to the handlebars as the Marlin leapt forward, the back end digging in deep, a great spray of water going up from either side.

Hepworth cut left and right across the water in tight curves, yelling with delight. The new, narrower seat design of the Mansory, and its special thigh pads, meant that more of the control came from the legs and you didn't rely on upper-body strength, so it was an easier ride for Hepworth, who didn't have Ray's muscle, but the insane amount of power meant he was always in danger of losing it.

Ray was on his tail, also swishing right and left, slicing across his wake, enjoying the bumps hitting the bottom of his ride, and they moved further out into the Straits, Hepworth shouting for Ray to keep up.

There aren't many tactics involved in a jet-ski race. Perhaps if it was a slalom and they were having to negotiate some obstacles and buoys it would have been different, but in a straight run you basically put the throttle on full and leaned into it. Whoever had the more powerful machine was basically the winner.

Ray was also heavier than Hepworth, which gave him an added disadvantage. He hung on to his boss's tail, unable to make up the difference. He wasn't slipping any further behind, though, which meant that Hepworth was holding back, the soppy twat, fearful of opening his machine right up. Too much power for him.

Ray was enjoying this. A good workout. Getting out of the house for a bit. He was worried about Sigrid. She'd changed in the last few days. Since that fucking incident in Corfu Town. What had that been about? Actually, he knew what it had been about – *fucking Lauren*. She was a liability. He'd have to do something about her. Her and Sigrid both. He couldn't keep the silly cow hanging on for ever, coming up with excuses as to why he hadn't put his plan into action yet. The problem was, if he just dumped her, she might get pissed off and start blabbing. It was clear Lauren knew all about it. Who else might she have told already? Ray had to fix the situation, no matter how much he enjoyed the free blow jobs. To be fair, though, they *were* getting a bit boring, a bit samey. She was just a kid and didn't really know what she was doing. And trying to talk to her before and after was torture. Plus, the tension of getting found out – which had added an extra thrill at first – was outweighing the brief pleasure. He was having to summon up increasingly outré fantasies to make it work. Which seemed to rather negate the whole point of the arrangement.

If she didn't get her shit together, he was going to have to properly shut her up. Her and Lauren and anyone else who got on his tits. Just like Pixie had shut up Natasha that time. Nothing was said about it. But Ray wasn't stupid. He *knew*. Pixie was dangerous. Maybe he should get Pixie to sort Sigrid out? Cook up some story.

No. The fewer people involved, the better. He didn't trust Pixie one pixel. Jesus. So much work. So much stress. So much to sort out. It was hard being a functioning psychopath.

He'd had his head down, concentrating on the Marlin, lost in his thoughts, but now he looked up to see a big ferry coming their way. He grinned. That would make things more interesting. Once they hit its wake, the water would become really choppy. Get your speed wrong, or your angle, and you could get slewed round in the water, or even be unseated.

He gripped the throttle tighter, keeping it maxed out as they passed the ferry. Thirty seconds later they hit the first of the waves fanning out from behind the big boat. You didn't want to meet them side on or there was a risk of capsizing, or your back end could lift out of the water and you'd lose traction. Ray steered into the wake, taking a more diagonal path than Hepworth, who looked like he was just steaming straight ahead, regardless. Ray manoeuvred into the centre of the wake and then came back at an angle the other way. He could see that Hepworth was struggling, could hear him swearing, and now Ray raced into a clear patch of water and came up alongside Hepworth, who'd had to slow down to regain control. Ray managed to turn his volume to full blast and sang along again – *duh-duh-daa-daa, da-da-daa-daa, duh-duh-daa-daa, da-da-daa-daa, diddly-oh, diddly-oh, diddly-oh, dah-dah!*

Hepworth lost his rag and speeded up too quickly, losing his grip. Swore as his machine spun out of control.

'Yeah!' Ray roared, pulling ahead.

He had a straight run now. He could already make out the writing on the big red and white buoy that marked the entrance to the mooring by the restaurant and was the official finishing point. He kept on full power 'til he was nearly there and then spun into a tight turn around the buoy and stopped, facing back the way he'd come. Waited for Hepworth, who arrived a few seconds later, still swearing.

'I told Lee to fix the engine. The fucking cooler's leaking.'

Ray laughed. 'Come on, boss, admit it. You misjudged the wake from the ferry.'

'Fucking ferry full of fucking halfwit lowlife plebs.'

Hepworth muttered something as he chugged past and headed for the small jetty by the restaurant.

They tied up the jet skis and walked along the planking to where the guy who ran the place was waiting for them. All smiles.

'Mister Hepworth, sir. How fantastic to see you again. Your table is, of course, ready.'

An informal place. Cushioned benches. Didn't matter if

you wore wet shorts here. Tiny little inaccessible bay. A few smart boats moored. Several customers already eating, outside, under a rush matting roof. Older men with younger women. Hepworth's table was set apart, at the end of the restaurant, over the water. Discreet.

There was a bottle of rosé chilling. A big platter of shellfish in the middle of the table. Ray and Hepworth sat down, and a waiter poured them both a drink. Hepworth wasn't looking at Ray. He waved the waiter away as if he were a fly. Ray should have let the fucker win. It wouldn't have mattered one small squirrel shit to him if he knew Ray had deliberately thrown the race. Being first, being on top, was all that mattered to him.

He was the human Vaporfly.

'This isn't just lunch, is it?' said Ray, helping himself to a prawn.

Hepworth cracked open a lobster tail.

'It's never just lunch.'

'Is it the party?'

'Why?' Hepworth looked over at him. 'Is there a problem?'

'No, but ...' Ray leaned closer, dropped his voice. 'With this drugs situation and all the Herberts out there running around trying to fuck each other up. Vlachos and the bloody Albanians. Are you sure it's wise to go ahead?'

'My annual summer party is the talk of the island, Ray. Talk of the fucking world. The highlight of my calendar. Pictures in *Vogue, Harpers, Tatler*. We've got some Big Guests coming this year. You want me to cancel them?'

'No, boss, but ... I'm head of security, it's my job to advise you – warn you – if I think ...'

'I'm not interested in what you think, Raymond. I don't pay you to think. You are muscle. Security. And you just don't get it, do you?'

'Get what, sir?'

'The purpose of security is not to *prevent* me from doing the

289

things I enjoy. It is to make sure I can *continue to do* them. And as you well know, I enjoy a party. I love to party. I live to party. I am the king of parties. I am Dionysus – the god of parties.'

'I can't argue with that.'

'Well, then, let's not hear any more about the party. That's not why we're here.'

'OK. Fine.'

But Ray had a headache. Thinking about the party. He could picture it now. There was gonna be all sorts of media camping out on the road trying to get shots of the guests arriving. Chartering boats to sail past so they could use their long lenses to snoop. There was so much to do. He was hiring in extra security to patrol the perimeters, to sort out the parking and the drop-off zone, to man the gates and check the IDs and the guest list and the fucking wristbands. Plus he'd had to vet the outside catering staff, the musicians and entertainers, the guys doing the fireworks – shipped over from Italy – the fucking close-up magician ... And then he had to sort out the extra girls Vlachos was bussing in ...

'So, what's on your mind, boss? What's up?'

'You know what's *up*.'

Ray shook his head. 'Trust me. I'm in the dark here.'

'You know my rules, Ray. Nobody fucks with me. Nobody fucks with my girls. Nobody fucks my girls.'

'I know the rules,' said Ray. 'I wrote most of them.'

'So, explain yourself.'

'I don't know what you mean, boss.'

'Yes, you do, Ray. You know the security I've got at the house. You are, after all, as you have just pointed out, *head* of my fucking security. So, tell me – what the fuck do you think you are doing ... ?'

37

AIMEE

'Did you know that Pythagoras was a Freemason?'

'That was quite a feat. To be a Freemason two thousand years before Freemasonry was a thing.'

'Two thousand years?'

'Freemasonry was started in the fourteenth century, Aimee. Pythagoras was 500 BC.'

'You see. That's the thing with you, Mac. Why are you never around when I need you to supply some cold, hard, dull facts? And why can I never get rid of you when you are?'

'Who the hell have you been talking to about Pythagoras?'

'Cindy. She's a flat-earther.'

'You should never engage with them, Aimee. Don't try to argue. It comes down to religious belief in the end. They're not interested in actual facts.'

'Yeah, well ... I like her. But she's very unhappy. It felt bad squeezing the juice out of her. Fabulous knockers, though.'

'You did well, Mrs Macintyre. We just need to secure some invites to Julian's party, and we're done.'

They were sitting in a swanky new rental, parked in the shade under some trees by the side of the road that led to the de Surmont estate, waiting for the tip-off. They had a clear line of sight in both directions and Pike was stationed at the turnoff from the main road, ready to alert them when the scooter boys came back from the beach.

Aimee was excited and a little jittery. Not sure how this was going to play out. Mac turned and smiled at her. Maybe he felt the vibes.

'You look good in a suit,' he said.

Aimee studied herself using her phone's camera. Made a face. Not convinced.

'You really think they'll buy this?'

'They're young, they're out of control, they'll probably be off their tits,' said Mac. 'We put the fear of God and all his angels up them, show them they're at the bottom of a very deep, very dark well with no way out, and when they're weeping and wailing and pissing into their boots, we offer them a rope. They'll be ours for life.'

'So, you want me to be scary?'

'You do good scary when you put your back into it.'

'Do I really want to be scaring a bunch of kids, though?'

'They're not a pleasant little gang. They've been breaking into all the holiday villas around here. Wrecking them, wrecking people's holidays, making them waste their days trying to get new passports. All just for kicks. They're not nice, Aimee. They need a scare. Good for their virgin souls.'

'I don't have to hurt anybody, though, do I?'

'Nope. No violence. You know that. They're going to be nervous as all hell. They'll go down without a push.'

'Maybe.'

'And there's the drugs, Aimee. Don't forget the drugs.'

They'd pieced it all together from what Ioannis had told Pike, what Cindy had told Aimee, what Mac had seen at Hepworth's and what they'd got from the Albanian's phone. The end was in sight.

Aimee checked herself again on her screen. Had to admit it

was pretty sharp. A cool grey suit with a pale blue shirt. Mirrored aviator shades. A little corny, but Mac was right – it was a good look for her. He was dressed similarly. Dark suit, white shirt, immaculate tie, opaque shades.

She was looking forward to the moment when he took his shades off and gave the French kids his dead stare. He'd spent a long time perfecting that stare. Nothing behind the eyes. A shark. Heartless. Worse than an angry or disapproving look by a million country miles.

He had a slight bulge on one side where he had a gun in a shoulder holster. He'd assured her it was just for the theatre. Wasn't even loaded. 'Everything has to be right,' he'd told her. We hit the kids hard from every side and they'll swallow it. He'd given her an impressive looking metal CIA badge in a wallet with her photo and agent number. Told her that in real life there was no such thing. If a CIA agent had any kind of ID it was a chipped plastic card to get in and out of official buildings. But a bunch of French kids brought up on too many Hollywood movies weren't to know that. They'd be expecting something like the badge. He'd bought a job lot of them on Amazon, apparently. Made in China.

She was Agent Horovitz and he was Oliver Pangbourne from MI6. They'd upgraded to this new car because it was bigger, more expensive and more impressive than the old one – more like the sort of car you saw agents use in the movies. Heavy and black with smoked windows. In real life, a British MI6 agent wouldn't have had the budget for something like this and would rent the cheapest heap of shit on the lot. Stay in the cheapest hotel, keep all his receipts carefully and note down all his expenses. The fake version was a lot more fun.

Mac's phone beeped and the screen lit up. He glanced at it.

'Here we go.'

He started the engine. Kept his eyes fixed on the road up from Agios Symeon. And soon they saw them. Riding three abreast.

The two de Surmont boys and another kid. Mac picked his moment and then pulled out so that their car was blocking the road from side to side. The French boys slowed, came closer and stopped, shouting angrily and making gestures.

'Hey, Fuckhead, get out of the road.'

Aimee and Mac looked at each other and then got out of the car. Timed it so that they were perfectly in sync, slamming the doors together. They walked over to the boys and looked them up and down.

'Gabriel de Surmont? My name is Oliver Pangbourne. This is Agent Horovitz. We'd like to talk to you in private, if we may.'

'What the fuck? Is this a joke? No way. You can fuck off.'

'We can fuck off, yes. But before that I'd like to say a few things.' Aimee was enjoying Mac's clipped, upper-class tone. 'In particular, I'd like to offer you boys a choice. You can talk to us here and now, or you can talk to the Greek police.'

'Or we can tell your parents and you can talk to them,' said Aimee, turning her American accent up to eleven.

'Or maybe you'd like to talk to the security team of Anatoly Kuznetsov.'

'What the fuck you talking about this guy for? Who the fuck is he?'

'Russian mafia,' said Macintyre. 'You may have seen his yacht around.'

'I ain't seen no fucking yacht.'

'He's a friend of Julian Hepworth. Due to be at his party.'

'Why are you talking about him to me?'

'We'll get on to that. But first we'd like to talk to you about several robberies in the area.'

'Fuck you.'

The kids exchanged looks. Laughed. Gabriel was holding up OK, but the other two were starting to look nervous, particularly the younger brother, Sacha.

Mac stepped closer to them, looked at Sacha's bike, where he had a portable JBL speaker fixed to his handlebars with bungee cords. Sacha looked away. Aimee reckoned it was time to flash her badge. As she flipped the wallet open, she could see a flicker of alarm in the boys' faces.

Gabriel squinted at them. 'Who you say you are?'

'Oliver Pangbourne, I work for MI6. Officer Horovitz is, as you've just seen, CIA.'

'We're working together on a case involving this Anatoly Kuznetsov,' said Aimee. 'Could we perhaps go up to your villa? Talk there? Where it's less public? Believe me, we don't want this to get out any more than you do. But if it does . . .'

'OK, OK, wait.' Gabriel peeled off and had a quick, quiet, slightly panicked conversation with the other two boys. Then he returned his attention to Mac and Aimee.

'You don't have any powers here.'

'Actually, we do,' said Mac. 'But we don't need to go into that now. It's very simple. As I said, you can talk to us, or you can talk to Anatoly Kuznetsov, or the local police . . .' He took off his shades. Didn't blink once. 'Or perhaps you'd like us to bring Genc Malecaj in on this?'

That was good – mentioning Russian mafia always put a sliver of fear into suggestible minds, adding in an Albanian gangster would only add spice to the mix. And now Mac casually let his jacket flap open, exposing his pistol.

Gabriel broke. 'OK. Move the car. We go in. You will follow.'

They drove slowly up the road like a cut-price motorcade, the French boys talking away furiously to each other. Waving their arms as they rode. They looked very young to Aimee, the oldest boy not much more than twenty. She had to keep reminding herself that they'd trashed Alan Human's villa. God knows how many others. The English had the perfect word to describe their type – *wankers*.

There were two big gates at the entrance to the estate that

opened automatically as the boys drove up. Mac and Aimee followed them in.

'Wow . . .'

The villa was old-school, built in the late fifties, so Mac had told her, in the old Venetian style, but on a grand scale. It was very smart and elegant, with a wide gravel driveway, formal landscaped gardens, cypress trees, statuary, clipped hedges, lawns and a fine view down over the countryside and out to sea.

The bikes stopped in front of the house and the boys kicked down their stands. Mac parked close by and he and Aimee got out, stood there, taking control of the space. Aimee did that wide-legged stance thing, the power pose. Had to admit it felt good. This really was turning into a scene out of a movie and Aimee was getting into her role. The boys stood around for a while, lighting up and looking shifty. Mac let them stew for a minute then strode over to them.

'Let's go inside,' he said. He was carrying a smart black leather briefcase. You never saw people with briefcases these days. It was all shoulder bags and backpacks. There was something grown up about a briefcase. Traditional, yet commanding and powerful. Went well with Mac's entitled, Hollywood villain, public-school accent.

It was dark inside the villa, took a moment for Aimee's eyes to adjust. Then she was hit with the full baroque experience. Polished tiled floors, lots of marble, a few statues, old oil paintings on the walls, wide, sweeping staircase, dried flowers in big vases, lots of fancy plaster work and gold leaf, even a mural on the ceiling. Cupids and naked-ass ladies. It was a touch of the *Ancien Régime* here in Corfu.

She and Mac followed the boys through to a living room. Again – *wow*. They'd turned it into a real tip. Obviously no parents around, maybe just some cowed staff, too scared of the consequences if they told the boys off or interfered.

There were dirty plates, bottles and cans everywhere, overflowing ashtrays, a couple of bongs and other drugs detritus, a giant TV surrounded by a tangle of gaming equipment. The curtains were drawn, and the aircon was on full, creating a frosty atmosphere. Aimee shivered, feeling the cold air getting down into her lungs.

Mac cleared some space on a leather sofa, sat down, cleared more space on the low table in front of him and carefully placed his briefcase on it. All very precise and deliberate.

He took his shades off again and slipped them into an inside pocket. Then he snapped the catches of the briefcase and flipped up the lid. Lifted out his laptop. Looked at all the wires and cables around the TV. The French kids had a laptop of their own wired into it. Mac nodded.

'Hook me up.'

Sacha scrabbled about, swapping leads, fiddling with remote control boxes. It took a couple of minutes, but he got there in the end and soon Mac's holding screen filled the TV screen.

Aimee watched his on-screen cursor moving around, clicking and scrolling, and then grainy footage of the living room in Alan Human's villa started to play.

'*Oh, merde,*' said Sacha, and Gabriel said something more complicated that Aimee couldn't understand.

The boys sat there, rubbing their faces, making vague noises, smoking hard. It didn't look good for them. They wore helmets in the snippet of footage, but they were still identifiable. Mac stopped the film before the camera was obscured.

'First thing I want to say is that you picked the wrong person to rob that day.'

'That's not us. You can't tell that's us.'

'Perhaps in a court of law it might take some doing. But we're not a court of law. We're right here, right now. But, to tell you the truth, I couldn't give a flying fart that you're breaking into holiday villas.'

'How d'you have this film?'

'The man you robbed, Alan Human, is a lawyer, and a thoroughly unpleasant man, who works for Anatoly Kuznetsov. We've had him under surveillance since he arrived here. You have blundered into the middle of a major international operation that we've been putting together for two years. We are seriously worried that the whole thing has been compromised.'

'We didn't fucking know.'

Aimee sighed. It was funny the way some foreigners used 'fuck' far too much when speaking English. It was her turn to speak again. Her dad's Chicago accent strong.

'You're very lucky that none of Anatoly's goons were there at the villa when you showed up,' she said, wondering if 'goons' was a bit corny, but she ploughed on. 'If they had been, you'd be somewhere at the bottom of the Mediterranean right now, with your balls sewn into your mouths. Headline news for a couple of days. *"Mysterious disappearance of French rich kids in Corfu"*. Anatoly wouldn't lose any sleep over that. To the best of our knowledge, so far he's killed twenty-seven people – including six journalists, three politicians, two police chiefs and a priest.' She'd got that one off the top of her head. Hoped it sounded OK. She was really getting a good picture of this imaginary motherfucker Kuznetsov. 'Those are just the ones we know about for certain. Now. Listen hard. What we need you to do is return the stolen property first thing. Right now. You got me? The passports, the cards, the portable speaker. Everything.'

'I'll get it – I'll get it!' said Sacha and he hurried out of the room.

'Why should we give it to you?' said Gabriel, still fronting it out.

'You give it to us, we get it to the police, and they get it back to Mister Human. Tell him, *don't worry, it was just a burglary, just some local kids, forget about it, we're taking care of it*. Because we really don't want this to go any further, Gabriel. We don't want Kuznetsov to start investigating this himself. We want it shut down. Before things get complicated.'

'Sure. Yeah. Sure . . .' Gabriel was beginning to break.

'Now, it could well be that you have been filmed by some of Kuznetsov's own surveillance equipment, in which case you are going to be written out of this series. Killed off. There's nothing we can do for you except shed a little tear.'

'It's here!' cried Sacha, bundling back into the room, carrying a black garbage sack. He tipped the contents on to the floor. A hoard of passports and wallets, watches, cameras and cell phones spilled out on to the tiles.

'You want to take it all?' said Sacha, trying to be helpful.

'Not particularly. Just find Alan Human's stuff.'

The three boys began to scrabble about in the pile of loot, opening passports and tossing them aside.

'Now let's talk about the drugs,' said Mac.

'What drugs?' Gabriel's head shot up like a meerkat spotting a leopard.

'The drugs you've been selling for Genc Malecaj.'

'No way. What the fuck. We don't sell drugs.'

He was clearly lying. And lying badly.

'I thought it would have been crystal clear by now that we're not bullshitting here. We know everything about what you've been up to. We know you sold those drugs that killed three clubbers.'

'Two. It's only two.'

'Another one died last night.'

'We didn't sell them.'

'Yes, you did.'

The French boys rattled on for a while, their stories becoming more and more disjointed and jumbled, adding fact upon fact to try to bolster the lies.

Didn't work.

Mac and Aimee sat there listening. Not saying anything. Finally, Mac stood up, walked over to where the boys were still sorting through their haul. Stared down at them, unblinking, until they eventually shut up and looked at the floor, ashamed. Sweating, despite the cold. Haggard. These guys were not cut out to be criminals. They'd grown up in a world with no responsibilities, no consequences. Their family money insulated them from the basic harsh realities of life. It was all just a game of GTA to them. Endless free lives. Reload from last saved game.

Sacha had started to cry.

Aimee knew that Mac needed the last few pieces of information, to tie everything together. And he was hoping to get it out of these kids. She looked at them. They'd hit the bottom of the well. It was time to scrape them off the floor and dangle the rope down towards them.

Aimee smiled. The closest thing she could approximate to something warm and motherly.

'We can help you,' she said. 'We can keep you out of things.'

'Yeah?' Pathetically hopeful.

'Listen carefully,' said Mac. 'We're not with the DEA. Interpol. Any of that. We're not police. We're not interested in the drugs – just the connections. We need to know if Kuznetsov is involved.'

'The Russian? No way, man. We don't know nothing about no fucking Kuznetsov. Never heard of him.'

That figured – as he didn't exist.

'OK.' Mac smiled as well, now. A breezy, confident, landowning-aristo kind of a smile. 'Why don't you hoover up a few lines? Have a little drink. Take a little hit. Pop some pills. Whatever it takes to straighten yourselves out. And we'll talk this through.'

The boys fell on their supplies like wolves among sheep. As Sacha carried on searching through the loot, the others chopped and rolled and snorted and puffed, gulping down tequila and brandy and Coke. They put on some loud Algerian rap as the freezing room filled with smoke. The atmosphere became clammy. The curtains remained closed. And the boys visibly relaxed. Their talk became freer, they laughed, they wanted to unburden themselves. There was a way out of this mess. They could restart the game.

'The only way we can help you,' said Mac, like they were all pals now. 'Is if you tell us everything.'

'*How much* can you help us?' asked Gabriel. Negotiating. Feeling more confident again, as if he was already halfway up the rope.

'Well. If it comes out that you sold the drugs, even if you didn't know what they were, even if you didn't have anything to do with the manufacture of them . . . '

'We didn't manufacture them. They were made at that place on the hill.'

'What place?'

'The science place. BOF?'

'BIF,' said Sacha.

'Everyone knows,' said Gabriel. 'Theo Vlachos usually sells them. They're usually shit. But Malecaj was the big man, joking about how he'd jacked them off the Greeks.'

'You sell a lot of stuff for Malecaj?'

'He has the best gear. And people know us in the clubs. They trust us.'

'You ever sold stuff for Vlachos?'

'Ah. A little. We get around. We know the best places.' Gabriel was proud of himself.

'Here . . . ' Sacha came over to Aimee and gave her a handful of Alan Human's stuff. She checked through it.

'So,' said Sacha. 'You got what you need. We told you everything. We are OK, now?'

'Do you know how we work?' Mac asked.

'Sure,' said Gabriel with a smirk. 'Sure, we know – *torture.*'

The boys laughed. Mac laughed.

'Ha-ha. Yes. Sometimes. When we feel like it. Not in the mood today. No – we mainly use informers, insiders. People who've got so much to lose, they figure it's a safer bet to work with us than against us. We will protect you. We will keep you safe from the fires of hell, and in return you will give us all the inside information and access we need – from now until the end of recorded time.'

'You mean become rats?'

'You already are a bunch of rats.'

'That's not a cool thing to say.'

'I'm not a cool person. I work for British intelligence.'

'James Bond works for British intelligence,' said Sacha. 'He's cool.'

'Fair point – but that's fantasy, Sacha. You are sadly caught up in the real world, here ...'

Oh, that was ironic. Aimee and Mac were both playing parts and she was starting to forget what was real and what wasn't. Starting to believe she really was some hard-ass CIA agent.

'The alternative is prison,' she said. 'Or worse ...'

'OK. OK. OK ... Chill out.' Gabriel put up his hands and made that dismissive French face they seemed to learn at school.

Sacha was still concerned for his welfare. His eyes red and haunted. 'If we do this, if we help you, we are not in any trouble?'

'Only with God,' said Mac.

'We didn't know those pills were bad. You have to believe us. We had no idea. We never would have sold them ...'

'I know you're good mama's boys at heart. And the break-ins?'

'Was just for fun, for kicks. You know?'

'Funnily enough, that's what I said last time I water-boarded someone.'

'That's different,' said Gabriel, lighting up another spliff.

'How so?'

'You work for the pigs. For the deep state. For the monolith. The one world government.'

'Ouch. You nailed us, Gabby. We're Illuminati. And you know what they say – never fuck with the Illuminati.'

38

RAY

'I really don't know what you're talking about, boss.'

You should never have beaten the guy in a race, you numbnutz, Ray. Thing was. They were the same. Him and Hepworth. Ray didn't like to lose either. Even if it meant a bollocking.

But what did Hepworth know?

Chances were it was nothing. Nothing concrete. And he wasn't going to give Hepworth any ammo. So he sat there. Saying nothing. Waiting for Hepworth to lay his cards out. Took another prawn. A sip of wine. Offering a cool, level gaze to his boss. Unflustered. Unmoved. Unscared. Determined to keep his balls in place.

He knew this game. He'd played it enough times himself. If you didn't actually know anything, but had your suspicions, you hit your victim with some vague but meaningful threats and left the poor sod to incriminate himself. Well, Ray wasn't about to do that, was he? He was an experienced player. He was going to enjoy the game. And somewhere down the line he was going to shift the focus and land someone else in the shit.

He kept quiet. Forcing Hepworth to make the next move. Finally he spoke.

'As head of my security, Ray, you must know that you can't do anything at the house that I don't know about.'

'Yes. I do know that.'

'Good.'

'Which is why I am clean, boss. I seriously don't know what you've heard. What someone might have said. There's always gossip, rumours, whispers. Too many women about the place. Not my job to track down rumours and suppress gossip. Too busy keeping a lid on things for you. Tittle-tattle does not interest me greatly.'

'Keeping a lid on things?'

'Yes, boss. What happens in Patia HepKat stays in Patia HepKat. Always has done. Always will do. As long as I'm on the case. You've never had reason to question my contribution to your health, prosperity and wellbeing. Your *security*. I keep things under control for you.'

'Shame you couldn't keep things in your pants.'

'What things?'

'Your dick.'

'That's only one thing.'

'Your dick and your balls.'

'They come as a set.'

'Fuck off, Ray. Don't you get fucking cheeky with me.'

'No, boss. But to be fair, I honestly do not know what you are talking about at this moment in time. What is it exactly you think I have done?'

'Are you calling me a liar, Ray?'

'No, sir. Far from it, sir. So far you have said nothing that could be construed as either true or false.'

'I'm saying you have been doing someone you shouldn't, Ray. Is that a lie? Am I a liar?'

'No. Not a liar. I am saying you are simply mistaken. That's all. You have made a mistake. And I am trying to get across that I cannot continue with this conversation unless you explain to me what you believe it is I have done wrong. What my misdemeanour is. Where I have transgressed.'

Hepworth smiled suddenly. Not a warm smile, but a smile at least. Took a glug of wine. Tore into a langoustine. He was using his Pantocrator smile – his world-eating smile. 'I am God,' he was saying, 'and you are shit, Ray.'

Ray wasn't bothered. Ray was happy lying. He was a good liar. He enjoyed it. He knew he didn't have any tells. Didn't do any of those stupid things they told you on YouTube in bullshit *'6 ways to tell if someone is lying'* videos. He could lie for hours on end and no one would ever know. He wasn't gonna offer anything to Hepworth. If Hepworth knew anything, he'd come out with it. And he hadn't yet. Which meant there was just some rumours circulating and Hepworth was testing him. Trying to get him to incriminate himself. Ray mentally checked his vital signs. His breathing was steady and even. Heart rate flat. No sweat. He was cool. Relaxed. He leaned back from the table, manspread his legs a little wider on the cushioned bench. Stretched out his arms. Crossing them would look defensive.

Bring it on, Mister Hepworth. You wanna fuck with me – I'll fuck with you.

Hepworth's smile widened.

'So, you haven't been getting too close to any of the girls on The Team?'

Ray was chewing on some hard Greek bread, holding Hepworth's gaze. He moulded his face into a little WTF frown – *what the fuck are you talking about?*

'You know me,' he said. 'I don't play tennis.'

'Not even with Lauren?'

Ray let out an involuntary snort of laughter. No acting required. *Lauren?* You misguided wanker. Holy cow. He took a nice swig of wine. Enjoying the taste. Shook his head. Now Hepworth laughed, too.

'I'm just rattling your cage, Ray. Keeping you on your toes.' The weak-ass fucker was backing down. 'I know what it's like at the house. The temptations. It's a candy store, and it's easy to be a little kid.'

'I've got my faith, boss. Lead me not into temptation. I shall not covet another man's property, or his wife, or his girlfriend – no matter how hot her arse – nor anything with a pussy that dwells under his roof.'

'These modern translations of the Bible are something else, aren't they?'

Hepworth and his girls. Made no sense to Ray. The guy was ultra-possessive, but then when he got fucked . . . *they all got fucked.*

That was going to be the other massive headache at the party. Organising logistics for the restricted access to the three guest tiers. The circles of hell as he called them. He'd have to man the invisible barriers most guests wouldn't ever know about. The wristbands they were given on entry weren't colour-coded. That would be too obvious. You didn't want the VIPs to know that there were VIPs above them and an even more select level of VIPs above *them.* No. The wristbands were chipped. And that had to be sorted, monitored. The wrong guest with the wrong wristband and it would not be good news.

All guests had access to the outdoor areas, the pool, the beach and the main reception areas indoors. The big living room opening on to the terrace, the snooker room, the sun lounge, the bath-rooms, of course. But there were inner rooms at the house that you could only get to if you were Chevalier Level. Why Hepworth couldn't simply call them gold and silver, or fucking platinum, Ray didn't know. It was just an extra layer of headfuck for him. Drove him nuts. Chevalier Level gave you access to the games room, the disco, the indoor cinema and the chill-out room.

And then there was Noblesse Level. Or Knob-less as Ray and his team called it. Noblesse was where the real knobs ended up.

Hepworth's inner circle. Very few guests were allowed into what Hepworth called his Fuck Palace. It was underground. Windowless. Dimly lit with black light, pink light, purple light. The place had the feel of an upmarket knocking shop. Which is pretty much what it was. It featured a playroom, a smoking room, a soft area, a spa and several bedrooms. There would only ever be between five and ten special guests in there and what they wouldn't know was that it was completely tricked out with hidden mics and cameras.

For insurance purposes.

Apart from his close circle of fuck buddies. If Hepworth clapped his eyes on anyone at the party who he was interested in, he'd give Ray the nod and he'd have a quiet word with them. Then they'd be discreetly given a new wristband and a set of special instructions . . .

And all that took a lot of organising. But Ray was properly relaxing now. Someone had tried to stitch him up. It was all just a lot of hot wank. Time to get things straight.

'We know each other, boss,' he said. 'We've been together a long time. I know everything that goes on. We both do. In that sense, and *only* that sense, we're both on the same level. If either of us was to step out of line, the other could make things very difficult for them.'

'Whoa-whoa-whoa-whoa-whoa – are you threatening me, Ray?'

'Am I?'

'I don't know.'

'Believe me. I'm not. Any more than you were just threatening me. Now, don't get me wrong. I know where I stand. I am your employee, your hard man, your enforcer. I am a hired hand. In short – I am *your* man. You can make or break me. You could make sure I never worked again. If you wanted, I'm sure you could make me disappear. And I know when I'm on to a good thing. I'm never gonna get a better job than this. Which is why I strive very hard not to fuck up, boss. Not to fuck you up.'

'OK.'

'I would like to ask one question, though.'

'Go on.'

'Someone has obviously said something to you, sir. Someone has made some insinuation about me and my behaviour. I'd like to know who that is. I'd like to know who has a grudge against me.'

'Come on. *Seriously?* They all do, Ray. They all hate your guts. Because you represent authority. An unbeatable power.'

'And that suits me just fine, boss.'

'You're the troll, Ray, the bogeyman. While I am Prince Charming.'

'Yeah, well Prince Charming needs the troll, doesn't he? He needs a counterpart, a shadow, an enemy. Without the troll, he's nothing. He has no role in life. He's just a fancy dick in tights. As I say, we both know where we stand. On each other's shoulders. And I wouldn't have it any other way, boss.'

'Good. I guess I'm just reinforcing some lines, here, Ray.' *Yeah. Back down, bitch.* 'So – all good for the party, yeah? We are ready to rock?'

'All good, boss.'

So, who was it spreading rumours? He had to find out what cunt had been talking about him. That hard-faced bitch, Miss Lily, probably. Out of everyone here she was the one who hated him most. Would just love to have his job. To be properly running this whole place, instead of just the girls. Well, he'd have to fix her bacon. He had to fix several people here. It was time for a major shake-up. Top to bottom. Sigrid, Miss Lily, Lauren, Pixie – Ray knew too much about her. He needed respect. Security. And as for Hepworth . . .

Ray thought he might just have to sort the fucker out along with everyone else while he was about it.

308

39

IOANNIS

'Go and see what it is, Ioannis.'

'Why do I have to go?'

'Because you're the man. That's what men do.'

'I thought you were this *thing* – a feminist – Cindy.'

'I'm only a feminist until I hear a strange noise outside in the middle of the night.'

'It's probably just a dog, or a cat.'

'In that case, you've got nothing to worry about.'

'You really want me to go down?'

'Yes, I really do.'

Ioannis sighed and hauled himself out of bed. Slipped into his shoes. And, grumbling and grunting, went downstairs. Pulled a jacket on over his vest. Grabbed the axe handle from by the front door. He'd had it there since this situation had started with the Albanians.

He went out into the night. The security light was on. Something had triggered it. He heard the noise again – a rattling and banging – walked around the side of the house.

There was some guy trying to get into their garage.

'Hey! *Malakas*! What are you doing? Get away from there.'

The guy turned round, squinted at Ioannis. It was the American stoner, Joliffe.

'Ioannis!' he said. Looking like he was pleased to see him.

'What are you doing?' Ioannis asked – this time in English.

'You've got to help me out here, man. You've got to get me some. You got some in here? I know you have.'

'What is it you want?' Ioannis moved closer to him. 'What are you looking for?'

'The drugs, man, it's the drugs. I need more Afters. I know they were put in your car. Have you got them here?'

Joliffe's eyes seemed to be moving independently of each other. Swivelling around in their sockets. Like a broken toy, or some creature that was being eaten from the inside. Ioannis had seen them in nature documentaries on Discovery. Some nasty parasitic bug laid an egg inside a bigger bug, and as the larva hatched it turned the host's flesh to jelly and started to eat its way out. Nature was worse than any horror movie. Ioannis wondered what was going to burst out of Joliffe. The way he was behaving, Ioannis reckoned it was going to be some kind of psychedelic butterfly.

'But that stuff kills you.'

'Do I look dead?'

'You don't look very well.'

'That's just on the outside. Inside I am ... *born again*. Next stage, man. I have been upgraded. I'm one of the angels.'

'Go away. This is my house. Go home.'

'No way. I've gone too deep. And I'm going ever deeper. Joliffe's Bane. The dwarves tell no tale – do you follow me?'

'No.'

'I delved too greedily and too deep, and disturbed that *thing* ... I have disturbed it and it has risen inside me. AND I AM FILLED WITH LIGHT ... '

'I don't know what you are talking about, Joliffe.'

'I need more gear. I need more Afters. You got to help me.'

310

Seems Ioannis was right. There *was* a parasite taking the poor bastard over.

'Come on, Joliffe,' he said, keeping his voice low. Not wanting Cindy to hear any of this. 'They were contaminated. Vlachos tried to warn Malecaj . . .'

'Shit, man. Cry tough. It ain't the drugs. The drugs are fine. Some people just aren't strong enough. The drugs are bigger than they are. You got to be bigger than the drug. You get me? I can handle it. I am a voyager on the seas of Narcopia. I have taken oo-koo-he and ayahuasca with shamans in the jungles of Bolivia . . .'

'Yeah? For sure? When was that?'

'Well . . . I watched a thing on YouTube – but I was *there*, man. You know?'

'Is that the same?'

'If you get the drugs right – you travel on the astral plane and your spirit is there in the jungle with the shaman . . . You take the trip together.'

'But surely the video wasn't live?'

'Ha-ha-ha . . . Everything happens at the same time. Didn't you know? Smart guy like you. Time is *fluid*, folded, flexible, all things are simultaneous.'

'Come on, it's late. I need to sleep. Get away from here. I don't have no more drugs.'

'You got to. I need more. Feed me.'

'Joliffe. The pills kill you . . .'

'No, no, no . . . They showed me how everything really works . . . Finally I understand, it all makes sense.'

'Why do I have the feeling you are now going to say something that makes no sense at all?'

'We have to keep watch, guard against the shapeshifters. It's all there, brother, online – if you know where to look. The Truth. The Certainty! That which is above is from that which is below, and that which is below is from that which is above. Yeah?'

311

'I have to go to bed.'

'The Lemurians, the reptiloids, the shapeshifters, they seem like people but they're not, they're aliens or something I think. Maybe demons? Are they demons?'

'Who?'

'I told you, man, the shapeshifters. They work for the devil. Let me tell you about the devil. The devil is a woman. The devil is a shapeshifter. Sometimes he's a man, sometimes he's a woman, a fallen angel, you see? The angel, you have to listen to her, she's filled with light. A light so bright if you listen to her, she will tell you the truth. Her father is the sun and her mother's the moon. But the devil's a shapeshifter, first one thing, then another. You can't trust him, and he always – he always has his hound with him. Oh, yes. The devil dog. And sometimes the dog is the devil, and sometimes the devil is the dog. I saw all this. And I understood.'

'How many pills did you take?'

'One ... and then two more ... and then five. Five in one hit. I was so close to the edge. I was at the edge of the disc ... '

'What disc?'

'This flat earth we live on. I'd climbed the ice wall, baby. I'd gone past the wall of ice and I was looking over the edge into the abyss. And you know what I saw?'

'I have no idea.'

'I saw myself looking back.' Joliffe stretched out his arms, smiling like a politician and nodding his head, as if he'd just shown Ioannis the deepest truths of creation.

'Please,' said Ioannis. 'It's too late for this bullshit. I've heard enough about the fucking flat earth.'

Joliffe began to scratch his scalp manically, lips pulled back from his teeth, face screwed up, like a dog tormented by fleas. His hair was falling out and his fingernails came away bloody. He looked at them casually, then sucked them clean.

'I lived an entire life that first night,' he said. 'Let me die now. I

312

don't care. I begged him. I begged Mal, I went down on the floor and kissed his feet. I said, "Mal – you gotta let me keep some – keep some of this holy shit" but he didn't want any of it anywhere near him. He was scared. Never seen him scared before. He put them in your car, Ioannis. You're the driver now.' And with that, he flung himself at Ioannis, got his hands round his throat before Ioannis knew what was happening.

'I need more fucking pills!'

Ioannis shoved him away and he fell down hard on his ass. Sat there, like a little boy. He looked around as if unsure of where he was. Lost. Broken. When he looked up at Ioannis, he was crying.

'I didn't kill them,' he said miserably.

'Kill who?'

'You know, man ... You know ... '

'I never said you did.'

'Mal gave them to me. I gave them to the French kids. I took some. I saw ... I saw ... I saw the devil ... AND I AM AT THE END OF MY FUCKING ROPE.'

Joliffe turned his face to the stars, shiny with tears.

'I *did* kill them,' he said quietly. 'I gave those drugs to the French kids to sell, sent them out into the world. I should have kept them all for myself. I am a worthless piece of shit. I didn't want this. You know what I want?'

'No. I don't know what you want.'

'I want to be back in Thailand. Turn of the millennium. First time I left America. It was all so simple. I spent three years living in a beachfront, bamboo bungalow. Dollar forty a night. I didn't have to do anything expect make sure the sun would set on time. Huh. Know what I mean? Kids from all over the world. We'd build a beach fire and sit around drinking cheap Thai whisky and smoking out of bamboo bongs. That was the good times. Later came the smack. The other shit. Came here to escape all that. Ha-ha. Came here for the sea, the sky and the sand, the green hills and the calamari. That's all. In the end, you know, smoking weed on a beach was all I ever asked. And now look at me. What am I doing, Ioannis? Why am I mixed up with a godforsaken, motherless soul-eater like Malecaj?'

Joliffe got out a battered cigarette packet. Fumbled a cigarette into life and smoked for a while, sitting in the dirt. Thinking.

'Fun, baby,' he said after a while. 'Does not exist.'

'I can get you more of the drugs, Joliffe.'

'Ohhhhh . . . ' Such a deep sigh of longing.

'But there is a price.'

'I always pay my dues, man. Name your price.'

'Malecaj.'

'Huh?'

'You will be the man on the inside. And you will hand me his head on a plate.'

'Huh? Seriously? You want me to rat him out?'

'That's what I want you to do. He fucked my car. Tried to fuck me. Now I will fuck him.'

'We-ell . . . now . . . We-ee-eell now . . . I don't know. Malecaj is a mean bastard, if he found out, he might . . . '

'You want the drugs, or not?'

'I want the drugs.'

Joliffe stuck out his hand. Ioannis hauled him to his feet. Joliffe leaned in close. His breath stank.

'I can tell you one thing straight away,' he said. 'A down payment.'

'Tell me.'

'Genc Malecaj is trying to move in on your whole operation.'

'I know this, Joliffe.'

'Uh-uh-uh.' Joliffe raised a finger. 'He's been talking to Hepworth. They're going to cut you out.'

'Hepworth?'

'Hepworth's guy. One of his lawyers. Smooth, shiny, shit-ball called Rex Adams.'

'I don't know him.'

'Oh, he's a piece of work. He's invited Mal to Hepworth's party. They're going to have a big old powwow. You get me? Your man Vlachos is being written out of the picture.'

40

HUMAN

Macintyre laid everything out on the table – wallet, passport, plane ticket. Alan peered at them with bleary eyes. He looked like he hadn't slept at all last night. The harsh morning light was streaming in, bouncing off all the hard surfaces, and Alan was blinking and rubbing his face.

'You OK?'

'Do I look OK?'

'No. You look like shit, but then you always do.'

'Thanks. Didn't sleep at all last night. Tried mixing sleeping pills and brandy. Didn't work.'

'Sleeping pills and brandy wasn't very wise, Alan.'

'I thought you'd have worked out by now, Macintyre, that I'm not exactly behaving in a very wise fashion at the moment. In fact, I'm being very *un*wise. I am behaving with a total lack of wisdom.'

'Yes. And it's got to stop. I mean – what do you want? For Lauren to see you like this when she gets out? A piece of shit in a flowery shirt? Even if you don't care about yourself, you've got to care about what *she* thinks. You've got to offer her stability. You've got to be what she needs right now – an ordinary, boring father.'

'But I worry, Macintyre. That's the thing. I worry that that's all

I am. That I'm nothing to her. I can't compete with Hepworth. The golden boy. When you said she might not want to leave him. I have nightmares about it. Going back to an empty house. How can I offer her what Hepworth can? That life. That world. When we were told Lauren didn't want to talk to us, didn't want to see us, was having the time of her life . . . God, that's preyed on my mind. She *so* wanted to go. Like a racehorse out of the starting gate. And we signed everything that Hepworth's lawyers put in front of us.'

'You said before, Alan. You didn't know anything at the time. It wasn't out there, Alan.'

'Maybe it was. Maybe I just wasn't looking. I have to take the blame.'

'That's how he works it, Alan. Undermining people. Spreading doubt. Putting out half-truths and lies and nonsense. Turning things around, making people doubt themselves. Doubt the truth. Making sure the victims get blamed for what happens to them.'

'But I lie awake and I go over it and over it – am I any different from the parents who let their kids have sleepovers with Michael Jackson? *"They fuck you up, your mum and dad . . ."'*

'I always thought that Philip Larkin poem was bullshit,' said Macintyre. '*Every* mum? *Every* dad? *Every* child? Really? You're telling me the whole world is fucked up? I mean. Come on. You look out there – it's mostly just ordinary families watching *Pointless* and buying shoes online. It really bugs me that the word "normie" has become an insult. Someone who's bought into the heinous lies that big government, and the mainstream media, and the international, one world conspiracy sell us. Often used alongside "sheeple". Being called normal should never be an insult. It should be a badge of pride. Because the alternative . . . The alternative is *Hepworth*. Hepworth is different. Hepworth *actually is* fucked up. And he really does fuck up everyone around him. I've seen him up close now, Alan. Classic narcissist. Classic sociopath. Full-blown psychopath, for all I know. Turning on his charm, trying to manipulate everyone. There's a monster in this story and if anyone has fucked up your daughter it's him – *not you*. You said it yourself when I first met you – you're a normal guy.'

'Has he turned her, Macintyre? Corrupted her?'

'Don't think about it. There's nothing you can do about that right now. Just concentrate on what you *can* do.'

'What?'

'You've got to provide a safety net for her to fall into. Offer her normality. It's the best any parent can do. It's your job. Be consistent. Be stable. Don't be weird. Don't do a Larkin on your kid. Don't be a Hepworth. He's got Lauren there and we're going to get her out and then you're going to be her dad. So, get your shit together. You understand me?'

'When are you going to do it, though? How long is this going to go on for?'

'Any day now. That's why I need you gone. Your flight's in the morning. Pour your booze down the toilet, shave and shower and brush your teeth. Make sure you've got some clean clothes. *Sort yourself out*, Alan. Fly home. And, the next thing you know, Lauren will be walking in through your door. And you're going to be what she wants. A normie.'

He wasn't going to tell Alan that everything was in place. That the operation was tomorrow night. Almost the last thing had been to meet up with the Albanian, Genc Malecaj. Macintyre had enjoyed playing a stone-cold humourless Yank lawyer with a steel rod up his ass. Rex Adams. If the timings all went to plan, Malecaj's arrival at Hepworth's party would supply the diversion Macintyre and his team needed to get Lauren out. And then only this morning he'd had word from his Korean hackers that they'd found the chink in Hepworth's armour. The moth hole in his security blanket. They'd got into the top level of his security system. So they'd got their ducks lined up as straight as you ever could with wildfowl and he just needed to get Alan out of the way. Gone. No risk of adding any of his up-fuckery into the mix.

'But what do I say to her, Macintyre? When I see her in the doorway? Standing there? My girl. *Home.* I don't want to be a disappointment to her. She needs to be sure she's made the right decision to come back.'

'I don't have any kids, Alan. You're asking the wrong person. How about something simple and unmelodramatic, like "Hello, Lauren, welcome home"?'

'No. That's too stiff-upper-lipped. Too English, repressed. These days it's all hugs and kisses and emoting.'

'Again. You're talking to the wrong person.'

Alan flung out his arms. *'Hello, baby, we've missed you. We love you so much ... '*

'I think *"baby"* is wrong,' said Macintyre. 'Considering what she's been through.'

'Is *darling* better? Or is that charged, too?'

'Alan. Please. You sort it out.'

'How about I just keep it simple? *"Hello, love. We're so happy to have you back home. Everything's just how you left it ... "'*

'Yeah. Sounds good. Now you've got your ticket. Passport. I've even put some more euros in your wallet ... '

'"Welcome home, Lauren. It's all going to be fine from now. We'll talk and you can tell us everything you want to ... But if you don't want to talk, that's OK ... And ... And ... "'

He stopped. Eyes popping. Mouth open. Like a dog had just bitten him. Grabbed Macintyre.

'You bring her home,' he said. 'You fucking bring her home to me.'

'I'll bring her home.'

41

PIXIE

Pixie had all afternoon to get ready for the party. Massage, bath, shower, sit down with her hair and make-up team. Hair, face, skin, nails, wax job. The full baby's bum. Then get dressed, take her pills, a toke, a line, a mojito and go out to face the degenerate fuckers.

So she had plenty of time to make her video. She was looking forward to using her new Smart light bulbs. She really liked them. They were so cool. She'd screwed three of them in around her room. You could dim them, make them flash or pulse, or change the colour with just a few simple swipes on your phone. Flip the mood in an instant. Red light for a whorehouse, purple for a drugged-up, night-club, pink for hentai, ice-blue for a cool, sophisticated, but slightly weird vibe – useful for when Julian wanted Pixie to take control – and green if you wanted to throw up.

She hadn't told Julian about them, yet. It was going to be a surprise. He liked it when she took the initiative. This video would be their first reveal. She was going full Hollywood! She checked the picture on her laptop screen, tried changing the colour to see the effect. Cool. This was going to be a good one.

Julian loved her videos, which always started the same way – 'Hi,

Daddy!' He'd whack off to them, sometimes with Pixie in bed with him. She was getting ready for a full performance, with the type of faked orgasms he loved. All cross-eyed and fluttery, like she was having a stroke. Did he know they were faked? Did he care?

He'd given her a new toy. A pink Shibari Halo. Looked like a microphone, or some kind of power tool, with a big vibrating head on it. You didn't stick it up yourself, thank God, you just pressed it into your clit.

Maybe this would be the one? Maybe this would kick-start her libido, and she could finally see what all the fuss was about.

Yeah. Right.

Her family home, the place she'd grown up, *The Schloss*, as the family called it, was a dump. Schloss von Crantz – to give it its full name – sounded grander than it actually was. It wasn't a palace, or a castle, it was just a run-down, faded old house with too many rooms and a leaking roof, standing in what had once been a small park outside the town of Esch-sur-Alzette and was now in the suburbs, with most of the grounds sold off long ago.

Her bathroom – cold and draughty, a short walk along a landing that felt much longer in the dark of night – had an ancient toilet in it. God forbid they'd instal a modern, push-button thing. No. It was, like, a hundred years old and had a handle. And when you pulled the handle it never flushed first time. You had to keep pulling and pumping and coaxing it until eventually, if you were lucky, you tipped it over the edge and there was a gush of rusty brown water into the bowl. That was how she felt about orgasms. She tweaked and coaxed and pumped and was always just the wrong side of flushing.

Sometimes with the toilet, if it was just pee, she'd leave it. The whole place stank anyway. Of damp and mould and dead mice. Her en-suite bathroom here at Patia HepKat was bigger than her bedroom. She spent hours in there.

Her father never fixed that toilet at the Schloss, no matter how many times she complained. She begged him to put in modern bathrooms, but he refused. He never replaced anything in the Schloss, never updated anything, never properly mended anything. Said it was common. They had a Rubens in the living room, a Fragonard in the entrance hall, a Max Liebermann on the stairs, but they didn't have a modern bathroom or central heating in half the house. There were clocks everywhere, one of them worth half a million dollars, but none of them told the right time. Furniture from the eighteenth century, carpets with holes in them, tarnished silver service, and a three-bar electric fire in the dining room.

It was a dump, big and cold and horrible, just like her father.

God, she'd been so happy when she'd left home at fourteen. Spotted in *Tatler* and taken to Paris to become a model. So, she had to do some pretty sleazy things in Paris, but at least the toilets flushed. But after three years of modelling, it was clear her tits weren't going to stop growing and she had the wrong look for the catwalk or the pages of *Vogue*. She wasn't weird enough. So, she danced off to America. Married the first rich dick she met. Arnold Biederman, better known to the world as DJ Buzznutz. And what an asshole he turned out to be. Liked to get fucked up and knock her about all over the place. Cheated on her. Every fucking night. She'd been so happy when his Piper Mirage went down over the Gulf of Mexico and he was never seen again.

And then there was Julian. A true British gent. A true British cunt. He'd been obsessed with her, had photos of her everywhere, right from when she'd first started modelling. Wouldn't leave her alone. Sent cars for her, helicopters, planes ... In the end she thought, what the fuck, and gave in to him. He'd never given her any real pleasure.

So why did she want him?

She had *no fucking idea*.

She'd tried therapy. Four of the useless bastards. And they'd all told her the same thing.

'What about *you*? You need to think about yourself...'

Either that or 'Be in the moment...'

But she didn't want to think about herself. She didn't want to think about anything. She didn't want to be in this moment or any other moment. All she took comfort in was *things*.

She looked around her room. Everything modern. Everything new. Everything worked. Depending on her mood, Pixie either loved this room or wanted to burn it down. Watch the pink walls blacken and peel. The stuffed toys burst into flames. The heart-shaped bed become a bonfire. She pictured herself lying there, hands folded across her tits. Her pink, silk, shortie nightie becoming a shroud of flames. Like Joan of Arc. Say goodbye to all this shit in style. Ever since she was a girl, she'd loved seeing things fall around her.

Her mood right now was pretty neutral. The burn/not-burn balance was level. She'd taken the right combination of pills to just exist. She was coasting, hanging around, mellow. How pleased her ex-therapists would be to see her being so in the moment. Her pink, Party-Time machine was on, filling the room with sparkly bubbles. She watched them floating about, popping, falling. That is the inside of my head, she thought, and laughed. Yeah. Sometimes she could be *so* fucking deep. She looked at her reflection in the mirror that covered most of one wall. Went cross-eyed and stuck out her tongue.

'I am the fairy princess,' she said in the voice of a five-year-old.

There were star-shaped fairy lights everywhere. Hentai pictures on the walls. Every fabric was printed with unicorns or teddy bears or big-eyed, little girls. It was her pink palace. The place Julian most liked to have sex. Listening to the soundtrack from *Bilitis*, or *Emmanuelle 2*, or Serge fucking Gainsbourg. Christ, if she had to listen to 'Lemon Incest' one more fucking time, she thought she might spontaneously combust.

Yeah. This was the place that Julian liked to have sex all right. To

323

have sex and then leave. He always slept alone. All this was for him. She even had that tennis poster on the back of her closet door. The one with the girl in white, scratching her naked butt in the late afternoon sun. Julian had given it to her. Claimed it was ironic. It wasn't ironic. It gave him a hard-on. He'd first seen the poster when he was a boy and she reckoned it had shaped his whole life. His whole *philosophy* of life. It was what he aspired to. The beautiful life, his own tennis court, drinking cocktails as the sun went down, a hot young blonde with no knickers on. His fantasy life. Just like the framed David Hamilton photographs he had around the place. That was the world he wanted to live in, a land where innocent, pure, young, half-naked girls wafted around the Mediterranean getting off with naughty, handsome aristocrats in palazzos and beach huts and by the side of swimming pools. Like something from an old-school dirty book. *The Lusts of Lord Percy*. From before the internet.

The girls in those Hamilton photos were all young. Underage. When he was eighty-two, some of them had accused him of raping them. And Hamilton had killed himself. Was found in his Paris apartment with his head inside a plastic bag.

They always get you in the end. Things fall . . .

Didn't bother Julian. He collected original photos. Signed and numbered.

'They're art!'

Didn't hang any of them in the public areas, though.

There were a couple in Pixie's room. She didn't even see them anymore. They were just wallpaper. They'd burn well, though, when she set fire to the place!

She'd fought to be here. The only girl in Patia HepKat with her own bedroom. In the main house. Not like Miss Lily, packed away in a tiny closet in the staff annexe. And she had to keep fighting. To keep all this. Couldn't allow anyone else to take her place.

It might so easily have been Natasha.

And Natasha knew it. She'd risen up and threatened to bring

324

Julian down if she didn't get what she wanted. Pixie had seen what a danger she was. But not Julian. He was in love with her. Obsessed. Just like he'd been obsessed with Pixie when she was younger. Before she'd got old and become just his wank sock. He was ready to give Natasha everything. The keys to the kingdom. Pixie knew that Natasha got as little out of the sex as she did. It was everything else she wanted. And she had the single-minded ruthlessness of a young teenager. She was a good actress. She could pretend well. Pixie had seen it first-hand. Natasha would eventually learn how to do what Pixie did, learn how to take her place, and that would be the end for Pixie.

But, when it came down to it, Pixie was a better actor. She'd got close to Natasha, groomed her, confided in her, flattered her, made her believe that Pixie was her best friend in the whole world. She'd got under Natasha's skin. Made plans with her. Julian kept the girls dosed up and docile with his synthetic shit. Pixie went further. Started to share smack with the girl. Only smoking it at first but moving on. And all the while she was creating a fantasy of escape. How Natasha would be a star outside, the girl who brought down the Sun God's kingdom. Stoked her fires. Filled her head with dreams. And when they'd all been in Paris for a tournament, she'd introduced her to Raul. Handsome, young, charismatic. He'd crammed more dreams of escape into her head.

And she'd done it. Natasha had jumped ship. Pixie had got rid of her. The threat was gone.

And that was when she panicked.

Natasha could bring this whole thing crashing down. And if Julian ever found out it was Pixie who'd made it happen . . .

She hated herself for what she'd had to do to Natasha. She knew she'd never stop thinking about that night. The press had been all over it. Was it accidental, suicide, murder?

Pixie had been terrified for a while, but the interest had fizzled out and the police never got very far with it. She worried about

Adrian at first. That he might sniff the heady stink of money and betray her. After all, he must have known. He'd supplied the smack that killed the poor girl. But it turned out he wasn't invincible after all. He was found a few weeks after that night with a scaffolding pole rammed through his rectum all the way up to his lungs. There had been speculation about that, as well. Was it Albanians? A rival drug gang? In the end, his lawyer was arrested. Had wanted to take over the business.

So, Natasha was gone, and Adrian was gone, and Pixie was in the clear. It was between her and God.

And Ray.

Ray must have known as well. She'd occasionally give him a little treat to keep him onside, but she was working on a more long-term solution.

Because now, there was Lauren. And it was starting all over again. The girl was getting too strong. Too powerful. Pixie wasn't going to let it go so far with her. She was gonna nip Lauren in the bud. Cut her down to size. But she had to play this one differently, had to be more careful, not be so reckless and go so far. She just had to make sure Julian's affections for the girl soured. Make sure that if anything happened to her it was Julian's doing. It was a long game, she had to play it slowly.

She'd started whispering. Spreading rumours. Put it out there, subtly, very subtly, that Lauren was fucking Ray. That was all it took. This place was wound so tight already. All you had to do was start tiny cracks. Just like the tiny cracks in her bedroom walls at the Schloss, growing up. She'd notice one and watch it grow, bigger and bigger, year by year. The one by the window got so big you could poke your fingers in it. See daylight through it.

Lauren was going to crack. And Pixie was going to fix Ray into the bargain. Big, stupid, muscly creep with his tiny head. He was going to fall as well. Him and Miss Lily and the rest of them. She was going to clean the house.

Miss Lily hated her. Miss Lily hated everyone. Everyone and everything. Probably hated herself. She was the most miserable, hatchet-faced fucker Pixie had ever met.

This whole place was going to come down and all that was going to be left was Pixie. She was going to be queen of the world. Empress of oblivion. Have this whole place to herself. A ghost among the ruins.

But first she had to make this stupid, fucking, lame video for Julian. Rolling around in a world of bubbles with the pink power tool and squealing while the lights flashed, and her heart shrivelled even smaller.

She turned on the shower and stripped naked. Laid out a choice of outfits and wigs. She was about to go back into the bathroom when she felt a tickle on her inner thigh.

A mosquito. No matter what you did, they always got in. She watched it as it crawled over her shaved crotch. It stopped. Rubbed its legs and then stuck its snout into her skin. The filthy little bastard. She smacked it and left a smear of blood across her stubble.

That – she thought – is life.

42

SHOTS

The French kids were swarming around the gate, making a lot of noise, getting in everyone's way. They'd obviously started the party early. If they were this out of it now what were they going to be like later? Ray and his team were trying to process them through quickly because it was chaos down here right now, but the wankers couldn't have been less helpful if they'd tried. Didn't help that the brothers, Gabriel and Sacha, were wearing evil bunny masks that covered their heads. Mad teeth. Big ears sticking up. Like from that film. What was it? *Donnie Darko.* They had to keep pulling them off to show who they were and swapping them among the other kids who'd arrived with them.

They'd rocked up in the biggest stretch limo Ray had ever laid eyes on, and it was right now stuck halfway round the turning circle, painfully inching backwards and forwards. Two other Greek drivers had got out of their cars and were standing there, waving their arms about and giving unhelpful suggestions, while one of Ray's guys – who actually knew how to get cars round the circle – which was really more of an oval – was trying to make himself heard.

To be fair, the turning circle had always been too fucking small.

Hepworth had insisted on having one. He thought it made him look important. *Look at me with my fuck-off turning circle!* But, although he owned the access road, it only came with a narrow strip of land on either side of it. The architect had tried to squeeze a turning circle in, between the outer gates and the inner gates, and it had not been entirely successful. They'd blasted some rock away to create a bit more room, but when it came down to it, the circle was just that bit too snug. Even when there weren't many cars to contend with, bigger vehicles had a hard time of it and the circle tended to get fouled up. AND THE FUCKING FRENCH KIDS SHOULD HAVE KNOWN THAT. They'd visited enough times, hadn't they? The twazzocks couldn't have hired a worse vehicle – AND THEY ONLY LIVED ROUND THE FUCKING CORNER. It was almost as if they'd done it on purpose, as some kind of hilarious, young person's prank to post on YouTube.

What made it worse was the line of expensive hire cars, private cars and taxis backed up all the way down the access road. The drivers leaning on their horns, or out of their windows, shouting, swearing, jeering. Ray had his SIG Sauer in a holster on the back of his belt. He was really tempted to go down the line and stick the barrel in their fucking faces one by one and tell them all to SHUT THE FUCK UP.

With so many people arriving at the same time, the road was totally snarled up. Some of the guests were getting out of their cars early and hobbling up the stony, uneven roadway in high heels and tasselled loafers. Others sat fuming. It was chaos. And Ray was sweating it. Getting ratty. It didn't help that Hepworth had got all his staff dressed up in nautical costumes. Ray felt like some twat out of a gay perfume ad in his stripy top and round sailor's cap. So far, when it came down to it, the whole evening had been one long shitfest. Why couldn't Hepworth have staggered the invites? He knew how it got at the turning circle. Plus, too many guests had driven their own motors here, even though they'd been warned not to. Ray was sick to the back of his arse of people asking him about the parking situation.

DIDN'T YOU READ THE FUCKING INVITE? YOU CUNT! THERE IS NO PARKING SITUATION.

They'd fight their way up the access road and he'd just have to tell them to turn around and drive back down into town. Tell them to find somewhere on the streets – which really pissed off the locals and the holidaymakers in their expensive rentals.

The idea was to keep things moving. You pull up to the drop-off point. Your guests get out and you drive away, freeing up the space for the next vehicle. But some guests, especially the women, took an age to get out of the cars, rearranging themselves, sorting out their hair and make-up, putting on uncomfortable shoes, finishing phone calls...

'Yeah – we're there – so cool – I'll call you later and tell you all about it...'

AS IF THEY HADN'T HAD ALL FUCKING DAY TO GET READY.

To make it even worse there was a crowd of rubberneckers and media crews crowding round the outer gates, further clogging things up. The police had laid on extra security for Hepworth – for an eye-watering sum – and were down there keeping the sheeple back. But Ray had seen the hayseed cops earlier trying to take photos of the guests themselves.

There were a few celebs in tonight. Some US and UK film and TV types. Some models. Media types. Business faces. Lesser royalty. A few musicians. Couple of comedians. Too many reality stars. But most of the guests were from the ranks of the idle rich – the sort of cunts you saw in the glossy magazines, lined up and grinning in photos taken at society parties, birthdays, openings, first nights, fashion shows and charity dinners.

The only thing that eased the jam was the fact that maybe a

third of the guests were arriving by boat. It gave Ray some comfort to picture Herve and Lee Morgan and their team having just as shit a time of it as him. Although, to be fair, it tended to be more civilised down at the beach. There was plenty of room for the boats and they didn't have to contend with a crowd of no-marks watching them and getting in the way. Ray kept in constant touch with Herve and Lee and everyone else through his earpiece. He liked the earpiece. It gave him authority.

He had to admit he got a kick out of checking everyone who came in, no matter who they were. They might be bigshots out there in Paris, or London, or New York, but this was Ray's domain. Ray owned the gate. If you wanted to get in, you had to get past him.

He looked over to see the coach arrive – with Vlachos's girls grinning out of the windows – a riot of make-up, cheap bling and hair product. It was directed up the side access road that – thank God – branched off just before the turning circle. Two young lads were in charge of that operation, keeping the entrance to the side road blocked with crash barriers, which they had to drag apart every time someone needed to get up there – caterers, musicians, the technical guys doing the fireworks, and, right now, the big coach. There were twenty-five girls on there, ready to make the party go with a swing. Ray caught a glimpse of Ioannis sitting up front with the driver, grim-faced and weary looking.

Good. The girls were here. That was one more thing Ray could tick off his list. He really wished he could have had the evening off to enjoy the party, but this was his busiest night of the year. Hepworth was having a smaller bash for the staff in a few days' time, once the dust had settled. Cheap booze and supermarket snacks instead of the lobster and champagne laid on for the guests tonight.

He looked at the big stupid fucking stretch fucking limo. It was gonna be another couple of minutes before it got round the circle.

331

Shit on the Frogs. Thousands of the fuckers had poured out of the car when it had pulled up. The de Surmont brothers, a couple of wide-eyed teenage boys, little more than kids, who'd be puking cocktails into the bushes and passing out well before midnight, the two naïve tourist girls from Agios Symeon – Juno and Taz – who Ray had told the brothers to definitely bring along tonight. And last to get out of the car were a couple of older American guests. Which had made Ray's heart sink.

Rich, entitled Yanks were always the hardest work.

The guy was your typical slick LA type. Longish, blond hair with an expensively messy Brad Pitt sort of styling. Dark plum polo shirt under a shiny, grey suit. Nicely cut. Italian. Aviators after dark. The wanker. Ray was pretty sure he'd seen him on TV somewhere, he looked familiar. He was on his phone now, not even looking at Ray. Offhand. As far as he was concerned, Ray didn't even exist. Sounded like he was making some kind of a deal. Shouting down the line. If Ray had had more time, he'd have loved to give the guy a full Stasi welcome, Checkpoint Charlie, metaphorical torch up the bum-hole, delay him getting in, but right now he just needed to shunt everyone through and clear the backlog. He'd enjoy taking his phone off him, though.

He liked that part.

The guy's name checked out but didn't ring any bells with Ray. Where had he seen him? Ray nodded to Beatty to give him a basic wristband. And then Ray held out his hand – he was going to do this part personally, not leave it to Beatty.

'Can I take your phone please, sir?'

'Say again?'

'No phones inside, sir. We'll bag it and tag it – if you need to make a call come down to the gatehouse and you can do it from there.'

'Seriously?'

He gave the jerk a big smile. 'Same for everyone, sir. You're here to party, not make calls. Mister Hepworth insists on it. He wants people to enjoy theirselves tonight. So, no selfies, and no snaps of other guests having a good time.'

Before the guy could protest anymore, Ray passed him along to the girls who were taking care of the phones.

Now Ray turned to address the crowd of guests trying to get in.

'You all have to hand in your phones, folks! No more Instagram pics tonight, I'm afraid. We'll keep them safe for you. There are a couple of photographers roaming around. There'll be a website with photos you can download if you want one to show your grandchildren.'

Blondie had gone in. The last of the de Surmont party to process was a fit black babe showing a lot of tit. Great hair. Probably a wig. Covered in tats and dressed in that glam/fetish way that meant she was either a hooker or an R&B star. She looked familiar, too. But, shit, there were so many of them – they had a couple of raunchy hits, thrust their crotch at you in some headache inducing, semi-porn video and you never saw them again.

Ray wished more than ever that he could be let loose tonight. This lady was begging to be ridden hard. Not Hepworth's style at all. Too scary for him. Too powerful. Juno and Taz would be upgraded to Noblesse wristbands later. Lured down into the basement. No doubt about it. They were right up Hepworth's strada. But not the soul diva. She would stay up top.

Shit. Ray was fired up now. He liked a challenge. A fuck that was more like a fight. This lady was going to be the life and soul of this one. Beatty strapped on her wristband. She handed over her phone without being asked, shook her booty and shouted –

'OK! Let's paaaar-tee!'

Lee Morgan's earpiece squawked as Ray said something unintelligible. Like one of the robots in *Star Wars*. Something about phones, maybe? Lee had other things to worry about. There were three launches backed up waiting to dock, but he was still process-ing guests on the jetty. Herve had a couple of extra guys who were helping out, but they were slow. They were hired muscle really. Paperwork was not their strong point.

Lee was not having a good night. That bloody Lauren. Why did she have to go and make things so difficult? What was it she'd said? *If Hepworth came crashing down, they all did.* It was that or help the girl. Either way could lead to ruin. There was only a very slim chance that Lee might not get rumbled and kicked out on his arse.

Not that that was the worst thing he feared.

There were a lot of rumours about Hepworth.

Lee was finding it hard to concentrate. He was going over and over the details of Lauren's plan in his mind. A fifteen-year-old girl, plotting like a hardened con planning a prison break. She was going to go far, that girl. Or end up at the bottom of the Straits wearing a concrete life vest.

He just hoped his mate, Pan, would be ready and waiting on his Monte Carlo hard-top out in the Straits as they'd arranged. Well out of the view of the cameras. Pan ran a charter business out of Kontokali and was always up for making a bit of money on the side. No questions asked. A little run over to Albania – the main-land – not check the passenger details too closely, or the cargo.

The guy was a pirate. But Lee trusted him. He was gonna take the girls into Corfu Town and after that . . .

Lee didn't know what happened after that, and he didn't want to know. He just hoped Lauren had it all figured out.

Let's face it, they'd probably never get that far. Never get off the beach. Security was super-tight tonight and Herve was itching for the chance to throw his weight around. It was all too risky. The route from the party down to the harbour was lined with cameras, and even if Lee did manage to get the girls out to Pan, he had to come back and face the shit that would be flying out of the fan.

334

Hepworth had all the CCTV footage backed up on his servers. If Miss Lily didn't spot the girls on the way down, hidden among other partygoers, it wouldn't take her and Hepworth long to find the relevant footage later, spool through to see them disappearing along the beach. And then they'd see Lee taking the ViperMax out. Two and two would add up to a royal bollocking.

Yes. Lee was fucked whatever happened. Maybe he should hop on Pan's boat with the girls? Get the fuck away from this place and never come back.

Best not to think about it. Maybe Lauren and Sigrid would never make it this far. Maybe they'd bottle it. Maybe Hepworth wouldn't let them out of his sight ...

Right now, he just had to get these folks off the jetty and sort the next lot out. Come on, Lee. Focus on the job in hand. Be in the moment. Wasn't that what they always told you?

He just wished he could be in a different moment to this one.

Miss Lily was sitting in the windowless control room in the basement, staring, unblinking, at the screens. Amazing, the things you saw when you watched closely. When you paid attention. The things you learned about people. The secrets.

She had a whole wall of screens. Scrolling and flipping, zooming, panning, black and white, colour, night vision, all linked up to the computer system. It had taken her months to learn the best way to use them, how to read them, to see the patterns, the details in the digital fog. She knew everything about everyone here. How one of the gardeners swam in the pool at night. How two of the male kitchen staff were having a thing. How some of the household staff were stealing booze and food. How Ray was abusing the Danish mulatto girl, Sigrid. How Pixie had some new doomed scheme on the go. How Lauren was plotting something with at least three of the other girls ...

So much going on. And Miss Lily was teasing it all out,

putting it all together. She didn't tell Mister Hepworth everything. Only what she wanted to tell him. She had the real power here. The information she was gathering as a weapon, to be stored and used only when the time was right. In the meantime, she sat here, hour after hour, watching. Nothing escaped her ever-moving eyes.

There was Ray at the main gate with his team, checking in the guests. A long line building up. Ray was too slow. She made a note of it.

There was Lee at the harbour. Smiling and joking as he processed the guests who'd arrived by boat. He was taking too long as well. He didn't have to bother with the chat. The banter. Didn't have to try to be liked. Nobody cared about him. Most of them didn't even see him. *Just get them through, Lee. Get them to the party.* He was nervous about something. She could read it in his body language.

She made a note of it.

There was Tokyo Masombuka, in the office, working late as always. One of Mister Hepworth's eunuchs, his harem guards, sexless and dedicated.

There was David Hamlish, the TV exec, talking to a bunch of money guys on the sofas inside the house. There was Karagiannis with two of the girls Ioannis had brought in. Did they know he was a policeman? Not that he cared.

The sprung dance floor, built out over the lawn, was heaving. So much flesh. So much hope and expectation. So much disappointment. There was the English actress, Sally Spence, dancing with a much younger man. Was she going to stay here for ever?

Beyond the dance floor was the stage. A band playing right now. Some Italian pop group Mister Hepworth had shipped over for way too much money because he liked their singer. A young girl with bleached blonde hair who dressed like a schoolgirl and sang about lollipops.

There was a famous American band on later. Miss Lily knew she should recognise the name, but she didn't know about these things. In fact, she didn't much like music, really. She'd heard too much of it in the girlie bars of Manila where she'd grown up.

And there was the tennis team, getting ready in their bathroom, chattering into the mirrors, putting on powder and paint and lip gloss, hair spray, nail paint. Like a bunch of tarts, smearing, smudging and yacking. Yack-yack-yack. So many words spilling out of their empty, half-formed little brains. Too much going on tonight, too much noise to listen in. But she'd be watching.

She zoomed in on Lauren. She'd been keeping a sharp eye on her lately. She'd been worried about her for some time. Didn't like to let her out of her sight. She was cooking something up, that girl, for sure, and Miss Lily was going to catch her out.

She wasn't going to let that girl out of her sight.

Lauren was next to Sigrid at the mirror, applying the finishing touches. They didn't want to risk talking now. When they were out there in the party, with the music blaring and the wall of chat, it'd be safe. For now, they just had to keep their nerve. She'd gone over the plan so many times. It *had* to work. The hardest part was going to be convincing poor Lee Morgan to take all fifteen of them. She hadn't dared tell him in advance.

He was going to have a fucking heart attack.

It was like looking into a beehive. Sooner or later you made sense of it all. The swarming, milling, crawling insects. And there was Julian himself, now. King Bee. Working the crowd. Never standing still, shaking hands, giving hugs and kisses, doing those ridiculous rapper hand-slapping greetings ...

His party, his world, his people. Miss Lily had never seen him happier.

*

337

Hepworth was moving, always moving, like a shark. Yeah. The Finn had sorted him with a special pill, cooked up just for tonight. Called it 'No More Party Fears 2'. And it was *working*. He was high and mellow and focused and crazy and buzzing and jitterbugging all at the same time.

He was like a spirit, a party deity, gassing his guests, firing them up, making sure they were happy . . .

Have you checked the cocktail bar in the grotto? All the drinks are fucking luminous . . .

You've gotta – you brought a swimsuit, yeah? – you gotta try the hot tubs. No swimsuit, no problem – we're all liberal here – gotta have an open mind – let it all hang loose and blow in the breeze . . .

Have you tried out the nail parlour and the glitter face painting?

You have *to try the moonlight woodland walk – there are surprises at every turn . . .*

Did you catch the Mariachi band? They're here all night! They'll be somewhere, check 'em out . . .

Anything you want, we've got it. Food from all round the world. Have you seen the guy making mozzarella? Amazing.

Don't miss the fireworks!

Macintyre was keeping a low profile. Chatting to people so as not to draw attention to himself as some weird loner. He was wearing the same microphone and battery pack transmitter they'd used for the interview with Hepworth, and was keeping in touch with his team via wireless ear buds concealed under his blond wig. The signal from the mics was being picked up by the drone – far enough above the party to be out of sight of Julian and his security. And the drone was transmitting the signals not only to his team at the party, but to the powerful satellite equipment on Pike's boat, sitting out in the Straits. Pike's gear instantly bounced the signal on to Korea – from satellite to satellite right around the world – where Macintyre's guys were processing all the data. They, in turn, were using the drone to hack into Julian's security. The Koreans had been working on it for days and had eventually found a way in *via a light bulb*.

Somebody in the house had installed a cheap, Chinese knock-off smart bulb system and it had been a tiny keyhole through which the Koreans had been able to open the door to Hepworth's network. They hadn't got very deep into his computer system yet but had access to everything connected to it. It meant that Macintyre and his team could listen in on all the walkie-talkie traffic at the estate, and, even more crucially, access the security cameras. It was only a matter of time before somebody at Patia HepKat found out about the bulbs and the miscreant got hauled over the coals, but, so far, they'd remained undiscovered. And Macintyre was in now, even if they locked the door behind him.

Hepworth had helped build the digital world and now it was going to bite him in the buttocks.

Macintyre looked at his reflection in the big sheet-glass window. Not sure if the blond look suited him. He had to admit that Aimee looked fabulous, though. She was out on the dance floor now doing her thing. Putting much younger girls to shame with her moves. She had the toughest job. It was down to her to convince Lauren to go along with their plan and not freak out. If Lauren didn't trust Aimee they were screwed.

Sacha and Gabriel de Surmont had rounded up a posse of young people. Were cruising the party, hoovering up drinks. Gabriel their leader. Loud. Shirt undone to his waist.

'I am going to get into the secret party tonight. *This time.* Yeah ... And I am not going to go home until I've got close to Pixie. She's a goddess.'

'Forget it, Gabriel. She is out of your league, man.'

'A kiss. I would settle for just a kiss. I would die happy if Pixie was only to kiss me ...'

One of the boys kissed Gabriel and Gabriel chased him across the lawn. Everyone laughing.

Sarah was on the *Louise B* flying the drone, eyes fixed on the laptop, keeping an eye on the flight time. Battery life was forty minutes. Didn't want to be out of commission changing batteries at a crucial moment. She was flying so high, the image on the screen was like looking at Google Maps. Pike was on a second laptop, looking at the security cameras and listening to the messages over the radio comms system. This was the modern world, that nobody had predicted. The digital world – everything connected. You never saw, in those old sci-fi movies, the people of the future in their silver suits wandering around staring at their phones. *Blade Runner, The Time Machine, 2001*, you never once saw anyone using Twitter.

Well, actually, when it came down to it, they wouldn't be, would they? Not in 2001. Hard to believe it, but the film was set in a time before Twitter. Facebook. YouTube. Tik-Tok.

2001 was already ancient history.

'Hey, Pike?' she called out. Hoping he could hear her behind his giant headphones.

'Yeah?'

'What do we do if there's fireworks? The drone could be knackered.'

'I was just thinking that myself. There's definitely talk of a display. Let's hope they hold off 'til at least midnight. But first signs of any sparklers and you pull the drone out of there.'

'Sure. Not much happening up there right now. I think this is a good time to bring her in and swap batteries.'

'Good idea, hon . . . '

Hepworth had found Juno and Taz, the young girls from the village Ray had spotted on their first night. What a pair they made. Juno with her dark skin and Taz so fair. He had them all to himself. They were glugging frozen margaritas and rocking backwards and forwards on the swing seat between the dance floor and the pool.

'So, what's Taz short for? No – let me guess. Anastasia?'

'Nope.'

'Tamsin?'

'Nope.'

'I got it – Theodora?'

'No way.' The two girls laughed.

'OK. You got me.'

'Tazmania.'

'Tasmania? You're kidding.'

'Nope. It's a nickname. My big brother gave it to me when I was teeny. He used to watch this kids' cartoon show ...'

'Tazmania!' Hepworth yelled, and giggled. 'Shit, I remember that. Why's it not on anymore? It was cool.'

'I don't really remember it, to be honest. But, apparently, I used to behave like the main character – Taz.'

'He was a Tasmanian devil,' said Hepworth. 'Used to go batshit crazy, smashing around all over the place, spoke this kind of mad, spluttery language. Hwabba-wrabber-thwubber-rrrrber ...'

'Well, that was *me*! Mini Taz. I used to entertain big bro for hours, apparently.'

'Who put the Taz in Tasmania ...?' Hepworth sang. The girls didn't join in.

'And what about you, Juno, how'd you get your name?'

Juno shrugged. 'Dunno. It's just my name.'

'Juno was the queen of the Roman gods.'

'Yeah?'

'And look at you – you're a queen.'

'Don't feel like one.'

'The two of you – you're a picture. A black and white picture! Ha-ha-ha-ha.'

341

'Funny,' said Juno, in a way that implied it wasn't.

Hepworth pressed on. The drugs didn't have any brakes.

'The two of you ... The two of you ... You're like a black and white sandwich – like an Oreo. You like Oreos?'

'Not really,' said Juno. 'They suck.'

'All American biscuits suck,' said Taz seriously. 'Their chocolate is cheap shit.'

'Yeah,' said Juno, warming to the theme. 'Oreos are just a cheapo American biscuit with fonky chocolate.'

'They're an institution!' Hepworth protested, sounding more put out than he'd meant to.

'I prefer British biscuits,' said Taz.

'Me, too.'

'Really?'

'Yeah.'

This wasn't going quite the way Hepworth had hoped. This was not sexy or glamorous. That was often the problem when talking to kids.

'I like chocolate digestives,' said Taz. 'They're the best. Everyone knows they're the top biscuit.'

'I like a Jaffa Cake,' said Juno.

'Ooh. Controversial. You've opened a can of worms, there. Is a Jaffa Cake a cake or a biscuit?'

'It's a biscuit.'

'How about a finger of fudge?' said Hepworth and he felt his face pulling a wide grin. Like the worst kind of asshole.

Juno gave him a long, level look.

'How old are you?' she asked, with all the scorn that a teenager could load into a sentence.

These girls were a touch more sassy than he liked. He'd have to teach them a little lesson. Get them fucked up and show them how the world worked.

'Listen,' he said. 'My guy, Ray, is going round handing out

special wristbands. Exclusive access. Noblesse. To my VIP area . . .
I'll tell him to look out for you, yeah?'

'Will there be biscuits?' said Taz and the girls laughed.

'You'll have to find out for yourselves . . . Go down the rabbit
hole into Wonderland . . . Oh, wait, you have *got* to come and see
this! It's the parade.'

The Eurotrash band had finished, which looked like it had come
as a big relief to many of the partygoers. It was certainly a relief
to Aimee, who hadn't taken to their mix of big hair rock, disco,
Latin and Italian reggae.

Now the deejay had gone into overdrive, pumping up the crowd,
shouting encouragement-to-party over an incessant, thumping,
electronic, bass beat that kept building up but going nowhere.

And now there were screams of delight and drunken whoops as
Hepworth took to the stage, clutching a cordless mic.

'OK, ladies and gentlemen, boys and girls, ladyboys and
trannies, crazies, animals, aliens, cyborgs, dwarves, orcs, elves,
hermaphrodites, non-gender aligned, black, white, yellow, brown,
pink and blue and green, rainbow alliance, unicorns, LGBT, BLT,
BBQ lovers, self-abusers and accountants!'

Whoop-whoop-whoop.

'And I apologise sincerely if I've left anyone out!'

'Hey! You left out the Inuit, you racist scumbag, Hepworth!'
came a raucous voice from the crowd and everyone roared with
laughter and cheered and whooped some more.

'It's the moment you've all been waiting for,' Hepworth yelled.
'As I present – all the way from the winners' podiums of every
major junior tennis tournament in the world – the reason we are
here tonight, the reason I get up in the mornings, the reason I built
this place, the stars of tonight's extravaganza, the most special,
the most precious people in my world – LET'S HEAR IT FOR
The Team!'

A massive roar and cheer. Spotlights came on and all eyes were focused on the huge, glass sliding doors to the house. Two flunkeys dressed as sailors pulled them apart with a theatrical flourish and the first of Hepworth's tennis players emerged, blinking into the light.

Music blared from the speaker stacks. Aimee recognised the intro. So familiar. And then the chorus kicked in . . .

Here come the girls!

Jesus. *Really?* How old was this song? For a while it had been the soundtrack to every reality show, strippers' convention and cheap advert trying to sell the concept of girl power – usually using half-dressed young women. Well, Hepworth didn't have any class. And none of his music choices were exactly cutting edge.

It worked for him. And it worked for the crowd.

A long, temporary wooden ramp, like a catwalk, had been installed. It started at the terrace by the house and jutted out towards the dance floor. It was covered in a purple carpet and had been slightly in the way all night. People had been having to negotiate their way round it or had been using it as a makeshift seating area. But now it came into its own as everyone stood back, clapping in time to the Sugababes, as the tennis team came out and strutted past them, half walking, half dancing, with fixed grins on their over-made-up young faces. They were all dressed in white, in different styles – short skirt, long dress, trouser suit, boilersuit, glammed-up tennis outfit with visor, short-shorts and halter top, T-shirt dress, nurse's outfit, princess, oversize man's shirt with a belt, sixties PVC with thigh-length boots, floaty diaphanous summer dress with wide-brimmed hat, cowgirl . . .

At a prom night, among other young people, this might have been fun for the girls, but here, tonight, on show, with a much older crowd, it was grotesque. Sordid. Like a knocking shop.

Aimee looked for Lauren. Despite their different outfits, at first glance it was hard to tell the girls apart. There was something about the spectacle that had robbed them of their individuality, like a chorus line. All wearing the same colour, the same make-up, the same forced expressions of FUN.

I am young and gorgeous, full of life, in my prime – and I AM HAVING FUN!

There she was – in the boilersuit. Athletic, like all the girls, medium height. Impossible to tell what she might be thinking. Dutifully going through the moves. Not the greatest dancer, but maybe her heart wasn't in it.

Never mind. They were a girl group. The overall mass effect was more important than what any one of the individuals did. In its way it was dazzling. Hepworth's fantasy world come to life. His id prancing up there like a pure white circus pony.

More 'sailors' were patrolling the catwalk, making sure nobody got too close. The two official photographers were flashing away. And Hepworth stood on the stage, entranced, legs wide in the power stance, exhorting his guests to cheer louder, to enjoy the show, to feel like they'd arrived.

Waiting for his girls to come to him.

Tokyo could hear the cheers and shouts from outside, that damned stupid track that Hepworth loved so much. He tried to shut it out. Deep into a long and complex legal document. Putting out fires again. It was getting out of control. There was a danger that Hepworth was going to go the way of Michael Jackson, and drown in NDAs, payoffs, buyouts, hush money, veiled blackmail threats, gagging orders, out-of-court settlements, golden handcuffs ... His fortune dribbling away to nothing. And the fact was that he hadn't ever actually had that much money to start with. It was a scam, a bubble, an illusion, a dream. As long as everyone thought he was billionaire, he could behave like one. The sad truth of this world was that banks bent over backwards to lend gold to people who they thought already had saddlebags filled with the stuff.

What Tokyo had seen of Hepworth's finances, they were an arcane mare's nest of debts, loans, dummy corporations, false fronts, weird offshore accounts, unpaid bills, legal battles and fantastical accounting. Hepworth really needed this new media deal to come through. Tonight was as much about impressing his potential partners and investors as it was about entertaining his so-called friends. The amount of dodgy money and debt that was going to be funnelled through this new venture was going to come as a kick in the balls to the other guys – if they ever found out.

Plan was. Day after tomorrow – they'd need a day to recover – they were all going to sit down together in the main living room and thrash out a deal over lobster, champagne, vodka and caviar.

But Tokyo wasn't stupid. He was making sure his insurance was all in place. Busy ferreting away various incriminating and eye-opening documents into secret files that only he could access. When they came for Hepworth – whoever *they* might be – the good, the bad or the ugly – Tokyo was going to be ready and eager to help out.

Cooperative.

The man with all the secrets.

'What is this, babe? What is this video you sent me?'

'It is what it is.' Grinning. 'Did you watch it?'

'Yeah, I watched it. I just watched it now.'

Pixie had sent it earlier – just as Julian was dressing for the party – to make sure he kept his eye on the ball. Knew what was on offer for him later if he finished the night in her bed and not with someone else. She'd put a lot into it. Best ever. Saying and doing all the things her daddy loved. And she'd programmed her new lights to keep switching up the mood. It was funny, too, though she said it herself. She was FUCKING ADORABLE and would be an adorable fuck. She'd kept it short, though. It promised a lot. Julian had to supply the ending himself. The climax. In person.

'The lights, babe? What's going on with the lights?'

'Do you like them? Aren't they wild?'

'What are they? What the fuck are they?'

'What's the matter? Don't you like them?'

'It's not a question of whether I like them or not – IT'S WHERE THEY FUCKING CAME FROM.'

'All right, all right . . . No need to lose your shit.'

'I will lose my shit if I want to lose my shit – it is my shit to lose and right now, yes, I am fucking losing it. So, tell me where those lights came from, before I break your fucking face?'

'I bought them. You can control them with your phone.'

'That's it. That's what I thought. That's why I am losing my shit, here. You can't just attach anything to the wi-fi, *darling*. The fucking Bluetooth.'

'I thought you'd be pleased. I thought you'd like my initiative. Making things fun for you.'

'Right now, the most fun I can imagine is squeezing your neck until your eyes pop out.'

'Why are you doing this? Why are you saying these things?'

'You have to lose the app. OK? Right now. Quit out of it and delete it. On all your devices. You have to lose the lights. You want fancy lights you ask me, and I'll sort it for you. I'll get you the best lights in the world. You don't use your own initiative. Understand? You don't ever use your own initiative. You are there to be fucked and to look good at my parties.'

'I don't know why you're so mad at me.'

'Because you have created a potentially catastrophic breach of security. If someone wanted to hack into my system . . . '

'Could they do that?'

'They could. They fucking could. If things aren't installed properly, if the correct protocols aren't followed, if they're not shielded, then a smart phone, a smart fridge, a vacuum cleaner, a car, a fucking light bulb, they can all become Trojan horses.

You follow me? A way in. I mean, Jesus, how long have you had them?'

'A little while, but, baby . . . '

'Oh, shit.'

'If you took more of an interest in me.'

'If I took more of an interest in you? MORE OF A FUCKING INTEREST! I've been a bit busy lately, babe, with this media deal, in case you hadn't noticed. I don't need to be distracted by having . . . FUCKING CONVERSATIONS with you? OK? Now go back to your room and obliterate everything.'

'Are we safe?'

'I don't know . . . Yeah . . . Yeah. OK. I'm sure we are . . . Yeah. Don't cry, babe. I shouldn't have sounded off like that. Someone would have had to get right up close and personal to hack in. And, even then, my computers have more levels of security than there are levels of hell. They're safe. They'll be safe. It's the peripheral stuff.'

'Like someone could have hacked in and secretly vacuumed your office at night?'

'Yeah – ha-ha-ha – something like that. But, please, babe, be more careful. Think of *me* sometimes instead of yourself.'

'I'm sorry, honey, I will *so* make it up to you later . . . '

'I know you will. But you may still have to be properly punished.'

'Promises, promises.'

'And you'll make it downstairs? For the real party?'

'I'm your slave, master. Tonight, I will grant your every wish.'

'Good girl. *My* girl. Love you, babe.'

'Love you more.'

'Love you squared.'

'Love you to the moon and back.'

Pixie blew him a kiss and he walked away, giving his arse a little comedy wiggle.

*

Aimee had managed to get close to Lauren. Danced her way through the crush on the bouncing dance floor and was now bumping hips with the girl in the white boilersuit. The two of them laughing. Aimee whooped and Lauren whooped. She was a better dancer when she wasn't being watched.

The music was booming, there was a babble of voices all round them, people shouting to be heard over the thumping beats. Aimee was ready to go for it.

'Lauren?' she said, as loudly as she dared, and Lauren looked at her, wide-eyed – *what was this?*

'It's OK,' said Aimee. Smiling, smiling, smiling. 'Don't get freaked. You don't know me. But I need to talk to you.'

'Er, cool – OK – this is weird – you want to go somewhere quieter?'

'Nope, I want to stay right here, girl. Whoo-hoo! This isn't for all ears.'

Lauren's face clouded. A frown, looking around. Should she put some distance between her and the weird black woman with the afro and the glittery face paint?

'Keep smiling,' said Aimee. 'Keep whooping, keep dancing and hear me out.'

'I'm listening. I'm still dancing.'

'You seen *Star Wars*?'

'Course I've seen *Star Wars*. Everyone's seen *Star Wars*.'

'You can't count on it these days.'

'I've seen it. I know *Star Wars*, OK?'

'Yeah, well, I'm Luke Skywalker. I'm here to rescue you.'

'Aren't you a little black for a stormtrooper?'

'Ha-ha! You *do* know your *Star Wars*.'

'Is this for real?'

'No. I was lying. My name's not Luke Skywalker. I'm not a stormtrooper. I'm Aimee, and I've been hired by your dad.'

'What? You what? You're really? Seriously? This is ... No way. Is he here?'

'He's not here. Whoo-hoo!'

'Whoo-hoo!'

'He wants you out of here, Lauren. And I'm here to make that happen.'

'You're shitting me.'

'I need to know it's what you want, though. I can't force you. I'm not some kind of Special Ops shit. If this is going to happen it needs to be done quietly and smoothly and with your full cooperation.'

'Look...'

'If everything goes to plan, you'll be back in England tomorrow. Back home. You just need to tell me – yes, or no. Are we on?'

'Yes, but...'

'Good girl. Whoo-hoo!'

'Whoo-hoo... There's just one thing I have to tell you...'

Ray was in Pixie's room, staring at the picture of the tennis girl hitching up her skirt. Looked like he'd been going through her closet. He was holding a waste bin with the shattered remains of her bulbs.

'Ray...?'

'Hepworth sent me.'

'I was gonna do that.'

'Beat you to it. We don't want to take any chances here, Pixie. We gotta be smart.'

'Like the bulbs.'

'Like the bulbs.'

He was still staring at the poster.

'You like that picture?'

Ray shrugged. 'She's got a nice arse on her.'

'I read somewhere that all the problems in this world are caused by the male gaze...'

'Yeah?' He was thinking hard about this. 'I don't have lot of time for them, but I can't see that...'

350

'Time for who?'

'The gays.'

Pixie sighed. 'Fuck off out of here, Ray.'

Ray stepped closer to her. In her high heels they were about the same height. He gave her a hard look.

'Don't ever try to fuck with me, Pixie. I know where the bodies are buried. I know what you did in Paris.'

Pixie smiled at him, gave him a big kiss. The full works. Tongues and everything. Grabbed his dick through the sailor pants and squeezed it. Felt it harden.

She stepped away from him. Smiled again.

'Fuck off out of here, Ray.'

'Mac. We've got a problem.'

'There's always a problem, Aimee. Our job is to just keep fixing them.'

'This one's pretty big.'

'How big?'

'Fifteen.'

'What do you mean, fifteen?'

'Lauren has her own thing going. She was planning to bust out of here tonight.'

'Tonight? Shit. OK. Right. Well, that shows some spirit. I like this girl.'

'But she wasn't going to go it alone.'

'Ah ... So, how many of them were planning to try?'

'As I said. All fifteen of them ...'

'All of them? OK. Well, that changes things just a little.'

'Just a little. What do we do, Mac?'

'We're only here for Lauren.'

'But, Mac, this could be ...'

'This could be the "all is lost" moment, Aimee. If we try to change too much at this stage. We stick to our original plan. OK?

We have to. It's thought through. Everything's in place. It can work. But fifteen . . . '

'We just leave them?'

'Once Lauren's out, once she talks, we can get this place shut down. The other girls can walk out of here. If they just hold on . . . '

'The bulls are running, Mac. This might be out of our hands.'

'What's the deal?'

'There's a track that Hepworth always plays at his parties, apparently. It's the trigger. The signal to the girls to set their escape plan in motion. As soon as that song starts, we'll have to move. Whatever.'

'How long have we got?' Mac looked at his watch.

'Don't know. But we have to coordinate with these girls, somehow, or it could get ugly. Can't we just scale up our plan, Mac? If it works for one it can work for more.'

'Two maybe . . . *three*. But *fifteen*, Aimee. We need to be driving this, not them.' He looked at his watch again. 'Shit. You know what makes it worse? The distraction's due to start any minute now. What if the track comes on before then? You've got no idea of the timings?'

'Nope. And Lauren doesn't, either. But they planned it to happen at a moment when everyone was distracted and Hepworth was on stage.'

'That's good planning – no help to us, though.'

'As you, said, boss, there's always a problem and our job is to fix it.'

'But fifteen, Aimee. Fifteen is too big a problem. Can't Lauren just tell her girls to call it off?'

'I don't know. They're all deliberately spread out. Not talking to each other. Keeping apart until the track comes on.'

'Yeah. I like the girl's style. When this is over, we need to recruit her.'

'She needs a simple life, Mac.'

'Yeah, it was kind of a joke, Aimee. I tend to joke when I'm stressed.'

'You need to tell me what we're going to do.'

'Let me think ... Let me think ...'

'You need a drink?'

'Yeah. Maybe. I just saw a troop of bar girls marching past with wooden trays full of tequila shots. I should've grabbed one.'

'Oh, fuck.'

'What?'

'I think Hepworth's about to pull the trigger ...'

'You – you – you – yes, you! All of you! Hey-hey-hey! Tonight, is going to be the best! Best ever! THE BEST EVER! Party on! Nobody goes home 'til the sun comes up. Sunrise over Albania is a million times more beautiful than it sounds. Don't take my word for it! You can see it for yourselves. And I can ASSURE YOU! There *will* be bacon butties for breakfast. With brown sauce! Woooooh!'

Hepworth was back on stage. A frustrated rock star. Strutting about. Nodding his head. Eyeballing the crowd. Starting to look a little sweaty and crazed. There was a stunning girl with him. Like a perfect, impossible, computer-generated image of a young woman. Wearing a wide grin, a tiny white bikini, thigh-length boots, a pair of small strap-on wings and a halo on a wire sticking up behind her head. Flashing lights all over it. She was dancing and waving around a bottle of Roca Patron Silver tequila in one hand like a trophy and clutching a terrified chihuahua to her chest with her other hand. The chihuahua was wearing little red devil's horns. The girl shrieked, moved the dog to one side and poured some tequila down her front. Hepworth licked it off.

So this was the famous Pixie. In the flesh. And Aimee, like everyone else, wanted her for herself. To be alone with her for just five minutes. *God ...*

Hepworth had one arm outstretched, now, pointing at people in the crowd.

'You! You! You– you – you – yes, you! I see you, Terrill. I see you, Nick. I see you, Kate, Belle, Gabriel – Patty! Hey, Bernie! Sacha! Sally S! Hamlish! Yo, Mands, I see you, in the zoo, having a poo! Are you ready to get this party started? Because right now . . . RIGHT NOW! I want to tell you – I'M FUCKED UP . . .'

There was a roar of approval from the dance floor. Some kind of Pavlovian response. They'd obviously heard this before. A catchphrase. Aimee had heard it, too. It was the start of the track.

Here we go . . .

'Yeah. Believe it, people. And – if you ain't gettin' fucked up, boys and girls – get orff moi land!'

An animal grunt from the floor – 'Uh-huh!' – like a herd of wildebeest, as a very basic beat started up. Insistent and throbbing with a sort of lo-tech home-made feel. The shots girls were circulating with their trays. Guests making a grab for the tequila.

'So let's do this!'

'Yeah!'

Harsh, ugly, rasping keyboard stabs, lots of shouting, half-rap, half-song, half-drunken rant, and Hepworth dancing on stage, swigging from the bottle of Roca Patron Silver. Pixie snaking her hips, arms above her head, eyes closed, tongue licking at her lips . . .

And then the chorus slammed in, and everyone was yelling and bouncing in unison. It felt like an earthquake as the dance floor jolted up and down while everyone chanted 'shots' over and over and over.

The mighty digital bass drum hitting every time they shouted the word.

The place had gone wild, and Aimee saw Lauren leaving the dance floor.

The girls were on the move . . .

*

354

'We're on the list.'

'You're not on the list.'

'Mister Hepworth invited us himself personally.'

'No, he didn't. He doesn't know you.'

Joliffe was handling this. Under control. Everything checked out, everything was cool. He just had to juggle the security guy on one side of him and Genc on the other.

'This is the local businessman, Genc Malecaj,' he explained, calm and straight.

'I'm sure it is,' said the security guy with the muscles. 'And who are you? Radagast The fucking Brown?'

'I am not a mythical wizard. I am Joliffe.'

'Joliffe what?'

'Just Joliffe. I am an associate of Mister Malecaj and as he doesn't speak English so good, I am also his major-domo and transistor.'

'Transistor?'

'Lator – trans-*lator*. His transcendental translator. Transmission, transubstantiation. His protection against the shapeshifters.'

'*What are you talking about, Joliffe?*' Malecaj butted in. '*Why is this taking so long? Just get us in there.*'

Joliffe processed the two languages at once. American and Albanian. Coping well. Handling it.

'*I am trying, Mal,*' he said in Albanian. And now back to the bouncer. Big guy with a small head and a clipboard. Not a great combination. 'Mister Malecaj wants to know why this is taking so long.'

'It's taking so long because you are not invited to the party, my friend.'

Malecaj made an angry hand gesture. Raised his voice.

'*Tell him to fuck himself, Joliffe. We don't need to speak to this pinhead. He is just a doorman. Show him this . . .*'

Genc had got his phone out and was waving it in Joliffe's face. It left streaks of colour in the air that captivated Joliffe for a moment. He took a deep breath and tried to concentrate. Took the phone. Showed it to the bouncer.

'What am I looking at?'

'The invite. Mister Hepworth's lawyer invited us.'

'Why would Mister Hepworth's lawyer invite you? It's not his party. It's Mister Hepworth's party. Mister Hepworth sends out the invites. Not his lawyers.'

'Yes, yes, I understand. But, you see, *my friend*, this is not just pleasure. We have a meeting set up with Mister Hepworth. We are going to discuss ... All manner of things. Which is no doubt why his lawyer got involved in the invitation process.'

'Yeah. Whatever. But you're not on the list, sunbeam. And if you're not on the list, you don't get into the party. It's as simple as that.'

'Show him the invite again, Joliffe. The invite on my phone.'

Joliffe smiled at the bouncer.

'I ask you to perhaps talk to Mister Adams.'

'Who?'

'Mister Rex Adams. He's Mister Hepworth's lawyer.'

'No, he's not. Hepworth has a lot of lawyers, but he doesn't have one called Rex Adams. Now fuck off out of here before I call the cops up from the main gate.'

'Why not just let us in? Yeah?'

'Look. Don't you understand English? I know *you* do, Catweazle, you're a Yank. But how many times, and in how many ways, do I have to say that I'm not gonna let in a scuzzy bunch of arseholes like you lot.'

Genc raised a hand, snarled at Joliffe.

'Tell him I will fuck him in the ass.'

'Don't think that's a good idea, boss.'

'Tell him I will fuck him in the ass and fuck his wife in the ass and fuck his children in the ass. Tell him I will fuck his dog in the ass.'

Joliffe translated. The bouncer gave his response and Joliffe passed it on to Malecaj.

'He says he doesn't have a dog. Do you want me to ask if he has a parrot?'

'What?'

'In case you want to fuck that in the ass, instead.'

'Tell him this is his last chance. And don't do any fucking jokes or I will fuck you in the ass.'

Suddenly there was a loud bang and a burst of light and everyone tensed. Arven and Costel went for their guns, before they remembered they'd left them in the car on Genc's orders.

The bouncer didn't miss the move. Gave them a sour look.

'I'll give you clowns one minute to get away from the gate before I call the police up.'

There was another bang and Joliffe looked up at the sky where a burst of shimmering light was opening up from the gates of heaven.

'Wow...'

Something clicked. Everything became clear.

The fireworks had started. The security cameras struggled to cope with the sudden changes of light intensity and flared to white, or else irised down and went dark. And now a couple of the screens snowed over. The one by the access area behind the kitchens went completely dead. Miss Lily swore. What was happening? There was a glitch. Half of the screens were juddering. Others were fuzzed out. Miss Lily clicked her headset microphone on.

'Ray. We got a problem with the security cameras ... Ray? We got a problem.'

She tried some switches. Fiddled with the control on her laptop screen, ran a quick diagnostic. Something was bugging out the system. Had the fireworks interfered with something? Perhaps a rogue rocket had hit one of the dishes on the roof?

'Ray? Mister Hepworth. Mister Hepworth? Somebody get Mister Hepworth. He's on the lawn. He's on the main lawn. Ray? We have a problem – here. Some of the screens have gone down . . . Ray . . . Mister Hepworth? Anybody?'

And then she saw it – on one of the few screens still working – Lauren and Sigrid, talking urgently together. Two more of the tennis team approached them. A black lady in an afro wig. What was that all about?

She swore. Zoomed in. Impossible to hear what they were saying with so much noise around. *That Lauren girl*. Miss Lily knew she'd been up to something, planning something.

She could hear the pop of fireworks in her headphones. See the flares. But no response from Ray or Mister Hepworth.

'Ray? Please answer me. Mister Hepworth? Lee? Herve? We have a situation . . . '

Genc Malecaj looked at the big man with the small head. Small head with no brains. He felt weary. Bitter. Acid in his guts. He'd had this sort of treatment ever since he'd left Albania. Nobody trusts you. Nobody wants to let you in. You were a second-class citizen everywhere you went. You are Albanian scum. You are all criminals.

OK. It was true, he *was* a criminal, but only because he'd had no other choice – he'd trained as an electrician, had tried to get work all round Europe – but tonight he wasn't a criminal, and he wasn't an electrician come to fix the fucking lights. Tonight, he was a guest, he'd dressed up. In a suit. A shirt and tie. They'd left their guns in the car. They were legitimate.

He grabbed the phone off the idiot Joliffe. Woke it up – showed the screen to the guy with the clipboard.

'Look,' he said, in English. The man looked. Interested. Frowning.

Ray shook his head. The Albanian was shoving his phone right in his face. He so wanted to clock the motherfucker but was trying to retain his calm and patient demeanour. It didn't help that Miss Lily was squawking in his ear. She so loved to sit there in front of those screens, in her own little world, like a little tinpot Buddha, shouting at them all the time about some stupid shit. And she had such an irritating voice.

With the fireworks going off and all, it was getting chaotic. He couldn't get over this Malecaj guy. He remembered Hepworth discussing him. Local drug dealer. Possible replacement for Vlachos. But, as far as he knew, the idea had been dismissed. He was too much of a liability. Well, he was certainly a trier. He had a plausible looking invite – with plus ones and everything – but it hadn't been generated here. How did he ever think he was going to get in with it?

OK. One last effort at reasoning with them.

'That invite's a fake. I've never heard of this Rex Adams. But I've heard of you, Genc Malecaj. If you want a meeting with Mister Hepworth, we'll sort something out, but not now. This is a *party*. Savvy? And you're not on the list.'

The Yank translated for his boss. His boss said something back and the Yank turned to Ray.

'He says you are lying to him. He says he won't stand for this. He won't stand here and be told what to do by a tiny-headed nobody like you.'

'What's that?'

'He said your head looks like a butt-plug.'

'I am going to fucking kill you.'

'I was just translating, sir. The thoughts and opinions expressed are not my own. I'm just like a . . . a mouthpiece. So, can we come in now? I'm seriously, like, getting quite itchy. Bored. Yawn.'

'*Ta qifsha Zotin tend*,' the Albanian said dismissively. Ray looked blank. That was the thing about Albanian. Nobody else spoke the language.

Except for freaks like Joliffe.

'What's he saying?' Ray asked.

'He's saying the time of retribution has come.'

'Don't you pull a shitter on me, you homeless looking twat.'

'The fire is in the sky, falling angels in flames, and I will draw down their power. This is the night I make a stand.'

'You what?'

'I can shoot darts from my eyes. I'm the thin white duke.'

'You're the skinny white dick, is what you are. FUCK OFF.'

'The power is in me. I am a power arranger ...'

The black lady had walked with Lauren and Sigrid away from the dance floor. Miss Lily had lost them for a moment but had soon picked them up again, heading across the upper terrace towards the beach steps. The black lady trying to shield them from the cameras.

Try again, lady. Not good enough, I got you!

It was just the girls' luck that the only screens still working covered the route down to the beach. The pictures were grainy and blurred, made worse by the constant flashes and flares from the fireworks, but Miss Lily could make out the black lady trying to keep the girls hidden, using what looked like a coat. Her efforts backfiring, only drawing attention to herself. To Lauren and Sigrid.

'Ray? Ray? Ray? Somebody answer me, please. We have a situation ...'

What was the matter with Ray? She glanced at the screen showing the gate. He was still arguing with a bunch of awkward looking men in cheap suits.

'Get rid of them, Ray. I need you. I need your team ...'

'Hello? Miss Lily?'

'Who is this?'

'It's Herve, down at the beach, is everything all right?'

'No. We have a situation. Two of the girls are trying to escape.'

'I'll talk to Ray.'

'I've been trying.'

'What about Mister Hepworth?'

'Somebody needs to tell him. The girls are heading your way. They will maybe try to steal a boat.'

'*Oui?* I wish them well with that. We got the harbour locked down tight.'

Genc was watching the argument and trying to understand what Joliffe was saying. He was ranting like a madman, now. The pinhead leaning back, arms raised in a 'Say what?' gesture. He'd only brought Joliffe along to translate. In case they had a problem like this, and now he looked like he was just making things worse. The pinhead was bracing himself now, looked like he was getting ready to hit Joliffe in the face with one of his big, meaty fists.

'Joliffe,' said Genc. 'You need to calm the situation. We simply need someone to come and verify our invitation.'

'Not this time, Genc. We are not getting pushed around anymore. There are signs in the sky. Clear instructions.'

'Those are fireworks.'

'They have been designed to spell out a message. Mister Hepworth is a powerful man. Connected. Illuminati. Illuminations? OK? He's the devil. He killed those kids.'

'You're not making any sense, Joliffe.'

'Forget that. I have gone beyond sense. I'm on a different plane right now – and the solution to our problems is clear. We gotta deal with the shapeshifters.'

'Joliffe, there are police around. Men with guns. I don't want any trouble. We will go.'

'I am gone, man, solid gone!'

And Genc watched helplessly as Joliffe pulled a gun from his pants. Some shitty old .38. Looked like a Rossi. Brazilian piece of crap. Tendency to go off when you didn't want it to.

'What are you doing, Joliffe? Put that away. Come on . . . '

No good. Joliffe fired wildly, three shots. They missed every-one and everything, but it freaked the security guys out and they backed away. One of them even threw himself into a flower-bed. It was enough to allow Joliffe to make a run for it up the driveway and into the bushes.

'Joliffe! Joliffe, you motherfucker!'

The pinhead was holding a lapel mic up to his mouth and shout-ing something into it. And now he unclipped a handgun from the back of his belt. Looked like a SIG Sauer. A much more serious gun. He sprinted after Joliffe.

Shit. This was not what Genc had wanted. A drink with Hepworth, a look at the pretty girls, a chance to move up in the world. Instead, it was turning into Gunfight at the Waco Corral.

He let out his breath with a long, slow moan. Turned to Arven and Costel.

'Come on,' he said. 'Let's go and get a drink.'

He started to walk away, back down the long drive.

Maybe he should go back to being an electrician.

'You're him! The shapeshifter!'

Macintyre had heard what sounded like shots and had hurried away from the party to investigate. But it had seemed all quiet. Nothing to see. He'd just been saying into his hidden mic that it must be fireworks when Joliffe had run out of the bushes and collided with him. He looked even more fucked than usual and was waving a handgun about. Now his eyes focused just enough to latch on to Macintyre.

'You don't fool me.'

'You've mistaken me for someone else,' Macintyre was sticking to his mid-Atlantic accent. Trying to defuse the situation. Not that he could say exactly what the situation was.

'You're Rex Adams, the lawyer, but you're not him. You're a shapeshifter. You're the devil . . . And I am going to fuck you up.'

'Yo! Joliffe! What you doin' here, man?'

Shit – it was the French kids. Sacha and Gabriel in their stupid bunny heads. Macintyre yelled at them to go back to the party. They ignored him. Came closer. And now Gabriel pulled off his head.

'Hey – it's me, Gabriel. You come to get the party started? It's *old*, man. Wow – hey – is that a real gun?'

Before Macintyre could do anything, Joliffe fired two shots. The first blew off one of Sacha's ears. The second hit Gabriel in the chest.

'Fucking shapeshifters.'

Pixie was trying to catch Little Pixie – the silly rat had got scared by the fireworks and slipped out of her hands. Was racing across the lawn away from the party, whimpering and squealing like a bitch. He ran through the legs of a small group of guests who were clustered around a churros stand. They laughed.

'Look at him go!'

'Little Pixie!' The name was too long to shout. She should have called him something else. One syllable. Two at most. But it was all she had right now. Not that he ever paid her any attention.

'Little P!' Sounded like she was shouting *little pee.*

And then she was past the guests and there was a crazy man with a pistol pointing into the face of a guest. The guy was wearing a shiny silver suit and an open-neck shirt. Sunglasses. Strings of beads. Wild-eyed, hair all over the place, missing a couple of teeth.

'Is this part of the show?' said one of the guests and the man spotted Pixie. Shifted his aim towards her. Someone screamed. There was a body lying on the lawn close to the crazy man, a group of kids clustered around it. It was too much to take in. Little Pixie stopped in front of the guy with the gun, shaking and shitting. Making a strangulated yowling noise.

Pixie stopped, too. The man looked down at Little Pixie, then back up at her.

'What the fuck is that thing?'

At that moment Pixie made a decision. This was all wrong. She was not happy. This was no way to live your life. Things had to change.

Someone shouted.

'I've got him! He's mine.'

Ray had lost the fucker in the woods at the edge of the lawn. And then, when he'd re-emerged, his line of sight had been blocked by a group of young kids, swarming in the driveway. He'd yelled at them to get out of his fucking way, there were two bangs, not even as loud as the fireworks, and then there he was – the Yank bastard. Standing there – arm outstretched. His gun inches from a guest's face. Looked like the Hollywood guy. And Pixie had got caught up in it, too. The French kids were on the lawn shouting about something. He had to shut them out. Shut the voices in his earpiece out. Concentrate solely on the crazy Yank. He wasn't moving. It was an easy shot for Ray. A clean shot. No chance of any collateral damage. His heart punched at his chest. And then he heard a buzzing in his earpiece.

'Ray? Please acknowledge me. This is Hepworth. Ray. I am fucked up, Ray. Everything is fucked up. What in the name of God is going on? We have to sort this shit . . .'

Ray didn't respond. This was *his* moment. All his life had been leading up to it. This opportunity. This point. *The point of a bullet.*

There would never be a better time. He'd be a hero, not a killer. A saviour. He would be talked about. He would save the girl. He would depress the trigger and his destiny would be fulfilled.

Drawn in a straight line from his gun to the American's head. The point of the bullet would follow that line. And it would penetrate his skull and flatten, turning and tossing, until it flew out the other side, sucking his brains after it.

That was the point of a bullet. It had no other function. And *Ray* had no other function. He was the hand of God. The One. A Pure Psychopath. You see the clear path. You take it. Nothing clouds your judgement. Nothing gets in the way of your actions.

Instant decision.

Life or death – choose death.

Yes. All he had to do was squeeze and he would move up to the next level. The killer elite. All he had to do was squeeze . . .

So why couldn't he squeeze?

God give me strength. Let me fulfil my destiny and do your work here on earth. Getting rid of the sinners.

Squeeze the trigger, Ray. Bring the bastard down. Why are you waiting, Ray?

'Ray?' Another squawk in his ear. Miss Lily again. And then, Hepworth.

'Ray. They're making a break for it. The girls. We have to stop this . . . I need you at the beach. Now!'

Ray didn't listen.

Everything hung. Frozen. The Hollywood guy trying to stay cool. The crazy American with the gun. Pixie frozen. The chihuahua crouching and shivering and making an unholy racket.

And Ray knew he couldn't do it.

He was a shit psychopath.

'Put the gun down.'

He was a boring cop, now. Killing the vibe. No witty quip before blowing the motherfucker away. Just – *Put the gun down* . . .

But the Yank didn't put the gun down.

He fired . . .

*

Pixie couldn't believe it. The twisted fuck had pulled the trigger.

'What did you do that for?' she said.

'He was the devil.'

'He was my dog.'

'Maybe I made a mistake.'

'I hated the stunted little bastard, but all the same – this isn't on. Now you listen to me . . . '

'I *will* listen. You're an angel.'

'You put that gun down. OK? Just drop it.'

The guy looked meek. Sad. Confused. He dropped the gun. There was a bang. A spray of blood. The guy roared, tipped over the low wall that ran along the edge of the lawn and fell out of sight into the bushes. Looked like he'd shot himself. *The dick.*

Two of the extra security guys were running down from the house. Ray was running up towards them, shouting.

'Sort this out! I have to help Hepworth! Sort this out! Shit-shit-shit.'

And he was gone.

With the fireworks still exploding, nobody, apart from the guests by the churros stall and the two security guys, had seen it all happen. They new guys were flapping about, not sure what to do. Pixie walked over to the wall where she'd last seen the shooter. There was a short drop down to a lower walkway. No sign of the guy. No sign of the blond guy he'd been about to shoot either.

She went back to Little Pixie. All the life was gone out of him. Looked like something you'd see on a supermarket meat counter. A dead chicken.

She felt like she ought to cry, but she couldn't be bothered.

'Gabby – Gabby – Gabby . . . ' Sacha was crying, his hands cupped around his brother's face. Blood dripping down on to his brother from where his ear had been. Gabriel was pale. Shaking. His eyes unfocused. There was an opening in his chest the size of a euro that was making a hissing, sucking sound. Pink, bloody foam bubbled from the wound. Gabriel coughed. Blood on his lips.

'Get him on his side!'

Sacha looked up. It was the British secret service guy, Oliver Pangbourne. Sacha did what he was told. Rolled Gabriel over. Pangbourne grabbed a bottle of vodka from one of the girls.

'This'll have to do.' He splashed some over Sacha's hands. 'Get clean.'

He quickly collected glasses, stacking all the ice cubes in one of them. Dropped a mangled piece of pink meat in it and poured more vodka over it. Gave the glass to Ennio to look after.

'It's Sacha's ear. What's left of it. They might be able to stick it back on at the hospital.'

A girl threw up and Pangbourne snatched a thick silk scarf from around her neck, wrapped it around Sacha's head. Sacha was so wired he couldn't feel any pain.

Now Pangbourne knelt down, tore the shirt away from Gabriel's wound, then took Sacha's right hand and pressed it against the hole.

'Don't let air into it. Press hard.'

Two security guys arrived. Stood there not knowing what to do. Pangbourne stood up. Shouted at them.

'Have you called an ambulance? – No – Then do it. There must be a qualified first aider on your team. A medic? – Yes – Get him – her – get them. Now! Go! Quick!'

One of the guys ran off. The other stayed. Pangbourne was still spitting out instructions.

'The wound needs to be taped up. Sealed. Water and airtight. But make sure the seal has at least one open side to let air out without letting any in. Your medic should know to look out for signs of a build-up of air in the chest. If the lung leaks, it's bad. Don't let him go into shock. Look for any signs he's turning blue . . .'

Sacha sensed a movement and saw that Pixie had arrived, his friends moving aside to let her come close.

Pangbourne nodded to her. 'You know how to do CPR?'

Pixie nodded back.

'Good. If he starts to go – you bring him back, yeah?'

'OK.'

Sacha put his face close to Gabriel.

'*Ne meurs pas pour moi, mon frère. Ne meurs pas. Rester. Tu n'es pas obligé de mourir . . . Je prie. Je prie pour toi . . .*'

And he was praying in his head as he spoke. The two happening together. It came easy. Even though he'd never prayed before.

When he looked up, Pangbourne was gone.

Aimee had made it to the harbour with the two girls. There was a guy with period-drama sideburns and a striped sailor shirt. Must be Lee Morgan – just as Lauren had described him. Another guy – squat and solid-looking, his sailor shirt stretched too tight over a beer gut. That would be Herve the Perve. Air-Vay the Pair-Vay. He had an ostentatious earpiece attached to a lapel mic and a look that said, 'You shall not pass!'

Through her own earpiece, hidden under the wig, Aimee had been keeping in touch with developments. Messages relayed by Pike and Sarah on the boat. She knew the guys down here had been warned of their approach. Best to take control.

'Lee Morgan,' she said loudly and firmly. Using her best fitness instructor's voice. 'I want your three-seater jet ski.'

'Technically it's not a jet ski,' said Lee. 'Jet Ski's a specific brand, like Hoover. Technically it's a personal watercraft. PW.'

'I don't care if, technically, it's a pedalo – just start it up for me.'

'Not going to happen, sister,' said Herve, stepping up to the plate. Smiling like he had this under control. All muscle and a bone head. 'What planet are you on?' Strong French accent. 'Let me show you how much black lives matter.'

He looked like he was going for a gun on his belt.

Fuck you, Herve.

All in one move, Aimee stepped towards him, squared up, aimed at a point about six inches behind his head, and drove her arm forward like a piston. Turning her body into it. Fingers up, palm flat, the heel smashing into Herve's nose. Down he went. Hit the ground with a heavy thump.

Basic palm heel strike.

'Lee,' she said. 'What are you waiting for? This is Lauren's gig – right? You know the plan, so get the fucking pedalo fired up. Go-go-go.'

'This wasn't exactly what ...'

'Don't hit me with any more technicalities, Lee. Let's do this. The three-seater.'

Lee did it. The big black jet ski, or whatever the fuck it was called, had been sitting ready at the jetty and Lee soon had the engine chugging.

Herve wasn't out, though. He'd got up on to his knees, dripping blood on to the ground from his nose, and was scrabbling for his gun again, muttering obscenities to himself. Aimee couldn't risk any shots being fired down here.

She walked back to him, raised her elbow and slammed a hammer blow into the back of his head. This time when he went down, he stayed down.

Aimee climbed on to the jet ski, strapped the kill switch cord round her wrist and shouted at the girls.

'Get on. We're going for a ride.'

The jet ski dipped in the water as they climbed on board.

'Won't forget this, Lee,' said Aimee as she rolled back the throttle. They moved away, slowly at first, but once they'd cleared the harbour wall, she opened her up and yelled in triumph as they shot away across the black water, the two girls clinging on behind her.

*

Ray was pounding down the harbour access road. Long, loping strides. Quicker than using the steps that zigzagged their way across the hillside, taking in the view at every turn. The concrete access road, hidden behind a high laurel hedge, wasn't built to be picturesque, but to make it easier to cart luggage and cargo up from the harbour. It went down straight and steep and Ray was almost flying.

Halfway there he lost his footing and went over. Smashing his knee and elbow and chin. Tearing his trousers. He swore. Picked himself up and pressed on, ignoring the pain. This was his chance to redeem himself. Next opportunity he got to shoot someone tonight, he wasn't going to hesitate.

Thirty seconds later, he was barrelling down the last stretch and out on to the beach behind the boathouse. He made his way round in time to see Hepworth arriving, with Tokyo and Captain Karagiannis. Someone was lying on the ground. Looked like Herve.

Fuck. Was he too late?

He walked towards them, trying not to limp or show any pain. It was hard work.

Hepworth was screaming at Lee.

'What do you mean, they took the Marlin?'

'I didn't have any choice, Mister Hepworth, sir. The black lady clearly knew what she was doing. Looked like Krav Maga – you know, that Israeli self-defence thing.'

'What?'

'Krav Maga – developed by Israeli Special Forces.'

'Lee, I don't need to know the history of unarmed combat.'

'She nearly killed Herve.'

'I can see that. We need to go after her in the ViperMax.'

'She told me she wanted to take the jet ski – I told her it was technically called a personal watercraft ...'

'What?'

'Not a jet ski, I tried to explain.'

'Lee! Get on with it! Stop wasting my time. We'll see to this shit when I get back. This has been a serious breach of security and you are at fault, there are protocols. There has been an infarction.'

'Do you mean "*infarction*", sir? Do you mean to use that word? Were you thinking of, perhaps, "*insurrection*"?'

'GET THE FUCKING BOAT READY. WE NEED TO HURRY HERE!'

'An infarction is an obstruction of blood supply to an organ.'

'And there has been serious loss of oxygen to your fucking brain, mate. I am so going to fuck you when this is over. You will see. Just you wait and see, Lee! We'll see. Get the ViperMax running. We can catch up with them. BUT ONLY IF WE GET GOING NOW!'

Ray made his presence felt with a throat-clearing noise. Hepworth turned and glared at him.

'Ray? Where the fuck have you been?'

'There was a separate incident, at the gates, sir.'

'Separate to what?'

'To *this* incident. Genc Malecaj and some of his men tried to get into the party – started shooting.'

'Shooting? Guns? You mean they were shooting guns?'

'Yes, sir. Guns. They were shooting guns. Well, *a* gun, singular. It all kicked off. It's suppressed, now. I suppressed it. It's over. So, I came down here as fast as I could.'

'Anyone hurt?'

'The shooter killed Little Pixie.'

'He killed Pixie! Shit . . . Shit . . . Oh, shit . . . '

'*Little* Pixie – the dog – he killed the dog.'

'He killed the dog?'

'Yes.'

'The fuck did he do that for?'

'I don't know.'

'He shoot anyone else?'

'The two French boys.'

'What? Jesus fucking Christ in a bike lane without a helmet. Are they OK?'

'I'm not sure – it's all quite confused. One lost an ear.'

'An ear?'

'The other one . . . I don't know.'

'Who did this? Who was doing the shooting?'

'Some crazy Catweazle Yank who was interpreting for Malecaj. It was him that kicked it all off. Shot the frogs . . . And the dog.'

'This is no way to throw a fucking party. FUCK'S SAKE, LEE – IS THE FUCKING BOAT READY?'

'Yes, Mister Hepworth, sir. Do you want me to take the helm?'

'No, I want you to fuck off.'

Hepworth, Tokyo and Captain Karagiannis tramped out along the jetty and climbed down into the speedboat. Ray followed, suppressing a groan as his knee buckled halfway down the ladder. He hopped the last few rungs into the boat. Nobody asked him if he was OK.

Hepworth took the wheel and looked up at Lee who was lingering on the jetty like a wet fart.

'You know, Lee,' he said. 'I sometimes think you must be autistic.'

'Not as far as I know, sir.'

'In that case you must just be a moron.'

'Yes, sir. Maybe.' Lee was trying to pass down life vests, but Hepworth told him to fuck off and threw one of them into the water.

'OK, gentlemen,' he said. 'Hold tight. We are going on a beaver hunt!'

Ray took a seat next to Tokyo, the cop behind them. He didn't look happy about any of this. He was on his phone, jabbering away in Greek.

Hepworth sped out of the harbour way too fast, nearly hitting the wall, and then put some music on.

Mission fucking Impossible. Pumping out at full volume. Hepworth sang along at the top of his voice as they bounced over the water, driving with the reckless confidence of a man who knew his boat couldn't be sunk.

'This is just like a movie!' he yelled.

Yeah, except when Tom Cruise went on a mission, he didn't take his sodding lawyer along for the ride.

And a bent copper.

There was just enough moonlight to see the Marlin up ahead, out in the deeper water. How far were they intending to get on the thing? All the way to Corfu Town? Maybe they were making a break for Albania?

They didn't stand a chance. They should have gone north into Agios Symeon, instead of south. Hepworth wouldn't have risked rocking up in the village, all guns blazing, not with so many people around tonight. He wouldn't want any weird scenes or violence in front of everybody. Out here on the water, though, in the dark, Hepworth had the upper hand. They were going to fix this. Hepworth's girls were not going to get away.

Ray smiled. Found himself singing along under his breath. This *was* like a movie.

Beatty was trying to make sense of things down at the turning circle. Police were making their way up from the outer gates, sirens wowing, lights flashing. Some confused party guests were trying to leave. Asking questions about what had happened, what was going on, which Beatty fended off like a politician.

The French kid was still lying on the lawn, Hepworth's medic tending to him. His brother sitting next to him, staring into a cocktail glass, a bloody scarf around his head. No sign of the ambulance yet. There was no sign of the wild and crazy Yank, either. Beatty still had guys out searching for him, but it was tricky in the dark, and it seemed half the security cameras were down and had missed it all.

With Ray gone and seemingly out of radio contact, Beatty wasn't 100 per cent certain what he was supposed to do – should he stop guests from leaving or let them out? The only thing he knew for sure was to keep the tennis team locked down tight.

There was the blare of a horn and he looked over to see the coach come down the access road and stop at the crowd-control barriers. Ioannis sitting by the driver looking white-faced and sick. Beatty trotted down. Signalled to Ioannis to open the doors, which he reluctantly did.

Beatty jumped on board, keeping efficient, keeping his energy levels high. The coach was full of Ioannis's girls, who crowded round him. A cacophony of voices as only a gaggle of girls can make. Angry, scared. There was a lot of flesh on display. In another life, Beatty would have spent the night partying with this clutch of cludge. But not in this life.

Ioannis looked done in.

'You have to let us out, Beatty. I can't risk any of my girls being interviewed by the cops. Wouldn't look good for Mister Hepworth, either.'

'Yeah. Good thinking. It surely wouldn't. You were never here. But, Ioannis ... '

'Yes?'

'You owe me a freebie.'

He jumped off. Told the lads to pull the barriers aside. Watched the coach trundle away, the girls pressed to the windows leering and pulling faces. Sticking out their tongues.

In another life.

Beatty ran back up to the gates, keeping snappy, sorting shit out, keeping things moving. He was good at this. Maybe Hepworth would take note. Maybe Ray would be out on his ear. He had sorely fucked up tonight. Three people and a chihuahua shot. So far only one of them was dead for sure, but it could have been a whole lot worse. Still might be if the boy didn't make it.

He waved a police car through. He was the man in charge.

'Go on in, fellas . . . '

Macintyre was making his way down the driveway with a small group of disgruntled partygoers. One of the women had her high heels off and was walking barefoot. They were all chattering away, discussing the events at Patia HepKat. Not that any of them really had a clue what had gone down.

Ioannis's coach went past, girls' faces pressed to the windows, and Macintyre waved at them. He was still listening to the comms in his earpiece. Aimee had made it to the boat with the two girls. Pike and Sarah were packing their gear away and getting ready to set sail.

Everything was going to plan. Albeit a slightly adjusted plan. He'd kept on top of things. Fulfilled his obligation. Done what he came here to do.

Now it was just a case of driving into Corfu Town and tying up the loose ends. Once he heard from Pike that he was all done, he could properly relax. A good night's work.

There was a cigar and a drink waiting for him.

'Ahoy! Ahoy! We are coming on board.'

'Ahoy yourself,' said Pike. 'What is this? Captain Pugwash?'

Pike was standing at the stern, giving Hepworth a dry look. Aimee was safely below with the girls. Sarah at the helm. The engine running. Everything was shipshape. Except for this bunch of nautical arseholes in the speedboat.

'I said we are coming aboard.'

'This is my boat, matey-boy. I am the captain and I say who comes aboard.'

'You know who I am?'

'I sure do. You are Mister Julian Hepworth. And, between you and me, admiral, you are well and truly up Scheisse Strasse without ein paddel.'

'Do you know who these other gentlemen are?'

'I'd hesitate to call them gentlemen.'

'DO YOU KNOW WHO THEY ARE?'

'Yup. Sailor Boy, there, that's Ray Jordan, your head of security. Then we've got Tokyo Masombuka, one of your lawyers, and Captain Karagiannis, of the Corfu police force. *Iasou*, Vassily.'

'Well, then, you will have to concede that you are well and truly outgunned, you old fart.'

Pike pointed back to the island. Far in the distance you could just see the party lights at Patia HepKat.

'Over there – on that little patch of land – you are lord of all you survey, Mister Hepworth. But right here, right now, out on the water, you have no more authority than a sea cucumber. Savvy?'

'Oh, I think you'll find we have jurisdiction here.' Turning to Karagiannis. 'Don't we, captain?'

'Well – I would have to know what crime has been committed,' said Karagiannis wearily.

'Don't you wimp out on me now, you heinous Bubble! You are my man. And don't you ever forget it.'

'I think he's trying hard to do just that,' said Pike, enjoying watching the captain squirm.

'I am only saying, Mister Hepworth, that . . . '

'You know full well that a fucking crime has been committed. Several crimes. Several counts. And I have my lawyer here to make it official. Count one – kidnapping. These people have abducted two of my girls and have stowed them away on this boat. That's people trafficking – count two. Yeah? Count three – they assaulted a member of my staff. That's assault. Ah, here they come, here come the cavalry!'

A Greek police launch was approaching from the south, lights flashing. Hepworth turned to Karagiannis with a triumphant sneer.

'Do you have the balls to get on board, now, Captain?'

The captain looked at Pike with a long-suffering expression.

'May we come aboard?' he asked.

'I guess I have no choice . . . '

'Ha! Yes.'

Hepworth looked smashed. Not in good shape at all. Probably on some kind of designer narcotic. Several kinds by the look of him. He was chewing his lips, baring his teeth. Pike felt a pang of nostalgia for his wild and wayward youth.

Karagiannis looked pissed. Pissed and pissed off. This wasn't the best way to end a party. Pike checked. The police launch was still a way off. He helped Karagiannis aboard and left Ray and Hepworth to fend for themselves. Tokyo opted to stay on the speedboat. He looked a bit seasick.

Hepworth paced the deck, jittery and fired up. Rubbing the back of his neck.

'I can assure you,' said Pike. 'There are none of your girls on board. Whatever you mean by "*your girls*". Do you own them? Are they not free to come and go?'

'They are athletes. On my tennis team. And have been taken from my promises under duress.'

'Promises?'

'Premises.'

'Well. There ain't no tennis players on board this boat. I mean, I used to play a bit. I was never any good. The wife, now, she's a demon. Maybe you should sign her up – or is she too old for you?'

'Shut the fuck up, Captain Birdseye.'

Aimee came up from below deck. She'd taken off her wig and put a wrap dress on over her party gear.

'Is there a problem?'

377

'These brave vigilantes believe we have kidnapped some of their tennis team.'

'Say what?'

'We clearly saw you on our CCTV – and we saw you steal our Marlin. That's another count. Take note, Tokyo. Theft of a PW.'

'You mean the jet ski?' said Tokyo.

'IT'S NOT CALLED A JET SKI!'

'I was going to take it back,' said Aimee casually. 'Lee Morgan said we could borrow it. I never knew they weren't all called jet skis, I always thought ... '

'I am going to sue your arses from here to eternity.'

'Fair enough,' said Aimee. 'But what's all this about a tennis team?'

Hepworth barged past Aimee into the living area, took a moment to get his bearings and then clattered down the steps into the starboard hull. Pike heard doors opening and closing and waited for him to re-emerge, knowing he'd find nothing of interest down there. He soon came back up and strode across to the port hull steps, muttering about how he was going to find them.

This time Pike went after him, Aimee following, just in case. It didn't take Hepworth long to find the girls, sitting on the bunk in the guest cabin, fiddling with their phones.

They looked up at Hepworth with looks of blunt indifference. 'Oh, hey.'

Then back to their phones. Pike could see Hepworth trying to compute what was going on. You could almost hear his brain whirring.

'What is this?'

'This is my daughter, Jessica,' said Pike. 'Though everyone calls her Taz, after the cartoon character. And her best friend, Juno. But I thought you'd already met them?'

'We got bored at your party,' said Juno. 'Asked Auntie Aimee to bring us home.'

'Home? What do you mean, home? What the fuck is going on?'

'You a fan of *Star Wars*?' Aimee asked him.

'What?'

'These are not the droids you're looking for.' Aimee left them to it and went back up the steps.

'Shit party, Julian,' said Taz, staring at her phone. 'The music was old. Sorry you didn't get to have your dick sucked.'

'Language, Taz.'

'Sorry, Dad.'

'My fault.' Pike offered Hepworth a smile. 'I tend to use overly colourful language in front of her. Now why don't you fuck off?'

'You haven't heard the last of this.'

'I think I *have*, actually. It's you who's gonna have to be answering quite a lot of awkward questions.'

When Pike returned topside, he found a comical tableau. Ray had his SIG Sauer out and was pinning everyone down, like a gunsel in an old Humphrey Bogart movie. His trousers were ripped and he was bleeding on to the deck.

'It's all under control here, Mister H,' he said when a bedraggled and shell-shocked Hepworth emerged, blinking and gulping and chewing, into the fresh air.

Pike glared at Ray. 'What d'you think you're doing, numb-nuts?' he said. 'Nobody pulls a gun on my boat.'

'Shut it.'

'No. It stays open.' Pike walked over to Ray, who shoved the gun into his stomach, and stood there, holding eye contact like a trouper.

Pike knew people.

Bad people.

He'd looked into the eyes of murderers, rapists, psychos, and even a cannibal, one time. People who would happily pull the trigger, stab you in the heart, break your neck, stick their hand down your throat and pull your guts out.

Then eat them – in one case.

It was not pleasant looking into their eyes.

And he knew what it was like to look into his own eyes. What was behind them. What he was capable of. How many people he'd killed in his time.

All he could see in Ray's eyes was defeat.

'Wanker,' he said, and shoved him overboard.

All the girls on the coach were singing along to the theme tune of *The Great Escape*. Lauren had found it on the driver's Spotify account, his phone wired into the sound system. The girls were throwing themselves into it, posing, grabbing each other, dancing in the aisles. Lauren was in the thick of it with Sigrid, laughing and yelling louder than anyone.

'I thought I was going to have a heart attack,' said Sigrid. 'Feel my heart. It's still beating hard.'

She clamped Lauren's hand to her chest and Lauren went wide-eyed.

'You could run a sound system off that.'

'Omigod. What a night!'

'I can't believe we did it.'

Roseanna and Issy came to join them. They sang together for a while. Ho-Sook, Carmen and Anne-Marie were in the next row, smoking cigarettes they'd bummed off one of Ioannis's girls. Avery and Chioma and some of the others were further down, dancing with the pack. The noise on the coach was deafening, their voices alone could have broken down walls. Patia HepKat had been like a nunnery. Vows of silence most of the time. Don't say anything and you can't be punished for what you've said. But now they could talk about whatever they liked to whoever they wanted as loud as they wanted. Some were chatting away to the local girls. Most of them spoke a bit of English and they were excited about being part of a jailbreak.

God, it had been exciting and terrifying at the same time. Hiding behind the seats and behind the sex workers when Beatty had got on board – and then Lauren had risked looking at him out of the window as they'd pulled away, grinning and pulling a face, sticking out her tongue. He'd looked right through her.

When lovely Aimee had come back to her and said they were all getting out, she'd been so relieved. She'd made promises to them all – all fourteen of them – and she'd kept her promise. To be honest, her plan to swim out off the beach and get Lee to pick them up at sea would probably have failed. But she'd put her plan together with Aimee's plan and now here they all were.

Here they all were.

Unbelievable.

Free.

43

AFTERS

The villa felt warm and stuffy as he came in, dropped the keys into a bowl with his wallet, watch and phone, and walked past the flight cases neatly packed and ready to be picked up in the morning. He went through to the kitchen where he'd laid everything out ready for this moment. Chopping board, knife, lemon, cigar, matches. He got the bottle of rum out of the fridge, the frosted glass out of the freezer, dropped some ice into it, added some rum. Listened to the ice cracking. He popped open a Coke, poured it over, sliced the lemon and chucked in a wedge. A squeeze of juice. Took a gulp. Smiled.

He took the drink and the cigar outside, stripped naked, put the pool lights on and threw himself into the water. A flat dive from the shallow end. Six quick lengths, front crawl, following the lights on the bottom of the pool. Washing away all the crap. Hauled himself out.

He put on the robe he'd left here earlier. Took another drink, lay down on a lounger, lit the cigar and watched the smoke as it curled up towards the stars.

Thought about the French boys. That was bad. He should have stopped Joliffe. He'd been too slow. But at least the kid with the chest wound was stable in hospital. The other one, the younger brother. His family could probably afford the best plastic surgery on the planet.

He had to let it go. Couldn't change anything now. When a job was over, it was over.

He let out a long sigh. Cleared his mind. Let the peace settle.

His gun was still in the safe. He hadn't had to fire it.

Yeah – screw you, Chekhov.

Joliffe was sitting on a rock halfway up Pantokrator, overlooking the sea. There was an intense, crippling pain in his belly that he was trying to set aside. He was using yogic breathing exercises and meditation technique to rise above it. Trying to coax his mind to lift free of all earthly concerns.

But it was a motherfucker.

A *total* motherfucker.

He couldn't move. Couldn't go any further. Not another inch. How he'd even got this far was something of a miracle. Something he couldn't really get his head round. The bullet had ripped up through his groin into his guts. As far as he could tell it was still in there. He was leaking pus and shit and blood and God knows what. After he'd fallen over the wall, he'd crawled and hopped and dragged himself round to the back of Hepworth's house. There was a service van there, looked like the guy was trying to fix a security camera. Joliffe waited, taking as many drugs as he could. He'd been prepared for an all-nighter and had various hidden pockets in his suit. His party suit. Eventually, the guy's phone went off and he was called away somewhere. Fired up and filled with a burst of superhuman strength, Joliffe made his move. He found the guy's toolbox in the back of the van, a loop of cable attached to it, threaded through various rolls of tape of all colours and sizes. He tore off some strips of duct tape and taped an old rag to his wound.

Then he put the guy's stepladder against the side of the house and somehow managed to climb up on to a low roof. He pulled the ladder up behind him and scuttled along the flat roof like a rodent, moaning from the pain, until he found a spot where he could put the ladder over from the roof to the top of the security fence. Then he shuffled out along it and dropped down the other side.

That had nearly killed him. Took him, like, *for ever* to recover.

He had to keep moving, though. He knew that much. He'd crawled through the woods and rocks and scrubland behind the compound, trying to get away, to get clear. It had been hard in the dark – he'd gone round in circles for a while – but once he knew to keep heading up, it had got easier. Up, up, ever up, crawl out of the swamp, evolve, climb free of the shit, get your head in the clouds. Fly away.

He'd come out of the woods, crossed a couple of back roads, more trees, a dirt track, even more trees, rocks, hard spikey shrubs that tore at you, across open ground, always climbing higher. Felt like he'd been climbing all his life. Maybe he'd find God at the top of the mountain. After all, one of his angels had sent him here, hadn't she?

But he knew he was never going to reach the top. Here he was. On this rock. And here he was going to stay. He looked down across the treetops to the sea. All grey and black in the half-light of dawn. It was cool up here. A light breeze rising up the slope. Boy, that felt good. He was burning up. A small voice kept telling him he should get to a hospital, but he had all the help he needed, really, didn't he? He had his own drugs. Ioannis had given him a whole bottle of the orange pills. They could cure you of anything because they took you outside your body, see, outside this world, on to another plane, a place where there was no pain, no misery and anguish. He didn't need this body anymore.

The pills could cure you of life.

Afters . . .

They would carry him gently, and kindly, to the afterlife.

He took a couple now. His mouth was dry. Took an age to get them down. Man, he was thirsty. There was blood trickling down from the rock. Like black oil. He could see a trail of it the way he'd come up the mountainside. He guessed they'd find him pretty quick once it was light. Would they have sniffer dogs? Magnifying glasses to follow the trail of blood. A helicopter?

The sky was getting lighter by the moment. The grey landscape turning to green and brown and gold. No two ways about it – the view was SPECTACULAR.

Just look at that sky! Darker overhead, getting paler and paler and paler towards the horizon, over Albania, where, right now, the rim of the sun was appearing. A hot, white line, fringed with red. Spreading a strip of deep orange all the way along the hills, soaking them in colour. The sky lightening by the moment, from black to purple to turquoise.

As he watched, the sun quickly emerged until it was like a red bullet hole burning white at its heart.

'Man, would you look at that,' he said. Everything reflected in the sea. Totally flat like glass. It looked like the end of *2001*. And the angel was part of it, spreading her wings and smiling at him. Everything was OK. He started to cry.

'What beauty ... What fucking beauty ... '

Pixie was cradling Julian's head in her lap. She'd fucked his brains out and he had no more fuck left in him. It had taken everything she had, all her skills, but she'd eventually given him a happy ending. He was still just awake. It was time for a nightcap. Even though the sun was burning through her pink blind.

The bed was wrecked. The room was wrecked. She was wrecked. Hurt all over. But she was stronger than him. She could push on. She heaved herself up and hobbled over to her vanity table. Mixed two drinks, sloshing in whatever she had to hand. Champagne, brandy, tequila, agave syrup, Dr Pepper. Stirred them with her finger. She took a sip from one. Not bad. What should she call it.

A Happy Ending.

Yeah.

She looked at Julian sprawled on his back, naked, tangled in the sheets, like an adolescent boy. Her little boy. Sweet. He wasn't going anywhere this time. She wasn't going to let him. He'd stay in her bed. With her.

She went to her vanity table. Pulled out the drawers until she found what she was looking for. Her first-aid kit. A big see-through plastic bag containing a big bottle of pills, a cigarette pack, some ketamine, a roll of tape and some superglue.

What a night it had been. Little Pixie killed. The two French boys shot up. Giving the older one the kiss of life for what felt like half the night. Police, ambulances. Julian's guys searching the woods. Chaos. Things falling. Watch it come down . . .

She got the big pill bottle out. Said *Probiotics* on the label. That wasn't what was in it, though. It was her special collection. She'd been putting it together ever since Paris. The right pills for the job. Enough heavy-duty sleeping pills and painkillers to knock down the Incredible Hulk, and the elephant he rode in on – benzos, barbies, Tic Tacs, she'd lost track of what they all were. They'd been a comfort to her, sitting there, knowing there was a way out . . . A happy ending.

She tipped some into a glass. Mashed them up with some lime juice. Poured the slush into one of the cocktails. Tipped in some ketamine crystals from the smaller bottle for luck. Swilled it around.

She looked back at the bed. Julian opened one eye and looked at her. Smiled.

'Goodnight, baby,' he said.

She raised the glass, held it up to the light, looked at the suspended powder, glittering like fairy dust. Cool. She slid an A-Bomb out of the cigarette pack. Hoped it hadn't dried out too much. Lit it up and drew the smoke down into her lungs. Coughed.

With the joint between her lips she carried the drink over to the bed. Helped Julian to sit up.

'A nightcap, baby. It'll help you sleep.'

'Good girl. You're good to me.'

'I'm the best. The things I do for you.'

She kissed him. Helped him drink. Wiped his chin. Kissed him. Stuck the A-Bomb between his lips. Made sure he took a drag.

He coughed, too.

Cute. They were so alike.

She straightened the pillows, plumped them, laid him back on them. He was smiling.

She went back to the vanity table to get the bag. Tipped the rest of the contents out on to the bed. Squeezed half the tube of superglue around Julian's neck. He giggled.

'That tickles. What you doing, babe?' Kept his eyes shut.

'Shhhhhh.'

She waited a couple of minutes until his breathing had slowed. Then slipped the plastic bag over his head, quickly taped it in place. Julian swam up out of his stupor and struggled for a few moments. One hand flapped pathetically at the plastic bag. She could see his face inside it. He opened his eyes briefly, stared at her, uncomprehending, but then he closed them again and seemed to float back, to go away from her, as if he was sinking into the sea. His legs twitched. He shuddered. Then lay still and quiet.

She downed half of the clean cocktail, fought off a wave of nausea, then lay down next to him. So tired.

She closed her eyes and had a sensation of falling. She jerked; her body flushed with adrenaline. Wasn't ready to sleep. She put her hand between her legs.

She saw the Hibachi on her bedside cabinet, reached over for it. Switched it on, felt it gently vibrating.

Maybe this time?

Maybe this time a happy ending...

Was it only last night? Not possible. Here she was, sitting at the kitchen table with Mum and Dad. As if the last two years had never happened. Weirdly normal. Pasta with pesto. Mum had got it into her head from somewhere that it was Lauren's favourite meal. Maybe years ago, it had been. Maybe it was now. Maybe it would be in the future...

It looked like Dad was going to go off on one. Mum exchanged a look with Lauren. *Let him talk.*

'Lauren. I can't tell you how lovely it is to have you home again.'

'It's unreal, Dad. In a nice way. I need to adjust. Get back to how things used to be.'

'Yes. And we just want the same as you, darling. We want to try and carry on and pick things up and get back to normal. I know, these days, everyone's supposed to do therapy and endlessly talk about things, and, yes, there'll be time for that – if that's what you want. If you're finding it hard, and I'm sure you will, anyone would, but if we can just get back into our groove, yeah? Least said soonest mended. You've had a traumatic experience. You've had a really difficult time and now you need to just get on with your life. This year's been hard, last year, too, this is *all* so hard, hah, but *next year* – next year is going to be different. Next year we'll be back on track. Next year will be normal and you can do all the things a girl of your age should be doing. You know? You can hang out with your mates. You can go to the cinema. Go to gigs or whatever they're called these days, just hang out in the park if you want. A boyfriend! And you'll go to school every day, and in the summer you'll do your exams, and I know what you're like, you're my little star, you're going to smash it. You take those exams and then next September you'll move up into the sixth form and you'll be like every other girl in England. You'll be free. Not locked up anymore . . . '

Cindy was sweating. She and Ioannis had just made love. The first time in a long while and it had felt good. That was one thing he'd always been good at. His hands were big and rough and strong, but they were also gentle, and he knew how to please her. She'd had to train him, of course, show him what she liked, how to go about it, but he was a good learner and he never forgot and never stopped trying to please her.

And he appreciated her body. Her breasts had lost some of their rubbery bounce – big breasts will do that as they get older – but, damn it, they were the breasts of someone half her age.

She and Ioannis lay there now, covered by a single sheet, looking out of the window at the night sky. It was the best thing about the house – the views. You couldn't see any other houses. Just the sky and the sea. And it was a beautiful night.

She felt there was a change in Ioannis. They'd talked over supper – she'd cooked him one of his favourite Greek dishes, lamb giouvetsi. She could sense he'd been wanting to tell her things and had opened up a bit, talked about Vlachos, hinted at some of the bad things he'd been getting into. Hinted that he wanted out.

Now he put his hand on hers where it lay on the sheet.

'I will change,' he said. 'I will say goodbye to that life. I will tell Vlachos that I can't work for him anymore.'

Cindy smiled. 'Next year's going to be better,' she said. 'Next year's going to be a good year. I just know it. I can feel it. The rentals will be coming in thick and fast. Your boat business will be back on track. We're going to get back on top of things. The world is going to be a sunny place next year, a happy place – don't you feel it as well?'

'Yes. I feel it. And I think I've understood some things these last few days – what I want from life, and what I don't want from life. I don't want the darkness. I want the light. I want a world of butterflies.'

'You big softie.'

'We'll work together. But there has to be a deal.'

'What do you mean? What sort of deal?'

'I'll do this for you, Cindy, I won't work with Vlachos anymore, if you do one thing for me.'

'All right. Of course, love. What is it? What do you want me to do for you?'

'Is simple. I want you to stop believing that the earth is flat.'

'Oh ...'

'Look – look out there – you can see the horizon. Yes?'

'Yes,' said Cindy. 'I can see the horizon. You know, I think, before, I was scared. Scared of what might be over the horizon, so I told myself there wasn't a horizon ... Does that make sense?'

'I think so. Perhaps.'

Cindy rolled over and turned to Ioannis, stroked his cheek.

'I needed something in my life, because I thought I was losing you,' she said. 'I felt so alone. I'd be happy to have you back, to have things back as they were, on a normal, round earth. And, as I say, next year is going to be the best ever. There's an auspicious feel about it – 2020 ...'

CREDITS